The Urbana Free Library

BOOTS AND SADDLES: A CALL TO GLORY

BOOTS AND SADDLES: A CALL TO GLORY

PAUL COLT

FIVE STAR
A part of Gale, Cengage Learning

GALE
CENGAGE Learning

Detroit • New York • San Francisco • New Haven, Conn • Waterville, Maine • London

GALE
CENGAGE Learning

LIBRARY OF CONGRESS CATALOGING-IN-PUBLICATION DATA

Colt, Paul.
    Boots and saddles : a call to glory / Paul Colt. — First Edition.
      pages cm.
    ISBN-13: 978-1-4328-2803-5 (hardcover)
    ISBN-10: 1-4328-2803-7 (hardcover)
    1. Patton, George S. (George Smith), 1885–1945—Fiction. I.
Title.
PS3603.O4673B66 2014
  813'.6—dc23   2013031780

First Edition. First Printing: December 2013
Find us on Facebook– https://www.facebook.com/FiveStarCengage
Visit our website– http://www.gale.cengage.com/fivestar/
Contact Five Star™ Publishing at FiveStar@cengage.com

Printed in Mexico
1 2 3 4 5 6 7 17 16 15 14 13

For Jack

For duty, honor and sacrifice for another. For the letter in the mailbox the day we laid you to rest. The canceled "stamp," written in your hand reads, "Free." I have it. I'll not forget. For you and all those whose names are etched on that black marble wall; and for all those who have or will defend our freedom; your courage and sacrifice preserve us. We remember. We owe you no less.

In Memory:
Sgt. Richard T. Jackson

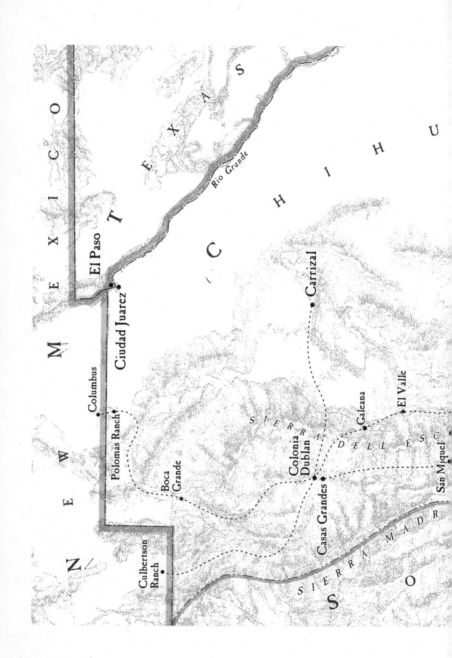

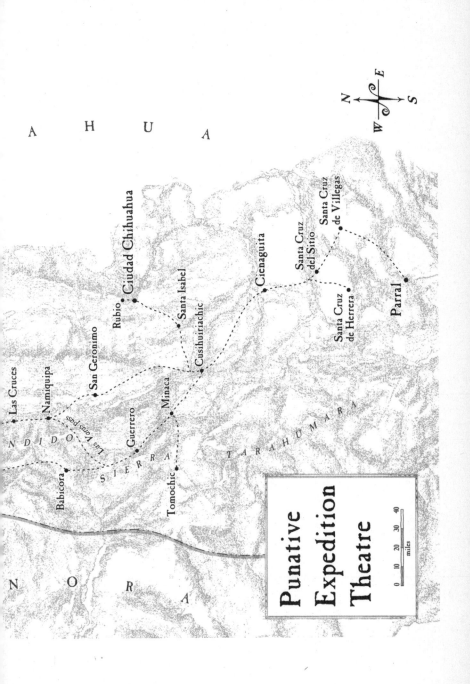

Punative
Expedition
Theatre

0 10 20 30 40
miles

PROLOGUE

Fleetwood Hill
Brandy Station, Virginia
June 9, 1863

Major Henry B. McClellan, CSA, swept his glass across the fields south and west of his position. Steamy summer sun beat the crest of the hill. The air hung thick and heavy. Sweat stained his blouse and tunic with discomfort. Distant dust clouds alerted him to the new threat. A dark line moving toward town confirmed a second Union thrust. The General had ridden north that morning to support Lee in response to a surprise Union advance. He'd left McClellan with a skeleton rear guard to hold the Fleetwood Hill headquarters and its stores. *Skeleton* might sum it up if he didn't get word to the General and fast. God knew he'd need reinforcements and judging by that dust cloud he'd need them damn soon. He scribbled a dispatch and handed it to the waiting courier. The young corporal swung into his saddle and galloped away to the northeast. The Major turned back to his vigil.

The dashing boy General, James Ewell Brown, better known as "JEB" Stuart, scanned the dispatch. With his headquarters and stores threatened, the morning thrust from the northeast suddenly struck him as diversionary. He turned to his adjutant.

"Yankees are moving at Brandy Station. We've got to hold the high ground. Order Jones and Hampton to fall back and secure

Fleetwood Hill. Get word to Rooney Lee. He's to fight a rear guard action and work his way back to join us."

"Very good, sir."

Stuart swung into the saddle. "Let's get the hell out of here."

Fleetwood Hill

An hour passed, then two. Little more marked the passing than heat and flies. McClellan wiped perspiration from his brow and lifted his glass as he had on the quarter hour since sending his dispatch to the General. Dust again, moving toward their position from town this time. *Shit!*

"Lieutenant Cahill."

"Sir?"

"Company's coming. Have a detail stand by to fire the stores. Deploy that six-pounder with whatever serviceable ammunition you can find. Form the rest of the men in line at the crest of the west slope."

"Anything else, sir?"

"If you're a prayin' man, I suggest you put in a word for reinforcements."

The column inched closer. McClellan made out Union cavalry, *likely horse artillery too*. The cavalry formed a battle line along the broad plain rising to the high ground. Nearly a mile off, it stretched across a wide section centered on the supply train.

"It won't be long now, Lieutenant." He snapped the glass closed. *Shit!*

Dust gave the first indication of movement along the battle line. It looked like little more than a trot across the grassy flats. The Yankees would hold to that until they took the slope.

"Prime that gun, Lieutenant."

"Gunners ready!"

McClellan let them close to the edge of the slope at a

thousand yards. "Fire!"

The little gun charged white smoke, bucked and roared.

Brigadier General William "Grumble" Jones halted his brigade east of Fleetwood Hill at the distant sound of cannon. A puff of smoke drifted against the pale blue sky. "Looks like the party's started without us. Battalion Commanders, form your lines!" He deployed the Eleventh, Twelfth and Thirty-fifth Virginia cavalry across a broad front in support of the hill ahead.

The Union line broke into a gallop, storming up the west face of the hill.

"Gunners fire when ready."

The six-pounder offered precious little resistance. McClellan let the Yankees come. The ground trembled under pounding hooves. Carbine and pistol fire would scarcely tamp the rolling thunder. "Lieutenant Cahill, prepare to fire the stores."

Sweet sound erupted to the rear. A lone bugle raised a clarion call. The ground shook violently under foot. McClellan turned to the roar of Rebel yells. "By heaven, Cahill, a chorus of angels couldn't sound no better. Give 'em hell, boys!"

Gray-clad cavalry swept past McClellan's thin line swathed in a choking dun cloud. They crested the hill and pounded down on the Union charge. Horses and riders plunged into the fray. Two great waves crashed against one another below the crest of the west slope. A roiled sea of blue and angry gray foam, churned on waves of chestnut and bay, black and roan. A forest of bright blades clashed, singing and dancing in the sun. Men sweat and cursed and bled. Pistol and carbine fire punctuated the din. Men fell. Horses reared, nostrils flared, wide-eyed in fear. Others bolted, their riders fighting for control. A blanket of gray powder smoke spread across the field layered on dust clouds rising from the melee. The crest of the hill and the combatants below disappeared under a canopy of yellow fog. The gray line pressed forward down the hill. The blue line pushed, held firm, slowed and bent.

Further south, Brigadier General Wade Hampton approached the south slope of Fleetwood Hill with four battalions. Observers reported a second Union column approaching from the southwest. Stuart also received the report. He ordered Hampton to let the Yankees commit to the hill and then turn their flank from the south, driving them onto the west slope.

A Union force of three battalions charged the southwest slope hoping to turn Jones' flank. Hampton struck across a broad front with the Cobb Legion, First South Carolina, First North Carolina and the Jeff Davis Legion. The Confederate charge smashed the Union right, pinning the federals against Stuart's seven battalions. The arrival of Rooney Lee's rear guard swept the federals from the field to a flourish and a chorus of cheers.

West Point
February 1909
0200 Hours
Cadet Adjutant George Smith Patton sat ramrod straight at his small desk despite the late hour. His cropped sandy hair glowed in a halo of lamplight. He closed the book, stretched his long athletic frame and yawned. His uniform pressed for morning assembly hung beside the bed, brass polished, creases straight. He'd achieved the cadet first rank despite his academic challenges. He took pride in that harbinger of a bright career.

He expected to be called on for his analysis of Brandy Station. He made no secret of his Confederate ancestry. The Patton line included officers who'd distinguished themselves for generations. He admired them. One day he would be numbered among them. He considered how to assess General Stuart's inspired performance. The text made a tediously dull tactical rendition, the art of war reduced to military science. True genius in the field was born of a feel for battle. Stuart had it. The instinct to go for the enemy's unprotected jugular. Cadet Patton admired bold genius, the essence of the horse soldier. Genius he would achieve again. Feel for the enemy came to him as naturally as Stuart's assessment of the tactical situation on the south slope.

He might have ridden with Stuart in that historic battle. One day cavalry under his command would perform to standards such as these. Caesar himself could attest to that. General Stuart broke the Union Cavalry with a decisive counter stroke. He achieved tactical supremacy with concentration of force and surprise based on speed. It was a lesson in military strategy for the ages. Caesar struck blows such as these. Stuart understood the principles. Despite his relative youth, Cadet Patton understood them instinctively. He knew one day the enemy he faced would come to understand them too.

He stretched again, time to get a few hours' sleep before reveille. He picked up the small filigree picture frame as was his custom each evening before retiring. The stiff formality of the photograph managed to capture her classic beauty. The very thought of her warmed him and softened the cultivated starch of his military bearing. Beatrice Ayer was bright, witty and well educated. She had the classic look of a Victorian portrait: rich auburn hair, a petite figure, heart-shaped face, rosebud lips and a porcelain complexion. The pose the photographer caught accented the graceful arch of her neck and the depths of her eyes with their ever-present hint of mischief. God, he loved her. "Beat," as he called her, gave voice to the poet in his soul as no one else could. She completed a side of him little known to those around him. He'd been smitten as a gangly youth not yet grown into his body. The fact that she was an expert horsewoman added to her attractions. While he'd dated other girls during his years at the Point, in truth all he ever wanted was to be Beat Ayer's Georgie. Courting her had only been a matter of admitting that. He replaced the photo on the desk beside his thumb-worn Bible and switched off the lamp.

CHAPTER ONE

White House
Washington, D.C.
March 1913

Bright morning sun streamed through floor-to-ceiling windows and glass doors leading to gardens ripe with green shoots and the promise of spring. The President took little note, his attention thoroughly absorbed in a draft of the Federal Reserve Act. A soft rap at the door announced his appointments secretary. "Secretary Bryan to see you, Mr. President."

Thomas Woodrow Wilson, twenty-eighth president of the United States, scratched a note in the margin. The authority to adjust bank reserves would become an important tool in managing the flow of credit and with it the nation's economy. It merited further thought. The legislation contemplated a federal bank that would tie the nation's banks together through reserve accounts maintained with the central bank. A central bank had powerful policymaking potential, all in the name of a safe and sound banking system. Who could possibly object to such a noble goal? The bank must appear independent with no direct connection between the executive branch and the levers that manipulate the economy. Apparent independence would shelter proximity to executive influence. In time that influence would confer control of the economy on the executive. He might never see the day, but one day a worthy president would. *Just the sort of evolution sound progressive policy should be founded upon,* he thought as he set the document aside.

A reed of a man, Wilson presented a sober thoughtful countenance. He'd made his climb to the presidency through the improbable halls of academia, rising to the presidency of Princeton University. Conservative elements of the Democrat party saw promise in his views on political science and public administration. They persuaded him to run for governor of New Jersey and from there to the presidency. He set his pen aside.

"Send him in."

Secretary of State William Jennings Bryan of Nebraska filled the office doorway. The three-time presidential candidate made an imposing presence, in many ways more impressive than Wilson's reserved and scholarly demeanor. His wore his once dark hair, now salted with gray, neatly trimmed. His square jaw and broad forehead gave a determined set to lively dark eyes. An accomplished orator, Bryan gave weight to his words with the seemingly effortless turn of a phrase. "Good morning, Mr. President."

"Good morning, William. Have a seat." Wilson gestured to wing chairs drawn up before his desk.

"Thank you for seeing me on such short notice. I'm afraid I have some rather disturbing news I thought you should know. I received a call from our Ambassador Wilson in Mexico City last night. He confirms that General Victoriano Huerta has seized power in the wake of President Madero's assassination."

Wilson steepled his fingers, touching the tips to his lips in thought, his eyes lost behind the reflected glare of his spectacles. "That is a shame. Had President Madero been given the time, he surely would have brought socially progressive reforms to Mexico of the sort we could fully support. Huerta, I fear, will prove to be just another repressive thug with brass buttons."

"I quite agree, sir. The question, of course, is what are we to do? Do we recognize Huerta? Is his government legitimate?"

"Madero's revolution overthrew Diaz. We approved of him because we agreed with what he stood for. Diaz was a tyrant. I find it hard to justify recognizing a usurper like Huerta. In all likelihood he represents a return to the abuses of the Diaz regime."

"Our ambassador tells me the situation in Mexico remains unsettled." Bryan referred to Ambassador Wilson by title, avoiding the mention of his name again. The president didn't approve of the man and bridled at the coincidental imposition on his name. "Madero's revolutionaries have only recently laid down their arms. If we withhold recognition of Huerta, it may encourage his supporters to resist a return to repressive government. If the people resist, Huerta may not be able to hold the army. If the army turns, democracy may yet prevail."

Wilson regarded the appointment of Bryan an uneasy political alliance with a former rival. He wasn't sure he completely trusted the man. Still the Secretary's advice in this matter appealed to his academic penchant for avoiding conflict. "That seems sound counsel, William. Let's give it a little time and see what develops."

Cavalry School
Saumur, France
August 1913

Steel clashed, the ringing punctuated by grunts and the slap of boot leather on the polished wooden floor. Afternoon sun spilled through high arched windows, warming the exertions of the sparring partners. Spears of reflected light flashed from arcing blades. Softer rays diffused to a tawny glow on rich oiled wood. The swordsmen circled warily, searching for an opening—feint, stroke, stroke, thrust, counter clash.

A distinguished white-haired gentleman with a crisply

trimmed goatee clapped his hands impatiently. "Monsieur Patton, where is your parry? You must parry. A counter stroke does not constitute defense!"

Patton welcomed the break. Sweat soaked his padded tunic. He lifted his mask to the top of his head and wiped sweat from his eyes. "I find little opportunity for victory in defense, Monsieur Clery." He inclined his head in the direction of his opponent. "To give a man of Monsieur Giraude's skill the opportunity to organize his attack is to invite disaster. I prefer to carry the attack to my opponent. Let him take defensive action. I shall grant him no quarter." He punctuated the statement with a wide, toothy grin.

"Aggression suits your nature, Lieutenant, but you've come here to become a Master of the Sword not to indulge your personality disorder. To truly master the sword, you must be a complete swordsman. You simply must have a defense. One never knows when one's life may depend on it."

"The man who relies on defense in combat is already dead. The only matters in question are the timing and circumstance."

Clery chuckled. "The brash exuberance of youth. Monsieur Giraude, if you would please give the good Lieutenant here an opportunity to learn some defense. Monsieur Patton, you will parry. En garde!"

Patton hated defense. He put his usual meticulous effort to the task for the good of the goal. He would be the army's first Saber Master. Once the goal was achieved, he resolved defense would be the condition he visited on his adversaries.

Loire Valley, France
September

A ribbon of steam rose from the stream running through the valley floor below. In the gray light before dawn the Hun *yurts* were little more than dark lumps on the plain beyond the trees

18

lining the banks of the stream. Here and there the dying embers of a fire added a wisp of smoke to the steam, like ghosts, dancing in celebration at the arrival of the nearly dead. Beyond the yurts, herds of squat, shaggy mountain ponies smudged the hillsides. Mounted, the Hun were a fearsome scourge. Sleeping off the effects of their drunken revelries, they were fodder for the legion.

The dark-eyed Centurion set his jaw. His hand rested on the hilt of his sword. His great white stallion tossed its head to the breeze and stomped impatiently. The quiet sounds of men and horses holding in wait behind him stoked the fire that burned in his breast. That the Hun outnumbered them mattered not. None could match the fighting discipline of the Legion. At the head of his cavalry, he believed anything possible. Caesar himself said it best. *"Audaces fortuna iuvat."* Fortune favors the bold. The Hun would taste their steel. Roman swords and lances would run with the enemy's blood. Little remained but for their heathen gods to welcome the dead to the hell of their choosing.

He drew his sword and extended his arms left and right. The legion responded to his silent command with the muted sounds of armor and tack, shifting to positions of readiness. Men and horses moved forward. The battle line spread across the ridge like a giant predator bird, spreading its wings in preparation to swoop in for the kill. Helms and blades glinted in the low light. Horses snorted and pawed the ground. Time stood still, waiting for the battle line to form. Silence fell. The Captain on the left nodded, his eyes hidden in the shadow of his visor. The Captain on the right crossed his sword to his breast. The Centurion raised his blade and thrust forward, forward into the valley.

He eased his horse down the ridge, picking his way at a walk. At the base of the ridge the valley floor stretched to the banks of the stream. He squeezed the prancing stallion between his thighs. The animal picked up his trot, tossing his head, nostrils flared to the scent of smoke mingled on the morning breeze with sour human smells. The sky turned crimson in the east, foretelling the plumbs and pennants of the force advancing before it. Sunlight spilled golden over the hills lighting the valley and the stream ahead in ripples of fire.

The Centurion raised his sword. Bright blades caught the sun up and down the line. He thrust it forward, putting his heels to the stallion's flanks. The line surged. The stallion stretched his powerful muscles, responding to his master as might a willing woman. Thunder rumbled through loin and breast as the battle line splashed across the stream, flashing through the trees.

Hun stumbled from their slumbers. Alarm spread. Dark figures ran for the pony herd. Short bows appeared, though few found teeth in the feathered flights. The Romans swept down on the camp, pounding hooves overran those scrambling to its defense. Blades flashed. Lances slashed. Hun fell before the onslaught as wheat before the harvester's scythe.

The golden tide washed over the camp, scattering the herds to the hills beyond. The line broke left and right, circling in a second pass of death and destruction. Slaughter met slaughter, warriors afoot no match for the mounted. Slowly the din quieted. Resistance faded to the death throes of the wounded. The legion stood tall. The stunned barbarians rendered humble in defeat.

The Centurion passed from his mind's eye, the valley below did not. The gray gelding stomped and shifted beneath him. His eyes swept the terrain west, north and south. Beat sat a pretty bay mare beside him. The French riding habit flattered her figure. She smiled that wistful smile of hers. Their summer in France passed too quickly. Soon they would sail for home.

"It's beautiful, isn't it?" Her voice floated, its timber soft as a flute.

"It is today with sunshine and birdsong in the air."

"You say that as though you've been here before."

"I believe I have. History has appointed these hills and valleys important battle grounds. Caesar met the Hun here, you know."

"I didn't know that. That was ever so long ago, I'm sure it must be a good deal changed."

"The hedgerows are new. They are important. Knowing the terrain is often the key to victory. I suspect one day I shall fight here yet again."

Beat's eyes narrowed to a slight squint, unsure. "What do you mean, George?"

He glanced at her as though returning from a trance. He smiled the smile she always brought to his lips. "Nothing, my dear, really, just a feeling I have." He gazed out over the valley, his eyes far away. "It all seems familiar, like I've been here before. Destiny has decreed I shall return again one day."

Carrizal, Mexico
November 14, 1913

Doroteo Arango stood beside Sergeant Luca seated at the telegraph key. He waited impatiently for a reply. Waiting annoyed him. The head-shot body of the station master lay in a corner of the small passenger lounge, a pool of fresh blood spread around the faceless body. Outside the cramped depot, a heavily laden supply train waited for orders. The engine idled, a thin column of smoke drifted on a light breeze. His troops strung out along the line of boxcars prepared to board. His message to the federal commander at Cuidad Juárez informed him the telegraph lines to Chihuahua had been cut. The report suggested Chihuahua may be under rebel attack. Arango expected the commander would recall the Chihuahua supply train. No point in adding spoils to the rebel prize, eh?

Born June 6, 1878, to an indigent sharecropper on one of the largest haciendas in Durango, Arango was the eldest of five children. He received no formal education. From an early age he worked the Patron's estate to support his family. At age sixteen an incident occurred that would change his life. The Overseer of the estate made an advance on the virtue of his younger sister. Enraged, Doroteo shot him. The boy escaped with his life by fleeing into the mountains. There he became an outlaw. A career that began with petty thievery grew in audacity and plunder. He found that by sharing the spoils with the poor, the people would protect him. He cultivated the reputation of a Robin Hood, taking from the rich and giving to the poor that which he did not keep for himself. The affection of the people naturally drew him to the revolutionary causes of land reform and social justice.

He supported the reforms of Francisco Madero's revolution. The Revolution thrust him into a position of leadership for his fearless daring. Madero's assassination angered him deeply. Huerta's treachery marked a return to the injustices inflicted on the people by the Diaz government. He'd thrown his support and his troops behind the self-proclaimed rebel First Chief, Venustiano Carranza. They'd overthrown Diaz. Now they would remove Huerta. The supply train made a good start to equip and provision his growing army. A good start, but he needed more, much more. He needed the prize in Cuidad Juárez.

The day grew warm, the small depot hot and stuffy. The telegraph key remained maddeningly silent amid the flies buzzing about the pool of blood. Waiting annoyed him nearly as much as disloyalty. The disloyal he could shoot. Waiting would not yield to a bullet. He hunched his sloped shoulders, clasped his hands behind his thick middle and began to pace. At thirty-two, the humble Arango had transformed himself from auda-cious bandit to charismatic rebel leader, a champion of the op-pressed. He had dark skin, wavy black hair, a thick moustache and strong jaw. His eyes defined him best. Dark brown, they possessed the hypnotic quality of a snake, a hair's breadth from a violent spark. He wore a rumpled khaki uniform and a dusty wide-brimmed sombrero. Bandoliers crisscrossed his chest. He wore a Colt revolver on his hip, a gun he used with the speed and accuracy of a fabled gunfighter. He could be affable and charming one minute and deadly murderous the next. He demanded respect born of traditional Mexican machismo. He prized loyalty in his men. He favored sweets, ice cream, soda, beautiful women and fine horses. An expert horseman, some called him Centaur of the North, others called him *el Tigre* or the Jaguar. All regarded him as mercurial and dangerous.

At last the line chattered to life. Sergeant Luca scratched the characters with a pencil as the message came in.

"What does he say?" Arango could not hold his impatience.

"Return to Juárez."

A slow smile lifted the corners of his moustache. He stomped out to the depot platform, his riding boots thumping the rough wooden planks.

"Mount the train." The order echoed up the tracks. He turned to the young officer awaiting his instructions. "Tell the engineer, we return to Juárez."

On November 15 the bandit Arango, better known as the rebel leader Francisco Pancho Villa and his *División del Norte,* rolled into an unsuspecting Cuidad Juárez. They captured the city without firing a shot.

CHAPTER TWO

Mounted Services School
Fort Riley, Kansas
February 1914

> *"Stand therefore, having your loins girt about you with truth,*
> *and having on the breast-plate of righteousness, and your feet*
> *shod with the preparation of the gospel of peace; Above all tak-*
> *ing the shield of faith, wherewith ye shall be able to quench the*
> *fiery darts of the wicked. And take the helmet of salvation and*
> *the sword of the Spirit, which is the word of God."*
>
> Eph. 6:14–17

Patton thumbed the favored passage in search of inspiration. He closed the Bible and returned it to its place on the desk. He used the second bedroom of the small on-post house accorded a junior officer as an office. He studied the draft before him by lamplight, illuminating the question if not the answer. The centuries-old debate turned on the merits of edge and point. *What best served the purpose of the weapon, cut or thrust?* The age-old question, of course, had a correct answer in the context of modern cavalry warfare. His distinction as Saber Master gave him a say in the matter. He reread the relevant portion of his analysis.

The point is vastly more deadly than the edge. The edge requires a strong cut, highly restricted by the press of ranks in the charge. The point provides tactical advantage for its economy of movement.

He sat back and drew his pipe from his pocket. He removed the lid from a desktop canister. He took a pinch of aromatic tobacco and tamped it into the bowl. *The 1913 model saber must be a thrust weapon first and a cut weapon second.* The pipe filled, he fitted the stem between his teeth and closed the canister. *Thrust concentrated the power of the horse behind a point of steel.* He scratched a match to light, allowing the bitter sulfur to burn off. He brought the match to the bowl and puffed a cloud of fragrant blue smoke. *The thrusting rider leaned forward with his mount, urging the horse into the charge while offering the lowest target profile.* Yes, that was the point. Still, the cut should not be abandoned, as the French once argued. He scratched a note in the margin of the manuscript. *Prefer the point, do not forsake the edge.* Design details must complement the weapon's intended use. The blood gutters had been added to facilitate withdrawing the blade. The weight of an unhorsed body would serve to withdraw it when coupled with the forward momentum of the horse. Still the cut remained a single edge. One couldn't count on a clean thrust and withdrawal. He read the specifications again through a veil of smoke, searching for the elusive detail he felt missing.

Overall weight: 2 lbs. Grips: black hard rubber, checking 13 per inch. Guard: 0.042-inch gage sheet steel. Blade: forged steel, 38 inches overall length, single edge, blood-letting grooves 4.75 inches from tip to hilt.

Single edge, hmm. He took the pipe from his teeth and scratched *double edge* in the margin. He set his pen down and read again. He nodded. Yes, that's it, the perfect edge to extract the blade with a cut. He scanned the specification again and smiled, satisfied. He closed his eyes. A regiment of bright blades aligned to the charge appeared in his mind's eye. Yes, that was it, a double edge. Model 1913 cavalry saber, his signature on the future of mounted warfare.

"George, it's getting late. Isn't it about time for you to take a moment's rest?"

Beat, ever the thoughtful one when it came to his obsessions. "Yes, dear." He tapped out his pipe in the tray. He placed the manuscript in his case and closed the cover clasps. Millie would make the changes in the morning. He rose from the desk and switched out the lamp. He left the darkened room for an easy chair across the small parlor from the sofa where Beat sat reading. He glanced at the newspaper waiting for him on the footstool. The headlines underscored his preoccupation with work.

European Tensions Grow
Wilson Pledges American Neutrality

Beat closed her book. "How is the saber coming along, dear?"

"Finished, I think. We'll revise the specification in the morning and submit it to the Cavalry Board. With luck it may see action in the coming conflict."

Beat tilted her head. "The President seems committed to keeping us out of it."

"His isolationist policy is naive and foolish. The Axis powers are ambitious. Europe is only the beginning of an imperial design. We'll fight soon enough. When we do I'll get the chance at a battle I've trained for my whole life."

"I don't like to think about that, George. It's so dangerous."

He hunched forward, resting his forearms on his knees in earnest concern. "You're a soldier's wife, Beat, for better or worse. Battle is the reason soldiers exist. Look at me, Beat. I'm thirty years old and haven't advanced beyond the second lieutenancy I was commissioned out of the academy. One cannot rise in the ranks on garrison duty. It takes combat. Danger is part of a soldier's job. Military men have faced it down through the ages. I have my own recollections. I've faced it before and come through victorious. I shall do so again. It is what I am born to do."

"Perhaps so, but I don't have your recollections. Those dangers didn't affect my life and my children."

"Would you have me be other than what I am?"

She bit her lip. "No." She shuttered her eyes. "Perhaps the President will have his way."

"The man is an idealist, a professor of the humanities. Man's inhumanity to man breeds war. Mr. Wilson deludes himself if he believes we can stand apart from it. He ignores reality. In the end, inhumanity will deny him the luxury. When that happens, I shall be prepared to fight."

National Palace
Mexico City
February 1914

Count Heinrich von Kreusen sat on an ornately gilded chair with red velvet cushions in the expansive black-and-white tiled reception to the president's office. He hated waiting. Waiting for a man of Huerta's Indian breeding grated, no matter the station he might have clawed his way to. Foreign Service, he'd found, could be far more tedious than the glamour of its reputation.

Tall and thin, von Kruesen cultivated the aristocratic bearing of his heritage. He wore his silver blond hair and goatee neatly trimmed. His brushed gray suit and Italian leather shoes befit the dignity of his office. A monocle hung about his neck suspended on a black velvet ribbon. It assisted his reading when needed but more often provided an affectation useful to emphasize a point. He'd been flattered when the Kaiser asked him to assume the ambassadorship to Mexico. A diplomatic posting to a warm climate was generally considered pleasant duty.

Mexico was peaceful at the time and removed from the tensions growing on the continent. That, of course, changed with the untimely demise of President Madero. Huerta's ascension rekindled revolutionary instability among Madero's former supporters.

With the risk of war growing in Europe, von Kreusen suddenly found himself in the midst of a diplomatically sensitive mission. Mexican oil would become important war materiel to Great Britain and the allies. The German high command pressed the Foreign Ministry to strike an alliance with Mexico and close down the flow of oil to the allies if possible. Huerta needed munitions to consolidate power and fend off nascent revolutionary forces. Von Kreusen had been authorized to offer German arms and support in return for Huerta's oil embargo. Making the offer would be easy. He fully expected Huerta to accept. Why would he not? The more difficult question remained. Could Huerta be trusted?

"*El Presidente* will see you now, *Herr* von Kreusen."

Presidente Victoriano Huerta retained the trappings of military command. As a general, he'd been a brutal instrument of the Diaz repressions before striking his alliance with Madero. The tiger retained his stripes. Tall and lean, he wore his military uniform and battle decorations even now as Mexico's President. He had a fringe of close cropped gray hair, accenting a bald crown and long features. He wore his steel-gray moustache neatly trimmed. Wire-rimmed pince nez spectacles gave the only concession to weakness in an arrogant presence born of absolute power and the violent cruelty required to preserve it.

He had no use for the prissy German ambassador. He suspected the man was homosexual. As such, the German offended his machismo. He agreed to see him for one reason.

Mexico was poor. The German Kaiser was not. If the Germans wanted something, he, Victoriano, would set the price.

"*Señor* Presidente, thank you for seeing me."

"*De nada.*"

The diplomat floated across the office in Italian slippers.

Huerta looked at his glass. Empty again. "I was about to have a drink. Would you care to join me?"

"A cup of tea, if you have it."

"Of course." He signaled his secretary.

"Milk and sugar."

"Of course." He splashed tequila into his glass from the bottle on his credenza. He directed the German to a settee and chairs clustered around a massive fireplace at the side of the office. They took their seats as the secretary returned with a fine china tea cup and saucer. He set it on a small table beside the ambassador and departed.

"Now what can I do for you and your Kaiser, Señor Ambassador?"

"Right to the point, I see. Very well then, we'd like to discuss your oil."

Huerta smiled to himself, taking a swallow of his drink. He'd guessed as much. He liked this bargain. It would be expensive.

"We'd prefer your oil did not find its way to the British and certain of her allies."

He pursed his lips, stroking his moustache with a forefinger. "We are a poor country, Señor Ambassador. As you know, we have recently fought a costly revolution. Even now rebel forces harass us. We sell our oil as a means to finance our defense."

The German touched his cup to aquiline lips, making a graceful arch of his little finger. "My superiors understand your predicament. We are prepared to offer you compensation and arms."

Huerta hid his disdain behind a forced smile. He met the

German's eyes across the rim of his glass. He tossed off his drink and rose to pour another.

"I think we may do some business."

CHAPTER THREE

White House
May 1914

The President sat in a wing chair at the side of the Oval Office, flanked by New Mexico Senator Albert Bacon Fall on the couch and War Department Chief of Staff, General Hugh Scott, on a facing wing chair. Scott was a bear of a man, with a thick body, round ruddy face, silver-blond moustache and intense bespectacled blue eyes. His presence filled a room, even one as pretentious as the Oval Office. Fall sat with his Stetson hat in his lap. He wore boots and a string tie appropriate to his cowboy senator image. Shoulder-length dark hair hung in waves turned gray at the temples. Sun-hardened features etched a lined mask. The gravel in his voice sounded rough as parched desert hard scrabble.

Scott puzzled over why he'd been summoned to meet with the President and the senior senator from New Mexico. White House meetings were not out of the ordinary for the General in Chief of the Army given the state of affairs in Europe and potential contingencies occasioned by an aggressive Germany. What made the meeting unusual was the presence of the somewhat eccentric gentleman from New Mexico. One had to wonder what the meeting could possibly have to do with the Army given a presidential election year in the offing. Scott kept his questions to himself. Good soldiers knew how to do that where politicians were concerned.

The President turned to Fall. "So Albert, why don't you fill General Scott in on some of the concerns you expressed last week."

"Thank you, Mr. President. In a nutshell, General, I'm concerned about instability in Mexico. The brand of violence we see from the rebels has the potential to spill over the border into our own country. Border security is worrisome for all the border states, New Mexico included. Beyond that, I have a number of influential constituents with significant business interests in Mexico. I'm concerned that we do everything possible to protect those interests. And, if I may remind you, Mr. President, many of those constituents are your supporters."

"I'm well aware of that, Albert, and the underlying risks that concern you. I'm further troubled by persistent reports that German agents are actively courting the Huerta government. Only recently our navy nearly intercepted a shipment of German arms bound for the Mexican government at Veracruz. German interest in compromising the Huerta government cannot be denied. The Germans must not be allowed to establish a foothold in the Americas. I can tell you in confidence that we are reaching out to the rebels who oppose Huerta in the hope of bringing about a stable government in Mexico, one that is more favorably disposed to our interests. That is a dicey undertaking, of course, with no assurance of success. If we offer the rebels support, it may encourage them to refrain from damaging our interests. That said, short of going to war with the Huerta government, I am not certain how much we can do to protect American interests. We can exercise all the diplomatic resources at our disposal and yet face forces at work inside Mexico over which we have no control."

"I understand the limitations, Mr. President. Still border security alone should justify a strengthened military presence.

Many of our vital business interests are located in northern Mexico. With troops on the border, the rebels and the *federales* will have to think twice about acting against our interests."

The President made a thoughtful steeple of his fingertips. "What do you think, General?"

Scott winced inwardly. The army was woefully undermanned and ill-equipped. Heaven only knew what would happen if hostilities broke out in Europe. Diverting assets to the border would only serve to exacerbate the problem. Then again, it might serve to expose the problem too. "The Senator makes good points with respect to border security risks and the deterrent effect of a nearby military presence. Once again, Mr. President, it's a question of manpower."

Fall nodded. "Thank you, General. I appreciate your support on this."

Scott didn't recall giving support. Fall took it for his opening.

"It may not be perfect, Mr. President, but a strengthened troop presence on the border is better than what we have now. You and I, at least, would have something to show our constituents."

And there of course is the nub of it, Scott thought. *Politics.*

The President turned to Scott. "What sort of presence would it take to secure the border in a meaningful way, General?"

Scott smoothed his moustache in the web of his thumb and forefinger, buying time to consider his answer. "I'd have to study the logistics, Mr. President. It's a sizable mission on the face of it. The areas at risk stretch from the Texas panhandle to California. We may not have enough men in uniform to secure the border adequately."

The President pursed his lips. "Deploying all our military assets to the border is out of the question, of course. Take a look at the situation, General. I'd like to review your recommendations for a reasonable response in two weeks."

Fall grinned. "Thank you, Mr. President. Thank you."

Hacienda de La Rosa
Ciudad Juárez, Mexico
July 1914

Villa drummed his fingers on the polished formal dining table. Carranza would make his grand entrance when the American arrived. For this he must wait. He hated to wait. The First Chief made certain no one overlooked his importance. Villa's presence here spoke only to the fact that Carranza needed him and his División del Norte to oppose Huerta. He needed him here to show the *Yanquis* he is First Chief and the one they should support.

He looked around the lavishly appointed room with its tiled floor and arched porticoes. Even this hacienda played a part in creating Carranza's show of importance. It belonged to a wealthy supporter. Wealthy supporter of a people's revolution against the abuses of wealth and power, the irony prickled Villa's preference for simple truth. Carranza was no Madero. He fought for power in the name of justice and reform. Wealth would corrupt him as it had Diaz and Huerta before him. Villa knew this. These trappings of wealth and power said as much. He would deal with it in time. For the present, he needed Carranza to bring down Huerta, one tyrant at a time. He needed the politician to gain *Americano* support. He needed arms and ammunition to sustain the revolution. Carranza's ambition may be corrupt, but for a time, he could be useful.

Footfalls echoed in the tiled hall leading to the dining room. "This way, Excellency." The maid spoke in accented English. She showed a sparrow-like man in a tan suit into the room and quietly disappeared. The man blinked behind thick wire-rimmed glasses, adjusting to dim light after the bright sunshine outside.

"Ah, General Villa, Zachary Cobb at your service." He offered the slender hand of a man who worked with papers. "A pleasure to meet you. I've heard so much about you."

Villa preened, dismissing the flattery with a casual wave. He took the offered hand. "Señor Cobb, welcome back to Mexico. My friends tell me you visit our country often and are, shall we say, connected."

"You flatter me, General. I am nothing more than a humble Customs agent."

Zach Cobb was more than a minor Customs official. He had a second mission through his contacts at the State Department. The slight, bookish lawyer cultivated listening posts along the border, eyes and ears to aid American foreign policy.

"A Customs agent who represents your Presidente Wilson."

Cobb bowed his head with a half smile. The brigand knew precisely why he was here, impressive for a peon in gold braid.

The staccato click of boots sounded in the hallway. Venustiano Carranza appeared in the entryway. "Señor Cobb." He flashed a bright white, welcoming smile as he strode across the room. Lean and angular, Carranza projected a confident demeanor. He wore his moustache and beard neatly trimmed in a fashionable goatee. His bespectacled eyes suggested the thoughtful wisdom of a professor, understating his more aggressive appetites. He extended his hand to the American. He glanced at Villa. "General, I'm pleased you could join us."

Villa inclined his head. *"Primer Jefe."* He performed his function for the meeting.

"Gentlemen, please take your seats." Carranza gestured expansively to seats at either side of the table. He seated himself at the head.

"Now, Señor Cobb, General Villa and I are at your disposal. How may we be of service to you?"

Cobb sat back, his hands folded in his lap. "I rather thought we might be of service to you, señor. As you know the United

States has withheld recognition of the Huerta government. President Wilson believes the Mexican people deserve a more representative and socially progressive government. It is our hope that your resistance will lead in that direction."

Carranza paused to reflect on the statement. "The Mexican people deserve a more representative government, one that does not impose policies as repressive as those of the Diaz regime. We continue the revolution to achieve that goal, though, as you know, Huerta has allied himself with certain foreign interests. The Germans now arm him against us."

"The United States is prepared to counter such assistance."

Villa hunched forward. "We need guns and ammunition. We do not need Americanos to invade our country."

"I assure you, General, the United States has no such intention toward your country."

"How then do you explain the recent presence of your navy in Veracruz?"

The Customs man squirmed. "Yes, well, Veracruz was merely an attempt to prevent German intervention in the Americas. It was not meant as a hostile act against Mexico."

Villa wagged a cautionary finger. "*Gringo* colonialism has no place in Mexico."

Carranza waved him silent. "General Villa has a point. Veracruz was an ill-considered infringement on our sovereignty no matter how noble the purpose. Your Presidente's interests would be better served by befriending loyal Mexican opposition. Leave Huerta and the meddlesome Germans to us. Your country can supply the money and arms we need to defeat Huerta and return stable government to your southern border. That is the message you should take to your Presidente Wilson."

"The President quite agrees. That is why I am here."

Carranza sat back with a satisfied smile. "Good. Then, as you Americanos say, I think we can do business."

CHAPTER FOUR

Mounted Service School
Fort Riley, Kansas
May 9, 1915

A late spring preamble to the long hot summer shimmered in waves over the training ground under a flawless blue sky. A brisk breeze stirred dust devils, providing some relief from the heat. A battalion of the Thirteenth Cavalry, four hundred strong, took the field. Companies formed in columns of four. Ranks of khaki-clad troopers sat astride a mottled tapestry of bay and chestnut mounts stretched over three football fields. Some two thousand yards across the broad plain, target dummies arrayed in ranks awaited the charge. Training maneuvers were under the command of Major Frank Tompkins, a crusty West Point veteran.

Patton stood on the reviewing platform reserved for the evaluators north of the field. The tactics chosen for the exercise exploited the thrust of his new saber design. He would evaluate the effectiveness of the saber work. Other instructors would evaluate horsemanship, efficiency of maneuver, discipline in formation and the speed with which the unit performed the planned maneuver. An involuntary shiver of anticipation crept up his back. He lifted his binoculars and adjusted the focus to the massed formation.

The column halted seventeen hundred yards east of the target objective. Muffled commands sounded. The troops reformed in a double column of fours. Eight abreast, they drew sabers with practiced precision. Bright blades flashed in the afternoon sun as lightning before a storm. Down through the ages, the raw power of the cavalry charge echoed through the pages of history. Glorious fields of yore flooded his senses with reflected vision. Force massed. Power and speed poised to strike the cavalry's signature blow. The saber, the ultimate symbol of glory, his saber would be put to the test.

The column surged forward at a trot, trailing a cloud of dust as they closed to one thousand yards. The bugler sounded the charge. Blades flashed forward to the thrust. The field shuddered as four hundred horses exploded into a gallop. Thunder stirred a feeling of power deep within him. The point of the charge closed on the center of the target ranks.

The column swept through the target rows. The primal cry of battle across the ages rang in his ears. Thrust after thrust shredded the targets, ripping a forty-yard gap in the target ranks. The column swept past the objective and divided devoid of command. Columns of four wheeled left and right in tight arcs as water falling from a fountain. Holding formation the columns swept back over the target flanks, repeating the destruction torn through the center until the objective stood shredded.

A bugle sounded Recall. The columns recovered, circling to the center in a double column of fours. Tompkins drew the column to a halt. He rode forward, wheeled his mount to the reviewing platform and presented his saber salute.

Patton released a breath he hadn't realized he held. His heart thudded in his chest. The weapon emblematic of the cavalry is his saber. Somewhere, an ancestor called. Glory rides at the head of the charge.

Beat bustled about the small kitchen preparing supper. Cooking hadn't come naturally to a girl of privilege. She'd learned to manage simple things out of necessity. A second lieutenant's pay didn't leave room for luxuries like a cook, even if you could find a good one in a desolate place like Manhattan, Kansas. Tonight she browned pork chops and skillet-fried potatoes with green beans. The potatoes sizzled in the skillet, filling the small house with the fragrance of cooked onion. Thankfully, Georgie appreciated the effort, or at least he said he did. Boots clumped on the front porch. The screen door squeaked and slammed.

"Home, Beat. It smells wonderful in here. What's for supper? I'm famished."

"Pork chops, dear." The ring in his voice answered the question before she asked. "How was your day?"

He filled the arched entrance to the kitchen. Beaming, he crossed the room in two long strides and swept her up in a bear hug. "The saber performed beautifully, Beat. As fine a weapon as I have ever seen put to the charge. It was a grand moment, a triumph. Tompkins' battalion performed first rate. Put that saber in the hands of a well-schooled cavalry and it is truly a thing of beauty. I shall report its performance to the Cavalry Board myself. All that remains now is to blood it in battle."

She winced at the mention of battle. The prospect of war in Europe seemed uncomfortably close with the news of the day. She turned her chops in the skillet. "Dinner will be a few more minutes, George. Why don't you take off your boots and put your feet up? The paper's on the dining room table. Oh, and a rather official-looking letter came from the War Department today. It's on the table with the paper."

He turned to the dining table and picked up the thick manila envelope. He tucked the folded paper under his arm and tore open the envelope on his way to the parlor. He withdrew the contents.

"Is it anything important, George?" she set out plates and napkins on the dining room table.

"New orders," he read. "I'm to report to Fort Bliss in September. I've been assigned to the Eighth Cavalry."

"Oh my. Where is Fort Bliss?"

"El Paso, Texas. This is great news, Beat, a line assignment at last."

She returned to the kitchen. *El Paso, Texas, wherever is that? Another obscure outpost. Didn't the Army have line assignments in Washington or New York?*

George removed his boots and set them aside for polishing after supper. Military discipline, as he practiced it, started with spit and polish. He expected it of his troops and those around him. He folded his frame into a stuffed chair, satisfied with the day, first the saber and now the prospect of a line command. He unfolded the paper. The headline assaulted him. "Son-of-a-bitch!"

Lusitania *Sunk!*
Wilson Lodges Formal Protest over U-boat Attack

"What is it, George?"

"Our damn pantywaist president is at it again."

"George! President Wilson is a Democrat. Your father would never condone such talk."

"He calls himself a 'Progressive,' whatever the hell that means. All I know is he doesn't act like any Democrat I ever supported."

"What's he done this time?"

Patton hoisted himself out of the chair and strode back to the kitchen scanning the article. "The Germans sunk a passenger liner. Nearly two thousand people lost on the *Lusitania* and our

Commander in Disbelief stiffens his spine enough to lodge a 'Formal Protest' with the murderers. That'll sure as hell put the fear of god in the bastards. The only threat there is that the Hun might hurt themselves laughing at our weakness."

"He is determined to keep us out of the war, George. He doesn't think it's our fight. I'm not sure he's wholly wrong in that."

"Aspirations to empire know no borders, Beat. Once the Kaiser has his way with the French and British, you can bet we'll be next."

"You can't be certain of that, George."

"It's greed, Beat. Greed and lust for power, empires are built on it. Empires breed aggression. It's been so down through the ages. Wilson sits in his ivory tower and denies the existence of man's basest nature. It'd be a damn sight easier to join the Franks and the Brits and whip 'em now on their soil before we have to face them on our own."

"You can't be serious, George, a German invasion of the United States?"

"I'm damn serious. To deny it is to deny history. Time was you couldn't have found a Roman willing to believe Hannibal could threaten the gates of Rome, but he did."

"I'm certainly not a military man, but I can't imagine a seaborne force sufficient to threaten the United States."

"Who says it has to be seaborne?"

She shrugged. "However else?"

"The Hun walk into Mexico for the promise of an alliance with the last dictator to win his revolution. They promise to return Texas, New Mexico, Arizona and California to the Mexicans in return for their assistance in conquering the United States. That promise would make a national hero out of whoever is El Presidente at the time. The *banditos* may not have any more to offer the Hun than a port on the continent, but that might be all the Kaiser needs."

"Oh my. Perhaps you should speak to the President."

"Second Lieutenants don't speak to the Commander-in-Chief, Beat. Besides, the stupid son-of-a-bitch wouldn't listen."

White House
August 1915

Secretary of State Robert Lansing thought he knew what he was getting into when President Wilson asked him to replace Bryan. Bryan resigned over differences with Wilson's positions on German use of submarines to disrupt allied shipping. Lansing agreed with Wilson's neutrality policy. He felt comfortable representing the President's policy before the powers in Europe. He hadn't prepared himself for this.

At fifty-one Lansing seemed well suited to the appointment. A trained international lawyer, he was no stranger to foreign relations and the State Department. Slight of stature he brought a serious, thoughtful composure in his dealings. His neatly barbered gray hair and moustache retained hints of a formerly darker hue. He had a square jaw, dimpled chin and disarming, almost feminine eyes.

At some level he'd known Mexico's history of political instability. Revolution seemed a way of life down there. It seemed like they had them with a regularity others reserved for elections. So they'd had another. He hadn't thought much of it. The United States hadn't recognized the Huerta government. The question now was how would the President deal with a Carranza government?

The appointments secretary called him back from his reflections. "The President will see you, Mr. Secretary." She stepped aside at the door.

Lansing found the President seated at his desk in his shirt sleeves, his jacket hung over the back of the chair. The lack of formality paid deference to the thick humidity brought on by late summer along the Potomac. Wilson rose to greet him.

"Robert, thank you for coming. Feel free to take off your jacket. Bloody damn hot this time of year and nothing to be done about it. I understand we've had a development south of the border."

"We have, Mr. President." Lansing peeled his coat off a perspiration-damp shirt.

"Please have a seat."

The Secretary settled in one of the wing chairs drawn up before the President's desk.

"Now what have you got, Robert?"

"Our attaché in Mexico City reports the city has fallen to General Obregon. President Huerta has been deposed. Venustiano Carranza has assumed the presidency."

"Hmm, somewhat less than we'd hoped for, but not altogether unexpected."

"Sir?"

"Oh, sorry, Robert. We supported Carranza's people with arms in the hope a more democratic government might be restored to Mexico. Carranza wasn't our first choice for President, but his revolution seemed the most likely means to that end."

"I see. Well, the question is what do we do now?"

"Like it or not, I'm sure he expects us to recognize his government."

"I should think."

Wilson drummed his fingers on the desk, weighing his options. "It's a trade-off. We need stability down there. Mexico could easily become a distraction. The Germans know that. They tried to curry favor with Huerta. If we don't recognize Carranza, we leave him susceptible to another German overture. If there were another obvious choice that would be one thing, but I don't see one. It's a case of the devil you know or the devil you don't." Wilson pursed his lips. "Recognize him, Robert."

"Very good, sir."

Ciudad Chihuahua

Black rage paled before Villa's mood. Colonel Nicolas Fernandez held his tall, lean frame erect and quiet. He wore the traditional Villista khaki tunic, crossed bandoliers, loose-fitting trousers and leather leggings. The sombrero pushed to the back of his head bore the distinctive silver insignia of the *Dorado*, Villa's elite cadre of personal bodyguards. Deep-set dark eyes followed Villa as he paced the hacienda great room, clenching his fists at his sides.

"No whore's son makes a fool of Pancho Villa! *El Presidente Carranza,* shit! He orders me south where I, Pancho Villa, won his revolution for him. Then he sneaks his tin soldier Obregon out of the west to capture Mexico City and the Presidential Palace. He steals the presidency like a thief in the night." Villa wiped sweat from his brow with a red bandanna. His eyes flashed black fire.

"And what do the Yanquis do? The second son-of-a-whore, Wilson, falls on his knees to kiss Carranza's piss-covered boots. He may choose to recognize his lap dog, but, Pancho Villa, will not. Division del Norte brought down Huerta and we will bring down the *bastardo* Carranza. I will expose him for hiding behind Wilson's skirts to do the Yanquis' bidding. He is a disgrace to Mexico. What reforms can we expect from a man who does the bidding of the landholders? None, I tell you. He will grind the *campesinos* to dust like Diaz and Huerta before him. Nico, will you fight with me?"

"Sí, Jefe."

"Will the Dorado?"

"You know they will fight, Jefe."

"Is Division del Norte with me?"

"Sí, Jefe."

"And the people, will they follow Pancho Villa?"

"Sí, Jefe."

"Good! Then we will bring justice to the Mexican people. Mexico will never be a Yanqui colony so long as I have breath in my body. Carranza and his Americano overlords will feel our vengeance. From this moment on, I pledge my life to killing every gringo in Mexico. We shall not permit them to occupy our country with their dollars. We will destroy gringo property in Mexico."

CHAPTER FIVE

El Paso, Texas
September 1915

Brigadier General John J. "Black Jack" Pershing sat erect in the back seat of the touring car watching the sandy plains of the west Texas panhandle roll by. *God-forsaken litter box, how else could you describe it?* The eastern base of his new assignment did little to improve his outlook on the situation. His orders were simple; secure the Mexican border. Easily said. The reality consisted of one thousand nine hundred fifty odd miles of mountainous desert. His command numbered five thousand troops. Practically speaking, he doubted you could secure the border effectively with ten times that number.

Then there was the question of the threat he was to guard against. The Mexicans were so busy revolting against themselves they could scarcely represent a serious threat to border security. U.S.-owned business interests in northern Mexico might be at risk from revolutionary instability, but they were beyond his operational authority. Protecting them was the Mexican government's job, whichever one happened to be in power for the moment. Once the facts and circumstances and logistics were clear, the whole assignment smelled like a politically symbolic show of force. It struck him as an odd gesture from an administration so loathe to favor military force. *What the hell do I know? I'm just a soldier.*

He squinted through the glare on the front windscreen. The road west stretched in a seemingly endless heat shimmer before disappearing in the distant smudges of the Franklin Mountains.

"Not much farther now, sir. You'll see the post come up south of the road."

"Thank you, Sergeant." Pershing shifted his gaze left. A dark ragged shape resolved out of the heat haze. A muscle clenched in the tight line of his jaw. *Home sweet home.* Pershing projected a larger presence than his five-foot nine-inch stature by using every inch of his posture. He wore his steel-gray hair cropped, moustache neatly trimmed. He had a prominent jaw and features lined by resolute purpose. A dimple appeared in his left cheek when he smiled, a disarming contradiction to an otherwise stern demeanor. Of late he'd had little to smile over. His wife and daughters had recently perished tragically in a fire. The desolate surroundings of this new assignment seemed a fitting venue for a man's grief.

The car slowed a mile east of the fort and turned onto a dirt road, making a straight run southwest to an arched gate. "Fort Bliss, Home of the Eighth Cavalry," the sign proclaimed. *Bliss* indeed. Marry into the right family and even a Lieutenant Colonel could get a fort named after him. Can flag rank be far behind? The post proper stood on a treeless arid plain. The rambling three-story clapboard headquarters building was flanked by two story barracks and mess. The dilapidated stables looked like a fire trap. The condition of a post often said much about the fitness of the unit calling it home. Pershing didn't know Colonel Taylor, the Eighth Cavalry regimental commander, but even a cursory inspection suggested he had some work to do to shape up the post and this unit. He hoped for better among the other units assigned to his command. He knew he could count on George Dodd's Seventh Cavalry. The Buffalo Soldiers of his old unit, the Tenth Cavalry had a tradition of excellence, owed to a steadfast dedication to prove the worth of an all black unit. Slocum's Thirteenth was less certain, though Slocum had managed to perform satisfactorily during the more recent years of his career. Time would tell. For now Fort Bliss and the Eighth presented the task at hand.

He wiped his brow and the sweat band of his Montana peak hat with a handkerchief gone damp from the task. The oppressive heat in the panhandle would not give way to a cooler fall for another two months. Phil Sheridan probably had it right. How had he put it? Something about given the choice, he'd rather live in hell than Texas.

Regimental Office
Eighth Cavalry
Fort Bliss, Texas

Patton stepped out of the taxi and retrieved his bag from the boot. He paid the driver. Gears ground, the cab sped off in a cloud of dust, leaving its passenger choking for breath. He hefted his bag and started up the crushed stone walkway to Eighth Cavalry Regimental H.Q. Scorching heat radiated from the stones like an oven. He paused at the bottom step, taking in his surroundings. Beat thought Fort Riley and Kansas barren and desolate. *She'll love this.* He didn't see much in the way of on-post housing either. She wouldn't like the idea of a long separation, but clearly this post presented some challenges. On the bright side, at long last he had a line assignment and a chance to make something of his career. He squared his shoulders and climbed the cracked but freshly painted wooden steps.

Late afternoon sun filtered through dusty windows, bathing the Regimental Offices in a golden glow. Even the regiment's newfound penchant for spit and polish couldn't control west Texas sand and wind.

"Sergeant Major, Lieutenant Patton reporting for duty." He slid his orders across an outer office counter that still smelled of varnish. The walls were freshly painted too and the floor polished. The grizzled Regimental Top opened the envelope and scanned the particulars.

"We've been expecting you, Lieutenant. Welcome to Fort Bliss. Colonel Taylor has assigned you to C Troop. The Colonel is away for the weekend. He'll want to see you Monday morning. In the meantime, Corporal Baxter will show you to your quarters."

A ramrod figure appeared in the doorway to the corner office behind the sergeant. Sunlight flared on a starred epaulette. Patton snapped to attention.

"At ease, Lieutenant." The gravel voice crackled with the edge of command. The General crossed the office at a brisk stride. Brushed uniform, polished brass and boots, every inch a soldier, he extended his hand. "John Pershing, Lieutenant. Let me add my personal welcome."

Patton accepted a firm handshake. "Thank you, sir. It's a pleasure to be here."

Pershing chuckled. "I've only recently arrived myself, but I've seen enough to suggest you may want to hang on to your pleasure until you fully form your opinion."

He allowed a wry smile. "I did notice conditions are somewhat spartan."

"Your reputation precedes you, Lieutenant. Olympic horseman, Saber Master, impressive achievements for a young officer, you are to be congratulated."

"Thank you, sir. You're too kind."

"I'm afraid you won't find much in the way of Olympic glory or saber ceremony in this assignment. The border regions we are charged to secure are vast and harsh. The west is still wild in some parts out here, downright lawless in some cases. It'll test our mettle as fighting men."

"I'm looking forward to that, sir. I've had enough of garrison duty and training assignments since leaving the academy. Sooner or later the Army will need fighting men. When that happens, sir, I expect to be ready."

Pershing studied the earnest young man, remembering a similar determination in his own junior years. "Yes, I'm sure you do. We'll talk again when you've settled in. Carry on, Lieutenant."

Monday
0700 Hours

Patton entered the office, came to attention before the desk and presented a crisp salute.

"Lieutenant Patton reporting for duty, sir."

Taylor glanced up from an open folder amidst piles of paper and clutter on his desk. "At ease, Lieutenant." He dismissed the salute with a wave. "Have a seat."

Colonel Charles W. Taylor, Regimental Commander, Eighth Cavalry, looked tired. Red-rimmed watery eyes stared out from behind smudged spectacles. His uniform looked rumpled, his tie slightly askew.

"Welcome to the Eighth, Lieutenant, and welcome to Fort Bliss. I hope you've made yourself at home over the weekend."

"I did, sir."

"I've been reviewing your record, Lieutenant, quite impressive for a junior officer."

"Thank you, sir."

"I see you're a Saber Master."

"Yes, sir."

"Don't know that I've ever met one before. Personally, I've never had much use for the damn things, all that brass to polish. I can never figure out what to do with it when I want to sit down."

"I think you'd find my new model a fine weapon, sir."

"Weapon, is it? I suppose at one time. These days I suspect its place is best suited to ceremony or the parade ground."

"It's done very well in training exercises at Fort Riley, sir. Perhaps you will permit me to give you a demonstration, once my troop is trained up on it."

"Trained up? I suppose. Let's see here, I have you assigned to C Troop."

"The sergeant major mentioned that. I'm anxious to meet my men and get on with their training. Are there any special weaknesses I should emphasize to improve unit fitness?"

Taylor furrowed his brow for a moment. "I suggest you conduct your own evaluation, Lieutenant. You can draw your own conclusions. Be quick about it though. General Pershing has ordered us to establish a series of outposts along the border. Your troop will draw one of those assignments within a few weeks. The sergeant major will introduce you to your first sergeant. He can take you from there. Glad to have you aboard, Lieutenant."

Patton stood and saluted.

Taylor's wave might have chased a fly.

CHAPTER SIX

Sierra Blanca
October

The C Troop, Eighth U.S. Cavalry wound its way through the foothills of the Finlay Mountains southeast of Fort Bliss. They'd covered over one hundred miles of relatively easy foothill terrain in three days. That morning the trail turned steep and narrow. The Troop stretched out in file, climbing and switching back as the trail meandered its way up Sierra Blanca Mountain. The air cooled with the climb, providing the promise of crisp relief from the desert heat. The sky, faultless blue, stretched unbroken to the horizons in all directions. Bright white sunlight splashed through broken clouds, painting sand and rock. Shade-mottled sage growth eked existence from the parched earth.

The General concluded the best use of his limited forces would be to establish a series of outposts along the border. Revolutionaries operating in the north disbursed in guerilla bands. They gathered in force to battle Federal troops only when targeting a prize of some worth. Pershing's strategy would strengthen border security with small, mobile units distributed along the border.

The mission was routine. C Troop would establish a border outpost in the mountain town of Sierra Blanca. The mission may be routine, but it was also duty in the field. Banditry among the revolutionary bands operating on or near the border happened. It posed a real threat that held out the prospect of action.

It felt good to be away from Bliss, or more particularly the dismal atmosphere surrounding the Eighth under Colonel Taylor. Taylor stood in sharp contrast to all he found admirable in Pershing's demeanor and command style. He found Taylor sloppy about his personal appearance and fitness. The example set a tone for the troops under his command. Patton had no use for it. He much preferred the discipline and leadership Pershing projected. The general had clearly raised expectations in regard to unit discipline, fitness and performance. It remained to be seen if Colonel Taylor could raise his unit to meet the new standard. Getting his own troop away from the post gave him the opportunity to instill some pride and discipline in a unit sorely in need of it. He'd not want his personal evaluations tainted by association with the rest of the Eighth.

The mountain trail descended to the southeast where the Chihuahuan desert spilled out of northern Mexico into west Texas. Scrub cactus dotted a sandy plain guarded by towering sentinel yucca. Hot dry wind whipped stinging gusts of sand and lazy tumbleweed.

"Sierra Blanca is up yonder." Lem Spillsbury, the scout, pointed to a dark ragged scar on the sandy plain ahead. Lean and sloe-eyed handsome, Spillsbury gave the impression of being quiet and laid-back. In truth he had a flair for adventure and a flamboyant streak when given occasion.

Patton nodded. At this distance the squat smudge didn't look like much. Close up, Sierra Blanca didn't look any better. It owed its existence to the southern routing of transcontinental rail service. The town spilled north from the tracks and a small weathered depot, a rag-tag collection of silvered clapboard salted here and there with adobe influence. Three cross-streets of a block or two intersected a dusty main thoroughfare with its hotel, saloon and general store. The side streets were more or less lined with residences, home to the town's three hundred and fifty or so citizens. The streets were near deserted save a dust devil and the occasional tumbleweed. Horses and wagons still served most transportation needs. It must not have looked much different to the blue-coated cavalry of the last century.

Patton squeezed his long-legged bay into a trot, pulling up alongside the scout. "It doesn't appear this town has much in the way of accommodations for a hundred troops."

Spillsbury spit. "Nope."

"What do you suggest?"

He shrugged. "There's water west of town. Camp there for now. Townsfolk will likely take the men in pretty quick, you bein' here to look after 'em and all.

"Sergeant O'Keefe, Mr. Spillsbury will select a campsite west of town. Get the men settled. I expect I should officially tell somebody we're here."

"Oh, they know." Spillsbury said. "You can't hide a cavalry troop in a town the size of Sierra Blanca." He glanced at the sun settling into early evening. "The Sheriff is Dave Allison. This time of day, you'll likely find him in the saloon."

"Thank you, Mr. Spillsbury." Patton touched the flat brim of his Montana peak campaign hat and jogged into town to the saloon hitch rack.

The saloon smelled of stale tobacco smoke and beer. Traces of smoke hung in the dim light of late afternoon with a curtain of dust mites. Burn-scarred wooden tables dotted a worn plank floor. A few local patrons scattered at tables or stood at a bar that stretched across half the room. A heavyset bartender in a soiled apron wiped glasses, chatting with a gangly rancher. Patton got an inquiring look as he swung through the doors.

"I was told I might find Sheriff Allison here." The bartender tossed his shiny bald head with its oiled fringe of dark hair in the direction of a corner table. Patton nodded his thanks and walked to the back table. Three men looked up.

"Sheriff Allison?"

"That'd be me, General. What can I do for you?" But for the star on his chest, he might have passed for a school master or undertaker. By reputation he had a closer association with the undertaker. He had close-cropped white hair, watery gray eyes and an earnest expression that gave no hint to a dry wit.

"Lieutenant George Patton, Eighth Cavalry." He offered his hand. "I'd like to have a word with you."

Allison looked him up and down with a half smile. "S'cuse me, boys." He scraped back his chair and rose.

The single-action Colt .44 holstered on his right hip looked like it meant business. *Welcome to the old west, George.*

Allison moved toward a table closer to the door. "Care for a drink?"

"No thanks."

"Tea-totaler?"

"No. On duty."

"Me too. Drinkin's just sociable in these parts." He pointed his chin at the bartender. "Tubby, bring us a bottle and two glasses."

Tubby arrived with the bottle before the chair got warm. Allison poured. He lifted his glass.

"Welcome to Sierra Blanca, Lieutenant." He took a swallow.

Patton returned the gesture. The whiskey wasn't half bad.

"Now, what can I do for you?"

"My troop is bivouacked west of town, Sheriff. We've been assigned to establish a border security outpost here in Sierra Blanca. General Pershing is concerned about Mexican bandit activity in the area."

Allison shrugged. "We get bandit trouble every now and then, but not much since them five revolutionaries came across last year. Made the mistake of takin' some horses didn't belong to 'em. Caught up with 'em down around Eagle Mountain, they ended up dead. Call me Dave."

Patton smiled. "Sounds like it will be kind of quiet up here then. And please, call me George."

"We manage to keep things quiet, George. Have for a good spell now."

"We?"

"Me and Buster."

"Buster?"

In the blink of an eye, the Colt appeared in Allison's hand. "George, meet Buster. Buster don't cotton to troublemakers. That's how they wind up dead."

Patton sat back, impressed. "I see your point."

"Most do. Word travels fast up here. Even Villa knows. Don't mess with Dave Allison."

"Villa, huh. You know him?"

Allison shook his head. "Don't need to. Don't care to, so long as he and his bandits steer clear of Sierra Blanca. It's all about respect. Them varmints know you mean business you can back up, they want no part of you. They teach you any of that shit at West Point?"

"How'd you know I went to the Point?"

"Spit and shine, George, spit and shine."

"Well, I believe one or two of my professors did touch on the topic of striking fear in the enemy, though I don't recall any of them putting it quite as colorfully as you, Dave."

"Colorful, is it?" Allison laughed and drained his glass. "Drink up, George. I don't know how long you're fixin' to stay, but we might as well have some fun while you're here." He poured another round.

★　★　★　★　★

"Again, Sergeant!" Patton prowled the field, balled fists pressed to his hips. O'Keefe circled the column of fours back to the start position. Patton stalked down the field after them. He addressed the column, his face red with the force of his displeasure. "Sloppy, gentlemen, sloppy. Hold your dress and cover, stirrup to stirrup, nose to tail. Sergeant, you set the pace. I want massed force, not a race to the finish. You may draw sabers when ready."

On Keefe's command, bright blades flashed to the ready.

Across the field at the edge of town, Spillsbury leaned against a fence rail, a blade of dry grass tucked in the corner of his mouth. Beside him an amused Dave Allison squinted under the brim of his hat.

"He's gonna wear them horses out with all that West Point bullshit."

Spillsbury nodded.

Allison spit a stream of tobacco juice. "What the hell does he think he's doin,' trainin' The Light Brigade?"

Spillsbury chuckled.

" 'Into the valley of death,' that's for damn sure. Cain't remember the rest. Don't need to."

A muffled command drifted across the broad plain. The formation moved forward at a trot. Another command, blades slashed forward. The troop let out a canter, pressed forward at a controlled gallop. The formation swept past the ramrod-straight figure in the Montana peak campaign hat. The troop slowed to a trot and recovered on a precise right wheel. He smiled to himself and folded his arms across his chest. They were rounding into shape. He might make a fighting force of them yet.

"Better! Once again, Sergeant!"

CHAPTER SEVEN

Sierra Blanca Hotel

A knock sounded at the door. Patton wiped the last of the lather from his chin with a towel. "Who is it?"

"Telegram for Lieutenant Patton."

He fished a quarter out of his pants pocket and opened the door. A young lad handed him the yellow Western Union envelope. He tossed the boy the coin and closed the door. He tore open the message.

Revolutionary forces reported south of the border in your area. They appear to be moving west. Mount a patrol to ensure they do not cross into U.S. territory. Do not engage unless fired upon. Do not enter Mexico even in pursuit.

Taylor

He left his room and crossed the threadbare hall rug. He rapped on the door. Muffled footsteps shuffled within. "Coming." The door swung open to Sergeant O'Keefe dressed in trousers and undershirt.

'Uh, excuse me, sir."

"At ease, O'Keefe." He handed him the telegram. "Send a wire to Colonel Taylor acknowledging receipt of his order. Alert the men. We leave at first light. If you need anything, I'll be in the dining room. The mayor is giving a dinner in my honor."

"Very good, sir."

Patton returned to his room. He donned his tunic. He'd adopted the westerner's practice of carrying his pistol at all times, concealed when not on duty. He slipped the heavy standard-issue .45 automatic in his pants pocket and headed downstairs.

The hotel dining room tables were set with linen, china, silver and crystal for the occasion. Cocktails were served there in consideration of the ladies present. Tom Tucker, full-time storekeeper and part-time mayor, greeted him, introducing his wife, a plain pleasant woman named Winnie. Tucker introduced him to two of the city fathers and their wives before Allison rescued him to a corner where he and Spillsbury already had their drinks.

"Lem, I'm glad you're here. We've got orders to mount a border patrol west in the morning. Bliss has some intelligence that revolutionary forces are moving west on the Mexican side of the border. We're to make sure they don't cross into the U.S."

Allison shook his head. "They won't cross. They're on their way to Agua Prieta. The Federales have a garrison there. Likely Villa figures he can take 'em."

Patton braced. "How can you be so sure?"

"I know how the sum-bitch thinks."

"Well, I hope he tries. I'd like nothing better than to give him a taste of U.S. Cavalry steel."

"That pretty pig-sticker of yours?"

"Damn right."

"Take my advice, George. Get yourself a close cousin to Buster. If you cross Villa's trail, shoot first. I hear he's a fair hand with a gun. Fast too. You'll never get close enough to cut that bastard. Save the pig-sticker for some Frenchman who smells good."

The Mayor clapped Patton on the shoulder. "Gentlemen, I believe they are ready to begin serving. Please, have a seat."

Over a fine steak dinner Allison recounted story after story of frontier law enforcement. Sometimes lawmen like Allison did the enforcing. At other times, rugged, law-abiding citizens took matters into their own hands when no one in authority could be found to do so. Patton listened. One of Allison's stories told of stopping a desperado's attempted escape by shooting his horse.

"You shot the man's horse?"

"Damn straight. Easier to hit a horse than the skinny bastard ridin' it. You'd do well to remember that, Lieutenant. You never know when it might come in handy."

You never know. These men reflected the spirit and courage that settled the west. They had character without pretense, character that deserved admiration. Sierra Blanca took him back to a time when the west was yet to be won. These men reminded him of a time when the United States Cavalry was the first line of defense for those hardy souls who ventured west. It may have been the golden age of the American horse soldier. It was a time in which he might have fulfilled his career ambitions. He felt comfortable in the company of these men, as he would have felt in the blue-coated service of the last century.

As the waiters cleared away the dishes, preparing to serve dessert, he pushed his chair back. "Excuse me for a moment." He left the dining room and found his way out back. The privy loomed ahead, a dark shadow in pale moonlight. The door creaked on a noisy hinge. He tugged at his trouser buttons.

The white-coated waiter was serving dessert when the shot rang out.

Allison reacted instinctively. "Everybody down! Kill the

lights." The room plunged into darkness as the diners dove under the table. "I'll have a look outside. Tom, stay with the women."

Allison rose. Dim moonlight showing through lace curtains glinted on Buster's blue finish as he started for the door. Spillsbury followed, his pistol drawn. "Lem, back door's next to the kitchen. Check things in back." Allison crossed the lobby to the front door.

Dim moonlight painted the yard in back of the hotel ghostly white. The privy cast its shadow twenty yards away. A dark figure moved out of the shadow. Spillsbury cocked his gun.

"Hold your fire, Lem, it's me."

Spillsbury let out his breath. "You all right, Lieutenant?

A chill mountain breeze cooled the heat on Patton's cheek. "I'm fine. Hell of a way to interrupt a man's business."

"Com'on, let's see if Dave's got anything out front." Spillsbury and Patton circled around to the front of the hotel.

"Nothin' in back, Dave."

Allison holstered his gun. "Damn strange. We don't get much shootin' in town these days."

Patton returned his pistol to his pocket. *Damn unreliable piece of shit! Jams when you need it, goes off when you don't. Perfectly good pair of trousers ruined too. Lucky I didn't shoot my balls off.* Allison's words chided him. "Get yourself a close cousin to Buster."

C Troop rode south the next morning. Spillsbury led them west along the border for three days. Patton spoiled for a fight every step of the way. *"Fancy pig-sticker," my ass. I'd love to show Villa and Allison good American steel at the point of a charge.* Rebel forces did not cross the border.

Fort Riley, Kansas
She curled up on the sofa and tore open the letter. Georgie.

Sierra Blanca

Dearest Beat,

We have just returned from a week-long patrol. We received reports of Mexican rebels moving close to the border. We made no contact and saw no action—most disappointing.

The men are beginning to understand what I expect of them. They will be a disciplined fighting force before I finish with them. Our time in Sierra Blanca has been useful to that end. As for the rest of the regiment, sad to say, the lack of discipline and attention to training is a shabby reflection on command. I must be diligent, lest the association tarnish my reputation. I hope the general recognizes my effort.

Sierra Blanca is a step back in time to a west still wild. Little has changed here in the last forty years. I believe I should have been quite comfortable living then. I quite enjoy the people.

The cavalry played a prominent role in settling the west. I am quite certain I should have acquitted myself adequately by the likes of that other George, Custer. We are to return to Bliss at the end of the month. I shall miss my friends here.

This separation grows long, my dearest. I shall use my time off to explore living accommodations for us as the post has little to offer. I hope to have some things to show you by the time of your Christmas visit. Perhaps Nita can join us. I'm sure her company would ease your travels. Until then, Georgie

CHAPTER EIGHT

Villa sat beside a small fire, wrapped in a *serape* against desert chill. The fire snapped, sending a shower of sparks into the darkness. The night sky glittered like diamonds scattered across a black velvet blanket. The fires of the assembled División del Norte dotted the rolling hills to the south and east. Colonel Nicolas Fernandez sat nearby.

"Do you feel it, Nico?"

He shrugged. "Feel what, Jefe?"

Villa tilted his chin, his face a mask of firelight and shadow. He arched a brow, a conspiratorial twinkle in his dark eye. "Destiny, Nico, destiny awaits us. Agua Prieta is the first prize, as it should be. Obregon is there. The thief who stole the revolution for Carranza will feel the force of our first blow. If there is justice, I will see him stand before a firing squad and pay for his part in Carranza's treachery. We must find a photographer. Yes, we must have pictures of Obregon standing before the wall. And the body, we must have pictures of the body. Pictures I can send to Carranza. Once his tin soldier is dead, he can begin numbering the days until he must pay for his crimes."

His gaze drifted to the darkness beyond the firelight. "We can do this, Nico. It is our destiny."

Agua Prieta
November 1915
Winter wind lashed the desert night in cold gusts. General Alvero Obregon's eyes watered. Nothing penetrated the darkness

in the hills east of town. He crouched below the low wall surrounding the flat roof. Shielded from the worst of the wind, he
cupped his hand around the tip of his cigarillo and scratched a
match on the adobe. The match flared. He drew the tip to light
before the wind snuffed it out. He stood again, straining to
penetrate the darkness. His smoke disappeared in thin wisps.
The Jaguar hunted at night. Villa hunted at night. He could feel
him.

Reports of his movements had been coming in for weeks. The
bandito couldn't hide the movement of a force as large as Divisíon del Norte. He took the reports seriously from the first.
The last one convinced him Villa would attack Agua Prieta. It
made sense. It fit the outlaw's machismo. He never turned his
back on an affront. He broke with Carranza over the taking of
Mexico City. He, Alvaro Obregon, made that possible. Villa
blamed him for taking the prize for Caranza after Divisíon del
Norte defeated Huerta's federal troops. Villa claimed Carranza
allowed him to steal the prize. Let the bastardo make all the
rash complaints he wished. It makes him predictable. Honor
would drive him to redress what he saw as insult. Let him come.
Obregon smiled. *We shall see.*

He'd prepared his defense with care. The jaguar knew only
one tactic, the charge. The bandito general favored the cover of
darkness. Obregon knew the value of stealth and surprise,
uncommon elements in a defensive strategy. He'd prepared a
sleeping flock. He'd given his sheep fangs.

Villa drew a halt on a low rise overlooking the town, sleeping
peacefully. Little more than shadows could be seen in the gray
light of predawn. The fat pig Obregon would pay for his
treachery this day. He signaled his troops. Tack jangled, saddle
leather creaked softly. Here and there a horseshoe clipped stone.
The column spread slowly left and right along the ridge. A line

of attack formed out of dark shadows.

Villa felt power spread along the line. He glanced left. He met Nico's eyes. To the right Candelario Cervantes nodded. He eased his horse down the ridge at a walk. The soft sounds of men and horses surged in his blood. The mesa leveled out at the base of the ridge. Sand, stone and scrub stretched to the shadows of the town. No light shown among squat ragged smudges before them. Villa squeezed up a trot, closing on the town. Dust clouds rose along the line like a morning fog rolling forward. He extended the trot to a lope. Horses sensed the charge. The ground picked up the beat. Thunder pounded under the hooves of seven hundred horses. Villa's blood ran hot with vengeance. The outskirts of the town loomed before them. He turned to his bugler.

"Sound the charge!"

The clarion bars of La Cucaracha shattered the cold night air. The line surged to a gallop. Shouts of "*Viva* Villa," drowned in a roar of primal lust. Muzzle flashes threw lightning to the thunder, storm and smoke. Wind-whipped ponchos, tearing sombreros to their throat strings, baring the heads of the horde. The charge closed to a hundred yards. Another fifty, the town waited. División del Norte bore in for the kill.

Darkness exploded in white light, catching the full force of the charge like fish in a net. Searchlights blinded men and horses. Somewhere beyond the lights a barrage erupted. Machine gun fire raked the line, streaming bright bursts of death left, right and center. Artillery roared and thumped, exploding over the massed Villistas in gouts of dirt and gore, indistinguishable for man or beast. Beneath the machine gun chatter and artillery bursts, devastating volleys of small arms fire rose from trench slits concealed behind the wall of light.

In the blink of an eye the plain east of Agua Prieta became a no-man's land torn from the battlefields of Europe. Men and horses shrieked and fell, screamed and died. The charge broke in a disorganized melee. Death rained in sheets. Lead and steel cut the attackers to shreds. Villa wheeled his horse to the rear. His exhilaration at the charge plunged to the depths of hell in a rage.

"Vaminos muchachos!" He spurred away to the shelter of shadow, leaving three hundred and thirty-six dead and dismembered. Mere moments in the rain of high-powered, precision fire sapped División del Norte of nearly half its strength.

Dawn broke over the ragged bloodied column clawing its way back into the hills. Horses plodded nose to tail. Riders swayed in the saddle fighting to hold their seats or slumped over their horses' necks. Few escaped without some injury. The nicked and flesh-wounded counted themselves near as fortunate as the few unscathed.

Villa rode by himself at the head of the column. His commanders gave room to his murderous rage. Only Nicolas Fernandez dared ride close enough to hear his wrath.

"Obregon! The bastardo pig hides in a hole with machine guns and cannon when real men come to fight. Coward shit Carranza won't even hide in a hole. He sits his presidential ass on a velvet cushion and lets his peons fight for him."

He turned in the saddle, saddened to see the pain born by his men. The once proud División del Norte straggled behind. An army reduced to a sorry parade of blood and mud. He held Fernandez' eyes and shook his head.

"The worst of it, Nico, are the Americanos. The gringos have no stake in our struggle. Still they sell electricity to the fat coward. Wilson treats Mexico as his footstool. He thinks the Mexican people are his gardeners. I would cut off his balls with a dull machete if he had any. He won't fight the Germans and he won't fight Pancho Villa. He is worse than that whore's son, Carranza. At least Carranza is Mexican."

German Consulate
Mexico City
November 1915

A light rap at the ornate gilt door echoed across the expanse of polished tile and stucco. Von Kreusen looked up from the week's Foreign Ministry dispatch, his brow arched over the gleam reflected in his monocle.

"*Fraulein* Leiben to see you, Herr von Kreusen."

Lady Love, he released the monocle to its velvet ribbon with a wave for his assistant to admit her.

Elsa Leiben crossed the spacious office with a confident stride, her sensual charms tastefully understated in a simple blue skirt, short matching jacket and crisp white blouse. Understated perhaps, but nonetheless stunning. Muted sunlight played golden light in her hair. She had smoky blue eyes, alert breasts and a figure sculpted to the perfection of a goddess. Von Kreusen found her striking in spite of his more sophisticated appetites. *If she had a brain, she would have the vulgar barbarian eating out of her.* He left the thought unfinished. Smiling, he extended his hand.

"Fraulein Leiben, I've been expecting you."

"Count von Kreusen, a pleasure to meet you."

"Please, have a seat." He held one of the gilt visitor chairs for her to grace the red velvet cushion. She smelled of the tiny lilies he remembered in the meadows of Austria. A lovely counter point to Mexico's less pleasant aromas. He took his seat behind the desk.

"I trust you had a pleasant journey."

"Quite restful, really, once one becomes accustomed to the

roll of the ship."

"No problems with illness then?"

She shook her head.

"Good. I trust you found our accommodations acceptable."

"Yes, quite, though I expect that is about to change."

"Yes, well conditions in the countryside can prove a bit more, shall we say, rustic."

She laughed, deep and throaty. "Rustic, is it? I'm sure."

"Down to business then, you understand your assignment?"

"I am to seduce Pancho Villa and turn him against the Americans."

"Very direct. I like that."

"Most men find me quite likable, Herr Ambassador."

Exception noted. "Good, then we understand one another. I will assist you by any means at my disposal."

She shifted in her chair, crossing a shapely leg. "First I shall need to know where to find this Pancho Villa. I shall require transportation and some pretense of an introduction."

"All that can be arranged. My sources tell me he retreated to Chihuahua after his defeat at Agua Prieta. He is rumored to be in hiding at Rancho San Miguel."

"I heard about Agua Prieta. It makes one wonder if Villa is up to poking the Americans in the eye. Wouldn't Carranza be a more suitable tool?"

Von Kreusen shrugged. "Carranza came to power with American backing. Wilson felt compelled to recognize his government, though I do not believe he supports it politically. Villa broke with Carranza after he allowed Obregon to take Mexico City. For better or worse, Villa opposes Carranza. It should be far easier to turn Villa against Carranza's American supporters than to convince Carranza to bite the hand that feeds him."

"I see."

"Actually, I believe you can turn Agua Prieta to your advantage."

"How so?"

"Villa blames the Americans for his defeat. Obregon lit the battlefield with searchlights powered by American electricity. After that, the matter was never in doubt. All we need is for Villa to target American business interests in Mexico. His desire for revenge should provide all the motivation he needs, with the proper guidance and encouragement, of course."

"Encouragement can be arranged."

"You might convince him to target oil interests in return for German support. Disrupting the flow of Mexican oil to the allies is vital to the Fatherland. If you can persuade him to raid an American border town or two, the resulting public outcry will force even the pacifist Wilson to act. With luck, we may provoke war."

She smiled. Eyes half lidded, she flicked her lip with a pink tongue tip. "I specialize in provocation."

"I'm quite sure you do. War with Mexico is the best way to keep the Americans out of the Allied war effort. Now, is there anything else you require, Fraulein?"

"Nothing."

CHAPTER NINE

Fort Bliss
December 1915

Candles decorated with holly boughs at the center of each linen-covered table suffused the officers' mess in a soft warm glow. They'd cleared the end of the hall near the entrance to accommodate a small orchestra stand and a dance floor. A buffet stretched along the far wall. Temporary bars were set in opposite corners on either side of a ten-foot Christmas tree that gave the room a festive hint of pine scent.

The Officers' Christmas Party was the highlight of the holiday season at Fort Bliss and a command performance for the officer staff. Party dresses worn by the officers' wives and guests painted a vivid palate of holiday color against a backdrop of dress blue uniforms. Muted conversation hummed as the guests mingled, the junior officers paying their respects while senior officers and their spouses held court.

Patton arrived with Beat on one arm and his sister, Nita, on the other. Both women had come to El Paso for a holiday visit. Heads turned. Beat wore a simple frock of dark green, a perfect complement to her hair and complexion. Nita, on the other hand, had chosen red, festive for the holidays to be sure, but a bold statement about her blonde hair and shapely figure.

General Pershing stood near the door, greeting the arriving guests, conspicuous by the absence of wife or guest. George knew of the tragic fire that claimed his wife and daughters earlier that year. The holidays, he knew, made times of loss all the more so.

"Lieutenant Patton, I'm pleased you could attend."

"Thank you, General. It's kind of you to offer your hospitality to the season. May I present my wife, Beatrice, and my sister, Nita Patton."

Pershing offered a slight bow. "Mrs. Patton, my pleasure. Miss Patton, is it?" Nita offered her hand with a nod. "How very nice to meet you, I'm pleased you could join us." Her handshake was firm, confident. He liked that. His smile revealed the dimple in his cheek, a warm blemish in an otherwise steel bearing.

Nita returned his smile. "It's a pleasure to meet you, General. George has told me so much about you. Thank you for having me."

"Enjoy the evening. Perhaps you'll save a dance for me later."

"I should enjoy that very much." The husky tone of her voice sounded like butter. She smiled again as George led them away to the obligatory introduction to Colonel Taylor and his wife.

Taylor looked pressed for once in the dress uniform that spent most of its days neatly hanging in a closet. Mrs. Taylor was a plain woman, made more so by the contrast to Beatrice and Nita. Still, she made both younger women feel welcome.

"Are you planning to move to El Paso?" she asked.

"George and I will look at off-post housing while I am here."

"It's unfortunate the post doesn't offer more living accommodations. Hopefully, you will find something suitable in town."

Beat smiled her thanks. George extended holiday wishes to the Colonel and his wife. They took their leave for the buffet line and an elegant assortment of hot and cold hors d'oeuvres. With plates filled, he seated the ladies at a table and fetched cups of punch from a cut crystal bowl set beside the end of the buffet. He then set off for the bar.

A familiar trooper serving as a bartender in a starched white jacket greeted him. "What can I get for you, sir?"

"Scotch and soda, please."

"I believe I'll have one of those, myself." Pershing stood at Patton's elbow. The bartender poured the drinks and served them.

"So tell me, Lieutenant, how was Sierra Blanca?"

"We used the time to good advantage training. The troop will be a disciplined fighting force in due time. The unit saber skill and strength of formation at the charge improved measurably by our time on the border."

Saber training, Pershing smiled. "Training and fitness are certainly in order. How is their marksmanship?"

"They are all qualified marksman with the exception of three new recruits."

"How many of them are qualified at long range?"

"Long range, sir?"

"One hundred yards or more."

"Isn't that more of an infantry skill? The cavalry training manual mentions nothing of long-range marksmanship."

"It should. The Springfield is a formidable weapon. It is highly accurate at long range. Modern cavalry tactic is more about speed and maneuverability than mass concentration of force. It places a higher premium on the trooper's marksmanship. If you've got a weapon like the M1903, that's effective at twenty-five hundred yards, it makes sense to exploit the capability."

"Thank you, sir, I shall look the training up in an infantry manual."

Pershing nodded.

"When should we expect to be deployed again?"

"That anxious to get back out there, are you?"

"We saw no action on our last deployment. We took the field once in regard to a report of bandits moving south of the border. I'd hoped we might blood our M-13s on the mission, but we saw no sign of them."

"Just as well. We know what that was about now."

"Sir?"

"Agua Prieta, Villa hit it last month. At troop strength you wouldn't have enjoyed the encounter, least of all with sabers. The M-13's your model, isn't it?"

"It is, sir." Patton beamed.

Pershing swirled the scotch in his glass, lifting an eye to Patton over the rim. "The saber is a storied symbol of cavalry lore."

"It's a fine weapon, sir, in the hands of a trained cavalry. The performance won top grades in the mounted exercises we conducted at Fort Riley."

"Mounted exercises, yes, I'm quite sure of that. As a practical matter, though, Lieutenant, the future of the saber is Olympic competition and ceremony. Its role as a weapon has passed."

"But, sir, you're a cavalry officer. You know the saber is emblematic of the cavalry. The saber is the point of the charge."

"I am a cavalry officer, Lieutenant. I am also a realist. Modern warfare is rapidly pushing the horse soldier into the pages of history. Look at what happened to Villa at Agua Prieta. Obregon prepared his defense and baited Villa into his signature charge. He then used searchlights, enfilade machinegun fire, artillery and high-powered small arms to cut Villa's cavalry to ribbons. Some estimates have the casualty rate as high as fifty percent for an engagement that lasted a matter of minutes."

"A poor decision by an untrained field commander certainly doesn't imply the end of the cavalry as a fighting force."

Pershing swallowed a half smile. Some might consider the Lieutenant's demeanor impertinent. He didn't. He'd had a streak of that himself once. "I'm afraid it does, eventually, George. Maybe not today or tomorrow, but the machine gun and ballistic advances in artillery are only the beginning of mechanized warfare. Study the conflict in Europe if you wish to see the future. Unfortunately, we're the ones falling behind. But enough shop talk. I've a mind for some holiday cheer." He drained his glass. "I believe I'll have that dance with your lovely sister, if you don't mind."

"Of course not, sir."

Pershing left him bewildered at the bar.

Beat looked radiant gliding across the floor with effortless grace. Patton managed the waltz.

"They make a lovely couple, don't they, Georgie?"

He'd tried not to formulate an opinion. After the fourth dance, he supposed he must. "The General does seems to enjoy Nita's company."

"Pshaw, George," Beat giggled. "Look at them."

They danced. Nita held his eyes in her smile. The General's dimple betrayed him. Generals weren't supposed to have dimples. There must be some regulation against it. It's Nita, for god's sake. She's in the arms of my commanding general. "How long is she staying?"

Beat laughed again, reading his thoughts. "Only through New Year's, George, unless I suppose El Paso should grow on her."

He winced.

74

CHAPTER TEN

Rancho San Miguel
Chihuahua

The sleek black touring car sped along the dusty road leading to the ranch. Elsa Leiben lounged in the soft leather upholstery. She'd seen to every detail of her plan with von Kreusen's help. Everything about Francisco Pancho Villa suited her purpose. His Latin machismo, his weakness for women, even his misguided ideas of social justice could all be used to manipulate the man. A child could do it. Well perhaps not a child. He was known to be a womanizer not a pedophile. If he were handsome it might actually be amusing. Sadly, she'd seen pictures. Handsome did not enter into the assignment. In war some things must be sacrificed for the Fatherland.

At last the monotony of the desert landscape beyond the dusty window began to change. The road climbed into foothills approaching the ranch. Waning sunlight painted the mesas and arroyos in long blue shadows touched by splinters of pink and gold. The hacienda appeared off to the right, a low sprawling walled adobe compound with a dull terracotta tile roof. The view fairly smelled of tortillas and beans. She withdrew a small mirror from her handbag for a last check of her lipstick and hair. Her golden tanned skin required little in the way of makeup. Perfect. She replaced the mirror in her purse beside the small pearl-handled revolver. Likely an unnecessary precaution, but in the realm of precautions necessity was best judged in the past tense.

The car passed unchallenged through an arched gate into a walled plaza. The driver circled a tiled cistern in the center of the yard and rolled to a stop in front of an arched portico with a massive double-door entry. Elsa smoothed her skirt waiting for the driver to open the door.

Villa stood, hands clasped behind his back, sloped shoulders hunched, deep in thought. The last rays of mountain sunset slanted through double doors open to the western peaks. The Germans wanted something. They always wanted something. Their Kaiser was ambitious to a fault. He'd corrupted Huerta, causing the Americanos to go over to Caranza. Now with Huerta gone, the Germans had no influence in Mexico. What else could they possibly want from him? He would never allow himself or the revolution to be corrupted by the interests of foreigners. That said it took fire to fight fire. Caranza had already turned to the gringos for help. The losses at Agua Prieta could not be restored without money, a great deal of money. The Germans had money. They shared a common enemy. The last rays of sunlight disappeared behind the mountains. He needed help.

Nicolas Fernandez could be remarkably quiet when Villa did not wish to be disturbed.

"Jefe, the German is here."

Villa turned to the intrusion in the vaulted entry to the spacious parlor. With sunlight gone, firelight from a massive fireplace dominating one wall warmed the room with a soft, flickering glow. Braces of candles supplemented the firelight, burnishing the heavy wooden furnishings with a polished glow. Cushioned chairs and a settee were arranged around the fireplace. A massive carved desk stood on the opposite wall

beside shelves lined with books. Villa liked the feeling of education the books lent the room. "Send him in, Nico."

Fernandez shook his head. "It is not a man Jefe. It is a
woman, *una mujer muy hermosa.*"

Villa raised a brow. A beautiful woman? He cocked his head,
interesting and so much more entertaining than some shriveled
old diplomat. The Germans must want something special. He
licked his lips. "Send her in, Nico."

Fernandez disappeared. Moments later he returned followed
by a golden goddess with the beauty to take a man's breath
away. And anything else she might want as well.

"General Villa, Elsa Leiben." She offered her hand with a
smile that brightened the room to a tawny gold.

He accepted her hand. "Señora or Señorita?"

"Does it matter?"

Villa shrugged, amused. "Not so much."

"Señorita."

"Please have a seat, Señorita. May I offer you some refresh-
ment?"

She took a seat on the settee in front of the fire. She smiled.
"What do you have?"

"For myself, a cola, but please feel free to have something
stronger if you like. I condone spirits. I simply prefer sweets."

"American sweets, I'm surprised."

"I hold many things against the gringos. Coca and Hershey's
chocolate are not among them."

"Good. Then I think we shall find much that interests us."
She crossed her legs.

He bowed stiffly. "I am sure." *The body of a goddess, the voice
of an angel, breasts of pure gold, dio mio.*

"Tequila over ice then, it helps me relax."

"Relax, sí. Nico, if you please, send for the drinks. Villa took
his seat beside her. "So, Señorita, how is it that I may be of

service to you?"

"Oh, General Villa, I think it is I who may be of service to you. And, please, call me Elsa."

"The pleasure is mine, Elsa. My friends call me Pancho."

"I know, but if you'll permit, I find Francisco so strong and so virile."

"Whatever pleases you."

"*Muy bien,* Francisco."

A dark-skinned serving girl in a long, colorful peasant skirt and white cotton blouse arrived with the drinks. She set them on the polished table before the settee and silently slipped away.

Villa lifted his glass in a toast. "So Elsa, since you are to be of service to me, what is it you find me in need of?"

She wrinkled her nose and took a swallow of tequila. Getting him to take a bath might prove a greater challenge than her diplomatic mission. "My government is prepared to supply you with arms and ammunition."

"These are always much needed by the people's revolution. Undoubtedly, you have a price for such aid."

"Nothing more than you already intend. Your revolution opposes both Carranza and his American puppet masters. Germany would like to disrupt the flow of oil to the Allied war effort. Americans own much of the oil production in northern Mexico. You wish to repay the Americans for supporting Carranza in that dreadful affair at Agua Prieta." She made a pretty pout and shrugged her shoulders. "If you take your vengeance on American oil interests, both our causes are served."

"So simple, is it?" He folded his hands in his lap.

She patted his hands. "It's a start."

"It is a start, but it takes more than guns and ammunition to wage revolution. It takes money. Money pays soldiers. Money buys supplies."

"Money buys larger interests for us."

"What interests?"

Her eyes turned smoky. "War between Mexico and the United States."

Villa laughed. "You don't ask much. Poke the sleeping gringo in the eye and find myself caught between two armies as though one is not enough."

"I told the Kaiser you were the *hombre* to do this, Francisco. Perhaps I overestimated you." She favored him with a wicked smile.

He caught the twinkle in her eye. He undressed her in his mind's eye. "You will find me more than satisfactory. You are only mistaken concerning the cost of such an enterprise. How can your Kaiser assure Pancho Villa his revolution will succeed? How can your Kaiser assure we bring justice to the Mexican people?"

"Spoken like a man of vision. I like that." She leaned forward to pat his shoulder. A tender breast brushed his arm. "Germany offers you a powerful alliance. If the Americans are held out of Europe, Germany will defeat the French and the British. We will come to your aid with the united forces of Europe. The people will rise up against Carranza. Together we will conquer the Americans. We will restore Mexico's rightful ownership to territories from Texas to California. The leader who brings such a victory to the Mexican people will be a national hero the likes of which is unknown beyond Montezuma himself."

Villa gazed into the fire, his black eyes aflame. Elsa downed her tequila and poured another.

"Your Kaiser dreams in bright colors, Elsa. I must think on this."

"See Francisco, I am not wrong. You are every inch the strong hombre I told the Kaiser you were."

"You are not wrong." He arched a brow playfully. "You know, I do my best thinking in the arms of a beautiful woman."

Elsa drained her glass. "I find a thinking man terribly exciting."

His *virilidad* stirred. "Then shall we let the thinking begin?"

"Sí, Francisco, but first, if you don't mind, it has been a long dusty journey. Do you have a bath I might use?"

"Sí." He grinned broadly.

El Paso
January 1916

Cold wind howled, rattling the window panes and ruffling the lace curtains where dry cracked putty surrendered to draft. The small parlor fought for warmth with the aid of heavy sweaters. Patton folded the newspaper. Beat sat across the room lost in thought over an unread open book. "What's wrong, Beat?"

"Nothing."

"I know nothing when I see it. What I see is something bothering you."

"Really, George, it's nothing."

"Is it that time?"

She forced a smile. "No."

"Then why so melancholy, my dear?"

"Oh, George, it's just, this."

"This?"

"Fort Bliss, El Paso, another remote post who's only redeeming quality is that it is not another long separation."

"You miss Nita, don't you?"

"I do miss her, along with the advantages of a city, sophisticated society and warmth in the air even if it's a fire in the winter. But it's more than that. This is your dream, George, but where is it taking us? You're bothered by General Pershing's views on the future of the cavalry. Is it really worth all this?"

The question struck him. He sat silent. Buried questions and doubts welled up. He'd had them. He hadn't wished to confront them. Now Beat had them too. Were they so obvious? Once exposed, they could not be denied.

Fame and glory had certainly eluded him. At thirty-two his career had not progressed beyond his rank at graduation from the academy. What had he truly accomplished? His Olympic riding garnered some notoriety. His accomplishments with the saber earned him distinction as the Army's Saber Master. Master of a weapon soon relegated to ceremony and parade. He was a cavalry officer, the proud scion of a long line of cavalry officers. He was bred to the cavalry. It was his life's purpose. And yet the officer he most admired doubted the future of the cavalry as a combat arm in modern warfare. Where did that leave him? Was he indeed a warrior trapped in a bygone age? He was a garrison soldier with no combat experience in an army whose political overseer seemed committed to policies of pacifism and neutrality. By any reasonable measure his prospects looked bleak. Beat had a right to expect more. Hell, he expected more.

He set the paper aside and went to her. He sat beside her and put his arm around her. She rested her head on his shoulder, welcoming the warmth.

"Wouldn't you rather raise horses? You've a talent for it, you know."

"You may be right, Beat. It's only that the army has been my dream as long as I've had one. I'm a soldier. Descended from a long line of soldiers. I'm born to it. I find the idea of giving up repugnant. General Pershing is the finest general officer I have ever encountered. I can learn a great deal from him. I see qualities in him I know I possess. It's only a matter of others coming to recognize them. In time, the general will see them."

She lifted her eyes to his, hands folded in her lap. "At least think about it. We only have so much life to live. Must we live it apart or in the El Pasos of this world?"

CHAPTER ELEVEN

Santa Ysabel
January 1916

Thomas Holmes took in the unfamiliar scene beyond the streaked train window. He knew rural train stations from his home in New Hampshire. Small clapboard depots freshly whitewashed or stained with neatly painted signs, announcing the location of the stop. The only thing Santa Ysabel had in common with those stations was wood and water up the tracks where the engine parked. The adobe depot looked like a brick oven. He could scarcely make out the badly chipped sign painted in faded letters beside the door. Waiting passengers shuffled across a rickety wooden platform bleached dry by desert sun. Laborers unloaded an odd assortment of crates and parcels, piling them on the platform for their rightful owners to claim. One crate contained a noisy cargo of live chickens. Dust clouds swirled here and there, whipped by a hot wind. Without air circulating from the train's movement, the temperature inside the car grew oppressive. Sweat matted the young engineer's shirt to his chest. *Hell of a place to make a living. And this is winter, what must the summers be like?* Why didn't they find oil in civilized places with modern comforts? He guessed fields like that, if there were any, must be reserved for more senior people. The crew he signed onto in El Paso was made up of mostly younger men with a sense of adventure.

He shifted in his seat on the hard bench as the conductor barked his boarding announcement from an unseen location up toward the engine. At last the train lurched forward at a slow roll past the depot. Two heavily armed horsemen sat astride hip shot sleepy horses in the shade beside the depot. Holmes had the uncomfortable feeling of being watched. Mr. Watson, the General Manager, had assured the crew the revolution was over and that it was safe to return to the field. It might be safe, but that didn't make those men look any less disquieting.

The countryside scrolled by the window as the train picked up speed. Vast desolate expanses of desert scrub gashed by ravines in some places or spiked by rocky outcroppings in others. Sand, nothing but sand, everywhere you looked, sand followed by more sand. Sand patched with gray-green sage, cactus and more sand. The rhythm of the rails and the heat tugged at his eyelids. His head nodded. *Siesta,* they called it. At least something in Mexico made sense.

The train slowed. Holmes jerked awake. He glanced at his watch, too soon for the next stop. Red rock walls appeared on both sides of the train as it slowed through a cut, gouged out of a great stone butte. Brakes squealed, releasing hissing gouts of steam. The whistle blasted a shrill protest.

"What the hell now?" Two rows in front of Holmes, Watson stuck his head out the window. "Damn it!" He pulled his head in, grabbed his coat and started forward in his sweat-soaked shirt sleeves.

"What's the matter?" Holmes called.

"It looks like a freight car blocking the tracks."

Veterans of the Mexican oil fields told stories. To hear them tell it, nothing down here ran smoothly. It sounded like this might be his first taste. Curious, he rose and followed Watson to the car door. The crew chief stepped down to the roadbed and set off toward the engine. *This should be good.* Holmes jumped down behind him. One car forward, shadows appeared on the side of the car from above. Dark sentinels silhouetted in bright sunlight.

"Viva Villa!" Shots exploded down the confines of the cut, reverberating off the stalled cars. A bullet struck the track, whining wildly away in a shower of sparks.

Watson turned, wide-eyed, ashen. "Run!" He pushed past Holmes, running to the rear of the train. Holmes followed. Shouts and shots pursued them, spitting and singing in the narrow channel between the rock wall and train. Watson broke past the caboose into the open. Another volley of rifle fire roared down the cut. Bullets ripped his body, jerking violently, his white shirt spattered in bright red patches.

Holmes stumbled, pitched forward and rolled down the roadbed's cinder embankment, cutting and scraping his skin. He crashed into a mesquite thicket, stunned. He lay still. The shooting fell silent.

Back up the line near the head of the train, harsh voices shouted in Spanish. Orders followed by the crunch of boots running on the cinder bed. More orders, shouted in broken English this time.

"Get up. Get off the train."

Holmes turned his head toward the tracks. His eyes adjusted to the shadows. Members of Watson's crew climbed out of the passenger cars, holding their hands in the air. Khaki-clad dark figures in wide-brimmed sombreros followed, holding the men at gunpoint. A gunshot exploded somewhere beyond his line of sight.

"*Muerte* Americanos!"

"Muerte gringos!"

"Viva Villa!"

The cries echoed down the rock walls. Along the train, prisoners were forced to kneel. A dark figure strode into view. He stopped at the first guard. He grabbed the man's rifle, leveled it at the kneeling oil man and fired. The body lifted off its knees with the force of a high-powered rifle fired at point-blank range and slammed to the ground. The shooter handed the rifle back to the guard and calmly moved on. Holmes closed his eyes to the grisly spectacle. Another rifle shot followed, then another and another. Fifteen shots in all until sixteen of the seventeen-member crew lay dead. When at last the shooting stopped, Holmes risked another look. A Mexican in a baggy khaki uniform with crossed bandoliers stripped the nearest victim. The glint of a knife appeared over the body. Holmes closed his eyes against the gore.

He lay still, listening to his heart pound in his ears. Time passed. Blue shadows drew a somber veil over the rock walls, as though slowly covering the train in a shroud. Somewhere in the darkness brakes released a shrill screech. Couplings clanked, a metallic chain reaction rippled through the cars. Steel-flanged wheels inched backward. The train rolled by, slowly picking up speed, car by car. The coal tender passed, followed by the engine, backing away from the horror-laid waste beside the track. The engine headlamp lit the tracks and mesquite thicket like a floodlight. Slowly it grew less intense, smaller as it retreated up the tracks, shrinking to a bright white spot that disappeared the way it had come.

He waited. He did not move. He listened. Shallow breathing roared in the stillness. His mind raced, formulating a plan. Sneak back to Santa Ysabel. Hop a freight to Juárez and the border. Darkness fell. Black shadow filled the cut, quiet and still. His eyes searched the gloom up the line. Nothing. He eased himself out from under the bush. Moonlight filtered through a blanket of cloud scudding out of the mountains. Naked bodies lay sepulcher white beside the silvered ribbon of track. Dark patches marked the passing of bullets and blades.

Bitter bile rose in his throat. He vomited, retching in spasms he could not suppress. He steadied himself, spit, turned his back on the dead and walked up the tracks.

El Paso
February 1916

Mexican Revolutionaries Execute Sixteen Americans
Villa Supporters Believed Responsible

Zach Cobb read the newspaper account. It described the cold-blooded murder of unarmed, innocent civilians as told by the lone survivor. He set the paper aside. Tensions long the border were not new. U.S. and Mexican relations had turned frosty, to say the least, after Vera Cruz. The continuing political instability in Mexico did little to improve the situation. The paper reported that the men who attacked the train shouted "Viva Villa" and "Death to Americans." Carranza's inability to control revolutionary elements operating in the north exacerbated border security problems. This incident would only add to the tensions.

People were angry. They wanted action. He'd seen them gathering on street corners and in vacant lots as he made his way to the office that morning. Small vocal knots shouted demands, raw emotion feeding on itself as the gatherings grew into crowds. He could hear them even now drifting toward the border. He looked out the office window, up the street into town. A handful of blue-clad police drew a thin line, talking reason and calm. Voices in the wind, he thought. If that crowd turned ugly and crossed the border, he shook his head at the diplomatic consequences of mob violence on Mexican soil. He went back to his desk and picked up the telephone.

"State Department, please." He waited impatiently, drumming his fingers on the desk while the connection went through.

Finally, the line rang.

"State Department."

"Under Secretary Armitage, please." More waiting and clicking.

"Armitage here."

"Charles, it's Zach. We've got a situation down here."

White House
February 1916

"It's an outrage, Mr. President, a damned outrage!" Senator Fall hunched forward, red-faced in anger. A small vein throbbed at his temple. "American citizens taken off a train and gunned down execution style, their naked bodies mutilated and left to rot in the sun. We must take swift and decisive military action."

Wilson held up his hand. "I understand your frustration, Senator, but we have a larger diplomatic context at work here."

"Diplomatic context my ass, with all due respect, sir, we have an obligation to protect those people."

"Secretary Lansing has received assurances from the Carranza government. They will see that those responsible are hunted down and brought to justice."

"That's pure sheep dip and you know it. The sole survivor heard it plain as day. 'Viva Villa!' We know who's responsible for this atrocity. Carranza might rule the Presidential Palace, but in outlying states like Chihuahua and Sonora, states that abut our border, I might add, he has no more control than the man in the moon. If Villa gets away with this, there's no telling what he may do next."

"Senator, are you asking me to invade a sovereign nation? That is an act of war. With conflict in Europe threatening, the last thing we need is war with Mexico."

"Interesting you should mention the European conflict, sir. I can't prove it, but the reports I'm getting from the border say that Villa's men are armed with new German Mausers. If that's true, the Kaiser may already be pulling the bandit's strings."

"We have reports that raise similar suspicions. Nothing would suit the Kaiser's purposes better than to have this country distracted by war with Mexico."

"If the Germans are behind Villa's aggressive behavior, why should we expect he'll stop at one atrocity? He's dangerous, Mr. President. What do you mean to do about it?"

"I mean to let President Carranza handle it."

"You do, of course, realize who those men worked for?"

Wilson removed his spectacles and rubbed the bridge of his nose. "I am well aware of those interests."

"Emotions are running high along the border. When news of the Santa Ysabel massacre broke, the governor had to declare martial law in El Paso. The police couldn't manage the mobs taking to the streets to demand action. Those citizens also vote, Mr. President."

"I'm aware of that too, Senator."

Fall clenched his jaw. *Nothing ruffles the man. He still thinks he's a tenured college professor.* "Are you prepared to throw away the border states come the next election? Think about it, Mr. President."

CHAPTER TWELVE

Rancho San Miguel
Chihuahua

The Dorado guard showed Elsa into the parlor. Villa sat in a cushioned chair beside the fireplace eating a large dish of ice cream, his boots propped up on the low table in front of the settee. She favored him with one of her most fetching smiles as she crossed the room. His eyes followed her filled with undisguised animal hunger.

"Señorita, would you like some ice cream?"

"Francisco." She bent to kiss his forehead. "Thank you, no. A girl must keep her figure, you know." She took a seat on the settee at his knee.

"Hmm, a little meat on the bones never hurts. So, how do you like our little venture into the oil business?"

"Oil and the Americans just as we discussed, you are so very clever, Francisco. The Foreign Ministry was very pleased by my report. How did your men find the Mausers? You certainly made good use of them."

Villa shrugged, licking his spoon. "They are very powerful. We could use machine guns and light artillery."

"All in good time, Francisco, all in good time. First I would like to hear your plan to avenge Agua Prieta."

"Your Kaiser wants this war with the Americans very badly,

doesn't he? This is a risky undertaking for a humble revolutionary."

"Francisco, I'm surprised to hear such talk from a man of your machismo."

"Revolution is expensive. War with the United States is very expensive."

"I'm sure I can arrange a shipment of machine guns and light artillery to go with those lovely rifles of yours."

"That would help the revolution. If I attack the United States and provoke your war, how does my revolution survive until you finish your war with the English and the French? The promise of your Kaiser's alliance may be more luxury than a humble revolutionary can afford."

"Nonsense, Francisco. I have seen how resourceful you can be. You are more than man enough to provoke the Americans. Once you do, Carranza will have no choice but to oppose them. If he does not, the people will see him as a vassal of American imperialism. The people will rise to your cause."

He scratched his chin, considering the possibilities. "War with the Americans is very expensive."

"How expensive?"

"Very expensive. Even if I had the money, I must think carefully about this. I cannot risk being caught between the Yanquis and Carranza. We must disappear while Carranza expends himself on the Yanquis and your Kaiser finishes his business with the English and the French."

"There," she purred. "That is just the sort of thinking we need."

"Do not forget the money."

"You drive a hard bargain, Francisco. I admire a hard man. I will get you your guns. I cannot promise money but I will see what I can do. While I do, think hard about how you will avenge the American insult done to you at Agua Prieta."

"Sí, I will think. But for now, I have something even harder for you to admire."

"You do drive a hard bargain, Francisco."

Fort Bliss
Reservation

Two dark riders swept across the sandy plain, horses stretched out at a gallop. Dun dust clouds trailed behind rising to a crisp cobalt winter sky. They climbed a low ridge and drew rein at the crest silhouetted to the sand dunes for miles around.

The horses snorted, tossing their heads, prancing and pawing, fighting the bit. "Nothing like a fast horse to fill a man with rightful purpose." Pershing patted his horse's neck with a gloved hand.

"I agree, sir. Winter doesn't improve the view out here, but a little cool air lifts the spirit. The horses feel it too."

Pershing scanned the horizon. "It is something of a kitty box, isn't it? A soldier's duty seldom lends itself to beauty. We're generally called to ugly things that need doing in not so pretty places."

"At least we should have the diversion of some action. Border patrol is garrison duty in desolate surroundings."

Pershing chuckled. "It seems so, so far. Shall we walk these horses back to cool them down?" Pershing wheeled his mount, picking up his thought. Patton followed. "I wouldn't get too complacent, though. I suspect Villa's only taking a breather to lick his wounds after Agua Prieta. The reports we get out of Juárez suggest he blames the U.S. for his defeat."

"The U.S., how so?"

"Obregon got the electricity for his searchlights from the power company in Douglas, Arizona. Villa is reputed to be a vengeful sort. If he decides to vent his frustrations against us, we may see some action yet. We have reports the Germans are courting him. They tried to persuade Huerta to cut off the supply of Mexican oil to the allies. We backed Carranza to protect our interests. Now the Germans are playing 'Your enemy is my enemy' with Villa."

"What's the point? We have no part in the European conflict. Our President has no stomach for it."

Pershing glanced at his riding partner. The statement clearly tasted sour. "We have longstanding sympathies and relationships with the British and French. The Kaiser is smart enough to read between the lines. For the moment he can only nip at our heels in the shipping lanes and hope we stay out of the war. Provoke a war with Mexico and we'd be far less a concern."

Patton turned Pershing's assessment over thoughtfully before changing the subject. "Sir, I've been thinking about our conversation at the Christmas party."

"Ah, the Christmas party, which conversation?"

"The one about the future of the cavalry. You said I should consider what is happening in the European conflict. I've been studying the newspaper reports and magazine accounts as best I can."

"And your conclusions?"

"I'm not sure I've come to any definitive conclusions. The accounts don't provide much military detail. It is clear the conflict is mired in a defensive stalemate. It is a war of attrition with no clear prospect for victory apart from one side bleeding its opponent to death. Cavalry movement is highly restricted as I read it. I see the dilemma. But surely, sir, modern warfare does not negate the tactical and strategic advantages of speed and surprise in offensive operations. Defense by its very nature produces no victory."

"You're right, George. Think of it as a temporary imbalance. Gunpowder changed the nature of war in its time. Today's advances in firepower and ballistics have gotten ahead of other developments in mechanized warfare. Time and invention will correct the imbalance. One can see the signs already. The use of motorized vehicles is an example. One by one the missions of the cavalry are being transformed. Command and control will pass from mounted battlefield couriers to more reliable applications of our wireless radio experiments. Reconnaissance will pass from cavalry patrols to the air service. Transport will pass from the mule-drawn wagon to the combustion engine."

"And the mobile fighting force, sir?"

"One can't say at this point with certainty. Both the French and the British are engaged in the development of a motorized, armored artillery piece they call a tank. They're not very fast or reliable as yet, but time and invention have a way of correcting such deficiencies."

Patton fell silent. His horse picked the way along on the general's flank. Beat might be right. The officer he most admired saw no military future for a man of his skills. "It seems we no longer fight the war I'm bred to fight."

Pershing cocked his head, taking the young man's measure. "I'll not comment on your breeding, George. Experience is a great teacher. Time has a way of correcting all manner of things. You may find your breeding, as you choose to put it, prepares you for some as yet undiscovered purpose."

Perhaps, Patton thought, but at age thirty-two and still a lowly second lieutenant, time was running out.

Pershing brightened. "On a more pleasant note there is a small matter I need to mention. General Scott has called General Funston and me back to Washington for a briefing on the situation here on the border. I'll be in Washington for a few days. I've invited Miss Anne to come down and join me. She accepted the invitation. I hope you don't mind my seeing your sister."

"Mind? Of course not, sir."

"Thank you. I know some might think it awkward, given our circumstances. But I must say George, I find your sister most pleasant and charming company. I know too, there is some difference in our ages, but I assure you my intentions are completely honorable."

"It never occurred to me that they would be anything but, sir."

He smiled. "I appreciate your confidence. And please, when we're off duty call me John. Miss Anne does."

Rancho San Miguel
Chihuahua

Villa slammed his fist in the palm of his hand. "Where are the guns, Nico?"

Fernandez shrugged.

"We paid the Russian gringo for guns and ammunition. Where are they?"

"Ravel says these things take time."

"Ravel is a thief! He took our money. He promised us guns. Where are they? I think it is time we take our money back."

"He will ask for more time."

"I, Pancho Villa, wait no longer. We will go to Columbus and take our money back."

"Take our money back? They have Americano troops in Columbus, Jefe."

"Sí, Nico, troops with horses, machine guns and ammunition for the taking. They have a fat bank with our money, Ravel's money and more money than that. It is a fat prize for the revolution. If we can take it, it is a poke in the Yanquis' eye. Our German friends will approve. They will give us still more money."

The woman, he shook his head. "Is this wise, Jefe? I mean to strike the Americanos across the border. They may pursue us. We could be caught between Carranza and the Americanos."

"I have thought much on this since the Kaiser offered us money to do this. The Germans will pay us to do it, hoping for war. But, there will be no war. Wilson is an old woman. The English and French are Americano friends. He refuses to fight with them, but the day may come when he must. He will not risk war with Mexico. He will leave it up to Carranza, as he did after Santa Ysabel. Carranza is weak. Even now, he does not come out to fight with us. No, Nico, this is a prize we can take from the weak on both sides of the border. It is a prize that will make us stronger."

"Sí, Jefe." He cast his eyes down with worry. *The whore blinds him.*

CHAPTER THIRTEEN

Northwest Chihuahua
March 1, 1916

Smoke rose from the cook fire of a small ranch house in the valley below. Early evening shadows draped the hacienda and its adobe outbuilding. The evening star winked in the east. Nicolas Fernandez turned in his saddle. His column straggled down the trail below, disappearing in shadow. The men were tired and hungry. The ranch offered an inviting rest stop. It looked like a poor ranch, but they must have food. They would not have much else. Even a small store was better than none.

He eased his sturdy gray gelding down the hillside. The valley floor leveled out to a low rise. The hacienda sprawled across the top. One window blinked to light. The cook smoke smelled of mesquite. Fernandez' stomach growled in anticipation. They made their way slowly, not wishing to raise an alarm. Fernandez drew the column to a halt at the base of the rise and rode on to the hacienda by himself. He stepped down at the porch and ground-tied his horse. His boots clumped on the plank porch, his spur rowels rang. He raised his fist prepared to knock.

The door swung open. Yellow light spilled out behind the figure of a woman, tall and sturdy. He blinked. "Colonel Nicolas Fernandez, Señora." He tipped his sombrero and bowed. "I wish to buy food for my men."

"We have little."

She had a good voice, strong and unafraid.

"I will sell you what I can."

"Muchas gracias."

She stepped back, allowing him to enter. In clear light, he found her comely, pleasant features burnished by desert sun and the hardships of life. A small boy, perhaps two years old, sat on the floor in one corner. He stared round-eyed at the tall khaki-clad stranger.

"My husband is away. He should be home directly."

No surprises, smart, he liked that.

"Conchita and I were preparing supper. Would you like something to eat?"

"Señora is most kind." He removed his sombrero. Outside a horse snorted. A bit jangled. Saddle leather creaked. Boots sounded on the porch. Two men entered, the taller one greeted the woman with his eyes.

"John, Colonel Fernandez is joining us for supper."

"You are more than welcome, Colonel. John Wright." He extended his hand, still wary.

The woman served beef stew, fresh bread and coffee. Fernandez wolfed down his food. The men ate. The woman picked at her bowl, exchanging worried glances with her husband. John Wright cleaned the last bit of stew from his bowl with a crust of bread. He wiped his mouth and pushed back from the table.

"We'd best see to the horses. Com'on, Frank."

Fernandez nodded. The two men left. Finished, Fernandez pushed back from the table. The woman rose to clear the dishes. He put out his hand.

"Show me the food you have to sell."

She led him to a small store room at the back of the kitchen. She lit a lamp. The supplies stored there would not go far among his men.

"Bring the child."

He caught the barest flicker of fear in her eyes. She knew. She gathered the boy and followed him out to the yard. Her husband and the other man sat on mules guarded by soldiers, their hands bound behind their backs. Fernandez jerked his head toward the hacienda. Six men scrambled inside. They stripped it of anything that might be of use to them.

"Leave the boy. You will ride with me."

She turned defiant as she handed her son to Conchita. "I have my own horse."

He half smiled. Spirited, he liked that too. "As you wish, but be quick about it."

They rode north through the night. Villa would be waiting for them south of the Boca Grande River. Jefe could decide what to do with the two gringos. He'd taken the woman for spoils. He expected Villa would grant him her fate.

They found the main body the next day. División del Norte numbered nearly five hundred men, a mere shadow of the force once many times that number. Fernandez' troops joined the camp. He ordered the prisoners delivered to Villa. The woman he placed under guard.

Villa sat beside the fire surrounded by his most trusted officers General Candelario Cervantes, Colonel Pablo Lopez and Fernandez. From a distance people sometimes mistook Cervantes' blocky stature for Villa. He had fleshy features and a misshapen eye that gave him a look of perpetual menace. He had a volatile violent temper to rival Villa's. Villa valued him as a fierce fighter. Lopez made his place in Villa's esteem as the butcher of Santa Ysabel. He had lean, sharp features and dark ferret-like eyes constantly flicking at those around him. Villa cast his eyes from one man to the next, confident in the loyalty of each.

"We have come far together." He held his voice low. The men

leaned forward, straining to hear him over the crackle of the fire. "We have lost many men. We have too little food, too little money. The German arms are needed, but we cannot eat bullets. División del Norte must grow stronger if the revolution is to grow strong enough to win. We need money for this. The Germans will pay money for war with the United States." He cut his eyes across the circle of firelight, reading the eyes of his men. War with the United States was a far different undertaking than a new revolution to overthrow the last. He came to rest on Nico. Candelario and Pablo would fight. Nico would fight. He would also think.

"Do we fight for the Mexican people, Jefe, or do we fight the German's war for them?"

Candelario and Pablo heard the question. Nico had their respect. Good. "This is the question that troubled me the first time the German asked our help in this. I have come to think of the two as the same. We need guns and men. Both cost money. Money we can take from the gringos and the Germans. Men must come from the people. We fight Carranza. We know he is Wilson's lap dog. If Wilson sends troops to protect him, the people will know it too. The Americano Presidente has no *co-jones* for war with Mexico. Carranza is too weak to fight if he did. It is a bold gamble, but it is one we can win. The reward is victory." He spread his arms wide, embracing the camp. "Look at us *amigos*. Do you see victory here?"

They looked from one to the other and shook their heads. They looked to Nico to speak.

"What is your plan, Jefe?"

Villa smiled. "Columbus, New Mexico. New Mexico, ripped from the fabric of our country by the Americanos. Columbus with its fat bank, home to that thieving son-of-a-whore, Sam Ravel. Can you think of a more just prize?"

Fernandez had hoped Villa would reconsider this. Regret-

1

tably, he had not. "There are soldiers in Columbus."

"There are, Nico. My spies tell me not many."

"They will fight."

"We have surprise with us. We will take them sleeping in their beds. If we move swiftly, they will not have time to organize a defense. We hit and we run back across the border. The Yanquis will not pursue us without the approval of their overlord *dons.*"

Cervantes' eyes flashed black firelight. "We can do this, Jefe."

Lopez agreed with a nod.

U.S. Customs
El Paso
March 3

The goose-neck desk lamp created an island of pale yellow light in the office gloom. A chill draft seeping around the door beat back the feeble heat coming from a small potbelly stove in the corner. Zach Cobb read the dirt-stained message from the operative known as Francisco.

Villa moves north toward the border along the east slopes of the Sierra Madre. His strength is five hundred men.

Cobb scratched his chin. What could he be after? He turned to a map on the wall behind his cluttered desk. He traced a line on the map with his finger. Nothing but desert all the way to— Columbus. *He wouldn't dare. Or would he?*

Columbus
New Mexico
March 4

Major Frank Tompkins stepped off the westbound El Paso & Southern train onto the plank platform. Raw gusty wind whipped his uniform, slapping his face with invisible blasts of stinging sand. *Welcome home,* he thought as he crossed the platform, valise in hand.

The rail line divided the town of Columbus on the north from Camp Furlong on the south. Deming Road ran north through town west of the depot and south along the west end of Camp Furlong to the border and Palomas Ranch beyond. North of the tracks, the center of town stretched five blocks along Central Avenue and Broadway a block further north. Residential areas north of Broadway housed the citizenry as well as most of the off-post officer cadre from Camp Furlong. Commercial interests included a bank, drugstore, livery, two restaurants, three hotels and a handful of mercantile stores anchored by Sam Ravel's general store. Ravel, a feisty Russian immigrant, had a reputation for being a tough businessman. He was believed to have had a hand in supplying Mexican rebels, including Villa. Suspected revolutionaries were known to have visited his store. He kept his residence at the Commercial Hotel, east of Deming on Central.

Tompkins walked west from the depot on Central. He turned south on Deming to Camp Furlong. He commanded First Battalion of the Thirteenth Cavalry under Colonel Herbert Slocum. A chiseled granite presence, Tompkins had thick wavy hair touched by premature gray at the temples. A confident, determined officer, he served under the West Point washout Slocum, largely owing to the fact the senior man had some success in the last days of the Indian wars. The old man could also put on a polished appearance in genteel surroundings and court goodwill up the chain of command. Tompkins thought it kissing ass. He bristled at the Army's capacity to weigh favor over fitness.

He turned off Deming into the camp compound. The Regimental Office, barracks and mess ran south in formation

Paul Colt

along the Deming Road perimeter. His boots crunched on the stony cinder path leading up to post command. He climbed the worn wooden steps and opened the screen door to the small office. Regimental Sergeant Major Bill Hastings looked up from his desk and started to rise. Tompkins waved him at ease.

"Sir, welcome back. How was your leave?"

"Very pleasant, Top, thank you for asking. Altogether too brief, as you might expect."

"They always are."

Slocum appeared in the doorway to his office, his features a sun-hardened mask. "Welcome back, Frank."

"Thank you, sir." *He looks like an unmade bed in that uniform. OK, so border patrol isn't parade duty. It's still no excuse for looking like one of the Mexican bandits we're supposed to guard against.* "Anything of import come up while I was away?"

Slocum scratched at a salted gray sideburn. "No more than the usual unconfirmed reports of Villa's movements. I think you'll find you haven't missed much." Slocum glanced at this watch. "I was just about to head home. The missus is planning an early supper. You can reach me at home if anything comes up, Sergeant Major."

Hastings nodded.

"See you in the morning, Frank."

Tompkins glanced at his watch, three o'clock.

CHAPTER FOURTEEN

Palomas Ranch
March 5

Division del Norte spilled out of the hills south of the Boca Grande River. The river formed the southern boundary of Palomas Ranch. The two-million-acre ranch stretched along the border from west Texas across New Mexico to eastern Arizona.

Nicolas Fernandez rode at the head of a formless mass, sprawled across a wide swath of desert. Guards held the woman at the back of his command. Not far behind, off to the west her husband, the other prisoner and their guards rode on the western flank near Villa. As they approached a low rise the guards peeled away with their prisoners, disappearing around the far side of the hill. Fernandez turned in his saddle. The woman rode straight in the saddle, eyes shaded under a sun bonnet. She showed no sign of emotion. Perhaps she did not notice the men leave the trail. Minutes later the guards loped out from behind the hill without their prisoners and resumed their position on Jefe's flank. No shots were heard. The guttering sounds of silent death did not reach their ears.

Sand hills dotted in gray-green sage and cactus fell away to the north. Horses flared their nostrils. They picked up a prance, fatigue forgotten at the scent of water. Dark clumps of cottonwood and willow tops bloomed above the hills along the river banks to the east, winding west toward purple mountain patches.

Fernandez gave his horse its head, allowing the big gray to pick up an easy lope down to the river. He stepped down at the bank. His horse stepped to the water's edge and dropped his head, drinking in noisy gulps. Fernandez squinted across the sun glare rising from the surface of the river. Far across the valley floor the black specks of two riders paused near the north valley wall. One rode off to the east. The other rode toward the river. At the far bank the cowboy splashed across the river toward Fernandez.

Tall and lanky with a crooked smile, the man stepped down.

"Henry McKinney." He touched the brim of his alkali-stained hat. "I'm foreman at Palomas Ranch over yonder. We try to be on good terms with all of our Mexican neighbors. You ride with General Villa?"

Fernandez nodded.

McKinney smiled a crooked smile. "Old friend of mine, is he around somewhere?"

"Where are your cattle?"

McKinney tossed his head east. "We're movin' a small herd up from the river."

"How many men?"

McKinney hesitated. These questions didn't feel like a social call. "Half dozen or so I reckon. Well I best be gettin' back to my crew. Give my regards to the general."

"Please, I must ask you to stay here. Jefe will want to greet you personally."

"I'd like to see him too, but I need to get back to my crew." McKinney turned to his horse.

Fernandez drew his gun. The metallic hammer cock froze McKinney.

"We will not detain you long, Señor, but you may not leave." Fernandez cut his eyes to two men on his left. "Hold him here while we find the cattle."

He mounted his horse and splashed across the river accompanied by a dozen men. A dust cloud a mile to the east led them to the herd. As they approached, all the cowboys driving the herd but one left the cattle and galloped off to the north. The one remaining rode out to meet them.

"Bill Corbett." He waved as he drew rein. "Where's Mr. McKinney?"

"We will take you to him." Fernandez smiled and drew his gun. "Drive the cattle back to camp. Juan, Chico, come with me and Señor Corbett." He wheeled his horse and galloped back to the river.

Fernandez sent word of the prisoners and cattle to Villa. He rode in within the hour and stepped down from a flashy black stallion.

"Nico, you have beef?"

"Sí." He tossed his head to the herd at the river.

"May I stay for dinner?"

Fernandez laughed.

Villa strode past him to inspect the prisoners.

"General Villa. Remember me, Henry McKinney?"

Villa squinted at the crooked smile and shook his head.

"We met at the ranch two years ago. I told your man here, we just come by to say hello. No offense, but it's getting late. We'd be obliged to head on home."

Villa looked at the sun. "Sí, it is getting late. We shall not detain you any longer, Señor. Hang them, Nico." He turned on his heel.

McKinney laughed. "So funny, just like I told you, Bill. It's always a joke with General Villa."

Fernandez jerked his head. Soldiers grabbed McKinney and Corbett. They threw them up on their horses and led them to a stand of cottonwoods at the river bank.

"You sure they're jokin', Mr. McKinney?"

"Sure, Bill. Once the General sees we ain't gonna piss our pants, he'll turn us loose right enough."

One of the Villistas pulled the reata off McKinney's saddle. He threw it over a cottonwood limb and slipped the loop over the foreman's head. Someone drew the rope taught around the tree trunk.

"They ain't jokin', Mr. McKinney."

"Sure they are, Bill. Villa's havin' his'self a big belly laugh over yonder."

A brown hand smacked the horse's rump.

"They ain't jokin', Mr. McKinney. I told you, they ain't jokin'. Oh God."

Someone jerked the hat off his head. A coarse stiff loop slipped around the drover's neck.

Department of State
Office of the Secretary
March 7
Secretary Lansing read the telegram from Cobb.

> *Ranchers report Villa and five hundred men camped at Palomas Ranch on the Boca Grande River sixty-five miles southwest of Columbus, New Mexico. His intentions appear hostile.*

"Bailey."

"Sir." Lansing's assistant appeared at the office door.

"Get this telegram to General Scott over at the War Department, now!"

"Yes, sir."

General Hugh Scott telephoned Cobb's warning to General Frederick Funston, Commander of the Department of the South at Fort Sam Houston in San Antonio. Funston called Pershing at Fort Bliss. Pershing telegraphed Slocum.

Camp Furlong
Columbus, New Mexico

"Telegram from General Pershing." Sergeant Major Hastings crossed to the desk and handed Slocum the wire. He looked at the telegram and yawned. It looked like the rumor mill had people riled up all the way to the War Department. Trouble is they were nothing but rumors.

"Anything important, sir?" Tompkins stood at Slocum's door.

"Apparently Villa rumors have made it all the way to Washington. Have a look if you like. That'll be all, Sergeant Major."

Tompkins crossed the office, reading trouble in Hastings' eyes as they passed. Slocum handed him the telegram.

"Palomas Ranch, sixty-five miles southwest, that's pretty specific. We should send a patrol out to have a look."

"Specific, shit, Frank, Palomas Ranch is two million acres. It'd be like looking for a needle in a haystack."

"Sixty-five miles southwest of here shrinks the haystack considerably."

"If Villa is out there somewhere, it's probably to steal a few cows or horses. That's Mexican territory. Not our problem."

"Five hundred men is a lot of rustlers."

"What else is he going to do? He's never raided across the border. He comes across now and then for supplies. He wouldn't dare attack Columbus. All that shit is nothing more than bureaucratic hand-wringing. All those stuffed shirts need to cover their asses." Slocum rose. "Time for supper, Frank, see you in the morning."

Tompkins read the telegram again. He shook his head. *If the old man is wrong, who's going to cover* our *ass?*

CHAPTER FIFTEEN

Five Miles Southwest of Columbus
March 9
0100 Hours

Small fires dotted the sprawling campsite. Chill night air flattened a thin blanket of smoke from the cook fires. Men bundled against the cold. Horses stamped impatiently. White steam clouds of collective breath hung in the air. Starlight played in smoke and steam. The last embers of a burnt-out ruin that hours before had been a small ranch house glowed orange, dancing in shadow. Villa rode into camp and stepped down. He called his commanders and sat down to warm himself by the fire. One by one they took their places, grim copper masks donned in flickering firelight. Villa nervously sipped a cup of coffee, the steam amplified by the cold.

"I have been to Columbus. The army there is much larger than our spies reported."

Pablo Lopez spoke first. "Are you saying they are too strong to attack?"

"I'm saying resistance could be stronger than we expected. I do not wish to ride into another Agua Prieta." He fell silent to the pop and crackle of the fire.

The bellicose Cervantes stuck out his chin. "The men are tired and hungry. We have come far. If we leave without a prize, the desertions will be worse than any casualties we might suffer

108

from the gringos."

"These are not Carranza's conscripts, Candelario. These are Yanqui regular army, well armed and well trained."

"Sí, Jefe. I know this. Are they on guard for us?"

Villa shook his head. "I did not see trenches or any other fortifications."

"We will take them by surprise while they sleep. This is our advantage. You said so yourself. We could have taken Agua Prieta in much the same way, if not for Yanqui treachery."

"Pablo, what do you say?"

"There is wisdom in what Candelario says. We need supplies. We need the money in the bank. We need the German's money. The people must see that Carranza is Wilson's lap dog. We can show them that Pancho Villa does not allow the Americanos to treat Mexico as a colonial footstool. These things will rally the people to our cause. The people will make the revolution strong."

"Nico, you agree?"

Fernandez met Villa's gaze. All these things might be true, but the fact remained they would face regular army. He looked from Villa to Candelario to Pablo and back. The die was cast. They could not turn back.

"Sí, Jefe."

Villa nodded. "It is settled then." He took a stick and drew a line in the sand. He drew ragged squares above the line with a circle and a square below it. "The railroad tracks come through here. The town is north here. The *soldados* are here." He pointed to the square south of the tracks. He moved the stick to the circle west of the town. "We will approach behind the hill here. Pablo, you will take your troops down the tracks into town. Stores and hotels are here and here." He pointed to street lines closest to the tracks. "The bank is here. Candelario, since you are so hungry to bloody the Yanqui soldados' nose, you take the army camp here. General Fernandez, take your men north. Do not allow the people who live there to mount a resistance."

Fernandez looked puzzled. "General, Jefe?"

"Sí, Nico, you are promoted. Any other questions?" He looked from one man to the next. Each nodded his understanding. "Good. We ride."

0200 Hours

Villa stood on his saddle, a ghost-like apparition silhouetted in starlight and steam. His troops arranged in three loose columns behind their commanders. Breath from men and horses floated in an ash-gray fog. He began slowly, his words sound shapes in the air.

"Muchachos, we have engaged in a long struggle. You were first called to revolution against the tyrant Diaz. Our beloved leader, Francisco Madero, promised you land reform and justice. They killed him for it. They replaced him with the whore's son Huerta. Again we defeated the usurper. Now the traitor Carranza has turned against us."

Emotion built as he warmed to his rhetoric. "Who is it that corrupts and controls our leaders? Who is it that enslaves the Mexican people? Always it is the imperialist Americanos. They do not do this with soldados and bullets like men. They do this with money, with greed and corruption. Wilson is the puppet master. Carranza dances to the pulling of his strings. Together they conspire to colonize Mexico and steal our riches, just as they stole Texas, New Mexico, Arizona and California from our grandfathers' fathers."

"Tonight, we begin the true revolution. It is not enough to defeat the puppet. We must defeat also the puppeteer. Gringo collaborators inflicted defeat on us at Agua Prieta. With their help, Carranza's stooges killed many of our brothers. The Americanos are the true enemy of the Mexican people. We must defeat them. Once the people understand this, once they understand the true prize is to return the lands stolen from us, they will rally to our cause. Powerful allies will join us in this. Already you have new German rifles. More aid is coming. With it we will defeat the puppet and his master. With it we will win true revolution. Are you with me, *compadres*?"

The massed force erupted in chorus.

"Viva Villa!"

"Muerte los Americanos!"

"Viva Villa!"

Villa raised his arms in triumph. "Let's ride, amigos." He dropped into his saddle. The horse reared. He collected his horse's head and wheeled away at the head of the column. He picked up a trot to the north.

Columbus, New Mexico
0400 Hours

Villa drew a halt. A train whistle hooted off to the east. The tracks could be no more than a half mile ahead, beyond the dark crest of Cootes Hill. Brakes released a faint metallic cry. The engine chuffed. Couplings clanked. He waited. A bright shaft of white light slashed the darkness east of the hill, a stark reminder of the bright light at Agua Prieta. The westbound freight gathered speed leaving Columbus station. Great smudges of gray smoke appeared behind the light, painting the night sky before waning to distant wisps in the cold. The beam disappeared behind the hill. Moments later it reemerged, slowly picking up speed. The engine rumbled, the whistle hooted again. The staccato click-clack of the wheels grew faster as the train gathered speed. The light passed into darkness as the train highballed west. Villa eased his mount forward toward the hill.

0415 Hours
Cootes Hill

He ordered a rear guard to hold the hill and the horses. The soft sounds of men on foot moved off to the north and south.

He climbed the hill to watch and wait. On his right, Cervantes' magnificent white stallion floated in starlight. It gave the appearance of a swan crossing a great black lake, the shadows of men trailing behind along Deming Road made ripples in its wake. The apparition circled south around the sleeping camp toward the black smudges of corrals and stables further east.

Pablo Lopez led his men across the tracks to the north. Starlight reflected on the silver ribbons of track, slicing the darkness. They followed the roadbed to the center of town, the only sound the soft crunch of boots on cinders.

Nicolas Fernandez led his column across the tracks with Lopez. He continued north on the west end of town. Four blocks north of the tracks he turned east, waiting for the signal to attack.

Lopez' men began the raid, smashing windows and looting stores. They fired no shots at first. No alarm sounded. Others rushed the Commercial Hotel. They stormed the lobby, silencing the sleepy desk clerk with the butt of a rifle. They charged upstairs to the guest rooms. Startled guests woke to the sounds of heavy boots running in the halls and harsh orders barked in Spanish. A few wide-eyed guests cracked doors open in disbelief. Villistas kicked open other doors, their locks torn from the frames. Gun-wielding raiders rousted guests from their rooms. Frightened women and children crowded the hallways. They cowered in their nightclothes, held at gunpoint. Sharp commands translated by the motions of rifles and pistols ordered the men downstairs. Lopez' troops forced the men into the street. The first gunshots shattered the quiet night as they executed the men one by one or in pairs. Muffled screams inside the hotel began as the women realized what was happening.

★ ★ ★ ★ ★

Lieutenant John Lucas woke from a sound sleep. *What the hell is that? Gunfire? Sure as shit is and a lot of it.* He jumped out of bed, pulled on his trousers and boots. He grabbed his pistol belt and ran through the barracks shouting to his machine-gun platoon. "Com'on boys, get your asses down to the armory."

He bounded down the barrack steps and sprinted across the parade ground to the armory. Muzzle flashes punctuated by small-arms reports pricked the darkness across the tracks in town. He reached the armory and burst inside. Padlocks fastened the weapons cases. *No time to look for the damn key.* He drew his .45 and fired.

Rifle reports reached the north side of town. Slocum snapped awake. Somewhere in the night bugle bars mocked him. *La Cucaracha,* Villa, shit!

Down the block from the Slocum house, Frank Tompkins leaped out of bed and threw on his pants and boots. He raced into the yard. Muzzle flashes up the street and the throaty bark of high-powered rifles spit death into the night like a swarm of rabid fireflies. Tompkins ducked behind the house and sprinted for Deming Road.

A block south of the Tompkins home, Lieutenant James Castleman hid his wife in the root cellar. He raced down the east end of town to Camp Furlong, dodging the fire storm working its way east on Central Avenue.

Cervantes' men reached the corrals bent on stealing as many horses as possible. Rifle fire spooked the animals. They charged from side to side in the corrals, snorting and bellowing. Dust clouds billowed like smoke in the night. One of the men opened a gate. The herd bolted. Beyond control, the horses galloped toward town. The stampede added to the chaos spreading through the camp and the commercial center of town. Shadowy men ran in all directions, shouting and firing at other shadows. A woman screamed.

Villa rode alone into town amid the shouts of his men.

"Viva Villa!"

"Viva Mexico!"

"Muerte los Americanos!"

Lopez' men owned Central Avenue, smashing windows and looting store after store. Finished with the slaughter at the Commercial Hotel, they doused the lobby in kerosene and torched the building. Women and children trapped on the upper floors fled down the fire escapes. Sun-dried timbers burned like matchsticks. The raiders' lust for plunder and vengeance doused better judgment in flame. An eerie orange glow slowly illuminated the street, bathing the raiders in searching light.

Lucas deployed three of his machine guns east of the armory along the tracks, using the roadbed as a makeshift emplacement. He drew a deadly curtain of fire across Lopez' flank, suddenly exposed in the firelight. He turned his fourth gun on Cervantes' line, advancing from the corrals behind the stampeding horses.

Other men poured out of the barracks into the armory as Tompkins and a breathless Castleman arrived to take command.

"On me, boys." Thirty-odd men fell in behind Tompkins. He deployed a skirmish line along the tracks, adding the steady pop of Springfield sharpshooters to the chatter of Lucas' machine guns. Villistas silhouetted in firelight suffered the effects of hastily arranged surgical fire.

Castleman led a squad of troopers east along the tracks, using the covering fire of Lucas' fourth machine gun to hold

Cervantes' men at bay. Beyond the depot he turned north into town. The Commercial Hotel fire billowed clouds of black smoke into the night sky. Flames spread to adjacent buildings. Frightened horses galloped through the streets under a hazy orange fog. Wood smoke mingled with the acrid smell, gun powder burned the eyes. He led his men past the chaos in darkness beyond the reach of the firelight. He deployed a skirmish line on Broadway between the Columbus State Bank and the Hoover Hotel.

Lopez led his men north to Broadway, away from the fires and the rain of death coming from the machine guns and sharpshooters across the tracks. They plundered their way door to door down the street on the way to the bank. A family fled their home caught momentarily in firelight, bleeding up the allies from Central. The man fell in a hail of high-powered rifle fire. The woman was thrown to the ground. Bullets picked up a child, clad in a thin nightgown aglow in orange light, and tossed it into the darkness like a tattered rag doll. Lopez scarcely noticed.

"The bank, Amigos, the bank!" He led a charge up the street.

Castleman and his men waited in the shadows between the buildings. Dark figures backlit in firelight charged toward them.

"The horseman," Castleman shouted to his sharpshooters.

The darkened street beside the bank erupted in muzzle flashes. The 30.06-round hit Lopez with a force that lifted him from his saddle and slammed him to the ground as though he'd been kicked by a horse. Yanqui marksmen picked away at his men. They fell around him one by one, the senseless silent, the tortured screaming in pain. Lopez struggled to his knees. His shoulder burned. A dark stain soaked his blouse, hot and sticky.

His horse reared and danced beside him wide-eyed with fright. One arm responded to his will, the hand grasped rein. He forced his body to follow the hand. It found the pommel of his saddle. A weak boot toe stabbed at the stirrup. It found no purchase. Bullets splashed gouts of dust in the street at his feet. The horse danced away. He nearly lost control of the animal. Somehow he managed to hang on. Orange light swam in his eyes. Smoke cast a pall over the shapes of the fallen. The angel of death breathed chill on his cheek. He summoned his last and caught the stirrup. A sharp burst of dread propelled him into the saddle. He released the frightened horse to its fears. *"Vaminos, muchachos!"* He slumped forward against the coarse slap of the horse's mane and raked the animal's flanks with his spurs.

Castleman watched the Villistas withdraw. He ejected a spent clip from his .45 and slammed home a new load. They'd saved the bank and spared the Hoover Hotel guests the fate of the poor folks at the Commercial.

Cervantes pulled back from the withering chatter of machine gun fire as gray light appeared in the east. His men retreated west toward Cootes Hill along the southern border of Camp Furlong in a ragged mob. Lopez' men straggled out of town along the tracks as dawn broke, badly battered by precision fire heaped on them by the foolish act that fired the Commercial Hotel. Shooting died out nearly as fast as it had begun in the center and south of town. Fernandez read the sign. His men had seen little resistance at the north end of town. They'd drawn little fire and sustained few casualties. He pulled his men back toward the rally point at Cootes Hill.

Tompkins watched the raiders retreat. "Round up as many horses as you can, boys! We're going after the sons-a-bitches." Men disappeared in the firelight and choking smoke.

CHAPTER SIXTEEN

Cootes Hill

0600 Hours

Golden spears of sunlight stabbed the hills east of the smoldering ruins and burning buildings in town. Behind him the firefight turned to fighting fire. Ahead yellow dust stained the blue morning sky where Villa's column retreated. Tompkins stood with his fists on his hips, black with rage. *Sons-a-bitches caught us with our damn britches around our ankles. Not like we didn't have any warning either. The old man got it wrong. Damn wrong and a lot of people died for it.* Boots crunched behind him accompanied by the huff and puff of exerted breathing. He glanced over his shoulder, *Slocum, late as usual, right on time.*

"Frank."

"Sir."

He pointed to the dust cloud with his chin. "That what's left of 'em?"

Tompkins nodded.

"How bad is it?"

"Fourteen of our men, eighteen civilians best I can tell. We got quite a few of them. Lucas and Castleman did a hell of a job. I've got men rounding up horses to mount a pursuit." He thought again. "With your permission, sir."

"Granted."

Tompkins turned back to camp. The less he had to do with the old man in this frame of mind, the better.

Forty minutes later Tompkins rode to the head of a hastily assembled force of thirty-two.

"Lieutenant Castleman, column of twos."

"Column of twos, forward, ho!"

They crossed Deming Road south of Cootes Hill. He set a brisk pace, alternating trot, canter and walk, to spare the horses. Villa's trail of animal waste and discarded or broken equipment led southwest toward the Sierra Madre. Three miles south of Columbus near the border, they came upon a woman wandering aimlessly toward them as if in a daze. Tompkins called a halt.

"Come along, Lieutenant." He rode forward accompanied by Castleman. He drew rein and stepped down. Tall and ruggedly handsome, she looked thin. She stared, vacant-eyed, likely in shock.

"Ma'am, are you all right?"

She registered surprise at the sound of his voice. She nodded.

"Castleman, get her some water."

Castleman removed the canteen from his saddle and offered it to her. She took a swallow, coughed and took another gulp. She handed the canteen to Castleman, wiping her cracked lips with the back of her hand.

"What are you doing out here?"

"They took me prisoner, killed my husband. I escaped."

"Can you ride?"

She nodded.

"Corporal Lewis." The young man rode forward. "Take this woman back to town. See that she gets proper medical attention and food."

"Yes, sir."

She looked at Tompkins, misty-eyed, realizing her ordeal had ended. Lewis gave her a leg-up to his saddle. She slid back to the cantle, making room for him to step up. He wheeled away at a trot back to town.

"Com'on, Lieutenant, let's get them sons-a-bitches."

Fort Bliss
Officer's Mess
0730 Hours

"Care to join me, Lieutenant?" Pershing gestured to the vacant chair across the table.

"My pleasure, sir." Patton set his breakfast tray on the table and scraped the offered chair back. "Nice taste of spring out there this morning. Good day for some mounted saber drill." He unfolded his napkin.

Pershing smiled. "Drill is good for discipline. Coffee?" Pershing held out the steel pot in an offer to pour.

Patton extended his cup. "You don't place much store by the saber do you, sir?"

"It's not that, George. I know the saber is important to you. I just wouldn't neglect other aspects of training by putting too much emphasis on it. The purpose of drill is to prepare us to fight. How are your men doing on their marksmanship?"

"I took your advice, sir. I got the infantry marksmanship training manual. We are working on qualifying Expert on the close combat range. I plan to have my best marksman qualify on the sniper range. I'd like one or two in each squad."

"Good. If it's mounted exercises you need, how is your Troop's proficiency with the .45? That's the mounted weapon your men must rely on in today's warfare."

"I see your point, sir, though, between the jams and the misfires, the reliability of the .45 leaves much to be desired. Damn near shot my leg off with one in Sierra Blanca. Never cut myself on a saber."

Pershing chuckled.

Hurried boots sounded above the low hum of conversation in the mess hall. Pershing checked the mess hall entrance over Patton's shoulder, sensing trouble. A young trooper stood in the doorway across the room. He glanced around the room, put off the reservation of the officers' mess by urgency. He spied the general and came forward at a brisk pace.

"Telegram for you, sir." He handed Pershing the sealed transcription.

Pershing tore it open and read. "Shit!" He threw his napkin over the remainder of his bacon and eggs and pushed back from the table.

"Something wrong, sir?"

"Villa hit Columbus this morning. I need to telephone General Funston." Pershing left the table on long purposeful strides trailing the orderly.

Patton absorbed the news. *There's going to be a fight. Not even Wilson can take this lying down. Pershing's command will get the call. Finally, he'd have a part in a combat mission.*

Northern Mexico

Tompkins' column crossed into Mexico. Three miles south of the border, the shooting started. Snipers picked at the column from a low hill west of the trail.

Lieutenant Castleman's chestnut pranced nervously at Tompkins' flank as harassing fire kicked up dust gouts. "What do you make of it, sir?"

"It looks like Villa's left a rear guard to entertain us. I don't think there's much fight in them greasy bastards. Form a skirmish line, Lieutenant. Let's give 'em a proper introduction to the United States Cavalry."

"Form skirmish line!"

The column spread left and right across the broad front of the hill, flexing its muscle in controlled preparation to strike.

"Bugler, sound the charge!" The blood-stirring call split the air. The line surged forward at a gallop. Thirty-two horses' hooves churned the dry ground, filling the air with boiling dust clouds. Pistol fire clawed at the crown of the hill as the troopers took the face, pounding their way to the crest. The Villistas broke and ran.

Tompkins broke the crest of the hill and threw up his arm. "Halt! Dismount! Fire at will!"

Cavalry turned infantry took up the chase. Marksmen rained a 30.06 torrent on the fleeing Villistas. Men and horses fell as they ran a losing race against the Springfield's devastating range. The bolt-action rifle with its five-shot clip and twenty-four-inch barrel gave a skilled marksman effective range up to twenty-five hundred yards, earning the weapon the nickname "Silent Death." At length, remains of the Villista rear guard outran the killing field.

"Cease fire!"

"Reload!" Bolt actions chattered. Clips clicked into magazines.

"Remount!"

Tompkins stepped into his saddle.

"Column of twos, Lieutenant."

Tompkins pursued Villa through the morning and into the afternoon. The rear guard mounted several attempts to delay the Americans. Each time Tompkins' men broke the resistance. At midafternoon Tompkins' relentless pursuit overtook the main body of Villa's force fifteen miles south of the border. Villa turned. The ragtag mob began to form what looked like a skirmish line.

Tompkins raised his arm. "Halt!"

121

"It looks like he means to fight, Colonel."

"Yeah. Bad as we got him, he must have us outnumbered ten to one."

"The horses are about played out too, sir."

"We've spent a good deal of ammunition already. Then there's the small matter of the fact we're on Mexican soil without authorization. Much as I hate to say it, Lieutenant, I think it might be time to head home, at least for now. After the stunt he pulled this morning, the son-of-a-bitch hasn't seen the last of us."

Columbus

Tompkins' column rode into Camp Furlong at dusk. The burned-out hulk of the Commercial Hotel and adjoining buildings smoldered north of the tracks. A pall of smoke hung over the town. The smell of burnt flesh told him the citizenry had made quick work of the fallen Villistas. He drew a halt at the corrals and stepped down. Lights burned in the Regimental office windows. Slocum hadn't gone home early today. *Day late and a buck short for that.* He crossed the stable yard to report in.

The screen door to the office swung closed with a squeak and a bang. Slocum appeared in his office door, haggard and unshaven, clearly shaken by the day's events. "Any luck, Frank?"

"Luck? I'm not sure what that means. We chased 'em fifteen miles into Mexico fighting skirmishes with a half-assed rear guard. Shot 'em up pretty good. I counted seventy-two bodies. We caught the main body around 1400. Villa decided to make a stand. We were badly outnumbered, low on ammunition and water with tired horses. I brought the troops home. We'll let Washington figure out what to do next."

"Sounds like you gave a good account of yourself."

"Too bad we couldn't have managed that ten hours sooner. What's the situation in town?"

"We turned the Hoover into a field hospital. The bank's a morgue. You can smell what's been done with Villa's dead."

"Any word of a response to this?"

"None yet. I notified Pershing this morning as soon as we got the worst of the casualties tended to. This one will go all the way up the chain. I expect there'll be hell to pay soon enough."

CHAPTER SEVENTEEN

White House
March 9
8:00 PM

"Senator Fall to see you, sir."

The announcement interrupted General Scott's briefing. Wilson shook his head, annoyed. "Tell him I'm in a meeting with General Scott."

The secretary paused. "He's, ah, quite insistent, sir."

"Oh all right, send him in. I'm sorry, General, but the Senator has a stake in this too."

Fall's lanky frame filled the office entry. "Mr. President, thank you for seeing me unannounced. I must know what's to be done about this outrage."

"Senator, thank you for coming. I'm truly sorry about the circumstances of your visit. General Scott and I were just reviewing the situation. Please join us."

Fall folded himself into the second wing chair set before the President's desk.

"Proceed, General."

"You are both aware of the general circumstances of the raid. A force of Mexican irregulars believed to be under the command of the rebel known as Pancho Villa attacked Columbus, New Mexico, and the army post at Camp Furlong shortly before dawn this morning. A good portion of the town was sacked and burned before the raiders were driven off. Colonel Slocum, the commanding officer at Camp Furlong, reports eighteen civilians killed along with fourteen men of his Thirteenth Cavalry."

Fall shook his head. "American citizens and soldiers murdered on American soil. Mr. President, this is an unspeakable outrage done by the same killer responsible for the mass murder of American citizens at Santa Ysabel. What is to be done about it?"

"We will determine that in due course, Senator. Please, General Scott, continue."

"Colonel Slocum reports seventy-six raiders killed during the assault and another seventy-three killed by pursuit as they fled back into Mexico."

"Fled to safety in Mexico. So, Mr. President, is this President Carranza's response to the Santa Ysabel massacre? He has no control over these rebels. Nothing will be done unless we do it. The question is what are you going to do?"

Wilson removed his glasses and rubbed the bridge of his nose. "Are you finished, General?"

"There is one more thing, sir." Scott gave Fall an uncomfortable glance.

Wilson replaced his glasses. "Go ahead, General, out with it."

"The cartridge casings found at the scene indicate the raiders were armed with German Mauser rifles."

"So now we know what's behind Villa's recent hostility toward Americans. I suspect we opened that door when we recognized Carranza. The Germans would like nothing more than to provoke war between the United States and Mexico."

"Mr. President, I'm not here to debate the merits of your neutrality policy. I'm here to tell you the people of New Mexico and those in the other border states expect action. If you look over your shoulder, you'll find the rest of the nation joins them in demanding that you defend the country and its interests."

Wilson braced. "What military options do we have, General?"

Scott blinked behind his glasses. "Damned if we do and damned if we don't, sir. Do too little and the Germans see us as weak. Their submarine aggression is trouble enough already. Do too much and we risk war with Mexico. The best option might be to persuade Carranza to undertake a joint operation to rid the border of Villa's bandits. Villa is a threat to his government. He can't seem to do anything about it. He might listen to that idea."

"You're saying send American troops into Mexico with Carranza's approval."

Scott nodded.

Fall hunched forward in his chair. "I'm telling you, Mr. President, if you do not act decisively here, you'll hand the border states to the Republicans in November, if not the whole nation. What if Carranza doesn't buy it? What if you go down there hat in hand and he says no? Then what?"

"We'll cross that bridge should we come to it."

Presidential Palace
Mexico City
March 10

"El Presidente will see you now, Señor Ambassador."

United States Ambassador to Mexico Henry Lane Wilson was not related to the President. In fact they weren't even on very good terms. Patrician in appearance, he projected a polished urbane presence dressed in a black suit with a dove-gray vest, matching cravat and black pearl stickpin. Carranza's Administrative Secretary led him into the expansive presidential office with its tiled floor brightly lit by floor-to-ceiling arched windows. Carranza sat at a massive desk, diminished in stature by its size. A large Mexican flag stood in a standard behind the desk.

"Mr. President, good of you to see me." Wilson crossed the

room, solemn in demeanor as befit the gravity of the circumstances. He could not dispel the vague sense of approaching a throne.

"Señor Ambassador, please have a seat." He gestured to his visitor chairs. "Let me first express my country's condolences over the regrettable events in your Columbus, New Mexico."

"Thank you, Mr. President. It is that matter, in fact, that prompts my visit."

"I thought as much."

"As you might imagine the Columbus raid is a matter of much concern to my government. Coming on the heels of the Santa Ysabel affair, it places a great deal of pressure on our government to take action. We made a good-faith decision to leave prosecution of those responsible for the Santa Ysabel murders to your government. Thus far, nothing has come of that. Now we believe elements of those same rebel forces are responsible for the deaths of eighteen of our citizens and fourteen of our brave men in uniform. President Wilson feels a great deal of moral and political pressure to take action against those responsible for these heinous crimes. For that reason, we respectfully request your permission to send American troops into Mexico for the purpose of bringing Pancho Villa to justice."

Carranza regarded the diplomat beneath bushy eyebrows. "This is a difficult request. It undermines Mexican sovereignty. Any suggestion of an American invasion would be cause for grave concern to my countrymen. Passive acceptance of such a thing would reflect poorly on my government."

"We understand the sensitivity, Mr. President. Villa is a problem for both of us. Still you must understand we cannot sit idly by while he commits atrocities such as these on our soil and yours."

Carranza made a steeple of his fingers. His gaze drifted over Wilson's head. "He is a problem for both of us, isn't he?" His words trailed off, as if the question begged no answer. He pursed his lips. "There is some precedent for that."

"Excuse me, Mr. President. I don't understand."

"Geronimo."

"Geronimo? Truly you have the advantage of me, sir."

"Yes, I believe this could work. Forgive me, Señor Ambassador. Some years ago our countries reached an accommodation to allow us to deal with the problem of renegade Apache operating in our border region. We made a reciprocal agreement to allow troops from both countries to cross the border in pursuit of the Apache. Such an agreement might also be used to deal with Villa. Because it is reciprocal, both countries are equal partners in the enterprise. Such an agreement can be explained to our people in a way that does us no harm."

"That is brilliant, Mr. President. It's perfect. Geronimo and Pancho Villa, the similarities are undeniable."

White House
March 10

Cherry blossoms added the promise of spring to a sunny warm day. Curtains in the Oval Office fluttered with a touch of breeze. It lightened the mood on the matter at hand. The President sat in a wing chair at the side of the office sipping coffee. Secretary of State Lansing sat on the settee at his right. Secretary of War Newton Diehl Baker occupied a wing chair across the coffee table opposite the President. A bespectacled former librarian with no military experience, the frail Baker suited Wilson's pacifist policies better than a man of competent military credential. Secretary Lansing had the floor.

"You may not care for Ambassador Wilson, Mr. President, but he's managed something of a coup this time."

Wilson lifted his gaze over the frame of his spectacles. "Go on."

"Carranza has agreed to allow our troops to enter Mexico in pursuit of Villa."

"Splendid, problem solved."

"There's more, sir. El Presidente was quite reluctant at first with concerns over Mexican sovereignty, but the Ambassador was able to reach an accommodation of some genius."

"And what, pray tell, is this master stroke of diplomacy?"

"Geronimo, sir."

"Geronimo, as in the Apache Geronimo?"

"The very one, sir. It seems some years ago we had a reciprocal agreement allowing our respective militaries to cross the border in pursuit of renegade bands operating in the border region. President Carranza has agreed to a similar arrangement in respect to Villa."

Wilson chuckled. "Geronimo. I'll give the ambassador credit, very clever, indeed. Well, Newton, there you have it. You have your authority."

"Very well, Mr. President. What orders shall I give General Scott?"

"The obvious, I suppose, send an expeditionary force into Mexico to kill or apprehend the bandit known as Pancho Villa."

Lansing raised a hand with a limp wrist. "If I may beg your pardon, sir, the mission may be a bit more delicate than that. This arrangement is politically sensitive for President Carranza. We must guard against the appearance of confrontation with federal troops. We must take care to avoid any action with respect to the civilian population suggestive of an American invasion."

"Yes, of course, Robert. Well said. Is that clear then, Newton?"

"I believe so, sir."

CHAPTER EIGHTEEN

War Department
March 11

"Good afternoon, Mr. Secretary." Major General Hugh Scott's presence filled the room, overpowering Baker despite the separation created by the Secretary's spacious office.

"Good afternoon, General. Thank you for coming."

"You remember my adjutant, Tasker Bliss."

"Why, yes, nice to see you again, General."

"Thank you, sir."

"Please be seated." Baker led them to a small conference table. "Let's get right down to business. The President has reached an agreement with President Carranza on how to respond to the Columbus raid. Both countries will allow the other to cross the border in pursuit of those responsible for the unrest in the border region. You may recall a similar arrangement some years ago for dealing with renegade Apache. You are to mount an expeditionary force to enter Mexico for the purpose of killing or capturing the outlaw known as Pancho Villa. The President insists that we remain courteous and deferential to the Mexican people and avoid any confrontation with President Carranza's Federal forces. We must give no suggestion that this operation in any way constitutes an invasion or occupation of sovereign Mexican territory. Is that clear?"

Scott pursed his lips, giving his ample features the appearance of a walrus. "Northern Mexico is mountainous desert, mostly uncharted. Finding Villa on his home ground won't be easy if he doesn't want to be found. The operation is reminiscent of Geronimo in more ways than one."

"Villa's recent activities have become politically sensitive for the President. We must put a stop to them. You are to use such means and measures as may be available to get the job done. Just mind the sensibilities of our relations with Mexico. We walk a fine line here between the situation in Europe and these problems along the border. The evidence may be circumstantial, but you can bet the Kaiser has his hand up Villa's back. Break a few German fingers in the bargain, so much the better."

Scott scowled. *Fine line,* diplomatic double-speak for one hand tied behind our back.

"Now to the next important question, who should command the expedition?"

"That's why I brought General Bliss with me, sir. Between the two of us we know the officers who'd be best qualified. On paper the nod should go to General Funston. He commands the Department of the South, which has responsibility for the border region."

Bliss shook his head. "On paper, yes, but given the sensitivities of the mission, I don't recommend him. Funston can be something of a hothead. Given the diplomatic situation, we don't need a bull in the china shop. Funston's talents would be better left overseeing the operation from his headquarters at Fort Sam Houston. He can raise hell when logistics snarl without ruffling diplomatic feathers."

"That's just the sort of thinking the President is after."

"You're right, Tasker. That brings me to Pershing. He's a fine combat soldier. He has also demonstrated considerable diplomatic savvy in his dealings with Moro tribesmen in the Philippines."

"Good point, General. He's served on the border these last few months so he is familiar with the situation and the troops stationed there. You may also recall he served under Miles in the later stages of the campaign against Geronimo. He knows something about northern Mexico. That could be of considerable value given your point about the difficulty of finding Villa if he doesn't want to be found. Miles, you will recall, had to talk Geronimo into surrendering."

"That's right. Capturing or killing Villa will be no easy matter."

"Then perhaps, gentlemen, we should amend the mission to kill, capture or neutralize the outlaw known as Pancho Villa. In fact, let's be very clear on the punishment point. We shall call it a punitive expedition. Now, time is of the essence. How soon will General Pershing be ready to march?"

Sierra Madre Foothills
March 11

The Villista camp sprawled along the floor of a deep arroyo. A trickle of fresh spring run-off spilled out of the mountains, God's blessing to men and horses alike. Lookouts posted in the rock ridges above had a clear view of their back trail. They saw no sign of pursuit. Purple shadows drifted down the walls, pooling along the floor amid the flicker of fires set to ward off the night chill. Villa gathered his commanders. Supper consisted of a meager ration of beans, tortillas and jerked beef.

The officers reflected the grim mood of the men. Anger and frustration smoldered. Columbus won little in the way of spoils. No victory tasted little better than stinging defeat. None of the officers would voice these things to Villa. He sopped the last of his beans in tortilla and set his plate aside.

"I waste no more bullets on my brother Mexicans. From now on, we kill gringos."

The officers sat silent, content to let the newly promoted Fernandez speak for them. "We poked the sleeping bear in the eye, Jefe. The Americanos will demand revenge."

Villa spat. "Let them demand what they wish. If Carranza pursues us, we are no worse off than we are now. The people will see him as the Americanos' lackey. If he allows the Americano army to enter Mexico, the people will see him as weak."

"Either way, we don't have much time. The men are tired. Our horses are spent. We have wounded to care for. We must find a place to rest."

Villa climbed to his feet, clasped his hands behind his back and paced in thought. He paused, squared his shoulders and faced his expectant generals with a broad smile. "We will send our enemies a little singing bird."

They looked from one to the other, confused.

"The bird will tell them we go to San Miguel for fresh horses."

Fernandez knit his brows. "Tell them where to find us? Surely you cannot mean that, Jefe."

Villa shrugged. "The bird will tell them we go to San Miguel. We will be in Rubio." They laughed.

Fort Bliss
Post Commander's Office
March 11
2030 Hours

Pershing sat at his desk haloed in lamplight. The darkened office cloaked him in a blanket of silence. The President's orders rattled down the chain of command at telegraph speed, reaching his desk in a matter of hours. He'd expected an assignment as part of a response to the raid. He hadn't expected anything on this scale. Forty-eight hundred troops, cavalry supported by infantry and artillery. He'd also have the Signal Corps' new First Aero Squadron. The nation's first use of motorized military aircraft gave the mission historic significance.

Then, of course, you had the mission. He puzzled over the ambiguity of his orders. *Enter Mexico with the sole object to capture or disburse forces operating under the command of the bandit known as Pancho Villa.* "Capture or disburse," what the hell did disburse mean? If Villa went into hiding, his forces might already be disbursed. What if Villa objected to being captured or disbursed? Did the Punitive Expedition have the authority to kill him? The order further stipulated that all of this should be undertaken with "scrupulous regard for the sovereignty of Mexico." Who had controlling authority over the operation, the President, the Mexican Government, who? What authority did he have as field commander? The unanswered questions added up to a diplomatic muddle calculated to give the appearance of doing one thing without clear direction to actually accomplish it. He shook his head. Clearly the president felt compelled to do something. That didn't mean he had to like it. He'd invested his conflicted purpose in a military operation where lives often depended on clarity. In effect, the politician dumped matters in the field commander's lap where they could take credit for success and deny responsibility for anything less.

At least they'd given him the troop strength to do the job, so long as Mexican Federal Troops didn't interfere. In addition to the units presently under his command, Scott had offered up the Sixth and Sixteenth Infantries and two batteries of the Sixth Field Artillery. The First Aero Squadron under Captain Benjamin Foulois made an intriguing addition to the so-called Punitive Expedition. Air reconnaissance and communication offered interesting possibilities given the difficulties of conducting military operations in northern Mexico. He'd have to give careful thought to the best use of that valuable asset in a theater of operation that encompassed fifty thousand square miles.

He turned to the more basic question, how to deploy the

cavalry at his command? Slocum and the Thirteenth are an obvious choice. He had his reservations about Slocum, but reports of the Columbus raid portrayed Major Frank Tompkins as a competent field commander. He had Custer's fabled Seventh under the command of Colonel George Dodd. Dodd may be nearing retirement age, but he remained a fire-breathing officer who knew how to fight. His beloved Tenth Buffalo Soldiers were now commanded by Colonel William Brown. He knew he could count on his all-black former unit when the going got tough in Mexico, which it would. That left a choice between Major Robert Howze' Eleventh and Taylor's Eighth. Howze may be the junior man, but he displayed the vigor to fight. With the exception of young Patton, Taylor's Eighth lacked the crisp discipline duty in the field demanded. He didn't have time to whip them into shape. Somebody had to hold the fort. That assignment would fall to Taylor. George wouldn't like it, but that's the way things worked out.

March 12, 1916

The mobilization order hadn't come. Why the hell not? Bliss buzzed with the news. The General had been given command of the Punitive Expedition. It didn't seem to matter to the Eighth. Something didn't feel right. Never one to wait patiently for anything, Patton headed for the Regimental Offices to see for himself what the hell was going on.

His boots crunched the crushed stone path leading to the office. He bounded up the two wooden steps and swung the door open. Sergeant Major Carson looked up from a stack of requisitions.

"Good afternoon, Lieutenant. Colonel Taylor is not in. What can I do for you?"

"What happened to our mobilization order?"

"Mobilization order, sir?"

"The Punitive Expedition, Top, surely the Eighth is included."

Carson shook his head. "The Seventh, Tenth and Eleventh will join the Thirteenth in Columbus. The Eighth is being held in reserve."

The news braced Patton like a slap in the face. He hesitated only for a moment. "Is the General in?"

"The General is extremely busy, Lieutenant. I'm sure you understand."

"I understand he'll see me." He opened the gate separating the office reception from the inner offices.

"Sir," Carson rose from his desk. "I must respectfully request . . ."

"At ease, Top." Pershing stood in his office door. "Come in, Lieutenant."

Patton crossed the outer office. Pershing closed the door behind him.

"George, I know you are disappointed. This is not about you. I have to leave a garrison. I had to make a choice. You can judge the fitness of the Eighth for yourself. What would you do in my place?"

Patton stiffened. "So I'm to be judged by the performance of others. Sir, you must take me with you. Appoint me to your staff. I'll do anything." Cold fire flashed his eyes ice blue.

"I have two staff officers."

"Leave one of them behind."

Pershing knit his brow. "Why should I do that?"

"Because I deserve it."

Pershing set his jaw, unaccustomed to such insubordinate behavior. Steel bearing met the force of iron will. Tension laced the silence separating the two men. Young Patton had determination. He of all people should understand that. He recalled a similar confrontation in regard to his joining the expedition to Cuba years before. In precious little time the nation would need combat-ready warriors. Experienced, disciplined officers were needed to lead. This army didn't have enough of them. It had grown weak in peacetime, old and top-heavy in command. Where would the warriors come from when inevitably the nation would need them? He nodded to himself.

"That will do, Lieutenant. How long will it take you to get ready?"

Patton breathed. "I'm packed, sir."

Pershing shook his head. "I'll be damned. You're appointed, Lieutenant."

"Thank you, sir." He turned on his heel and left the office. He jogged down the stone path all the way home. He burst through the front door to the small frame house.

"Hear that, Beat?"

"Hear what, Georgie?"

He swept her up in his arms and swung her off her feet.

"Boots and Saddles, at last I hear the call to glory."

"Whatever do you mean?"

He set her down. "The Punitive Expedition, we're going into Mexico after Pancho Villa."

"Are we at war with Mexico?"

"No, the diplomats have worked out some sort of agreement that allows us to go after him."

"Will it be dangerous?"

"I'll be serving on the general's staff. I won't be leading my troop in the field."

"Will you be gone long?"

"Villa and his men are irregulars, bandits really. They'll be no match for the United States Cavalry. I don't expect we'll be gone long at all."

She made a pretty pout.

"Don't you see, Beat, this is a chance to make something of my career. You can't do it drilling on a training field. This is a combat mission. Combat is where careers are made. If I'm to make something of myself, now is the time."

CHAPTER NINETEEN

Columbus, New Mexico
March 13
Sand and scrub rolled by the dusty window of the westbound El Paso & Southern train. Little distinguished it from the sand and scrub of the west Texas panhandle, save the ragged fringe of mountains to the north and west. Patton sat watching Pershing's expression reflected in the window glass in the row ahead of him. The whistle hooted, announcing the approach to Columbus. The scene beyond the window changed. A sea of materiel and equipment spilled along the tracks. Pershing's expression darkened as the train slowed. Haphazardly off loaded trucks, wagons and canvas-covered pallets spread across the depot yard and platform. Men milled around among the stacks in an unhurried crowd. Patton watched the color rise above the general's collar, the only thing lacking wisps of smoke at the ears.

"Look at this mess. Who the hell is in charge here?" He glanced back at Patton. "Don't answer that." He got out of his seat as brakes screeched. The train slowed, jerked to a stop at the platform. He strode up the aisle, spitting orders over his shoulder to Patton as he trailed behind.

"We've got twenty-four hours to get this mess straightened out. I'll be in the regimental office over at Camp Furlong. You find Dodd, Brown, Howze and the other unit commanders and get their asses over there as fast as they can move." He bounced down the steps to the platform. Colonel Slocum waited to greet him.

"General, welcome to Columbus."

"Welcome, hell. Look at this mess, Slocum."

The colonel braced, ill prepared for a brusque greeting.

"Meet my aide, Lieutenant Patton. You can assist him in locating the rest of the unit commanders. I want to see them at your HQ now." He turned on his heel and strode down the platform toward Deming Road, leaving a slack-jawed Slocum gaping after him.

Pershing fairly took the warmth out of the sun. And then it dawned, the sun ducked behind a thick deck of patchy cloud. The minute it did, warmth disappeared with it, the wind chilled noticeably. Patton didn't recognize the first taste of what was to come.

"Sir, where can we find Colonel Dodd, Colonel Brown and Major Howze?"

Slocum blinked back to Patton. "Ah, this way, Lieutenant."

Thirty minutes later they assembled in Slocum's small office.

"George." Pershing extended a hand to his former colleague. Lean and fit, sixty-three-year-old Colonel George M. Dodd shifted his perpetual cigar from one side of his mouth to the other and took Pershing's hand. A veteran of San Juan Hill, the feisty Dodd spoiled for one last fight before he retired.

"Bill." Pershing turned to Colonel William Brown. Brown followed Pershing in command of the Tenth Cavalry Buffalo Soldiers. Like Pershing, Brown maintained strict discipline though quiet and understated. Little distinguished him apart from lively blue eyes and prominent ears.

"Major Howze, we haven't had the pleasure, but we shall remedy that." Howze had established himself as something of a rising star in the cavalry officer cadre, gaining a unit command before attaining a rank appropriate to the assignment. He had an athletic frame and an energetic demeanor his men found inspiring.

"Yes, sir. Thank you."

"Major Tompkins, thank you for coming. You're to be congratulated for your response to the raid."

"Thank you, sir."

"Down to business, gentlemen. We are off to a ragged start with this expedition. The condition of the men and materiel I observed on my arrival is a disgrace. We march day after tomorrow, which means we have forty-eight hours to get this mess cleaned up. Colonel Slocum, your men are settled. That makes you quartermaster. Get the equipment, materiel and supplies inventoried and ready for distribution. Lieutenant Patton will take responsibility for organizing logistics. Major Tompkins, if you would please show the Lieutenant around."

"Certainly, sir." Tompkins nodded.

"The rest of you get your troops settled. Major Howze, bivouac the Eleventh east of Camp. Colonel Brown, take the west side of Deming Road between here and Cootes Hill. Colonel Dodd, bivouac the Seventh south of Camp. I'll expect a full report from each of you at 0700 tomorrow. Any questions? Good. Let's get to it."

The officer cadre filed out of the office, chastened. The old man was pissed. Tompkins fell in beside Patton as they headed up Deming Road to the depot.

"Is he always so prickly, Lieutenant?"

"No sir, it's just that the general has a way of doing things that doesn't tolerate sloppy."

"Good, I prefer a tight ship."

He glanced at the senior man. "Then you and the general will get along fine, sir." *If that's a comment on Slocum, the colonel might not.* "I saw wagons and trucks north of the tracks when we arrived. If we are going to move things, we better start there."

March 14

0700

The officers crowded into Slocum's office again. A potbelly stove in the outer office struggled to chase the night chill. Patton stood in the center with a clipboard and his tally sheets. "Two batteries of field artillery, twenty-seven trucks and two wagon companies totaling fifty-four wagons, seventy-two men, one hundred and twelve mules and six horses."

Pershing nodded and glanced around the room from man to man. "Good, gentlemen. It seems we've made progress. We march tomorrow." He stepped to a map of northern Mexico tacked to the wall. He picked up a rubber-tipped hickory pointer from the desk and traced as he talked.

"Gentlemen, the theater of operation is fifty thousand square miles bordered on the east by the Mexican Northern Railway and on the west by the Sierra Madre. Most of it is uncharted desert and mountains. There are few towns and little to sustain us beyond the supplies we carry with us. We will enter Mexico in two columns. The east column under Colonel Slocum will consist of the Thirteenth and Major Howze's Eleventh accompanied by the Sixth and Sixteenth Infantries. A Battery Sixth Field Artillery will support the column. This column will also include the supply train. Herbert, you will proceed south to Colonia Dublán by way of Palomas Ranch and Boca Grande."

He turned to Dodd. "George, you will lead the second column west to Culberson's Ranch. From there you will make a fast sweep south to Casas Grandes and on to Colonia Dublán. We believe Villa fled into this region. With luck we may catch him there and put a quick end to this business. Bill, you and the Tenth will accompany George's Seventh supported by B Battery of the Sixth. I will also join the west column.

"The order of the day is to draw your equipment and supplies. Lieutenant Patton will oversee those operations. Any questions, gentlemen? Good. Be back here at 1900 hours to review our marching orders. Now, let's get to work."

1000 Hours

Patton scanned the equipment requisition. He furrowed his brow and read it again.

Each Trooper is to be issued one Springfield rifle, one .45-caliber semi-automatic Colt pistol, one canteen, one mess kit, toiletries, shelter half and blanket. Cavalry requisitions include one feedbag. *It must be some mistake.* He left the supply depot and crunched up the stone path to Regimental HQ. The screen door swung open upon a hive of activity. The room buzzed with muted conversation punctuated by the jangle of telephones. Officers, non-commissioned officers and enlisted men hurried in and out. Slocum's small office had become the hub of the command center. He found Pershing in the center of the storm, his tunic thrown over the desk chair, working in his shirt sleeves. He waited until the general finished signing a document and sent it off with the waiting orderly.

"Excuse me, sir."

He glanced up. "What is it, Lieutenant?"

"It's about the equipment requisition, sir, there must be some mistake."

"Mistake?" Pershing frowned. "Let me have a look at it."

Patton passed over the form.

Pershing shrugged and handed it back. "Look's fine to me."

"Sir, the cavalry haven't drawn sabers."

"That's right, Lieutenant. We don't need the weight."

"But, sir—"

Pershing cut him off with a razor-wire glance. "I understand

143

your devotion to the tradition, George, but this is a combat mission." The howl of an arriving train whistle cut short the exchange. "Now, if you'll excuse me, Lieutenant, carry on." He turned to the door. The screen slammed, leaving Patton groping for a response.

"Don't need the weight," the damn thing weighs two pounds. A cavalry riding to battle with no sword, the centurion blinked in disbelief.

1015 Hours

Winter chill clung to a brisk breeze scented with creosote and sage. Patton followed Pershing up the road to the depot for the arrival of the westbound train. He made no effort to catch the general or argue his point further. Disappointment made a bitter broth. He'd put his heart and soul into the design of that saber. Now, at the first opportunity to see it in combat, the cavalry had no plan to use it. What was the cavalry without the saber? The realization hit him. He was the army's first Saber Master. He would also be the last. The bright blade was part of him. Losing it felt like losing an arm.

The engine ground its brakes with a screech at the crossing. Couplings clanked, a metallic wave rippled through the cars. The train stretched past the depot platform to the east. He counted eight flatcars between the passenger cars and the caboose, each loaded with one of the new Signal Corps aero planes. The wings had been removed and lashed to the sides of the fuselage for transport. They looked like great gray sea birds, sleeping on a dock. Curiosity called him away from his disappointment. An important piece of the future had just arrived on the scene.

The Curtiss JN-3 "Jennie" was a two-seat biplane equipped with a powerful ninety-horsepower engine. The frame and fabric structure measured twenty-seven feet in length with a forty-seven-foot wingspan. Wheeled landing gear distinguished this model from earlier craft that relied on sled-like runners. Landing gear gave these birds the ability to take off and land on roads, in fields or from any reasonably smooth surface. This feature coupled with speed, maneuverability and range gave the aero plane important advantages in reconnaissance and communication, missions traditionally performed by the cavalry. On the heels of the saber disappointment, it felt like a prize fighter's one-two punch.

Pershing climbed the depot platform. His boots clipped the planks as he made his way to the passenger cars disembarking the pilots and mechanics of the First Aero Squadron. Patton picked up his pace. Beside curiosity, he had a job to do. They reached a knot of men shaking off the stiffening effects of a long train ride.

"Ten-hut," someone barked. The sixteen pilots and copilots of the First snapped to attention. A puckish wiry aviator wearing a long silk scarf thrown over the shoulder of a belted leather jacket with captain's bars stepped forward with a crisp salute.

"General, Captain Benjamin Foulois and the First Aero Squadron reporting for duty."

Pershing returned the salute. "At ease, gentlemen. Captain, I should have recognized you even without the introduction. May I present my aide, Lieutenant Patton."

Somehow the general knew he was standing behind him.

"Lieutenant Patton will help you get your gear unloaded and settled. We don't have much in the way of amenities here. Columbus took a hell of a beating in the raid. They do have the Hoover Hotel dining room reopened. I hope you and your men will join me for dinner this evening. It will give you a chance to meet the rest of the officer staff."

"We'd be pleased to join you, General."

"Good. Shall we say 19:00 then? I'm most interested in hearing your thoughts on how best to employ your rather unique capabilities."

"Very good, sir."

"George, notify the staff please."

"Yes, sir."

Pershing walked off down the platform to have a closer look at the first of the Jennies.

Patton consulted his clipboard. "Captain, we plan to park your aero planes south of the barracks along Deming Road, which should give you the most serviceable runway we have. Will you require wagons or mules to assist in the transport of your aircraft?"

"No, Lieutenant. We'll roll the fuselages and carry the wing assemblies. They're quite light and that will reduce the risk of damaging the fabric."

"You and your men will be housed in barrack five. Let me know if you need anything. I've got requisitions to fill."

1900 Hours

The Hoover put its best face on a bullet-pocked facade to roll out VIP treatment for the Punitive Expedition officer cadre. Good whiskey set a convivial tone for building camaraderie before taking the field. Pershing counted that important. Most of these men, with the exceptions of Dodd, Slocum and Tompkins, had no idea of the harsh conditions they would face in the deserts and mountains of northern Mexico. March probably meant spring to most of them. In the mountains it meant hot days and brutally cold nights and that was before making allowance for sand, insects and snakes. These men would have plenty of hardship over which to reflect on a good steak dinner with all the trimmings.

Pershing invited Captain Foulois to his table along with Dodd, Major Howze and Patton. Colonels Slocum, Brown and

Tompkins spread themselves out at tables of junior officers. The General plied Foulois with questions from the serving of the soup. He plainly aimed to understand the aviator's vision of the fledgling air service. Patton hung on the Captain's every word as though having a sneak peek at a fortune teller's taro deck.

Foulois parsed his views between spoonfuls of soup. "I expect this expedition to make the Signal Corps' case for an expanded air service. One has only to observe the war in Europe to see that the aero plane is coming of age as a war machine. We need to make a strong case for expanding the air service. We are quite far behind the British, French and Germans in developing military aircraft. In this campaign we will be limited to basic reconnaissance and communication."

Pershing paused, a spoonful of soup stalled short of his mouth. "What's the speed and range of the Jennie, Captain?"

"She can make a top speed of seventy-five miles per hour with a sustained cruising speed of sixty. Range is two to three hundred miles, depending on speed and altitude. Her ceiling is eleven thousand feet."

"Impressive."

"It's really only the beginning, General. She'll earn her keep in recon and commo. One day the command and control advantages of radio communication will find their way into the air. Imagine what commanders on the ground could do with immediate and accurate information about enemy troop movements or the effect of artillery fire?"

"You don't think small do you, Captain?"

The waiter cleared away the soup bowls and delivered sizzling plates of thick-cut steak served with fried potatoes and hot biscuits.

Foulois warmed to the center of attention. "The day's coming when we'll see aero planes serve in combat missions. In the European Theater, air crews already exchange small-arms fire.

Both sides are working feverishly to successfully mount machine guns on aircraft. We'll see planes that are smaller, faster and more maneuverable than the Jennie with the ability to fight in the air and deliver devastating ground support. Bigger planes with higher-altitude capabilities will have the capacity to drop explosive projectiles. Many see this as a way to extend the range and precision of artillery bombardment in support of ground operations."

The questions and vision droned on into the apple pie. *"Don't need the weight."* The general's dismissal ate at Patton. *Where is the horse soldier in all of this? What is the use of a Saber Master to a force that fights without blades? He'd been bred and trained to fight in the nineteenth century, not the twentieth. Perhaps Beat was right. Much will be told of the future by this Punitive Expedition. Much will be told.*

CHAPTER TWENTY

March 15
0700 Hours
Pershing and Dodd sat at the head of the column watching Slocum and the slow-moving east column march south toward Palomas Ranch. Slocum's cavalry headed the column followed by the wagon companies, artillery and truck convoy. The infantry column brought up the rear. Patton sat his mount off Pershing's flank as the morning sun slowly burned off the night chill. He squinted southwest to the ragged fringe of blue mountain peaks. Somewhere out there Villa had already made good his escape, a phantom vanished in the clouds hugging the mountain tops.

"Ready, General?"

Pershing nodded to Dodd.

Dodd turned to his second. "Column of twos, Major." He squeezed up a jog southwest.

The column reached the eastern boundary of Culberson's Ranch in two days and turned south into the Sierra Madre the third. Canyons and arroyos honeycombed with caves gashed the hills. Northern Chihuahua offered a myriad of hiding places. Patton had studied enough of the Apache campaigns at the academy to understand the difficulty of finding a man like Villa in this hell-scape if he didn't want to be found.

Men and animals faced scorching heat, dust and wind-driven

sand during the day. Sunset brought long, bitter cold nights. Rain turned trails to muddy slop. Flies harassed men and horses. Rats prowled food stores, searching for any breach in the protections given them. Tarantulas, centipedes and scorpions infested bed rolls and empty boots in the night. Rattlesnakes threatened any lapse in vigilance by men and animals. Intestinal problems from bad food and water set in from the start and became constant companions on the march.

The sparse local population distrusted the Americanos out of fierce national pride. Attempts to recruit local guides produced mixed results. Conflicting and deliberately misleading reports from popular resistance led to one false trail after another. The people amused themselves by deceiving the Americans. Within days the pattern became irksome.

Boca Grande
March 17
The east column plodded south through Palomas Ranch, the wagons and trucks slowed by roads so poor, in stretches they amounted to no more than ruts. Troops suffered blistering days and freezing nights. Swarms of flies and storms of blowing sand turned to a muddy slog by torrential rain. Infantry could sustain a faster pace than the wheeled vehicles, transporting supplies and artillery.

A rider galloped forward from the rear of the column. Slocum turned in his saddle. "Now what?" He signaled a halt.

The corporal drew rein and saluted. "Sir, we've got one wagon with a broken wheel, two trucks with flat tires and a third with a dead engine."

"Any more good news, Corporal?"

"Sir?"

"Never mind." He turned to Tompkins. "Frank, we can't afford any more delay. Have those vehicles pulled out of line with the necessary repair details. Make sure they have adequate security. Close ranks and let me know as soon as we are ready to move out. The stragglers can catch up when the repairs are complete."

Tompkins threw up a salute. "Follow me, Corporal." He spurred his horse into a gallop to the rear.

Hours later Slocum looked off to the slanting sun and stroked his chin. "Far enough for today, Frank."

Tompkins nodded and signaled a halt. He wheeled away to the rear and the nightly ritual of making camp. They circled the wagons and trucks, establishing a security perimeter after the fashion of the covered wagon trains of the last century. Machine-gun batteries deployed around the perimeter. Horses and mules were picketed in the center of camp. Troopers pitched tents and built cook fires.

Tompkins and Howze joined Slocum at a camp table in front of his tent as the last touches of orange melted from the purple peaks in the west. The regimental mess sergeant and two cooks arrived with their trays. The officers pulled up camp chairs and dug in.

"Damn slow going," Slocum groused, out of frustration at falling behind schedule.

Tompkins soaked a bite of biscuit in gravy. "Not much we can do about it. We're dragging a lot of supplies and equipment over some mighty tough terrain. Wagon and truck breakdowns are a fact of life. The longer our supply lines get, the worse the problem will be."

Howze spoke up. "If we establish a base camp in Colonia Dublán at least we can get rail service to supply us there."

Tompkins turned cynical. "From what I hear about Mexican railroads, a man might starve waiting for a shipment to arrive."

Howze looked to Slocum. "That bad, sir?"

"Frank's right. I haven't experienced it firsthand, but the oil and mining men I've met in Columbus depend on the railroads. They bitch about them all the time. They never run on time. Breakdowns and derailments are a way of life. The farther south we go the worse it is likely to get."

Casas Grandes
March 18
1930 Hours

They drew camp chairs up around the fire, wrapped in coats and blankets against the cold. Pershing held court, joined by Colonel Dodd, Colonel Brown and Patton. Patton jabbed at the steam from his breath with the stem of his pipe, his expression dark with frustration.

"You can't believe a word the lying bastards say. He could be hiding over the next hill and they wouldn't tell you if you offered a king's ransom in gold. He's a bandit and a murderer and they treat him like a hero."

Dodd exhaled a puff of cigar smoke. "The Lieutenant has a point, John. We've run patrols on one goose chase after another with nothing to show for it. This is supposed to be the warmest part of the trail. It's not likely to improve in the days ahead."

Firelight mottled Pershing's features in shadow. "No one said this would be quick or easy." He glanced around at the darkness beyond the firelight. "I know these mountains. It took years to bring Geronimo in and we never actually did catch him. He gave up."

"We don't have years, General," Brown said.

"I know, Bill. I'm simply saying I doubt we can find him without the cooperation of Mexicans sympathetic to our cause. Right now, we don't have any such allies. We will have to recruit them and that will take time. Understand we are dealing with a cultural adversary. These people distrust our presence here.

Deeply held beliefs cannot be discounted in military conflict. It is similar to the problem we faced with the Moro tribesmen in the Philippines."

"What can we learn from that, sir?" Patton asked.

"The Moro are Filipino tribesmen steeped in ancient traditions and a rudimentary practice of the Muslim faith. Moro oath-takers, so-called *Juramentados,* are ferocious fighters. They take an oath to kill as many infidels as possible to gain their place in paradise. I studied the Koran to understand their beliefs. They'd kill you if they could, but they respected strength. Ultimately we were able to pacify the Moro out of respect for our strength. We approached it in much the same way General Crook earned the trust of the Apache. I'm not suggesting we have that kind of time in this case, but I do think the Mexican people distrust our presence here. As long as they do, they will continue to harbor Villa as a matter of national pride. We are more likely to gain cooperation if we befriend some of them."

"I hope you're right, sir. With your permission, though, I'd like to recruit reliable scouts once we reach Colonia Dublán."

"I think that would be helpful, Lieutenant. People familiar with the locals may help us identify the right Mexicans to befriend. I've already requested help from Fort Huachuca."

"Fort Huachuca, sir?"

"The White Mountain Apache scouts are stationed there. Nobody knows mountain scouting like the Apache. We couldn't find them, but maybe they can find Villa."

He turned to Dodd. "Now about the column, George. What good is artillery support if it lags so far behind? Our vanguard could be wiped out before the guns could be brought up and deployed."

Dodd squinted behind a veil of cigar smoke. "I know, John. The terrain's a bad-ass problem. It takes ten mules to move one damn gun up these trails. Then you have to feed all those mules.

We can't carry enough fodder. Foraging in this desert is practically a full-time job. The animals fall behind or founder and have to be replaced. I question the value of dragging all this iron around under these conditions."

Pershing shook his head. "Maybe the French have the right of it."

"The French? The last time the damn Frogs got anything right, Napoleon wore knee pants."

Pershing laughed. "I know it seems that way when they've managed to let their country get overrun the way they have, but they have done one interesting thing. They've mounted light artillery and machine guns on a motorized armored vehicle they call a tank. They expect it to provide the speed and maneuverability of horse-drawn artillery with superior firepower. Self-propelled firepower like that creates offensive options in the defensive stalemate of the trenches."

Dodd shook his head. "Motorized artillery. It's time for this old soldier to retire, John."

"Oh com'on now, George. It's invention. We're never too old to learn."

Patton drew on his pipe. *"Motorized artillery creates offensive options." "Time and invention have a way of correcting such imbalances."* He let his eyes wander the darkness beyond the firelight. The future lay out there somewhere, unseen, uncertain. Could he conceivably pick up the trail here in these godforsaken mountains? *"We're never too old to learn."*

San Miguel
March 19
"Ahgh!"

The hulk of dark sweaty flesh hovering in the dim light resolved in the shadow of a rutting boar. She braced herself. *She should have had a third tequila.* The bed shuddered. He collapsed beside her like a fallen tree, spent. She eased back against the pillow and reached for the glass on the bedside table. She downed the fiery liquid and poured another.

"How can you drink that shit?" His words muffled in the bedclothes.

"You have your sweets, Francisco. I have mine. We have much to celebrate now that the Americans have invaded Mexico." She took a cigarette from a silver case beside the tequila bottle and lit it.

"Carranza tells the people the Americanos are here with his permission. He has no intention of challenging them. He lies to save his skinny ass."

She released a cloud of smoke, calming the harsh echo of sex. "Yes, well, it is up to us to change that now, isn't it?"

"Up to us, you mean up to me. Tell your Kaiser war is expensive."

"You shall have your money, two hundred thousand pesos now, more when the fighting begins. Now tell me how you plan to make Carranza fight. I need to show my superiors progress."

Villa rolled on his back. He stared into the ceiling shadows. He shrugged. "Carranza, I know. This one they call Black Jack, I must meet."

"Meet him? You think that is wise, Francisco?"

"Only if he does not know we are meeting. Colonia Dublán is not far. My little bird will tell him I am here, while I meet him there. Then I will know how to make Carranza tweak his nose."

"Carranza?"

"Carranza, Villa," he shrugged again. "We are all Mexican to the gringos."

"Ah, Francisco, you are so devious. That is what I admire most about you."

His lips turned a fleshy pout below the shadow of his

moustache. "And all this time," his eyes drifted suggestively behind drooping half lids. "I thought you fancied my machismo."

"Hmm." She stubbed out her cigarette and reached for the glass.

CHAPTER TWENTY-ONE

Colonia Dublán

March 21

Patton sat at a camp table. Sun beat the canvas tent top to a starchy smell, the only distraction provided by a fat black fly. "Ahem." He looked up at three men.

"Lem Spillsbury, what the hell are you doing here?"

The sloe-eyed, laconic Texan grinned. "Nice to see you too, Lieutenant. When I heard you boys was comin' down here, I figured you'd be lookin' for scouts before long."

"It's a long way from Sierra Blanca. What do you know about this country?"

"Enough. Spent time scoutin' down here. You might even be interested in the man I scouted for."

Here it comes. "Who might that be?"

"Pancho Villa."

He chuckled. "I might have guessed. Lem, you're either a Texas tall liar or you just might be able to find the son-of-a-bitch. Even if you're lying, we're no worse off than we are now."

"Been lost some, have you?"

"Not lost as much as misdirected."

"Amounts to the same thing, don't it?"

He chuckled. "You're hired."

Spillsbury tipped his hat. "Much obliged."

"Who might these two be?"

"Thought you might like to meet them." He tossed his head in the direction of another lanky cowboy. "This here's Henry Vaughn. He's another Texan. Don't s'pose you'll hold that agin' him. He rode with Villa's Dorado for a spell." He tilted his jaw at a wiry man with chiseled granite features and long, straight black hair. "This here's Bill Bell, former Deputy Sheriff in Columbus and a pretty fair tracker for a Chickasaw."

"You recommend these men, then, I take it."

"For what it's worth, Lieutenant, though like you said, if I'm lyin', you're no worse off than you are now."

Patton chuckled again. "A man can't buy references as good as those. All right then, Mr. Bell, report to Colonel Brown's Tenth. Mr. Vaughn, you'll report to Colonel Slocum's Thirteenth when they arrive. They're coming down from Boca Grande somewhere. Actually, you'd be of service if you rode up that way and let us know when we might expect them."

Vaughn nodded. "Easy enough, Lieutenant."

"Thank you. Lem, you got the short straw. You report to Colonel Dodd's Seventh. See if you can keep them out of the sort of mess Custer got into."

Spillsbury took his turn to chuckle. "I'll do my best."

"You can go along and introduce yourself to Colonel Dodd. In the meantime you and Mr. Bell can get to work on figuring out where to find Pancho Villa. Talk to the folks you know. Make them understand we're here to do a job and go home. The fastest way for them to get us out of Mexico is to help us find the man we came for."

"Sure enough, Lieutenant."

Spillsbury and the others set off to their various assignments past a short lean trooper in a rumpled uniform. Patton sized him up. He had deeply etched copper features and bright black eyes set in a weathered mask. "First Sergeant Chicken, reporting for duty."

"First Sergeant Chicken? What the hell kind of a name is that, Sergeant?"

"Army give Chicken name. No can say Eskeh-na-destah."

"I see. Where you from, Sergeant . . . Chicken?"

"Fort Huachuca, White Mountain Apache Scouts."

"Ah yes, General Pershing told me about you. We've been expecting you. I guess you know these mountains then?"

Chicken shrugged as though there were no point to the question.

"Report to Major Howze at the Eleventh. Glad to have you with us, Sergeant."

March 23
1930 Hours

Patton crunched out of the darkness into the halo of lamplight. "Vaughn found Slocum's column, General. He estimates they are a day's march north of here."

"What the hell is taking them so long, George?"

"Bad roads, sir. That's the nut of it."

"That's our supply line."

Patton nodded. "It is. The farther south we go, the longer it gets. The longer it gets, the greater the risk it can be compromised or cut."

"Imagine trying to live off the land down here with a force of this size."

"I'd rather not, sir. Tonight, I'd rather go to the movies."

"Movies?"

"Yes, sir. Thursday nights they set up an outdoor theater in town and show movies on the wall of the jail."

"You're joking."

"No, sir. Tonight they're showing a Tom Mix film, 'Pony Express Rider.' Care to come?"

Paul Colt

"Why not. If Tom Mix can find his way to Colonia Dublán, we should be able to manage a few supplies."

The soft ring of spur rowels shuffled through the dust toward the makeshift theater. Wooden folding chairs stood in ragged rows in the shadows of a dusty lot beside the adobe jail. A crowd gathered slowly, talking in small groups or taking seats to await the feature. Street vendors hawked soda, beer and ice cream. Children laughed and played tag, enjoying an evening without the rigid discipline of bedtime. Soldiers of the Punitive Expedition mingled with the local citizenry. The man in a black sombrero bought ice cream and studied the enemy. They looked fit and well fed, unlike his ragged band.

He slipped into a seat near the back row away from the dim streetlight. Wrapped in the anonymity of the crowd, he waited. They appeared near the jail wall moments before the film started. The insignia at his collar twinkled in the low light, oddly like the star it represented. Lean and hard, he stood straight—a confident man, a man of strength. He must not underestimate this hombre. A tall young aide accompanied him. They slipped into seats near the front just as the jail wall came to light in flickering images.

The action on the screen captured his attention. The handsome gringo cowboy racing across the west on a fine horse that might rise to the standard of his own well-bred mounts. A fast gun and a sure shot, Villa admired these things. He, of course, was faster than this Tom Mix.

He glanced at Pershing's profile silhouetted in streetlight. What would he think if he knew Pancho Villa sat within a split-second pistol shot of killing him? What would he do? He considered it briefly. The Americanos would only send another general to pursue him with even greater vigor. No, better he know his adversary. This one would behave like a soldier.

160

Soldiers were predictable. Revolutionaries counted on that. Better this Americano soldado than their Tom Mix with his fine horse and fast gun. This way, Pancho Villa gets the girl. He thought of Elsa's golden skin, so different from his other wives. The German thought she used him. A smile lifted the corners of his moustache.

Mix brought the bandits to justice, won the heart of the girl and rode off into the sunset. Pershing and Patton filed out to the street.

"Hollywood makes their heroes handsome and fancy, but the men of the west do know how to handle their guns. The Sheriff in Sierra Blanca wasn't pretty, but he could ride and shoot like a Tom Mix."

Pershing clasped his hands behind his back, pacing back to their bivouac. "We could use a man like that to help bring in Villa. A Hollywood script wouldn't hurt either. Real conflict isn't often so tidy."

"No, sir. It's not."

"By the way, have you heard from Miss Anne lately?"

Spur rowels jangled in the dust as the stocky slope-shouldered figure in a black sombrero disappeared into the shadows, whistling softly like a bird.

Pajarito

The Little Bird cantina was a sprawling adobe with a large patio covered in thatch. The patio stood empty as night chill descended on Colonia Dublán. Inside the crowd consisted mainly of locals and a table of NCOs with the night off. Spillsbury stepped into the guttering smoky light. The scent of mesquite from a cheery fire at the far end of the room mingled with the smells of tobacco smoke and beer. He sidled up to the bar. A pot-bellied bartender in a badly soiled apron met his eyes expectantly.

"Tequila."

The bartender set the bottle on the bar along with the usual bowl of salt, a freshly cut lime and two glasses. Spillsbury smiled to himself. He felt a warmth at his back with a light scent of orange. He glanced over his shoulder and gave her his sloe-eyed smile.

"Señor Lem, how long has it been?"

She had a voice like honey on a warm pastry, black diamonds for eyes and a rich mane of blue-black hair. He took it all in, remembering. She had a figure descended from some primal paradise long ago denied mortal men.

"Too long, Rosa. You are more beautiful than memory can behold."

She laughed deep in her throat. "Always a flower for the ladies, you don't fool Rosa, but I like it." She tipped up her toes and kissed him on the cheek.

Soft warm breast pressed against him, stirred other memories. She handed him the glasses and the bowl, picked up the bottle and took him by the arm. She flashed him a smile, bright white against dark copper skin.

"Come." She shaded her eyes with dark lashes. "We have so much to . . ." she bit her lip. "Catch up." She led him to a corner table. She pulled out his chair and drew another beside it. She made a show of her hips, straightening her skirt to sit beside him.

He poured tequila. She lifted her glass, holding his eyes.

"Welcome back to Mexico, Señor Lem."

Welcome back, indeed.

They tossed off the fiery liquid chased with salt and lime licked from the back of her hand. "So what brings you to Colonia Dublán?"

"You have to ask." He said in mock disappointment.

She shook her head with a twinkle in her eye. "More flowers for the ladies. I don't believe you. Still, I like it." She kissed him. Longer and slower, she tasted of salt and lime.

"I know you look for the Jaguar. Do you join the revolution again?"

He weighed his answer. He read her eyes and shook his head.

She smiled. "I like it when you tell Rosa the truth, hombre." She poured two more drinks and salted her hand.

"Do you know where to find him?"

Her eyes smiled. "Rosa only knows what Nico tells her."

"Nicolas Fernandez, the Dorado?"

She smiled again.

"And where does Nico say he is?"

She lifted her glass to his. "Come along to my room, Señor Lem. If you live up to Rosa's memory of you, perhaps she will tell you."

She smelled of oranges. She tasted of salt and lime.

CHAPTER TWENTY-TWO

Colonia Dublán
March 24
1800 Hours

He closed the well-worn Bible and placed it on the cot, newly arrived with Slocum's supply column. The favored passage spoke of men prepared to meet the enemy. So it was he prepared only to find his preparations ill suited to the enemy. Horse soldier, Saber Master, *centurion,* faded glory cloaked in uncertainty. Dim tent shadow comforted him as other tents comforted warriors down through the ages, giving refuge before the storm. The battlefield beyond this shelter rose up as a new age. He sensed it all now, the glory, Cesar's Legions, the epic struggle, Brandy Station, clashing bright blades, all gone. The horse soldier, the Saber Master, seemingly had no part in the future of armed conflict. Slocum's labored column rolled on motorized wheels. For all the difficulty, the machines succeeded. *"Time and invention,"* the general had said. The inventions would only grow stronger with time. Preparation rendered him unprepared. The die was cast. Beat saw it. He saw it too, without the conviction to accept it. He glanced at his watch for reprieve, time to leave.

"Lieutenant Patton." Lem Spillsbury stood just beyond the tent flap.

He crouched over, parted the flap and stepped out.

"Beggin' your pardon, Lieutenant, I come by some information I reckon I should pass along."

"What is it, Mr. Spillsbury?"

"It's Villa, sir, he's at Rancho San Miguel southwest of here."

"How do you know?"

Spillsbury grinned, a knowing twinkle in his eye. "A, ah, señorita told me."

"A señorita?"

The scout nodded solemnly.

Skepticism settled over the prospect of yet another false report. "And how might this 'señorita' have come by such important information?"

"She got it from a Dorado officer of her acquaintance."

The Dorado, Villa's elite bodyguard. "And she felt compelled to share this information with you?"

"She did." He grinned, cock-sure.

"Very well then, General Pershing has called a meeting for this evening. Come along. You can tell him yourself."

The officer staff gathered around two camp tables set outside Pershing's tent. Oil lamps lit a map spread on the table, masking faces and features in light and shadow. Pershing brought the meeting to order.

"Gentlemen, be seated." He turned to Slocum. "Herbert, nice you could join us."

"Sorry for the delay, General. I must say the terrain is less than hospitable to transport."

Boots crunched out of the darkness. Patton stepped into the halo of light accompanied by Spillsbury.

"Excuse me for being late, General. Mr. Spillsbury arrived with a most interesting report."

Pershing cut his eyes to the scout. "Mr. Spillsbury?"

"It's Villa, sir. He's at Rancho San Miguel."

"You have this on reliable authority?"

"I believe he has, sir." Patton cut off the lurid detail.

"Good. We have something to go on. Where might we find this Rancho San Miguel?"

"If I may, sir?" Spillsbury gestured to the map.

"Please."

The scout bent over the map. "The ranch sits on a mountain table here." He stabbed the map with a cracked, stained fingernail some forty miles southwest of Colonia Dublán.

Pershing bent over the map beside the scout. Dodd rose from his place across the table. Colonel Brown leaned in beside Dodd. Pershing traced the line.

"You know the area, Mr. Spillsbury?"

"I do, sir."

"And Mr. Bell?"

"Like the back of his hand, sir."

"All right, the Seventh and the Tenth have this one. George, you hit him from the north. Bill, you cover his escape routes to the south and east. If he runs west into the mountains, he can't get far very fast. Let's try to get a leg up on the march south by taking the train. Lieutenant Patton, see to those arrangements."

"Yes, sir."

"Very well, gentlemen, let's get to it in the morning."

Patton hung back as the others departed.

"Is there something you need, George?"

"I was just thinking, sir, given the difficulty of dealing with the railroad, maybe I should go along on the mission."

Pershing half smiled in the shadows. "Spoiling for a fight, are we?"

"Sir?"

"Look George, you signed on to this outfit as my aide. That's your job. You do it well."

"But, sir, I was only thinking, if I could see some combat."

Pershing held up his hand. "Your heart is in the right place, I'll give you that. Getting forward with the troops is key to effective command and control. This theater of operation is so large and fluid we can't do it from a conventional base of operations. I've given the problem some thought. Here's what I want you to do once you get the Seventh and Tenth aboard that train. I want three—no, make it four—touring cars."

"Touring cars, sir? You mean like Sunday drive touring cars?"

"No, I mean like mobile command touring cars."

"Mobile command? I'm not sure I understand."

"I intend to follow my forward elements as closely as possible. If we can stay within twenty-five miles, we should be able to maintain radio contact. If we lose contact out here, we lose control over operations."

"I see, sir. Is that all, sir?"

Pershing nodded. He turned back to the map.

Patton trudged back to his tent. Touring cars would get them forward, closer to the chance of a fight, but not in one. Even in the field, he found himself stuck in a staff job. The realization roiled him yet again. That'd be fine if his pay-grade ambition stopped at regimental top sergeant, but he was West Point. He belonged in the command ranks, not pushing paper. The dead end had to end, or the dream would.

El Valle
March 25
The train south made agonizing progress through stifling heat and wind-driven dust that blew through cracks in the car window frames. Dodd chaffed at the incessant delays. A broken-down engine, cows on the track, freight loading and unloading at siesta pace, the hours mounted. He paced the cars carrying his men, chomping a cigar. Conditions deteriorated. The cars became sweltering ovens during the prolonged delays. Sweat

stained his uniform blouse. Finally, his patience exhausted, he made his way to the back of the last car. Lem Spillsbury dozed on the last bench with his hat pushed down over his eyes.

"Mr. Spillsbury." Dodd slid into the bench across the aisle.

The scout snapped awake. He pushed his hat back and blinked. "Sir?"

Dodd spread a map on the bench beside him. "Where in hell are we?"

"It is hot, isn't it?" He bent over the map. "Here." He pointed.

"And Rancho San Miguel?"

"Here."

"Can you get us there overland?"

He nodded.

"Good. We're getting off this godforsaken rattle trap."

He marched forward looking for Brown. He found him in the first car staring out the window at another decrepit station platform with its haphazard collection of bales and crates being pushed or dragged up and down wooden ramps to the waiting freight cars.

"This is bullshit, Bill."

Colonel Brown glanced over his shoulder, mopping sweat from his brow with a damp handkerchief. "It is for a fact."

"You can't move a troop train through the heart of Mexico this slow without the son-of-a-bitch hearing we're coming. I'm taking my men off the train. We can cover as much ground on horseback as we can in this slow-rolling oven." He spread the map across the seat beside Brown. "We're here." He stabbed their location with a finger. "San Miguel is here. Spillsbury says he can lead us there overland. We've got the north. You've got the south. Go on a bit further. Talk to Bell and pick a good spot to head west."

"The general did give us the south. I guess the Tenth got the short straw this time." He rose. "I'll go find Mr. Bell. You have a nice ride. We'll see you at the ranch."

The Tenth

By the time the last of the freight was loaded, Dodd had the Seventh off the train, tacked up and prepared to mount. Brown watched with envy. He'd trade this damn bench for his saddle in a minute. Train men stowed the loading ramps in the freight cars with a noisy clatter. Car doors slammed shut and latched with a metallic complaint. The whistle bellowed, giving some of the horses a start. The engine chuffed, couplings clanked, the train inched forward. Behind him, muffled commands ordered the Seventh into column.

Brown sat back on the hard bench, waiting for movement in the air and a bit of relief from the heat. Twenty miles to the next stop, he resigned himself. In twenty miles they'd be off this godforsaken torture rack. He closed his eyes as the train picked up speed. The car swayed gently to the rhythmic rattle of the rails. His head dropped to his chest. Time dissolved.

A sudden jolt cascaded through the train in a violent wave. The car pitched awkwardly to the side. Men were thrown from their seats or slammed into the sides of the car. Brown woke, hit the bench across the aisle and landed on the floor.

"What the hell was that?"

Bell staggered to his feet and stuck his head out the window. "Engine's off the tracks up ahead." He looked to the rear. "Couple cars are down behind us."

"Son-of-a-bitch! Does nothing work in this hell-hole?" He got to his feet and stumbled for the car door, bracing himself on the benches. He climbed down to the roadbed. Men spilled out of the train along the tracks. One of the stock cars was down. The horses trapped inside kicked and bellowed in panic, compounding their injuries. Brown strode to the rear, barking orders to his troop commanders. Clear the train. Tend the injured. Destroy the injured animals.

"Where are we, Mr. Bell?"

"Hanged if I know for sure, Colonel."

The realization settled in. By the time they sorted this mess out, the Tenth would never make it to Rancho San Miguel in time. Dodd and the Seventh were on their own.

The Seventh

Spillsbury led the Seventh west into the mountain passes twenty-five miles east of San Miguel. Dodd pushed the column hard, hoping to recapture some element of surprise. Despite the dramatic beauty of panoramic mountain vistas, harsh raw terrain made for a difficult march. Physical discomforts tortured man and beast. Sun scorched the eyes. Stinging wind whipped; sand coated everything in a gritty film. Swarms of biting flies descended on rest stops and meals.

The sun climbed into the peaks above. Spillsbury paused at the head of the column and turned in his saddle.

"It'll be dark soon, Colonel. What do you want to do about camping for the night?"

Dodd looked around. "Camp where? Perched on this mountainside? I don't see anything that remotely resembles a campsite, do you, Mr. Spillsbury?"

"No, sir. Not unless we park on the trail."

"Shit! We might as well keep going. Maybe we can still surprise them."

"Trail's a bitch, sir. Ain't easy in daylight, never mind at night."

"Take it slow. Just make sure we don't fall off the mountain."

Spillsbury tilted his head in disbelief.

Night fell. Temperatures in the mountain passes plunged, turning canteen water from musty hot to ice crystals. Wind howled. Needles of icy rain lashed the column in sheets. Steep rocky trails turned slippery and froze. The trail grew so narrow in places the men dismounted and led their horses, holding their reins in one hand and the tail of the horse ahead in the other. One slip by man or beast might pull others to their death. Step by step, turn by switch, the column snaked its way up the mountainside to the summit.

March 26

San Miguel

Night sky faded to predawn gray light. The trail crested a high mountain plateau. The climb eased. Tensions ebbed. Fatigue seeped into the exhausted column. Dodd drew a halt. Across the misty high desert, the black ranch silhouette slept. He set his jaw.

"Looks pretty quiet, Mr. Spillsbury."

The scout nodded and spit. "Too quiet for my likin'."

"Maybe we've caught him napping after all."

The scout shook his head. "More likely he give us the slip."

"Only one way to find out, we'll move in at first light. The column will rest here. Take a swing south to see if you can contact the Tenth. I'd sure hate to stumble over them in the dark."

Spillsbury touched his hat brim, heeled his horse and peeled away at a jog.

The scout returned just before dawn. He'd seen no sign of Brown. Dodd deployed a skirmish line and advanced at first light. Jaws closed. The steel trap empty.

CHAPTER TWENTY-THREE

Rubio

One hundred miles to the southeast, the small town of Rubio turned out a hero's welcome for División del Norte. *Mariaches* struck up a chorus of La Cucaracha. Villa rode astride a prancing black stallion. He led his troops toward the center of town, waving his sombrero to joyous crowds lining the dusty streets and rooftops of squat adobe buildings. The crowd chanted, "Viva Villa! Viva Mexico!" Women and children followed the troops in a spontaneous atmosphere of fiesta.

The Alcalde waited on the steps of the village hall in the central plaza.

"*Bienvenido,* Jefe. How may our humble village serve you?"

Villa accepted the mayor's greeting sitting his saddle. "Muchas gracias, Alcalde. My men are tired and hungry. Your generous hospitality would be most welcome."

"Sí, sí, we are honored to have you here. *Mi casa, su casa.*"

"Viva Villa!" Cheers filled the plaza.

Villa stepped down. He handed his rein to Fernandez and climbed the steps to the village hall. He turned to the crowd and raised his arms for quiet.

"Amigos, you have with you today the only force for true revolution in Mexico."

"Viva Villa! Viva Mexico!"

"The traitor Carranza has summoned his Yanqui masters.

Even now the Americanos assault Rancho San Miguel."

"Muerte a los Americanos!"

"They come to steal our land. They come to loot our treasure. They come to steal our country. They come at Carranza's inviting."

"La muerte de Carranza!"

Villa pumped his fist. Guns fired into the air, punctuating the strains of La Cucaracha. A young woman burst from the crowd, her eyes bright. She gathered her skirt about her knees and dashed up the steps, firm brown breasts bobbing in her thin white cotton blouse. She threw herself into his arms."

"Marry me, Jefe!"

He laughed. "Tomorrow, Conchita. Today my heart belongs to another." The girl pulled back with a saucy pout.

She stepped out of the shaded veranda behind the Alcalde. Villa felt her presence. He turned his gaze on the golden body of Elsa Leiben. Her eyes smoldered, half-lidded in invitation.

"Francisco, you have the silver tongue of an orator. I had no idea."

Villa glistened. "*De nada,* señorita. Silver, gold, I am a treasure whichever part you choose. Come let us refresh ourselves out of this sun."

Colonia Dublán
1730 Hours

Patton entered the quadrangle at the center of base camp. He spotted Pershing seated at a camp desk in the shade of a shelter half. His boots scuffed the hard baked ground. He read the general's mood from a distance. Whatever the cause of his foul humor, this news wasn't likely to improve matters.

Pershing set down the telegram he'd been reading and drummed his fingers on the desk. Patton stopped beyond the shade of the shelter half. He waved him in. "What is it now, George?"

"The station master refused to load the supply shipment for Dodd and Brown."

"What?"

"It seems word got back to Mexico City that we used the train to move the Seventh and Tenth south. Someone decided the Mexican government didn't like that. The railroad's been ordered to refuse our requests for service."

Pershing shook his head. He picked up the telegram. "This just came in. Dodd left the train at El Valle. He's marching west on San Miguel. Brown stayed on the train. Fifteen miles south of El Valle the damn thing jumped the tracks. The Tenth took some casualties. Brown returned to El Valle. Dodd's on his own. Brown needs supplies. Dodd will too. Now you tell me we can't ship supplies."

"We'll get supplies to Brown and Dodd, sir. I've ordered them loaded on trucks. I propose to take the convoy down there myself."

Pershing admired the initiative, though he suspected it played to Patton's desire to get closer to the action. He'd allow it in the larger context of his next moves. "Very well, George, you take the convoy to El Valle. It'll give you a firsthand feel for the logistics we face. I'll see what Washington can do to get Carranza's railroads to cooperate. If Dodd doesn't get Villa at San Miguel, he will need relief. We need to position troops to take up pursuit wherever he goes. I intend to deploy Tompkins in command of the Thirteenth along with Howze and the Eleventh. You'll need to organize supply support for those columns as well. Get back here as quickly as you can."

"Yes, sir."

The Seventh
San Miguel
March 26

"People say they're southeast of here at Las Crusas or maybe Namiquipa. That's Cervantes' hometown. They'd be welcome there."

Dodd mulled the scout's report. They were already low on supplies. He needed to let Pershing know they'd missed him. "How far to Las Crusas?"

Spillsbury scratched his chin. "Thirty miles or so. Trail crosses them mountains yonder." He pointed southeast with his chin. "You know what the mountain passes are like this time of year."

"Yeah, the other night was a walk in the park."

"This climb is worse. The elevation is eleven thousand feet most of the way, more in some places."

"What's the alternative?"

"Go back to El Valle. Maybe catch a train."

Food and communications didn't improve either way. Brown and the Tenth should be out there somewhere. Villa might even have run into them. "We're here to catch the son-of-a-bitch, Lem. Let's get after him."

The column moved out. Spillsbury led them down the southeast slope of the plateau and up the mountain side beyond. The narrow winding trail and rocky terrain made for a difficult climb. The scout hadn't sugar-coated that part. He didn't predict an early spring storm either.

Gray leaden clouds boiled out of the mountains, driven by winds whining through the chasms and passes. At times wind-driven snow laced with sand became so strong, men and horses were forced to turn their backs into it to absorb the buffeting. Thin air at altitude made slow going for men and horses. Graze disappeared. Men could go hungry on short rations. Horses didn't handle it well. The trail climbed into the clouds, further eroding visibility. Troopers relied on the horses' instincts for footing. Still, the Seventh plodded nose to tail up the mountain-side.

Storm-darkened day faded to night. Snow-covered trails, treacherous in daylight, became impassable in darkness. Dodd called a halt. The mountain afforded little fuel for fires and no shelter for the men. They wrapped themselves in bed rolls and shelter halves and gutted out a hard bitter night strung out in column along the trail.

Galena
March 27

The convoy rumbled through town on the road to El Valle. Ten truckloads of supplies strung out in a massive dust cloud resembled a giant fire-breathing serpent. A company of the Sixth Infantry accompanied the convoy with troops assigned to each vehicle.

Patton rode in the lead truck. He took some satisfaction from the speed with which he'd adapted his logistics plan to Pershing's troop deployments. This column would support the Seventh and the Tenth. He assigned five trucks to support Tompkins' Thirteenth riding southeast from Colonia Dublán. Five more would support Howze and the Eleventh on the march southwest from Galena. He had seven trucks in reserve to rotate in relief of the support columns. He'd sent one of the wagon companies south with Tompkins and one with Howze. They would take over supply operations when the columns traversed country too rough for the trucks.

Mile after mile the desert rolled by the dusty windscreen. In good weather the trucks could make fifteen miles an hour. He had to admit the truck's speed and capacity to carry material to troops who needed it made the operation impressive. Mule-drawn wagons could never match the performance of this convoy. Mules needed fodder and rest. Trucks packed their own gasoline. Mechanical breakdowns were a fact of life. They hampered the dependability of the operation. Then again, wagons broke down too and mules came up lame. It brought to mind the general's observation *"Time and invention have a way of correcting such things."*

Harsh conditions took a toll on men and machines. Choking dust and heat made the best circumstances. Rain and mud slowed the operation to mule pace. As the miles rolled by the reality of the logistics problem grew increasingly clear. The farther the columns penetrated into Mexico, the longer the supply lines became. Operational difficulty increased with every mile. Bad as conditions were, he expected the operation to continue indefinitely. Unless Washington cleared use of the railroads diplomatically, he had no other option.

El Valle

The Tenth camped south of town. Black troopers created a curiosity among the locals. Some were reluctant to trade with the Americans at first, until money lubricated basic commercial interests. Tortillas, vegetables, fruit and fresh "deer meat" suddenly appeared in abundance. Some speculated that the sudden increase in the local deer population could be traced to an equally sudden decline in the number of stray dogs roaming through town. Despite the abundance of local fare the troopers were damn glad to see the supply convoy's dust cloud roll out of town.

Patton turned the convoy over to the Tenth's supply sergeant and went off to find Colonel Brown. Brown sat in the shade of a shelter half. He greeted Patton with a smile and returned his salute.

"Lieutenant, those trucks of yours are about as welcome as

Christmas morning. My gut's been complaining about the food since the day our rations ran out."

"Glad we could help, Colonel. Any word from Colonel Dodd?"

"Not a peep, though I don't know why I would expect any. He's probably wondering where the hell we are. I take it the General hasn't heard from him."

"He hadn't before I left."

"He's probably made San Miguel by now and then some."

"With luck, we can hope Colonel Dodd got him."

Brown shook his head. "I'd be surprised. We'd have heard something if he had. The locals would know. Colonel Dodd left the train because it was moving too slow. You can't hide two regiments of cavalry on a train that doesn't need a watch to hold a schedule when a calendar will do. Word travels fast. We don't."

"So you think Villa had enough warning to get away."

"I'd bet a month's pay on it. How was the trip down here?"

He knit his brow. "The trucks are faster than mules on a decent road. They break down more, but they're easier to feed."

Brown chuckled.

"The deeper we go into Mexico, the tougher the supply problem will be, unless Washington can persuade Carranza to let us use the trains."

"What do you mean?"

"After your ride, somebody decided the Mexican government didn't like the idea of us using their railroads. That's the reason for the truck convoys."

"Well, Lieutenant, you may think the trucks are unreliable, but you haven't ridden the Mexican railways, either. Did the general give you any orders for the Tenth?"

"No, sir, he's sending the Eleventh and Thirteenth forward to relieve you and Colonel Dodd. I think he plans to establish a series of base camps."

"This supply business of yours looks like a full-time job."

He winced to himself, *Riding shotgun on truckloads of potatoes and beans, hell of an assignment for a fighting man.*

The Seventh
Las Cruces
March 27

The Seventh column spilled out of the mountains, trading icy winter winds for a desert blast furnace. Las Cruces shimmered dark and ragged in the distance as they descended through the foothills. Dodd felt cut off from the rest of the expeditionary force. They'd seen no sign of the Tenth. Something must have happened to Brown's regiment. The unknown gnawed at his gut. He needed to report in and find out what the hell had happened.

"Lem, we're going to need food for the men and forage for the horses. I need to find a phone or a telegraph to report in. Ride on ahead and get a start on that. We'll bivouac west of town."

Spillsbury touched the brim of his hat and squeezed up a lope through shimmering heat waves.

An hour later Dodd drew a halt west of town. They began to arrive almost before the men could dismount and get to the business of making camp. Donkey carts loaded with meat the purveyors called beef. The carts were followed by women carrying baskets of tortillas, pots of beans and roast peppers. One large cart carried great jars filled with water. Most of that went to the stock. The demand for water turned that commodity into a steady business, filling every bucket, jar and container to be found in Las Cruces. Coarse dry prairie grass provided poor forage for the horses, but to a hungry horse, poor forage was better than no forage.

Spillsbury rode in at midday. He found Dodd's tent marked by the Seventh's standard. "They don't have a working phone in town, but they do have a telegraph, Colonel. If you give the *Carrancista* commander a good explanation for why you're here, I'm guessing he'll let you use it."

"Good work, Lem."

"Don't thank me just yet. Let's see how the men do on them *frijoles.*"

Spillsbury knew his business. Between the water and the local fare, latrine construction scarcely kept pace with demand.

CHAPTER TWENTY-FOUR

Colonia Dublan
March 27

Desert wind ruffled the stack of paper on the camp desk. Pershing's pistol lay atop the stack, holding it in place. He scanned Dodd's telegram for the second time. Villa escaped. He nodded agreement at Dodd's assertion. The slow-developing operation afforded Villa's sympathizers too much time to warn him. Rumors in Las Cruces said he'd gone further south to the town of Namiquipa.

Time, distance and terrain were Villa's allies. You couldn't hide troop movements from sympathetic eyes. *Villa enjoys that advantage, for the moment.* He scratched a note on the pad at his elbow.

"Lieutenant Collins."

"Sir?"

"Get this telegram off to Camp Furlong." *Now let's see what those birds of yours can do, Captain Foulois.*

Camp Furlong
Columbus
March 27
1500 Hours

Captain Benjamin Foulois tested the column tension on the Curtiss JN-3 controls. He nudged the wheel forward, watching the flaps come down. He eased the column back. The flaps returned to level and continued to lift. Left rudder, right rudder, the wheel turned smoothly. He eased himself out of the front cockpit onto the fuselage frame. "She's ready, Ted." He gave the mechanic a thumbs-up. He glanced at the barracks to his right. A man jogged his way, holding a yellow sheet, unmistakable for a telegram.

"Telegram for Captain Foulois."

Ted gestured to the cockpit.

Foulois swung his leg over the side, found the iron stirrup and stepped down. He took the telegram, tore it open and read. His chiseled rock jaw broke into a gleaming white smile.

"Thank you, Corporal. Ted, get these birds ready. We take off within the hour." He hurried up the road to the barracks and dashed up the steps two at a time. "All right, fly boys, this is it. Roll your asses out of bed. We're going to Mexico. We take off in an hour."

"Where we headed, Captain?" Lieutenant Herbert Dargue led First Aero Flight Group Two. A darkly handsome New Yorker, he had a quick wit and a devil-may-care attitude that belied a thoughtful second nature.

"Colonia Dublán."

Dargue looked at his watch, puzzled. "Don't you think it's a bit late, sir? We'll never get that far before dark."

"We might make it. Let's show the General what the First can do."

Dargue shook his head as the barracks exploded in frenzied activity. Pilots and co-pilots scrambled into their flight gear. Mechanics and ground crew hurried down the stairs and ran for the planes. Sixty-five minutes later seven of the eight Jennies idled smoothly in their blocks beside Deming Road.

Foulois sat in the forward cockpit of his Jennie, buffeted by prop wash. He looked down the row of aero planes at the thick carpet of dust streaming behind them. He made goggled eye contact with each pilot. One by one they gave him a gauntleted thumbs-up signal. He turned to Ted and nodded. The mechanic pulled the chocks out from under the carriage wheels and ducked under the bottom wing.

The Jennie rolled onto the road. Foulois swung the tail around, pointing the nose south. He jammed the throttle to the floor, beginning his take-off roll. The second Jennie taxied into position behind him. JN Alpha rolled down the road, picking up speed. The tail lifted at take-off speed. He eased the column back. The nose came up as she rotated airborne. The ground fell away. She climbed like a sleek gray goose set against soft white puff balls in the late afternoon sky. He banked a lazy wide circle over Columbus. The burnt shell of the Commercial Hotel reminded him of the reason the First Aero Squadron had this chance to prove itself.

Below workers busily disposing of debris or rebuilding the damage stopped what they were doing to look skyward. People came out of houses and stores, drawn by the throaty rumble of powerful engines filling the sky. One by one the great gray birds lifted off Deming Road to circle the town. The display of U.S. military might was a breathtaking sight. The townsfolk looked on, satisfied Villa and his bandits had no idea what a hornet's nest they'd stirred by their foolhardy attack on Columbus. Well, they'd know soon enough.

Foulois watched his birds fall into formation, two flights of four minus one. The mechanics would deal with the engine problem on Flight Group Two JN Delta. Mechanical failure was a fact of aviation life. Regrettable, but he couldn't wait. He completed his circle. He pointed the nose of his ship at the southern horizon and crossed into Mexico.

The Jennies leveled off at four thousand feet and settled in at a comfortable cruising speed of sixty miles an hour. A mottled carpet of sand, sage and scrub passed below. Mountains smudged the horizons to the west and southeast. Little else disturbed the barren landscape. Foulois let his mind play ahead. Out here, a column of cavalry would stand out for miles from the air. The mountains might be a different matter. Mountains had air currents that would test an aviator's skill. They didn't have a training manual for that, just instinct, reaction and a bit of luck.

Foulois pushed past Palomas Ranch and on to Boca Grande. Slowly the sun sank toward the mountain peaks in the west. He checked his watch, 17:30. Purple shadows spread over the landscape with little more than an orange glow clinging to the mountain peaks. Disappointed, he resigned himself to the fact they would not make Colonia Dublán before nightfall. He gave his flight the hand signal to land. He peeled off and swooped low, looking for a favorable place to set them down.

Flying above the lead flight, Bert Dargue missed the hand signal and continued south into darkness. The three pilots in Flight Group Two soon lost visual contact with one another. Running low on fuel, one by one they brought their ships in to land at scattered locations. A drainage ditch stripped the undercarriage off JN Beta. She skidded to a stop on her belly, severely damaging the fuselage.

Rubio
March 28

Villa and Candelario Cervantes bent over a map spread on a table in the village hall. The Alcalde gave him use of the hall as his headquarters while División del Norte remained in town. Hollow footfalls announced a new arrival. Across the sun-splashed floor, Nicolas Fernandez climbed the steps from the entry foyer. He crossed the hall on long fluid strides, his boots clicking an urgent pace.

"Jefe, the Yanquis are in Las Cruces."

Villa pursed his lips, impressed. "They made good time returning from San Miguel."

"We have other reports of reinforcements moving south from Colonia Dublán. The second column remains in El Valle."

Villa rubbed his chin, studying the map. "Four regiments of cavalry can cover much ground. We may need to scatter into the hills for a time."

Cervantes puffed a cigar. "The men need food and supplies for that."

"Sí." Villa nodded. "These we can take from the Federales in Minaca and Guerreo." He stabbed the map. "From there we are a whisper of smoke."

Colonia Dublán
March 28

It started like a swarm of bees that rose to a throaty rumble. All over the camp men paused to look up, shading their eyes with their hands. Pershing squinted off to the north beneath the brim of his Montana peak. Four dark spots hung in the faultless blue vault. Patton watched the spots take shape, wings spread in pairs. The Jennies banked in a graceful arc to the east, circling the little town surrounded by the sprawling patchwork of the Punitive Expedition's base camp.

"Damn impressive, aren't they, George?"

"Yes, sir." He remembered dinner that night at the Hoover. The First Aero Squadron commander's vision of the air service began with reconnaissance and communication. Could these ungainly aircraft relieve the cavalry of these core missions? Many thought so, the general among them. Some believed the air service might prove its merit in this very campaign.

"Do you agree with Captain Foulois that the aero plane will

be used in offensive combat operations?"

Pershing arched a brow, reading his question. "With all that speed and range, consider the tactical possibilities. Conventional cavalry operations have ground to a halt in European-style trench warfare. It's a defensive stalemate. Armed aircraft have the potential to break that stalemate."

"They're so fragile, how will they stand up to modern ballistics?"

The general smiled. "Time and invention, George, these things have a way of taking care of themselves."

He looked away. His trucks were parked in orderly rows in the field north of the quadrangle. What of the horse soldier, then? He felt tired, discouraged. He'd tried to deny the realization. The mirror didn't lie in the morning when he shaved. His hair thinned, mocking him noticeably. He felt old, damn it. George Patton felt old.

Overhead the leader circled them into line over the Galena road south of town. Slowly they drifted down, riding unsteady wind currents. The line wavered, the planes slipping from one side of the road to the other. The first touched down, the wheels finding the road at the last in a cloud of dust. Flight Group One snaked out of the sky, touching down one behind the other.

Pershing looked back to the north. "No sign of the rest of them. I wonder where they are. Com'on." He set off down the road.

JN Alpha turned off the road onto a dusty flat. Foulois brought the tail around, pointing the nose back to the roadway, and shut down the engine. One by one the pilots brought their ships into line.

Foulois lifted himself out of the cockpit and dismounted. He pulled his goggles down around his neck and freed his hands of their gauntlets. He removed his leather helmet and ran his fingers through wavy hair as Pershing crunched up the road with Lieutenant Patton at his heels.

Foulois saluted. "First Aero Squadron reporting as ordered, General."

Pershing returned his salute, "Captain. Welcome. Where's the rest of your unit?"

"We had one mechanical problem in Columbus. Flight Group Two missed the signal to land last night. I expect they'll be along directly. You don't fly these birds unless you can land and take off when you need to."

"How soon can you be ready to mount a reconnaissance operation?"

"It depends on what you need, sir. Get these pilots some lunch and a full fuel tank and we can get back in the air this afternoon. If you want a sustained operation we'll need our mechanics. They're coming down from Columbus on the next supply convoy."

"For now, I'll take what I can get. We have a report that Villa is in Namiquipa. Colonel Dodd is close on his trail. My guess is he'll be on the move soon. I want you to find him. Give Dodd the benefit of your eyes in the sky."

"Where is Colonel Dodd now?"

"The seventh is bivouacked at Las Cruces, just north of Namiquipa."

"Let me have a look at a map. We may need a refueling stop south of here."

"El Valle," Patton offered. "I'll get word to Colonel Brown to expect you."

"Good. I can have two birds in the air in about an hour."

Pershing nodded. "Excellent."

CHAPTER TWENTY-FIVE

Sierra Madre
March 28

Foulois leaned out from behind the windscreen into the icy prop wash. The patchwork hash of Rubio's streets passed beneath his left wings at the southern mouth of the mountain pass. Mountains to the east fell away. The small town of Santa Ysabel lay across a flat expanse of desert dead ahead. Instinct told him no. If Villa left Namiquipa, he'd head west into the mountains. He brought the Jennie's nose around to the southwest, circling along the slopes of the western peaks. Spencer, his wingman in JN Bravo, followed his lead.

Foulois banked JN Alpha full circle to the north. The engine coughed in the cold, thin air. The cold seemed to reduce her effective ceiling. He took her down to get a good look at the eastern slopes. The updraft hit the Jennie hard, throwing her up and right in a violent lurch that shuddered through the fuselage and wing struts. Foulois' gut slammed into his groin. He fought the rudder, bringing her back level as he eased her off the face of the mountain toward the pass.

Lieutenant Doug Bassett, Foulois' second seat, tapped his shoulder. He pointed to JN Bravo off the left wing. Spencer's second seat observer waved frantically, pointing at the ground. Bassett handed Foulois his binoculars. He scanned the mountainside. A long column of Mexican irregular cavalry wound its way up the slopes below. *Villa, it had to be.* Foulois handed the glasses back to Bassett. He checked the map. The line of march crossed the front range toward the towns of Minaca and Guerrero. They needed to get the information to Dodd fast. He waggled his wings to get Spencer's attention. He signaled a return to Las Cruces.

Spencer returned a thumbs-up and then peeled away in a dive, apparently to take a closer look at the column. Foulois watched wide-eyed behind his goggles. The mountain air currents were dangerously unstable. *Pull up. Pull up, we've seen enough!* He screamed soundlessly above the roar of the engine and the blast of the prop wash.

JN Bravo swooped down and leveled off over the column, buzzing it southwest with the slope of the mountain face. Suddenly, the plane shook visibly. She struggled to bring her nose up. The engine coughed a puff of black smoke. The attempted climb stalled. She slipped back momentarily, rolled over and spiraled into the mountainside, erupting in an orange ball of flame and clouds of oily black smoke.

Foulois circled back, giving Bassett a good look at the crash site. Behind his binoculars the co-pilot searched the crash site, praying for any sign of survivors. Horsemen peeled away from the column and headed for the wreckage. Bassett tapped him on the shoulder. The observer's goggles turned misty. He shook his head.

"Americano." Fernandez delivered the expected news regarding the identity of the aero plane. Villa scratched his chin absently.

"The other one returned north. They know we are here. We need to move fast, Nico. Send Beltran and his company to Minaca. The town has no Carrancista garrison. Tell him to take what they have. The Federales hold Guerreo and San Ysidro. You and your men attack San Ysidro. I will accompany Candelario and his men to Guerrero. We must get the supplies we need and disappear before the Yanquis reach us."

"Sí, Jefe." He wheeled his horse at a trot to the rear.

Villa's orders passed to his officers. The column moved out, pushing its pace with a new sense of urgency. *Aero planes*, Villa thought. This Black Jack gringo has many tricks up his sleeve. He should never have gotten this close. We must not take this hombre for a fool. We have poked a sleeping bear. Four regiments of cavalry with eyes in the sky, how many more of these aero planes might he have? División del Norte must disappear. Even eyes in the sky cannot find smoke in the wind.

Las Cruces

The Jennie swooped out of the late afternoon sun, a giant black bird set against the mountain haze. Dodd watched the plane circle the camp. Just one, what the hell happened to the other one? The Jennie lined up on the road south of town and began its descent. These landings never failed to amaze him. The aircraft slid left and right, buffeted by wind gusts, seemingly unable to hold the line of the road. Somehow the pilots managed to get the nose over the hard-packed dirt surface just as the wheels touched down in an explosion of dust. He watched the pilot taxi to a parking place beside the road. The tail swung around, the nose pointing west. He recognized First Aero Squadron leader Foulois. The pilot climbed out of the cockpit the moment the propeller shut down. He pulled at his goggles and gauntlets as he strode purposefully across cracked desert ground. Dodd waited with Spillsbury.

Foulois threw up an anxious salute. "He's on the move, sir."

"Where?"

"East slopes of the Sierra Madre, a day's ride southwest of Rubio. It looks like they're headed to Guerrero. I make it the whole damn outfit."

"You know the area, Mr. Spillsbury?"

"I do, sir."

"Where's your other plane, Captain?"

He shook his head. "Crashed on the mountain, sir." Silence followed. The risk early aviators accepted there for all to consider.

"I'm sorry, Captain."

"Thank you, sir."

"We're going after him. Get your report to General Pershing at Colonia Dublán, Captain."

"Yes, sir." Dodd turned to go. "If I may, sir?"

He paused with a nod.

"Mr. Spillsbury, by what route do you plan to lead the pursuit? It may be important if General Pershing has orders for the Colonel."

"Good point, Captain." Dodd turned to Spillsbury.

"With the Colonel's permission we'll skirt the Federal troops at Namiquipa with a stop in San Geronimo. That'd be the best place to catch up with us before we head into the mountains."

Foulois turned to Dodd. "I'll be on my way at first light, sir."

"So will we, Captain, so will we."

Colonia Dublán
March 29
0900 Hours

Foulois reported to Pershing's tent within minutes of landing. Patton listened to the aviator's report. They'd located Villa in difficult mountain terrain, notified Dodd and brought word to headquarters. The reconnaissance and communication missions covered nearly five hundred miles in the span of twenty-four hours. Truly an amazing accomplishment when compared to conventional cavalry recon and couriers. Dodd might have scoured those mountains for weeks without ever finding Villa.

Speed and distance, decisive strategic elements for centuries, suddenly had new meaning. The tragic crash was sobering. The men who flew these machines did so in the face of terrible risks. Mechanical failures were troubling and dangerous. The aero plane may be unreliable at present, but the capabilities were truly amazing. Time would surely bring further invention. The general broke his train of thought.

"Excellent work, Captain, the results are truly impressive."

"Thank you, sir."

"I'm sorry about the loss of Lieutenant Spencer."

"Spencer was a good man, sir. We all understand the risks."

"Your Flight Group Two reported in while you were gone. All the men are accounted for. One plane was damaged on landing. Your mechanics and parts depot are on their way down from Columbus."

"Thank you, sir. I noticed the planes when I landed."

"You say Colonel Dodd marched south after Villa."

"He did, sir. We can reach him at San Geronimo day after tomorrow should you need to."

"Send someone down there to advise him a relief column under Major Howze is on its way to him."

"Very good, sir." Foulois saluted and went off in search of his men.

Minaca
March 29

Francisco Beltran and his company rode into the small village unopposed. The Village headman came out of a rundown one-story adobe dressed in the loose-fitting shirt and pantaloons of a peon. He met them at a well in the central plaza, his sombrero in hand, dark sweat glistening in his hair.

"How may our humble village be of service, Jefe?"

"My men are in need of food, water and fodder for our horses."

"We are a poor village, Jefe. Water and fodder we have some. Food," he shook his head.

"We shall see. Summon the people."

A shadow of fear crossed the headman's dark eyes. He went to the well. A bell hung from the rafters of the thatched roof. He rang the bell and waited. Flies gathered to the scent of men and horses, buzzing noisily and feasting on fresh droppings. The villagers came shuffling through the dust. Old men and women bent with age. Children stared wide-eyed at the mounted solda-dos. Men came from the fields.

Beltran's eyes danced over the gathering crowd, *no young women*. These people would hold out on him. He looked down at the headman.

"Tell them."

He turned to the people with a shrug. "Jefe wishes water and fodder for his horses. I told him we have some of this. He also wishes food. I told him we are poor."

Beltran drew his gun. "You lied, señor." He fired.

The headman's eyes froze below the gray splatter where his forehead had been. He pitched forward, blood spattered in the dust.

"Now, you," Beltran crooked a finger to the most able look-ing of the field hands. "Come."

The man looked from side to side as though someone else might heed the command. He removed his sombrero and stepped forward.

"Please, Jefe, I am but a humble peon."

"Tell them. I need food for my men, water and fodder for my horses." The man's eyes filled with fear. Beltran cocked his gun. "Tell them."

"Compadres, Jefe needs food, water and hay. Bring them

here." They started to go.

"Wait!" The villagers hesitated, watching the Villista in terror. "Your wives and daughters are hidden. Summon them here. No one will hurt them unless you hold back the supplies we need." He leveled his gun at the new village speaker.

"Do as he says, amigos." He crossed himself. "Dio mio, do as he says."

San Ysidro
March 29

The small town huddled beside the Federale barracks and corrals in the shelter of a shallow valley. The town was little more than a dusty cluster of adobe, tile and thatch-roofed buildings loosely arranged around a small plaza. Fernandez considered his options. The townspeople would offer no resistance. He must first deal with the garrison. He saw none of the defenses that turned Agua Prieta into a wasting slaughter. Then again, he saw little of the garrison. *Draw them out.*

He left a detachment of ten men with instructions to ride into town in two hours' time. Their purpose, draw the Federales into the open. Fernandez took the main body south, below the valley wall to a position flanking the barracks. With his men in position, he waited for his decoys to advance on the town.

Guerrero
March 29

The town sprawled across a high mountain plateau forty-five miles west of Rubio. División del Norte climbed through the morning hours as the heat of the day set in. Villa halted the column below the east rim. He continued on with a small party of Dorado to scout the village.

A river gorge bordered the plateau on the south. Three deep arroyos gashed the gently sloping plain, leading to the outskirts of town. Villa used one of these to move in for a closer look. At a distance of perhaps a half mile the floor of the arroyo began to rise to the level of the plain. Villa dismounted and climbed the rest of the way on foot. He hid in the rocks, looking up at the squat adobe buildings at the edge of town. Sentries patrolled the perimeter. He saw no sign of fortification. The Carrancista *Commandante* must consider such a remote outpost in little danger of attack. He would pay for his foolishness. Off to the north a second arroyo approached the village in much the same fashion as this, creating the potential for a two-pronged assault. Guerrero looked like a ripe melon ready for picking. He returned to the column and gathered his officers.

He crouched in the sand and drew with a stick. "Guerrero is here." He traced a rough outline crosshatched by streets. "The river gorge is here. This trail leads into an arroyo that runs up here." He drew lines in the sand leading to the village. "A second runs here. Pablo, take your men and circle north to the mouth of this arroyo. Candelario and his men will proceed up this one. We will charge the town together. The sentries may sound the alarm, but we will overrun the town before they can mount a defense." He looked from one man to the next. Candelario spoke.

"Should we not wait to attack until the dark hours before morning?"

Villa shook his head. "The arroyos cover our approach. We know the Yanquis are coming. If we wait, we give them more time to reach us. This way we take our prize and disappear into the hills before they reach us. Now, go find your position and send word when you are ready to move forward."

San Ysidro
1300 Hours
The decoys rode into town during siesta. A stray yellow dog, sleeping in the shade of a donkey cart, sounded the alarm. As

prearranged, the Villistas drew a halt east of the plaza and waited. The barracks came to life. An officer emerged. The brass buttons and insignia on his tunic and epaulets flashed in the sun. Two squads of riflemen followed him out into the yard. They fell into rank and advanced on the decoys.

Fernandez waited. He saw no stronger Federale presence. He smiled. He returned to his waiting men and stepped into his saddle. He squeezed up a prance over the crest of the valley wall. His men spread a skirmish line as they advanced down the shallow fall to the valley floor on the flank of the unsuspecting Carrancistas. Fernandez picked up a lope toward the garrison and the center of town.

Suddenly, the scene before them changed. Troops poured out of the barracks. Still more appeared from the buildings in town. They fell into ranks, advancing south on Fernandez' main body. The first rank dropped into firing position. The volley erupted along the line. Powder smoke bloomed behind a hail of high-powered bullets lashing Fernandez' line. Horses bellowed and reared. Men fell. The second rank advanced. A second volley exploded. A third rank stepped forward, closing on Fernandez with yet a third volley.

Beyond the first ranks, more than one hundred blue-clad Federales filled the plaza. Fernandez halted his charge. He counted San Ysidro too well guarded to be taken by his forces. He wheeled his horse, put spurs to flanks and bolted for the safety of the valley wall. He led his men east to Guerrero where División del Norte would fight for the largest prize.

Guerrero
1415 Hours

Villa rode at the head of Cervantes' column. The arroyo floor climbed to a point just below the surface of the plain. He called a halt. He imagined the Federales' surprise when División del

Norte rose out of the ground before their very eyes. He chuckled to himself. The swift power of the charge would overwhelm a weak defense, slow to react.

"Candelario, sound the charge when you are ready."

"La Cucaracha, La Cucaracha." Clarion notes split the air.

Two columns surged out of the arroyos onto the plain. The charge spread a ragged line from two files bursting out of the ground. Volleys of pistol and rifle fire punctuated cries of "Viva Villa, Viva Mexico." The charge swelled its numbers, horses' hooves pounded the ground, rolling thunder before a boiling dust cloud. The Villistas bore down on the seemingly defenseless town, slumbering in siestas under the afternoon sun. The vanguard closed to less than a hundred yards before the Carrancista Commandant revealed his hand.

Rooftops across the edge of town exploded in a rattle of machine gun fire. A carefully laid wall of enfilade fire raked Villa's ranks. Men and horses screamed and fell. The force of the charge broke against a wall of death. Light artillery thumped and whined. Explosive concussions sucked life out of the air, spewing gouts of dirt, rock and steel on the attackers. Salvo after salvo of precision artillery fire pounded the mouths of the arroyos, staunching the assault as a cork might stop a bottle. The barrage cut off the advance elements leading the charge. The void behind them blocked retreat to the shelter of low ground. Sharp-shooters picked at Villa's forward line, thrown into disarray in the vicious crossfire. A heavy-caliber bullet ripped Villa's leg below the knee. His horse reared. Miraculously, he held his seat.

Cervantes seized the moment. "Retreat! Retreat!" He wheeled his horse and galloped to the rear, leading a frantic route to escape the deadly rain of fire. Villa followed Cervantes, slumped over his horse's neck, his leg dangling useless.

★ ★ ★ ★ ★

Fernandez' retreat crossed trails with Cervantes' battered column east of Guerrero. He swung his men into the line of retreat to Minaca. The sight of a seriously wounded Villa disturbed him greatly. He was Jefe, the face of the revolution. Without him, who would lead? Worse than that, they had suffered another stinging defeat, further depleting their ranks and denying them the supplies they so desperately needed. Worse still, the Yanquis were coming. They had little time to recover and escape.

They reached the ranch of a sympathizer not far from Minaca. They carried a despondent Villa into the hacienda, crying in agony. A runner was dispatched to summon the local healer. The shriveled old man could do little more than clean and bind the wound. Villa suffered the dual scourges of black rage at his defeat and the extreme pain of his wound. Cervantes and Fernandez stayed at his side, grim-faced with worry.

Cervantes offered a bottle of tequila. "Jefe, just this once, for the pain."

Villa's eyes fluttered open, hard bright pits of black fire. He took the bottle and drank. He coughed and drank again. He passed the bottle back. "Nico, do not tell the men I have been shot. Tell them I was thrown from my horse."

"Sí, Jefe. Now you must rest."

He closed his eyes. They left the room.

"How much time do we have before the gringos come?" Nico asked.

Cervantes shook his head.

CHAPTER TWENTY-SIX

San Geronimo
March 30

Dodd pushed the Seventh south, skirting the Carrancista garrison at Namiquipa. He halted the column outside the village of San Geronimo. He rode into town accompanied by Spillsbury. The Alcalde met them at the outskirts of town. Dodd stepped down. Spillsbury followed his lead.

"*Buenos dias,* Alcalde."

"Buenos dias, *Coronel.*"

The exchange exhausted Dodd's command of Spanish. He turned to Spillsbury. "Tell him we have President Carranza's permission to pursue the bandit Pancho Villa. Tell him we would like to camp outside the village tonight."

Spillsbury translated. The old man looked troubled, but he could do nothing to object if he wished to.

"Ask him if he knows anything of Villa's movements."

The Alcalde listened. His eyes blinked, uncomfortable with the question. He mumbled his reply.

"He says he knows nothing."

"I don't believe him."

"Me, either, Colonel. Let me go into town. I'll get more information in the cantina than we'll get out here."

"Very well, Lem, I'll see you back in camp." He touched the

brim of his hat to the Alcalde, stepped into his saddle and rode back to make camp.

Spillsbury returned to camp an hour later. He rode directly to Dodd's tent and dismounted.

"What did you find out?"

"Plenty. Villa attacked Guerrero about forty-five miles west of here yesterday. Word has it the Federale garrison there put one hell of a whuppin' on him. Some say Villa was wounded. Others say he was thrown from his horse. That sounds like a cover to me. The man who said he was wounded says he got it from the healer who treated him."

"How long will it take us to get there?"

Spillsbury scratched his chin. "Tough ride over the mountains again, Colonel. Day and a half if we push it."

Dodd clenched his jaw. "Can nothing be done quickly in this godforsaken country?"

The drone of an approaching aero plane intruded on Dodd's frustration. He looked north, shading his eyes. The ship's shadow passed overhead in a sweeping turn to the southeast. She circled around to the west, made a tight turn to the north and dropped her nose, lining up to land on the road south of camp. A curious crowd poured out of the village to watch as the aero plane touched down in a cloud of dust. The pilot taxied up the road to the south end of the Seventh camp. He brought the tail around and parked in taxi position beside the road. The engine shut down. The pilot climbed out of the plane, dropped his goggles and started up the road to camp, removing his leather headgear.

Dodd hurried down the road to the aviator, trailing Spillsbury at his heel.

"Colonel Dodd." The flier saluted. "Lieutenant Herbert Dargue, First Aero Squadron. I have a dispatch for you from

General Pershing." Dargue handed Dodd a leather case he carried under his arm.

Dodd withdrew Pershing's order and read. "The General wants us to stand down, Lem. Howze and the Eleventh are on the way to relieve us. If we do that, Villa's trail will go cold. Lieutenant, how soon can you get my reply back to the General?"

Dargue checked his watch and glanced at the slant of the sun. He shook his head. "Not enough daylight left to get back to him before morning."

"All right, let's get you some supper and a place to sleep. I'll compose a reply advising him of the situation here. Lem, we ride for Guerrero at first light."

Minaca
March 30
"Jefe, the Yanquis are coming. We must depart."

Villa's eyes fluttered open. Dim candlelight pricked the shadows. His leg throbbed. His voice rasped little more than a croak. "Yanquis, Nico?"

"Sí, Jefe. Here, drink this." He lifted Villa's head to the cup of water.

Villa choked on the swallow. He slumped back on the pillow, his skin and hair damp with sweat. "I cannot ride, Nico. Leave me."

"We have a carriage for you to ride in. We cannot wait any longer. Candelario and his men will create a diversion to slow them down, but we must leave now."

Four men crowded around the bed. They took the corners of the bedclothes to form a makeshift stretcher. They lifted. Villa cursed through clenched teeth. They carried him into the predawn chill and passed him up to other men waiting in the carriage. He ground his teeth against a painful groan. They settled him on the hard leather-padded seat. The men scrambled down from the carriage and disappeared into the shadows. The pain ebbed. All around him the sounds of men and horses prepared to depart. Fernandez climbed into the carriage. The rocking carriage springs sent bolts of pain shooting up his injured leg, promising a torturous ride.

"Rest, Jefe. We will do our best to find a safe hiding place for you to heal."

He nodded and closed his eyes. Fernandez climbed down. The carriage lurched forward. Villa passed out.

Colonia Dublán
March 31
Pershing handed Patton Dodd's dispatch. He bent over the wind-ruffled map spread across the camp table in front of his tent. He drew his pistol and laid it on the northwest corner, intent on locating Guerrero.

Patton finished Dodd's report. "If he is wounded, that should slow him up some."

"You'd hope so. Damn, the action is getting away from us here. These supply lines are overextended. The relief columns can't keep up. They'll be ready for relief themselves by the time they catch up with Dodd. Communications work because of Foulois' people, but he's down to five functioning planes. At this rate they may not last another month."

"You do agree Colonel Dodd made the right decision to press his pursuit?"

"Of course I agree under the circumstances. I'm just saying logistics and command and control are a concern. I need to get closer to the action. It's time to activate our mobile command, George. If Dodd doesn't get Villa at Guerrero, we're going south."

"Yes, sir." *Closer to the action. Good.*

Guerrero

April 1

1700 Hours

The Seventh stumbled out of the mountains, exhausted after thirty-six hours of bone-chilling cold followed by an anvil of desert heat. Dodd drew a halt in an arroyo below the Guerrero plateau. Spillsbury read the sign. A large force stopped there several days ago.

"How about I ride in and have a look around, Colonel? I won't get the Federales all excited like the full column might. If they give Villa a lickin', he's left the area. They'll likely have some idea of where he went."

"All right, Lem, but get after it. We're running out of daylight."

"Beggin' your pardon, sir, take a look at these men and horses. After climbin' up and down mountains for two days, these boys need a rest."

"That may be so, but when you're hunting wounded game, you don't show them any quarter."

Spillsbury returned in little over an hour. He found Dodd resting in the shade of a rock ledge at the head of the column. He sat up, alert as the scout stepped down.

"What did you find out?"

"The Carrancista Commandante seems quite pleased with himself. He figures Carranza will give him a medal for the beating he handed Villa. Stung him as good or better than he got at Agua Prieta. He told me all about it. Villa come busting out of this arroyo and another one just north of here. The Commandante had his machine guns on the roofs of the buildings. They put down a crossfire that cut Villa's men up fierce. He figured an attack would come up the arroyos so had his artillery zeroed in on the mouths."

Dodd got the picture. "Son-of-a-bitch probably should get a medal. Glad you went to town before we showed ourselves. If he took offense to us, we'd a' been round two. Did he give you any idea where Villa went?"

"He seemed more cooperative than most. His reports say they went southeast toward Minaca. He's got some sympathizers down there."

"How far?"

"Five miles."

"If we get moving we can be there by sundown."

"Not interested in spending the night with the Commandante's artillery trained on you?"

"He might forget his good humor."

Minaca

The trail down to Minaca was covered in signs of Villa's withdrawal. Dodd halted the column northwest of the plaza. The sleepy village showed no sign of Division del Norte. He shook his head.

"Well, he passed through all right, but he isn't here now. You couldn't hide an army in a place that size."

Spillsbury spit. "These folks likely know more than we do."

"We'll bivouac here for the night. Let's ride in, Lem, and see what they'll tell us."

They left the column to make camp west of the village and rode into the noticeably deserted plaza. They drew rein beside the well and stepped down. Spillsbury knelt to examine a dark stain in the dirt.

"What is it, Lem?"

The scout stood. "Blood stain by the look of it."

A lone man in the loose-fitting clothes of a peon appeared in the doorway of a squat adobe building across the plaza. He came toward them hat in hand, wide eyes darting nervously from the troops encamping at the edge of town, to the Americano officer, to the scout and back to the officer.

"What is it you want of us? We are poor. We have nothing. What little we had has already been taken from us."

Spillsbury translated.

"Tell him we mean his people no harm. We seek only information about the bandit Pancho Villa."

The man's eyes darkened at the mention of Villa's name. "Muerte Villa." He spat.

Spillsbury glanced at Dodd. "Seems like he's been here."

"Ask him what he knows."

The scout interrogated the new headman for the next several minutes. "Well he's been here all right, twice. Four days ago some of his men came. They shot the village headman. That's his blood stain. They cleaned the place out of anything they had to eat. They came back through again three days ago, the whole army this time. He says they had a big fight at Guerrero. They had another smaller fight at San Ysidro. The Federales beat them both times. Villa is wounded. He rode in a carriage and seemed to be in great pain."

"Does he know where they are going?"

He shook his head. "They traveled southeast."

"Ask him how many people live in the village."

Spillsbury translated. "Fifty," he said.

"Tell him we will send food for tonight and more when we reach our supplies."

CHAPTER TWENTY-SEVEN

Cusihuiriachic
April 1
The carriage plodded south lashed by stinging sheets of sleet mixed with cold rain. Villa's painful groans were a constant reminder for the driver to avoid as many rocks and frozen mud ruts as the roadway allowed, the task rendered nearly impossible by a freezing mud slurry.

Villa gritted his teeth. "Nico!" He rasped.

Fernandez reined his horse aside at the head of the Dorado escort. He drew rein and waited for the carriage to roll alongside. Villa sprawled on the carriage seat, his injured leg supported by the seat cushion. The bandages below his torn trouser leg turned a brown-mottled yellow. Below the bandage his flesh had turned purple and black. His head lolled on his chest, his eyes and jaw clenched against the pain. He shivered with cold. He breathed steamy ragged gasps. Fernandez feared he might die.

"Sí, Jefe?"

His eyes fluttered open. He squinted against the rain and sleet. "Nico, for the love of your sweet mother, shoot me now."

Fernandez closed his eyes against the sight of Pancho Villa reduced to pleading for final grace. What to do for him?

"Jefe, you must not say this. You cannot die. The revolution needs you. The people need you. This is only the pain talking."

He reached into his saddlebag and drew out a bottle of tequila. "Here, Jefe, for the pain, it is all we have."

Villa raised a brow to the bottle handed down to him. "Shit, if I must live I need my wits."

He extended the bottle. "Use it for the pain, Jefe. Use my wits for a time."

He accepted the bottle, took a long pull and closed his eyes. "Nico!"

"Sí, Jefe."

"Keep your wits about you." He took another long pull.

Colonia Dublán
April 2
0900 Hours

Patton crunched up the path to Pershing's tent lost in thought. He missed Beat. Separations were always difficult. This one seemed the more so for the heavy burden of doubt that weighed on his future. He carried a routine progress report for the general.

The general sat at his camp desk, his chin propped in one hand. He absently smoothed his moustache with his forefinger, deep in thought. He held a telegram in the other hand.

"They're here, sir."

Pershing looked up, puzzled.

"The touring cars you requested. Brand new Dodge models arrived in Columbus by rail. I had them driven down here. They arrived last night."

"Good, just in time for us to move out."

"Move out, sir?"

"Here, read this." Pershing slid the telegram across the table.

Patton glanced at the signature line. Dodd sent it from Guerrero. He scanned the cryptic message. "Son-of-a-bitch."

"Missed him by hours. So close, so damn close."

Patton handed the telegram back. "What now, sir?"

Pershing took a deep breath and sighed. "Dodd needs relief. He's pushed his men and horses to the point of exhaustion. He's moved so fast the relief columns can't catch up with him. The best we can hope is that Villa's wounds slow him down until our relief columns can get into the action.

"I need to get closer to the forward elements. Command and control are too difficult from here. Telephone and telegraph services are sparse and unreliable in the field. We've got telegraph stateside, but they don't know any more than what we tell them. I need contact with the troops on the ground. Foulois' First Aero Squadron helps, but there aren't enough of them. They can't land everywhere. And then there are the mechanical problems. As of yesterday, three of the eight planes in the Squadron are still operational. If we get closer to the action, we can make greater use of wireless communication."

"At a range of twenty-five miles, conventional couriers could do that job."

Pershing half smiled. "They could, but wireless is fast and you don't have to look for it."

"The wireless units take mule-drawn wagons and a crew to raise the antenna."

"I'm aware of that. It's not perfect, but in this enterprise you take what you can get. Have radio crews deployed with the forward elements."

"Yes, sir."

"How soon can you have Mobile Command One ready to roll?"

"We should be ready by morning. How do you want them deployed?"

"Each vehicle will carry an officer, a driver and three riflemen. You'll take the lead, George. I'll take the second car with Lieutenant Collins in the third."

"What do I do with the fourth car?"

"I ordered it for parts, but here's a challenge for you."

"Sir?"

See if you can figure out how to mount a wireless on it. If we're going to be mobile, we need to take our wireless with us."

"Wouldn't somebody from Signal Corps be better equipped to do that?"

Pershing grinned. "Time and invention, George, necessity is its mother."

"What about my logistic duties?"

"Colonel Slocum will stay here and take over your supply operation while you are in the field. Find Captain Foulois. It seems his squadron can get in and out of San Geronimo without much difficulty. I'll send him down there to find Dodd. Tompkins can relieve him there. Carry on, George."

"We'll be ready to roll at first light, sir." *Time and invention, hell I thought I was a cavalry officer. Now I'm wet nurse to a damn wireless.*

2000 Hours

Dearest Beat,

These days of separation already grow long. My thoughts as ever are with you and little Bea. I continue to reflect on our future, as I am daily confronted by conditions that demand such reflection. Each day that passes reminds me that I am no longer a young man. I cannot read or write these lines without the aid of my spectacles. The mirror at my morning shave shows a man whose hair is thinner than the day before. I remember thinking brashly that I should be a brigadier by twenty-seven. I am now thirty-two and still the second lieutenant I was commissioned out of the academy. Even here in a combat theater I am assigned administrative duties. Opportunities for glory and advancement elude me.

I am not the only one beset by the passage of time. The army

I have trained for is changing. In fact, the very nature of war is changing. I am bred to be a horse soldier and yet newspaper accounts of the war in Europe report that cavalry is of limited use in modern trench warfare. Pancho Villa, villain that he is, is a bold cavalry commander. His use of the cavalry's most glorious charge in two engagements against machine guns and modern artillery has nearly decimated his command, and we have yet to encounter him. Even the traditional cavalry missions of reconnaissance and communication are changing. The aero plane affords speed and range the horse cannot possibly match. The aero plane is plagued by mechanical problems, but as the general says, time and invention have a way of correcting such things.

Tomorrow we depart for the south to engage the general's command closer to the action. The purpose of getting closer to the action is to permit greater use of wireless communication. The wireless is heavy and clumsy. It depends on erecting a tower for its use. Even at that the range is limited to twenty-five miles. Time and invention shall surely deal with that too. We do not travel by horse. We travel by motor car. Trucks supply the troops in the field. As I look again at the war in Europe, artillery is being transported by motorized vehicles. The French are developing a motorized armored vehicle mounted with light artillery and machine guns that is effective against entrenched defensive positions. They call it a tank. It has the speed and maneuverability of horse artillery with superior firepower.

And so dearest, Beat, I am left to ponder. Where is the future of the horse soldier in all of this? Where is the future of the saber? Where is my future? I have always believed myself destined for the greatness of past glories. I am disturbed by the appearance it may not happen in this age. Perhaps we shall reach some conclusion by the time of my next leave.

Love,
George

Hacienda Cieneguitta
April 2

The air hung warm and heavy in the candlelit room. Villa's dark skin glistened with sweat in the muted light. His chest heaved, his breathing ragged gasps against the white sheet. The white-bearded doctor snapped his bag closed. He turned to Fernandez, his expression grim. His eyes glittered beneath shadowy folds of brown wrinkles. He nodded to the door and led the way out of the room. He closed the door behind the Dorado.

"The leg should come off."

"Jefe will never permit it. He ordered me to shoot him on the journey here. I talked him out of it, but he will do it himself if you attempt to do this."

"The wound is infected. I have cleaned it as best I can. If it goes bad, he will die."

"Did you tell him this?"

The doctor shook his head. "I must do that now. If he agrees, I can do it."

"Save your breath, *Medico*. I will tell him when he wakes. If he does not shoot me, it is in God's hands.

The physician shrugged. "I have done all I can. If this is his wish, *via con Dios.*"

Fernandez followed him to the door. He stood on the veranda and drew a cigarillo from his pocket, watching the old medico shuffle across the plaza to his carriage. Beltran rose from a chair at the end of the veranda.

"How is he?"

Fernandez shook his head. He blew a cloud of blue smoke and flicked out the match. "The medico says his leg should come off."

"Jefe will never permit it."

"That is what I told him. Jefe is too proud to live life a half man."

"Sí."

"He needs rest."

"This is so, but we cannot stay here. The men and horses are rested. The *haciendado* had ample stores. We have corn, beans, slaughtered cows and pigs. Our bellies and packs are full. The Americanos are coming. Two more columns are coming down from the north. We must go to Parral. The people there will protect us. We can disappear in the countryside. Jefe can rest there."

He dropped his cigarillo and ground the butt in the polished flagstone with the toe of his boot. "It is in God's hands. Let us pray he survives the journey."

CHAPTER TWENTY-EIGHT

San Geronimo

April 3

The mobile command wound its way south through hot dusty desert surrounded by the majesty of the Sierra Madre. The panorama seldom varied, sand followed by more sand. The dun channel flowed between towering mountains, swirling a gray-green flotsam of chaparral, cactus and mesquite. Windscreens shielded drivers and front-seat passengers in the open-top touring cars from the worst of the dust, though drivers were forced to dry-wipe the gritty film periodically to maintain visibility. Patton had to admit they'd made good time, covering distances in the span of two hours that might have required a full day's ride on horseback. The eastern range gave way to desert as the dark ragged outlines of San Geronimo came into view.

Approaching the town from the north, a field of gray canvas tents sprawled out to the west. Dodd's Seventh, Patton reckoned, had withdrawn from Guerrero to await the relief column. He nudged his driver, indicating they should skirt west of town to the campsite. As they rolled past rows of tents, the feeling of fatigue became almost palpable. Men attending the daily business of waiting paid scant heed to the dusty black motorcade. Patton pointed to the red and white pennant, hanging limp on its standard at the south end of the camp. The driver veered toward Dodd's command tent, slowed and braked to a stop. Patton jumped out of the car and hurried back to open the car door for Pershing.

Dodd rose from the camp table set beside his tent in the shade of a shelter half staked overhead. His rumpled uniform, sun-reddened face and white stubble beard stood out by contrast to the clean-shaven and polished Pershing party. No matter how rough the circumstances in the field, Pershing made it his daily habit to shave and present a proper military appearance. The officers and men who rode with him followed his lead. Patton understood the connection between discipline and morale.

Dodd saluted. "General, welcome to San Geronimo, the finest resort accommodation in northern Mexico."

Pershing chuckled, returning the salute. "Resort, George?"

He jerked his head west. "If you'd climbed those mountain passes in storms cold enough to freeze the balls off a brass monkey, you'd understand resort living when you see it."

"That bad, was it?"

"Worst I've ever seen. We climbed through wind, sleet, ice, mud and then the weather got bad. The nights are blacker than the inside of a hangman's hood. The trail is so narrow you have to hold the tail of the horse in front of you to keep from falling off the damn mountain. After all that, the son-of-a-bitch got away."

"You gave it a hell of an effort, George. You and the Seventh are to be commended. Any idea where he went?"

"We hear lots of stories. No one knows if any of them are true. Most agree he's wounded and headed south. If he's wounded, he's probably headed for Parral. He's got sympathizers there. It's a big town, should have medical help and plenty of people willing to hide him and his men. If I had to bet, that's where I'd put my money."

"Did Foulois and his squadron arrive?"

"Four of them flew in early this afternoon. He's got the planes parked south of town. He and his men are camping down there to watch over them."

Pershing turned to Patton. "George, head down there and find Captain Foulois. Bring him back here for supper." He turned back to Dodd. "I hope you don't mind my inviting guests to your evening mess?"

"Not if you don't mind eating it. We've been living on watery stew ever since our supplies ran out. Cookie throws a little jerky in the pot for flavor along with whatever vegetables he can barter from the locals. Goes through you like shit through a goose."

"Sounds delightful. I can hardly wait."

"You eat it and trust me, the last thing you'll do is wait."

They ate a bland nondescript stew for supper, gathered around a small campfire. Pershing finished first, setting his plate and spoon aside. "This is the end of the line for the Seventh for awhile, George. We've got three columns coming down from the north. We need to bring them all in here. Captain Foulois, I'd like you and your men to track them down and send them this way."

"Very good sir."

"You'll find Major Tompkins and the Thirteenth somewhere north of Cuidad Chihuahua. Colonel Brown's Tenth is somewhere between here and Namiquipa. Major Howze and the Eleventh should be around Providencia west of here." He turned to Patton. "George, see if they've got a telephone or telegraph in town. Get a hold of Colonel Slocum and see if you can figure out something to do about the supply situation. You can't run an army on a belly full of this, ah . . ." He groped for a word.

"Shit, sir," Dodd volunteered.

"No disrespect to your cook, Colonel. George, see if you can figure a way out of this mess."

Mess detail front and center. "Yes, sir."

Foulois rode second seat behind Dargue as they circled Chihuahua City searching for sign of Tompkins and the Thirteenth. Either Tompkins hadn't reached Chihuahua or he'd already passed on further to the south. No point in guessing which. He tapped Dargue on the shoulder with a hand signal to take her down.

Dargue dropped the Jennie's nose approaching the northbound road out of town from the west. At five hundred feet he slipped the tail around, aligning her nose with the road into town. A startled peon leading a donkey cart loaded with melons scrambled off the road as the great dark bird settled in a cloud of dust and rolled toward town. Dargue taxied off the road a quarter mile north of town. He swung the tail around to the east and shut down the engine.

Foulois pulled his goggles down around his neck. "Stay with the ship, Bert. I won't be long." He climbed out of the cockpit and stepped down. He threw the tail of his silk scarf over his shoulder and started up the road toward town. Curious pedestrians gathered to stare at the aviator and his plane, most getting their first close look at one of the ungainly flying machines. Foulois approached a compesino dressed in loose-fitting shirt and trousers. He sat astride a sleepy-eyed donkey, his eyes shaded by a wide-brimmed straw hat. "Amigo, American soldiers?" He tried to question the man. He got no response. Somewhere in the gathering crowd someone shouted.

"Gringo, go home."

Foulois smiled and waved, dismissing a pang of unease. He walked on toward town where a dust cloud rose under the feet of townsfolk rushing out to see the curiosity. A squad of Federal troops appeared among the crowd at the edge of town. They jogged double time, rifles at port arms. Angry shouts from the crowd behind him grew louder. A stone thudded against the hard cracked ground nearby. He looked over his shoulder and ducked as another rock sailed out of the crowd. They moved across the road, effectively cutting off his path back to the plane. He turned back to the Federal troops, hoping they would restore order. He watched confused as they deployed a skirmish line. He spun around and shouted.

"Bert, get the hell out of here!"

Dargue stood by the plane, seemingly in shock.

"Do it now!"

Dargue cranked the prop and scrambled into the cockpit. He taxied out to the road and brought the tail around, pointing the nose north. The rock-throwing crowd disappeared in a cloud of dust as Dargue gunned the engine into his take-off roll. A ragged volley of Mauser fire erupted behind Foulois. He turned on his heel and dropped to his knee. The Federales ejected spent casings and bolted new rounds into their weapons, preparing another volley. Foulois sprinted toward the squad, waving his arms and shouting, "Wait! Stop! Don't shoot!" The squad commander stepped forward, pistol drawn.

"*Detener! Usted esta bajo arresto!*"

Dargue circled back over the angry crowd. Foulois stood hands in the air as the Carrancista soldiers took him into custody. North, he guessed. He had a dispatch to deliver. He'd worry about his squadron commander later.

Thirteenth

Tompkins called a halt in a mountain pass southeast of Namiquipa. He drew binoculars from his saddle pouch and swept the sun-drenched chasm ahead. A chill mountain breeze licked at the heat rising above his collar. He shook his head. A vein throbbed at his temple fanned in fury.

"This smells like another wild goose chase, Mr. Vaughn."

Vaughn nodded. "I was afraid it might be. Namiquipa is Candelario Cervantes' hometown. Most folks there is loyal to Villa."

"The question is where do we go from here?" He glanced over his shoulder at his adjutant. "Have the men dismount, Major. We'll rest the horses here." Tompkins stepped down. "Come along, Mr. Vaughn, let's have a look at the map."

He climbed the rocky hillside beside the trail to a large, flat rock. He withdrew a field map from his tunic, squatted down and spread it on top of the rock. Vaughn crouched beside him.

"I reckon we're about here, Colonel." He stabbed the map with his forefinger.

"So what do we know? We know he's not in Namiquipa. He's been moving south. The rumors say he's had another rough go against the Carancistas at Guerrero."

"Guerrero's further south and west, about here."

"So, Mr. Vaughn, you know the son-of-bitch. Where does he go?"

The lanky Texan pushed his hat back and scratched his head. "I can figure it two ways. If he was smart, he might be backtracking from Guerrero to Namiquipa. They got friends there who'd hide them."

Tompkins knit his brow. "That would be smart, but I don't think so. We've got a lot of men in theater. That line of march would put him across Major Howze and the Eleventh. What's your other idea?"

"Parral would be my other thought. You're probably right about him staying away from the pursuit. He's got informants. He knows where we are. That pushes him south and that most likely means Parral."

A distant hum intruded on the thought. Tompkins looked off

to the south. A black spot skimmed the east canyon wall. "Looks like one of Foulois' boys." As the plane drew closer, it swooped down into the pass, dropping below the canyon rim.

The Jennie waggled her wings as she passed overhead. She climbed to a sweeping turn north of the column and came around to the south for a second pass. She came in low over the column, following the pass. Troopers scrambled to quiet their nervous mounts. As she approached the head of the column, the pilot tossed a leather dispatch case over the side with a wave.

Tompkins waved his acknowledgment. A trooper scrambled to retrieve the case.

Tompkins opened it and scanned the dispatch. "It looks like General Pershing agrees with the notion he's headed south. We're ordered to proceed to San Geronimo."

CHAPTER TWENTY-NINE

San Geronimo
April 7

Howze' Eleventh finally arrived along with a supply convoy from Colonia Dublán. To Patton's frustration the supplies didn't go nearly far enough given the numbers of troops now assembled. They did provide an all too brief respite from the local stew.

Pershing brooded over his next move. Rumors of Villa's whereabouts were as numerous and scattered as sparrows in a high wind. He and Patton studied a map spread on the hood of his command car when a dust cloud rumbled out of the east. A rust-bucket truck rattled to a stop at the edge of camp. A somewhat worse for wear Captain Benny Foulois tumbled out of the back bed. He gave the driver a dismissive wave and made straight for Pershing's car. The driver ground the truck into gear, lurched into a wide turn and drove off through the same dust cloud he arrived in.

Pershing sized him up, guessing at conditions in a Mexican jail. "Welcome back, Captain. Is it the U.S. Ambassador's influence with the Carranza government or time off for good behavior?"

Foulois came to attention and saluted. "No idea, sir. They just let me go. Did Lieutenant Dargue make it back safely?"

"He did. Found Major Tompkins and the Thirteenth too as

luck would have it. By the look of you I take it the accommodations were somewhat crude."

"Crude, shit. Ah excuse me, sir."

"Quite all right."

"Let's just say I'll never complain about our mess again, even if it is the local stew. I thought I'd shit my guts out the whole time they had me in that hell hole. I assume you got a report from Lieutenant Dargue."

"We did."

"Then the only thing I have to add, sir, is that nothing Carranza tells the President or the Ambassador in Mexico City matters. His policy is to oppose us every step of the way. Villa may be a revolutionary bandit, but he's Mexican. The Federales in Chihuahua knew who we were. They opened fire on us. The Commandante didn't do that on his own authority."

"You're right, Captain. Unfortunately, my orders are clear. We are not to provoke a confrontation with the Mexican government."

"Sir, if we get Villa, it will be in spite of Carranza."

"I'm afraid I have to agree. Now, if you'd like to ah, clean up."

"Thank you, sir." Foulois turned on his heel and set off for the squadron bivouac.

Pershing watched him go. "Truth is Carranza's no better than Villa, he's just cleaner and happens to live in the Presidential Palace. We won't have any real border security until they have a stable government in this country. We'd be better off to forget Villa and simply occupy Mexico's border-states until that happens. Unfortunately, President Wilson doesn't have the stomach for anything as decisive as that."

"If you ask me, sir, the President doesn't have much stomach for anything."

Pershing lifted an eyebrow. The lieutenant had a point. Saying it out loud could get a military man in trouble.

1800 Hours

The officer cadre gathered around a camp table spread with a map. Kerosene lamps held the map against the early evening breeze, lighting the represented terrain. Pershing glanced around the table from face to face.

"We believe he's wounded and headed south, gentlemen. Not much to go on, is it?" Heads shook. "All we can do is keep up the pressure. Bill, I want you to take the Tenth southeast through Rubio and Santa Ysabal. Major Tompkins, I want the Thirteenth to ride south through San Antonio and Cusihuiriachic. Major Howze, the Eleventh has the mountains west and south. Captain Foulois, I expect your squadron to support each of the columns between here and San Antonio. The mobile command will stay as close a possible. We'll use Captain Foulois' men to stay in communication when we can't maintain radio contact. We will do the best we can to keep you supplied, but experience says you will have to live off the land much of the time. After our recent encounter in Chihuahua City, you should not expect much in the way of help from the Carrancistas. Avoid them whenever possible. If you encounter hostilities, take defensive measures and make every effort to disengage. Under no circumstances are we to provoke confrontation with Federal troops. Is that clear?"

Heads nodded.

"Any questions?" Pershing paused. "Good. Get some rest. We move out at 0600."

The officers drifted off to their respective bivouacs.

"Will there be anything further tonight, General?"

He shook his head. "No, that will be all, George."

He started to take his leave.

"Oh, just one more thing, have you made any progress on that radio project?"

"No, sir, sorry to say. The antenna is the problem. The damn thing is so big. We could train our riflemen to pull the guy wires to raise it. We can adapt the boot of one of the cars to accommodate the transmitter. I just can't figure a way to transport the antenna. The damn thing is too big and heavy. We may have to conclude that mules are good for something after all."

"It may be too much to improvise here in the field, but all in good time. Invention will solve the antenna problem too."

"You place considerable store by that principle, don't you, sir?"

"Experience is a great teacher, George. You'll come to appreciate that for yourself, I'm sure. Now get some rest."

Eleventh

April 8

The White Mountain Apache scout known as Sergeant Chicken picked up the trail of a large party of horsemen southeast of Minaca. Howze pushed his column forward, confident they had cut Villa's trail at last. The icy blasts of mountain March gave grudging way to April chill. Wind and drizzle made the going uncomfortable. Softened ground made tracking good.

To an experienced scout like Chicken, the trail read like an elementary school primer. He set a brisk pace for the better part of a day. At midafternoon, the trail forked. Chicken stepped down from his horse and crouched, studying the sign.

Howze waited impatiently. From his cursory inspection, Howze could see that the party divided. The main body took a southeasterly route while a smaller party split off on a more southwesterly course. Chicken straightened up, looking off to the southwest.

"He goes there."

Howze furrowed his brow. The main body had clearly taken the east fork. "How can you be sure, Sergeant?"

The Apache pointed east with his chin. "False trail."

"False, it looks plenty real to me."

"Many horses have no rider."

Howze shook his head. He acts like he stood here and watched them go by. How could he be so cock-sure? Villa would never abandon his troops. "Follow the east fork."

The scout suppressed a smirk with a shrug.

Evening shadow appeared on the east face of the western slopes when the trail spilled out of the hills near the small town of San José del Sitio. Over the last hours the trail gradually dissolved. The sign melted into the rocks and arroyos. Howze came to the bitter realization. He might have gotten it wrong. Chicken waited expectantly, reading the Major's indecision. He could press on and search the town or turn back to the fork and pick up a trail five hours colder than the rain. Five hours, that is, if they had enough daylight to get back there, which they didn't. A nine-hour halt for daylight added insult to injury. Villa could be warm and dry in Santa Cruz de Herrera by now.

Approaching San José del Sitio at dusk, a low rumble off to the north caught Howze' attention. He drew a halt. A dust cloud approached, lighted in the early evening shadows by the beams of headlamps bouncing over rough road. Pershing's mobile command braked to a stop beside the column. The General stepped out of the second car. Howze wheeled his horse out of the column and rode back to meet him. Patton waited at the fender of his own vehicle, close enough to hear what was said should the General require anything of him.

"Major, have you got anything?"

Howze stepped down. "We picked up a trail this morning. It came to a fork midafternoon." He jerked his head back toward the mountains. "The main body came this way. It's my intent to search the town."

"Very well, carry on. We'll tag along if you don't mind."

Howze' search proved fruitless. He delivered a succinct report to Pershing.

"Nothing, sir."

"Is it possible you took the wrong fork?"

"It sure looks that way."

Patton caught Sergeant Chicken's eyes behind the Major. Chicken nodded and shrugged. *He took the wrong fork all right and likely Sergeant Chicken told him so.*

"So where do you go from here?"

"The other trail headed for Santa Cruz Herrera. Maybe we can head him off there. We'll ride down there in the morning."

Santa Cruz Herrera
April 9

Beltran dozed on the veranda of the hacienda they commandeered on their arrival. He'd sat his vigil wrapped in a serape well into the night before giving up to some sleep in the small hours of early morning. The crushed butts of his cigarillos counted the hours he'd waited. Fernandez stepped out of the hacienda into the pale gray predawn chill. His boots scraped softly on the tiles. Beltran snapped awake.

"What is it, Nico?"

Fernandez yawned. "He sleeps."

"At last, he needs his rest."

"The fever has broken, though, the wound smells foul."

"Will he live?"

"It is in God's hands, Francisco."

"If only we could rest here longer."

"What do you mean?"

"Word came last night. The Americanos know of our decep-

tion. They are coming, no more than a day behind us. We must
be away at first light."

Nico sighed, shook his head and returned to Villa's bedside.

The Eleventh reached Santa Cruz just before sunset. Major
Howze ordered a search of the town. They discovered camp
sign around the once-occupied hacienda. The trail beyond
vanished into the rocky hills southeast of town. Howze realized
his mistake. So close, if only he'd listened to the scout. Villa
eluded them again. Sergeant Chicken pointed his chin toward
Parral.

This time Howze took him at his word. He ordered the wireless deployed. If he could get word to Tompkins, the Thirteenth
might head him off there. They tried to raise a contact signal for
two hours. Nothing.

Parral
April 11
Not even the welcoming sight of Parral improved Villa's mood.
With the fever broken, the wound gave him less pain. His temper
grew evermore foul with each tedious mile. Fernandez reined
his horse back beside the coach.

"What is it now, Nico?"

"Pardon, Jefe. I don't mean to disturb you."

"You already have."

"I think it is best if we do not take you into town. The fewer
people who know you are here, the better."

"So where am I to go? Am I to hide from the Yanquis under a
rock?"

"No, Jefe. Rancho Rodriguez is not far from town. The
household is small. Felipe is the soul of discretion. You will be
safe there."

"Sí. Send the men into town. They can disappear there and

be less noticeable than if we all went to Felipe's."

"That was my thinking, Jefe. You shall have a safe place to rest soon."

San José del Sitio
April 11

Patton arranged the three cars and four trucks making up the convoy in a defensive perimeter. The men pitched their tents near their vehicles. The mess sergeant set a detail to work building a cook fire. The general and his aides sat on camp chairs beside a small fire. Patton filled his pipe and struck a match. The flame set the bowl aglow, reflecting off the lenses of his glasses.

"We're close, George. I can feel it. He's in Parral. We've damn near got a loop around it. Soon we'll draw it closed."

Patton puffed fragrant smoke into the evening chill. "I hope you're right, sir. He's proven himself one slippery bastard so far."

"That he has. Not surprising, though. We're fighting on his home ground. The people are his friends. We haven't had time to turn them to our way of thinking."

"You think we can do that, sir?"

"These people are poor. Villa promises to fill their bellies. They love him for it. If we had the opportunity to feed them awhile, they'd love us too."

"Is that how you dealt with the Moro?"

"Something like that. There are many ways besides combat to obtain a desirable military outcome."

"I'm learning that. I'm also learning my training has little prepared me to fight in the modern military."

"It's the nature of change, George."

"I understand that, but in this age it seems everything is changing." Patton relit his balky pipe. "Do you remember the dinner we had at the Hoover the night Captain Foulois and his men arrived?"

Pershing nodded.

"Foulois said that aero planes would be fitted with machine guns and soon would have the ability to drop explosive projectiles on the enemy."

"He did say that."

"Well if the Captain had such armaments the day he sighted Villa in the mountains on the way to Guerrero, this mission might have ended then and there."

Pershing considered the possibility for a moment, then nodded. "It's certainly possible. We are only beginning to understand the fighting potential of the aero plane. I believe it will have a significant impact on modern warfare, but I don't see it ever replacing ground combat if that's what you mean. As much as I see their value, they cannot yet be considered a reliable weapon with all the mechanical problems. I'd be reluctant to put fighting men in a tactical situation that depended on air support."

"You said yourself, sir, 'time and invention have a way of correcting such things.' "

He chuckled. "I do say that, don't I."

"If I may make a personal observation, sir, I'm a cavalry officer, a trained horse soldier. I haven't been on a horse in a month. I'm a Saber Master in an army that no longer fights with them. I'm surrounded by all this new-fangled war-making capability that leaves me to wonder where I fit."

"Don't take it too hard, George. You're learning. You see the future. You just described how armed aircraft might have ended this campaign. Learning is the human form of invention. If you're patient and willing to learn, time will reinvent you to some new purpose."

He tapped out his pipe. *One can hope.*

CHAPTER THIRTY

Parral

April 12

Major Tompkins drew rein between two hills overlooking Parral, shimmering in heat waves to the southwest. His advance company of the Thirteenth easily outdistanced the other two columns, methodically making their way south, searching the villages and hill country along the way. Parral looked like many other towns they'd encountered in northern Mexico, a dusty warren of narrow streets and bleached adobe, differing only in sprawling a bit larger than most.

Henry Vaughn drew a chapped leg up and crooked the knee over his saddle horn. He fished in his shirt pocket for the makings. He shook a line of tobacco onto his paper and made a deft roll with one hand. He pulled the tobacco pouch string closed with his teeth and deposited the sack in his pocket. "Don't look like much, does it, Major?" He scratched a match on his boot heel and drew the light to his smoke.

"Nothing special."

"Don't be too sure. Villa always considered Parral safe. If he's down there, you can bet he's well protected.'

"What do you suggest, Mr. Vaughn?"

"Let me ride on in, nose around a little bit, and see what I can find out. I expect Carranza's got a garrison there. I won't be no threat."

"The Federales are supposed to be in this with us. I say it's time they show Villa and these people we mean business."

"Suit yourself, Colonel. We just best hope the Carrancista Commandante sees it that way."

"Forward, ho!"

Word spread through town before the column reached the outskirts. A crowd built along the narrow streets and fell in behind Tompkins' troop as the column jogged their horses toward the center of town. A Carrancista officer with a token squad of riflemen blocked passage to the village square. Tompkins drew a halt and stepped down.

"Major Frank Tompkins, Thirteenth U.S. Cavalry." He saluted.

"General Ismael Lozano. What is the meaning of this incursion into my city? Why was I not told you wished to enter?"

Tompkins ignored the belligerent tone of the questions. "We are here by permission of President Carranza. We have reason to believe the fugitive Pancho Villa is in the area."

"We have no knowledge of this. If we did, he would be under arrest. Now I must ask to you leave at once."

"Not so fast, General. We are here at the invitation of your government. Our countries have a mutual interest in capturing or killing a bandit who terrorizes our border. I expect your cooperation in this. If you are confident Villa is not hiding here, I will accept that. Before we leave, however, I need feed and water for our horses."

"That is a civil matter you must take up with the Alcalde. I have nothing to spare."

"Very well, where do I find the Alcalde?"

"This way." Lozano led the way across the plaza to the village hall.

Tompkins followed, leading his troop into the town square

until they fairly filled it. A crowd built in behind them growing in numbers, soon surrounding the plaza, spilling into the side streets leading to it.

Elsa recognized opportunity when she saw it. She stood in the shade of her contact's veranda near the village hall. She'd made contact with a Villista sympathizer who promised to take her to him if he approved the visit. The wait bored her until good fortune dropped an American cavalry detachment right in front of her.

"Juan Carlos, do the people know the Americans mean harm to Francisco?"

Her dark-skinned host shrugged. "Sí."

"The Carrancistas are in league with the Americans. The people are the only ones left to protect Pancho Villa. Send your people out into the crowd. They have stones. They have sticks. They have rakes and hoes. They can drive the Americanos out of Parral and save their liberator."

Her host disappeared with a nod. Villa's Dorado guards stripped of their bandoleros and insignia slipped unnoticed into the crowd.

"Alcalde, General Lozano has requested that we leave Parral. I will comply with his request, but first I must have feed and water for my horses."

The shriveled little man with a wrinkled prune face fidgeted with his hat. His eyes wandered the dimly lit small room with its head table and broken-down benches. "You have many horses. We are a poor village. I do not know that we can spare so much feed."

Lozano drew himself up to the full measure of his height, his eyes not quite reaching Tompkins' chin. "Please, Major, I must again ask you to leave. You place a great burden on these poor people."

The silence that followed admitted voices of protest rising in the plaza. The door burst open. Vaughn's silhouette filled the splash of sunlight. "Major, you'd best come out here."

Angry crowd noise poured through the open door with the sunshine. Tompkins turned on his heel and strode to the door. General Lozano followed. In the time Tompkins had spent with the Alcalde, the crowd surrounding his men had grown to fill the plaza and streets beyond. The mood grew more hostile by the minute. Lozano's presence on the Alcalde's veranda served only to raise the tenor of the crowd's displeasure. The first stone struck a horse near the front of the troop formation. The horse reared, eyes wide, nostrils flared trumpeting alarm. More stones followed, raining confusion on the American ranks. Lozano stepped in front of Tompkins.

"Please, you must leave now. Come with me. My men will hold the crowd."

The situation irritated Tompkins. He had no desire to turn tail and run from rock-throwing peons. Even so, he realized the ugly situation had nightmarish diplomatic implications.

Lozano did not wait for a response. He set off through the ranks to the rear of the formation. Tompkins mounted his horse and followed, ordering a column of twos on his lead. The last of the column left the plaza as shots rang out. Lozano turned to Tompkins.

"Get out of the city as fast as you can. My men will control the crowd." Lozano did not wait for an answer. He expected Tompkins to comply.

Tompkins stifled a chuckle. The General's gait as he jogged back to the plaza belonged in a Keystone Cops movie. Amusing or no, he led his men out of town. Moments later sporadic gunshots could be heard behind them in the direction of the plaza. He picked up a canter, realizing the risks of being caught in the confines of narrow streets by hostile fire. Anxious minutes later, they cleared the edge of town. Railroad tracks from the north ran along the east end of town. An embankment running along the roadbed afforded ample cover. Tompkins pointed the position out to the company commander.

"Captain Johnson, fix a rear guard there. We'll deploy the main body in the hills up the road until we are sure the Carrancistas bear us no hostile intention."

Johnson saluted and wheeled away. He deployed a squad, covering the rear as ordered.

Tompkins' precautions proved prescient. Shooting in the plaza fell silent. A dust cloud boiled over the rooftops south of town as a large force of Federal troops advanced from their encampment. Johnson's rear guard offered little challenge to so large a Federal force. Lozano's men opened fire.

"Captain, recall the rear guard. We're getting the hell out of here." Badly outnumbered, Tompkins withdrew up the road to the north. He deployed a rolling rear guard to cover his withdrawal. Squads alternated firing and falling back at quarter-mile intervals to slow the Federales' pursuit. Lozano's cavalry quickly outdistanced the infantry. The superior force threatened to overrun Tompkins' rear.

The outbreak of hostilities with the Mexican nationals troubled Tompkins. He understood the diplomatic sensitivity, but what was he to do? The Carrancistas pressed their attack despite his best efforts to disengage. He could not allow his men to be shot down in retreat. If they could reach the small town of Santa Cruz de Villegas, they could take defensive positions Lozano would have to respect. The question was, how to get there? *The same way Villa did on the road south of Columbus.*

"Captain, call a halt. Deploy skirmish lines. Prepare to fire on my command."

Johnson could scarcely believe his ears. This tactic hadn't been used since the Civil War.

Lozano's cavalry pressed forward. They could not believe their eyes. The Yanquis dismounted. They formed in ranks, barring the road north. They took no cover, waiting, begging to be overrun. The Carrancista commander drew his sword. The long, bright blade flashed in the sun. *"Carga!"* The Federale cavalry pounded up the road trailing storm clouds of dust.

At three hundred yards the powerful Springfields bloomed fire and smoke, spraying the road with a volley of death. The fusillade ripped the vanguard of the Carrancista charge. Horses and riders fell in a hail of bullets. Others stumbled over them from behind. The Federales charged on. At two hundred yards, the second rank fired to devastating effect. Ghostly clouds of blue-powder smoke shrouded the American ranks. The third volley at one hundred yards broke the charge, leaving Lozano's cavalry in confused disarray.

Tompkins raised his arm. "Enough Captain! Mount up. Let's get the hell out of here."

The cavalry pursuit broken, the Thirteenth retreated up the road in orderly fashion. They reached the small town of Santa Cruz de Villegas. Tompkins took over the settlement. He turned the adobe buildings into fortified positions where the superior firepower of the Springfield and the marksmanship of his men persuaded Lozano's Federales to abandon their pursuit.

CHAPTER THIRTY-ONE

War Department
Washington, D.C.
April 13
0900 Hours

The telephone jangled. The annoying demand intruded on his train of thought. *Damn it.*

"Scott here."

"Please hold for Secretary Lansing."

The clerical voice on the other end sounded as mechanical as the instrument. He could be interrupted to take a call the Secretary couldn't be bothered to place.

"General, what the hell is going on in Parral?"

Scott took a breath, measuring his response to the prissy bureaucrat. "I'm sorry, Mr. Secretary, I don't know what you are talking about."

"I've just received a formal protest from the Mexican ambassador. It seems some of your troops invaded the village of Parral yesterday. A riot broke out among the local populace. Mexican Federal troops in the area intervened to quiet the disturbance. A fire fight broke out between Mexican and American forces. President Carranza is demanding a formal apology and the immediate withdrawal of our troops. Pershing has specific orders to avoid such confrontations at all cost, does he not?"

"He does, sir." Scott swallowed his anger. *Why the hell didn't*

John report any of this?

"I'm on my way to brief the President within the hour. It might be best if you joined us."

The phone went dead. Scott slammed the receiver down on the cradle. "Davis, get Funston on the phone—now!"

White House

Wilson could be peevish when annoyed. He sat at his desk plainly bothered, bracing Lansing and Scott in the facing wing chairs.

"Have you any explanation for this, General?"

"I'm afraid not, sir. Neither General Funston nor I have a report on the incident. We were able to contact General Pershing's base camp in Colonia Dublán. They haven't received a report either. General Pershing is in the field further south. Elements of the expedition are known to be operating in the vicinity of Parral. It's a remote area, Mr. President. Communications can be difficult. It's possible General Pershing doesn't even know what happened as yet."

"Well, President Carranza's communications seem to work well enough. The question now is what is to be done about it?"

Lansing cast Scott a sidelong glance and waded into the void. "Mr. President, I think it is clearly time to bring this so-called Punitive Expedition to a close. We've not been able to so much as contact Villa. Now we've provoked an incident that might be considered an act of war. Mexico is a sovereign nation. She has formally requested we withdraw our troops from her soil. They have withdrawn the authority that permitted our forces to cross her borders."

Wilson drummed his fingers on the desk blotter. "It's scarcely been a month. We still have civilian and military blood on the streets of Columbus. I can't imagine the public mood has been satisfied so soon and with so little result."

Scott felt uncomfortable. Here he sat with no firsthand knowledge of the situation on the ground. How was he supposed to respond to the political winds blowing through the Oval Office? If the Mexicans want us to withdraw, that'll be all Lansing needs. Wilson demonstrated little political will for armed confrontation to start with. He had men in the field with their hands tied behind their backs. The prudent course might be to declare victory and bring them home.

"If you recall, Mr. President, our mission is, in part, to disburse Villa's forces. If we can't find him, it would seem we've accomplished that part of our purpose. Perhaps Secretary Lansing is right. If we heed President Carranza's demand, we can accomplish our mission with no further risk to peace with Mexico."

Wilson weighed the suggestion. On balance, Mexico was a trifling matter in the broader context of his progressive agenda. He had considerable work left to do, work that would carry over to a second term, if there were to be a second term. Mexico might be a trifle, but trifles had been known to tip scales.

"I need to give the matter some thought, gentlemen. Mr. Secretary, General, you shall have my answer in the morning."

"Thank you, sir." Lansing said. He and Scott rose in unison and left the office.

Wilson followed, waiting for them to leave the outer office. His appointments secretary looked up expectantly.

"Call Senator Fall's office. See if he might spare me a few minutes later this afternoon."

Oval Office
4:00 PM

"Senator Fall to see you, sir."

"Send him in."

Fall appeared in the doorway, hat in hand, boots out of place in the refined trappings of the presidency.

"Albert, good of you to come on such short notice."

"Mr. President, when your office calls, the nation answers."

"Please have a seat." Wilson indicated the wing chairs and settee at the side of the office, disdaining the more formal seat of authority at his desk.

Fall noted the gesture, taking his seat. The President wanted something.

"What can I do for you, sir?"

"You westerners are so direct. Straight to the point, is it?"

"Pretty generally works best that way."

"Yes, I'm sure. We've a situation in Mexico that demands some attention. You are close to the mood of your constituents on the matter. I'd like the benefit of your perspective."

"Shoot."

Wilson smiled wryly. "Yes, well that is some of it. It seems we've had an incident in Mexico. Our forces pursuing Villa had an armed confrontation with Mexican federal troops. President Carranza has asked us to withdraw our troops. Secretary Lansing doesn't see much to be gained by continuing the expedition. General Scott points out that our stated purpose for pursuing Villa was in part to disburse his forces. That objective seems to be accomplished. I'm considering what to do about withdrawing our troops. The last thing we want is open war with Mexico."

Fall sat back, extended his legs and crossed his boots at the ankle. "If you're asking how the border states would take to withdrawal, all I can say is badly. We had citizens and soldiers die in Columbus. How's that for an act of war?"

"Villa's a bandit."

"Yes, sir, and Carranza ain't much better."

"Isn't."

"Have it your way. The only difference between the two of

them is that Carranza sits in a Presidential Palace. He has no more control over the revolutionaries and bandits running loose in Mexico than I do. Until law and order is brought to that country, our citizens are at risk. They look to the federal government to protect them. They look to you to protect them, Mr. President, or somebody who will. Withdraw now and you walk away from that responsibility. Truth is, if we really want to solve the problem, we ought to occupy Mexico's northern states until such time as the Mexican people start deciding who governs with ballots instead of bullets. Until that happens, the only government in Mexico is the bandit with the most guns.

"Oh, I know you don't support armed conflict, Mr. President. It doesn't suit the niceties of your progressive ideals. But let me tell you something, the world ain't all that progressive. There's plenty of bad people out there, people who do bad things. The only thing most of 'em understand is force and deadly force at that. So, if you're askin' my opinion on what you should do, I'll tell you what the people of New Mexico and the other border states would say. Get Pancho Villa. Put him away dead or alive and secure the border. That's why we pay taxes and that's why we elect people to represent us. Now, you got anything else you'd like my opinion on, Mr. President?"

"Not just now, Albert. You've made your position quite clear. Thank you for your candor."

State Department
6:00 PM

Early evening light streamed through the windows, holding off the need to light the desk lamp. The Secretary glanced out the window, *a sure sign of spring.*

"The President is on the line, Mr. Secretary."

"Lansing here."

"Robert, I've made my decision. I want you to apologize to

the Mexican government. Assure them that we will do everything possible to avoid any further confrontation, but it is in our mutual national interests to neutralize the threat posed by Pancho Villa. If President Carranza wants us to withdraw our troops, all he has to do is kill or capture Pancho Villa."

"Are you sure, Mr. President? What if Mexico declares war?"

"They won't, Robert. Carranza is weak. He can't possibly defeat us. He has more to lose than we do, unless of course we send a message of weakness to the Germans. We both know they are watching the situation in Mexico. We know they're agitating to provoke a war if they can. We don't dare embolden them further. I will reiterate my orders to General Scott and the rest of the general staff in regard to avoiding conflict with the Mexican nationals, but we will press on in our search for Villa. Any questions?"

"No, sir."

"Good night, then."

The line clicked dead. Lansing replaced the receiver. His eyes drifted to the world map, prominently displayed on his office wall. He picked out Mexico City and sighed to himself, *election year diplomacy.* Carranza may indeed be weak. Let's hope he's not foolish. One can almost hear the Germans bait him from here.

CHAPTER THIRTY-TWO

San José del Sitio
April 14

The Jennie dropped into view below a fluffy white cloud deck running east in the late morning sun. She circled on her landing approach. Patton guessed the unexpected arrival meant some sort of news. Pershing came up to stand at his elbow.

"What do you make of it, sir?"

He shrugged. "We'll find out soon enough."

The plane touched down in a billow of dust as she taxied up the road toward the encircled mobile command. Foulois waved from the cockpit as he swung the tail around and shut down the engine. He scrambled out of the cockpit and dropped his goggles as he jogged over to the general and threw up a salute.

Pershing returned the salute. "What have you got for me, Captain?"

"A message from Colonel Slocum, sir. I had my bird in Colonia Dublán for maintenance yesterday. Colonel Slocum got a call from General Funston. Washington is up in arms over the firefight in Parral."

Pershing wrinkled his brow. "Firefight in Parral, what firefight in Parral?"

Foulois shrugged. "I thought you knew. The Carranza government filed a formal protest. Apparently there was a firefight in Parral two days ago between some of our men and Mexican

241

Federales. General Funston and General Scott want to know what happened."

Pershing rubbed his temples, shaking his head. "We've got men in the area, but I haven't heard anything of the sort." He turned to Patton. "I'm guessing its Tompkins, George. We'll split up to speed things up. You get down to Parral and find him. Tell him reinforcements are on the way. I'll go after Colonel Brown. Collins can track down Howze. Captain, give me a few minutes to compose a report you can take to Colonel Slocum. He can pass it on to General Funston."

Southern Command
Fort Sam Houston, Texas
  To: Major General Frederick Funston
  Southern Command
  From: Brigadier General John J. Pershing
  Mobile Command, San José del Sitio
  14 April 1916
Sir,
  We are investigating the Mexican government claim that advance elements of this expedition encountered hostile action involving Mexican Federal forces in the vicinity of Parral on 12 April. At this time I cannot confirm such action took place, or if it did, report the circumstances that may have given rise to it. I will report same, as soon as reliable information becomes available.
  Communication in this theater is limited by considerations of distance and terrain. Telephone and telegraph services are unreliable or nonexistent. Mexican national forces are uncooperative and potentially belligerent. We are denied use of rail service in our supply operations. Overland logistics and supply operations are difficult and inadequate due to distance, terrain and climate.

The objectives of this mission are further obstructed by a hostile populace.

I respectfully suggest that the objective of securing our border would be better served by a full-scale military occupation of northern Mexico until such time as a stable government is established in the country. Our current base of operations provides the first step. I am able to dispatch forces west to secure Sonora. A second strike force moving south from El Paso into Juárez and Chihuahua should fully secure our border.

Respectfully,
John J. Pershing

Santa Cruz de Villegas
April 15

Patton's car rumbled down the road under a desert sky so hot the blue burned white. He ignored the heat. Here was his first chance to get near the action in a combat operation and his job was to settle a diplomatic shit-storm for a panty-waist President. If Carranza wanted to pick a fight, we sure as hell ought to oblige him. Reason required resignation. Like it or not, he had his orders.

An hour later Santa Cruz de Villegas appeared up ahead. As the car approached they found the road blocked. A pair of sentries stood guard at a makeshift barrier. The driver slowed the car. "They're ours, sir."

Patton nodded. The car braked to a stop. One of the sentries stepped around the barricade. He recognized the Lieutenant and picked up his salute. Patton returned it.

"Where can I find Major Tompkins, Trooper?"

He thumbed his shoulder. "South end of town, sir." The second sentry lifted the barricade.

The driver engaged the gears and accelerated into town. Dusty adobe dwellings lined the narrow streets. Sleepy-eyed women and children paused to stare at the sleek black car, bringing still more Yanqui soldiers to their town. They drove through the deserted plaza with its central well. South of the plaza, they slowed for troopers walking the streets and manning buildings commandeered to form a defensive perimeter. Tompkins wasn't hard to find.

"Major." Patton saluted.

"Lieutenant, nice to see the General hasn't forgotten us."

"Oh, he hasn't forgotten, sir. You've made quite a lot of noise down here, enough to reach all the way to Mexico City and Washington."

"I'm impressed."

"Not as 'impressed' as the general when he got the news from Washington."

"Oh." Tompkins sobered.

"What happened?"

"We have reason to believe Villa is hiding in Parral. I entered the city to look for him. The Carrancista Commandante, a General Lozano, asked us to leave. I agreed if I could get feed and water for my horses. While we were trying to work that out, a crowd gathered. They got ugly, started throwing stones. We left town. We heard some shooting as we were leaving. We took up defensive positions north of town. The Federales called out their garrison and started after us. They had us pretty badly outnumbered. We retreated north under harassing fire. I made a stand when their cavalry tried to overrun our withdrawal. We broke the charge and made it to defensive positions here. The shooting started on the Mexican side."

"That detail didn't make it into the protest that wound up in Washington. The General caught it topside from Scott and Funston."

"Ouch."

"It gets worse. Scott caught it topside from the President."

"So now what?"

"The General is on his way down here with reinforcements."

"Good. We'll head back down to Parral and take the hills north of town. They won't be expecting that. Adequately reinforced we can take the town and do a thorough search for Villa. I think Lozano may actually be hiding him. Why else would he pick a fight with us?"

"You can't go back to Parral, Major. The General intends for you to hold your position here."

"*Intends,* Lieutenant? You mean he didn't specifically order it. Don't go getting ahead of yourself, Lieutenant Patton. I'm in command here. If I say we ride back to Parral, the Thirteenth rides back to Parral."

Patton stiffened. "Major, I must respectfully request that you hold your position here. General Pershing's intentions were quite clear. We've stirred up enough of a mess down here without serving up a second helping."

Tompkins took his turn at stiffening. *Who the hell did this shave-tail pup think he was talking to?* Patton never wavered under Tompkins' glare. His eyes held cold steel.

"You better be right, Lieutenant. You better be right."

"I am, sir."

CHAPTER THIRTY-THREE

War Department
Washington, D.C.
April 16

Scott set Pershing's report on the desk and picked up the telephone.

"Put me through to Funston." He tapped the miniature saber on his desk he used as a letter opener, waiting for the connection to go through.

"Funston."

"Frederick, its Hugh."

"Good afternoon, General. What can I do for you?"

"Thanks for sending Pershing's report along. It makes interesting reading."

"Interesting and disturbing, it doesn't appear the Carranza government can be trusted."

"No, and according to Secretary Lansing's report, relations aren't likely to improve. Carranza isn't happy with our response to the Parral incident. The President is betting he's too weak to do anything about it. I suspect he's right, but I'm worried Pershing is overextended. We've already been bitten in the ass by communication problems. His supply lines are in no better shape. He's in the middle of a very hostile environment down there. The people don't want us there. Villa still commands a fighting force and the Carrancistas have proven they can't be trusted."

"You make a good argument for bringing our troops home, Hugh."

"Maybe so, but the President says we stay. With our hands firmly tied behind our backs, of course."

"What do you propose we do?"

"At the least, Pershing needs to pull back. Consolidate his communication and supply lines."

"That's not likely to advance the mission."

"If the mission is to kill or capture Villa, you're right. At this point I don't know what the hell the mission is, other than to get the President re-elected. We watered down the mission to disband or disburse Villa's forces, or some prissy wording like that. For now he's gone into hiding, so you could say we've done that. We need to keep enough pressure on him to keep him away from the border. As long as the border is quiet, we can wait this out. Once the election is over, our Commander-in-Chief will be more than happy to get us out of Mexico."

"Son-of-a-bitch. Is that what you want me to tell Pershing?"

"Hell, no. Tell him to pull back, consolidate his communication and supply lines. Keep enough pressure on Villa to keep him away from the border. If he gets lucky, fine, but he's not to turn the country inside out trying to find the bastard. And above all, avoid any further hostilities with Carranza's people."

"That's a hell of a thing to tell a commander in the field."

"Tell me about it. But that's the situation in the marble palaces."

Santa Cruz de Villegas
April 16
16:00 Hours
Pershing arrived with Brown's Tenth. Patton came out to meet

him as Colonel Brown set his men to work making camp northwest of town.

"Where's Tompkins?"

"He's made a defensive perimeter on the south end of town. I can take you to him, sir."

"What the hell happened?"

"As you might imagine, sir, Major Tompkins' version of the events isn't quite the same as the Mexican's. I think you'd best hear it from the Major directly."

"All right, let's go find him. Any sign of Major Howze?"

"No, sir. I expect he'll be along directly. We sent a courier advising our position at the same time we sent the information to you."

Pershing led the way to his command car. He climbed in the back seat. Patton took the front passenger seat to direct the driver. They found Major Tompkins at his makeshift command post in a small adobe at the south end of town.

Tompkins saluted. "General, welcome to Santa Cruz de Villegas."

"Spare the formalities, Frank. Is there someplace we can talk?"

"Right this way, sir."

"Excuse us, George."

Tompkins led the way inside the adobe. Patton waited with the car. Twenty minutes later, Pershing returned. He climbed into the back seat and motioned for Patton to join him.

"Where do we bivouac?"

"Near the road, just north of town, sir."

The driver nodded and engaged the gears.

Pershing looked around as if taking stock of the town for the first time. "All things considered, I can't say that I'd have handled the Parral situation much differently. Damn messy business when both sides find themselves in positions they don't like. Politics don't play well on the ground in an armed conflict."

"So what do we do now, sir?"

"Damned if I know just yet. If Villa is hiding in Parral, the mission says find him. If the Federale commandant has decided to protect him, I don't know how we do that and not provoke another firefight." He fell silent for several moments of brooding thought before setting the problem aside.

"You don't back down, do you, Lieutenant."

"Back down, sir?"

"Major Tompkins tells me you had a little disagreement about returning to Parral."

"No disagreement, sir, the Major didn't understand the sensitivity of the situation."

"And you did."

"I did, sir."

"Do you make it a practice to countermand your superiors, Lieutenant?" He couldn't hide the twinkle in his eye.

"Only when I'm right, sir."

"I shall have to remember that."

The car braked to a stop.

Dargue arrived just before sunset with Funston's order. Pershing fumed. Tompkins had the right of it. Taking out the Federale garrison at Parral would make a good start. It would mean war, but the war wouldn't last long. Carranza was weak. As President, he was no more than the latest two-bit despot in a long line of two-bit despots. Instead of orders to do the job that needed to be done, he got orders to pull back and sit on his ass while the flies and scorpions made a feast of his command. He half crumpled the telegram Slocum received at Colonia Dublán.

"Something the matter, sir?" Patton could read Pershing's mood like a book after these long weeks.

"We've been ordered to pull back." He handed the telegram to his aide.

"Bullshit! If you'll pardon me, sir?"

Pershing dismissed the outburst with a wave.

"If you don't mind my saying so, sir, this mission is political cover for the President and not much more. He sends us down here with our hands tied behind our backs to stem the public outcry after the Columbus raid. He had to do something for the border states in an election year and that's about all he has the stomach for. A half-hearted gesture that gets good men killed to no good purpose."

"That's political reality, George."

"Maybe his infernal European peace policy is better than going to war if this is the only kind of war he's prepared to wage. If you're going to send troops into battle, the least you owe them is the conviction to defeat the enemy."

"As a soldier, I agree completely. As an old soldier, I can tell you it doesn't always work that way. It takes courage to be Commander-in-Chief. Not all the politicians who aspire to that office have it. Unfortunately, some of them become President. When that happens in the face of conflict, the lack of political will is a burden born by the military."

"It stinks, sir."

"Damn right it stinks. It always does, but in our democracy the majority rules. Sad to say, sometimes the majority gets it wrong."

"So we're pulling back."

"Those are our orders."

"But sir, if Major Tompkins is right, Villa is hiding right down the road in Parral. How is it in Carranza's interest to protect him? If the Carrancista commandant is hiding him, I'd wager Carranza doesn't know it. Don't those diplomatic channels communicate both ways?"

"Are you suggesting that I object to my orders, Lieutenant?"

He suppressed a mischievous glint. "Only if you're right, sir."

Pershing arched a brow, suppressing a glint of his own. "Find Lieutenant Dargue, Lieutenant. I have a message for General Funston."

Fort Sam Houston
San Antonio, Texas
April 17

Funston stood at his desk unable to sit as he waited for the infernal connection to go through.

"War Department."

"Put me through to General Scott, General Funston calling." Another silent pause.

"Scott here, what's on your mind, Frederick?"

"It's Pershing, Hugh. He's got a problem with the order to withdraw."

"What kind of problem?"

"He has reason to believe the Mexican garrison at Parral is hiding Villa. If that is the case, he believes they are doing it without Carranza's knowledge. It doesn't make sense for Carranza to hide him. John thinks we should contact the Mexican government through diplomatic channels to expose the situation before he and his troops withdraw."

Silence followed.

"Hugh, are you still there?"

"I'm thinking. Pershing is sure about this?"

"You know John. He's not given to take matters lightly."

"True. OK, I'll give it a try, but no promises."

State Department
Washington, D.C.

The Secretary stood at the office window, his arms folded. Dark felt clouds muted the District in the gray afternoon light. Sheets of rain lashed cobblestones, concrete and stone. Puddles collected on the streets and walkways connecting the institutions of national power. "General Scott is on the line, Mr. Secretary."

Now what? In this job, calls from the War Department seldom meant good news. "Lansing."

"Mr. Secretary, thank you for taking my call."

"What's on your mind, General?"

"We've heard from General Pershing in regard to his order to withdraw from Parral."

"Yes."

"The General believes that Villa is hiding in Parral under the protection of the Federal garrison there. He believes they are protecting him without President Carranza's knowledge."

"Why would they do that?"

"Villa is something of a folk hero in Mexico, a Robin Hood if you will. Whatever the reason, General Pershing suggests that we notify the Mexican Government before he withdraws his troops."

"The president has made his position on this quite clear. He wants General Pershing to disengage. Tell General Pershing that we will send a note to the Mexican Embassy."

"What should he do in the meantime?"

"He has his orders, does he not, General Scott?"

"He does, Mr. Secretary."

Santa Cruz de Villegas
April 19
The telegram from Funston lay on the desk. Head down, the general pressed the bridge of his nose between thumb and forefinger. Patton read the telegraphed message from ten yards away. *The order to withdraw stood.*

CHAPTER THIRTY-FOUR

Namiquipa
April 25

The Punitive Expedition withdrawal made its way north. Pershing determined his strategy on the move. He'd withdraw all right. He just wouldn't concentrate all his forces in one place and nowhere near as far north as Colonia Dublán. Dodd had the Seventh camped in San Geronimo. He made that his forward outpost to the south. Well back from Parral, it afforded a forward base Foulois had demonstrated his squadron could reach.

He halted the column at Namiquipa, home to the Villista general, Candelario Cervantes. After evening mess, he spread a map on a crate lighted by the headlamps of his command car. Patton sat across from him, a garish mask stoking his pipe in the bright beam. Pershing studied the map, refining his strategy for the disposition of his troops.

"Namiquipa is a hotbed of Villa sympathy. Carranza thinks enough of it to place a garrison here."

"A garrison that's plenty suspicious of our withdrawal I've noticed."

"So have I. That's why I plan to establish a second base camp here under Major Howze. It could be an important observation post."

"Aren't you concerned about the potential for trouble with

the Federales?"

"I'll talk to the Commandante. Howze will have strict orders to avoid provocation. More important, I don't want the bastards to forget we're here." The crunch of boots beyond the head-lamp glare brought him up from the map. Tompkins and Henry Vaughn stepped out of the darkness.

"General." Tompkins saluted. "Mr. Vaughn picked up some rather interesting information in town tonight."

"Not another of those 'Sí, Patron' tips, I hope."

Vaughn tipped his hat back. "Not this time, General. I know the man I talked to. He didn't know I'm scoutin' for you. Far as he knew, I'm still ridin' with Villa. Anyway, he told me Cervantes is holed up in Tomochic with a hundred fifty or so men. It ain't Villa, but Candelario's a big fish and a hundred fifty men would put a hell of a dent in División del Norte."

"Permission to go after him, sir?"

Tompkins was an eager fighter, his request predictable. More importantly, the information gave him the opportunity to test his new strategy. "Permission denied, Frank. You're going on to Colonia Dublán with me."

"But, sir."

"You heard me, Frank. We've been ordered to pull back. We are going to do that. We are going to pull back to base camps that position us to cover as much of the theater as possible. When an opportunity for action arises it will go to the unit responsible for that sector." He consulted the map again. "That town must be pretty small. I don't see it."

Vaughn bent over the map, tracing a line with a dirty fingernail. "It's about here." He pointed southwest of Guerrero.

"That's Dodd's sector." He marked the location with a pencil stub. "Lieutenant Patton."

"Sir?"

"Get word to Colonel Dodd. He's got a bandit in his sector."

"Yes, sir."

The Seventh
April 27

Dodd demanded speed. Spillsbury did his best. Sixty miles of mountainous terrain tested man and beast. At lower altitudes on the way to Minaca, the trail passed through lush forested hills, plentiful with game. The last thirty miles made an arduous climb of nearly nine thousand feet beset by cold and strong winds. You couldn't move a regiment of cavalry up that trail fast. A nimble native with knowledge of the back trails could cut the climb by hours.

Tomochic nestled in a high mountain valley. The Seventh reached the valley wall in the gray light of predawn. Dodd sent C Troop circling the Valley to the south. E Troop circled to the north. He expected these units to cut off escape routes. He deployed the main body in a skirmish line and advanced on the outskirts of town.

Shots rang out to the north. Dodd halted the main body advance. Sporadic fire suggested E Troop had encountered some resistance.

"It looks like we may be on to something. Captain Sparks, take G and K Troops to support E Troop." Sparks saluted and spurred away. Dodd never hesitated.

"Bugler, sound the charge!"

The clarion tattoo of the charge rang in the morning air. Dodd's line surged forward at a gallop. The ground shook under the thunder of pounding hooves. They swept over the sleeping town scattering pigs, chickens and dogs. They rousted sleeping villagers out of their beds.

Having assured Cervantes his escape, resistance in the north melted into the mountains. Among those sleeping peacefully in the town, eighteen-year-old Miguel Ramirez smiled at his knowledge of the back trails between Minaca and Tomochic. He rolled over and fell back to sleep, still tired from his night's work.

April 28

Flushed out of the safety of Tomochic, Cervantes led his men northeast toward Guerrero. He dismissed the main body of his men to return to their homes or the homes of nearby sympathizers. He continued on with his closest cadre of Namiquipa men. He expected he'd find safety at home with family and friends. Thirty miles southwest of Namiquipa, one of his scouts returned to the column.

"Jefe, Yanquis!" He pointed north.

"How many?"

"Twenty."

Cervantes nodded. The odds suited him. "Show me."

The scout wheeled his horse and galloped to a nearby rise. Cervantes followed. The scout drew rein below the crest and stepped down. He led Cervantes into the rocks above. He pointed to the trail below. The Americanos wound their way along the base of the foothills in a column of twos. Cervantes cut his eyes south, anticipating the path the patrol would travel.

"There." He pointed to a low hill overlooking the trail. He swung back into his saddle and galloped back to his men. "Vamos muchachos!" He waved. They sleighed and slid down the ridge. He picked up a lope around the base of the next hill to the south face of the hill he'd sighted from above. He drew a halt, swept his rifle from his saddle boot and dismounted. He scrambled up the hill followed by his men. They spread out below the crest, waiting in ambush for the Yanquis to pass below.

He looked left and right down his line, catching the eye of each man. "Hold your fire until I shoot the officer." Each man nodded in turn. He crawled to the crest of the hill on his belly. Sun-scorched red rock scraped his elbows and knees.

Below the Yanqui soldados picked their way along the trail at a walk. Dark shadows from the slanting sun followed the column like death stalking its prey. The patrol leader rode at the head of the column. Cervantes fancied it an easy shot. He levered a round into the chamber of his Winchester. He preferred the lighter American weapon to the heavier German Mauser. He shouldered the rifle and dropped the sight on the lead horseman.

The snake struck without warning. *"Serpiente!"* Someone screamed. Cervantes rushed his shot, missing as the startled lead horse shied away from the scream. The hidden Villistas opened fire wildly as the Yanquis leaped from their horses and took cover at the base of the hill. Cervantes held the high ground and tactical superiority. They had the Yanquis pinned down with no lines to return effective fire.

Silence followed the initial volleys. Neither side offered targets. Cervantes expected the Yanquis to mount a flanking maneuver. He signaled three of his men to slip around the south slope. He sent three others to the north. Loose stones rattled down the hillsides in spite of the men's best efforts to move quietly.

Minutes passed slowly. The snake-bitten man moaned softly. Cervantes sweat, burned by the sun and consumed by rage. He drew his pistol and shot the snake-bitten man to silence his crying. The pistol shot echo died away, as shots exploded along the north slope of the hill. He waved two men to follow him.

Crouching low, he ran toward the sound of the shots. He rounded a sentinel rock, nearly stumbling over the body of one of his men. He jumped back behind the rock and pressed his back against the rough stone. He held up his hand to halt the two men following him. He listened. His pulse beat in his ears.

Sweat trickled down his forehead, burning his eyes. Boots crunched on stones.

Yanqui troopers popped up from the rocks below Cervantes' men, Springfields spit death at close range. High-velocity .30-06 blasts lifted both men off their feet and slammed their blood-splattered bodies against the hard-scrabble hillside. The shooters disappeared before the bodies hit the ground. Cervantes waited, listening. He heard nothing over the thud of his heart in his chest. He levered a round into the Winchester. He took a calming breath and let it out slowly. He spun around the rock.

Time froze. The young officer aimed his pistol, steel eye, black bore, white flash, red mist, dark light.

CHAPTER THIRTY-FIVE

Colonia Dublán
April 29

The Punitive Expedition established permanent base camp in Colonia Dublán. With supply lines shortened, supply operations improved, though shortages continued to plague the expedition. Local peons and merchants rushed to fill the void of unmet needs. Cantinas sprang up, serving oceans of Mexican beer. Street pimps offered "virgin" sisters. Brothels seemingly appeared out of thin air to offer more experienced companionship. Campesinos pushed carts loaded with fresh vegetables and more of the savory "deer meat." Life settled down to garrison routine.

A signal corpsman entered the dimly lit command tent from the sun-splashed quadrangle. He came to attention at Patton's desk.

"Telegram for General Pershing."

"At ease, Corporal. I'll take care of it." He took the envelope and crossed the tent to the general's desk. "Telegram, sir."

Pershing glanced up from his reading and took the envelope. Patton retrieved the coffee pot from the nearby camp stove to refill his cup. He ran a finger under the flap, removed a sheet of yellow foolscap and read. "Got him!" He held the telegram from Howze in the air triumphantly.

"Got who, sir?"

"Cervantes. Dodd missed him in Tomochic. One of Howze's patrols got him near Namiquipa. He tried to ambush the patrol. Our boys killed him and five of his men. They also took a couple of prisoners."

"That's good news, sir."

"It is. The strategy is working even if we had to pull back. If we keep our wits about us, we may even lure Villa out of hiding. If we can get him up and moving, we may yet have a chance to get him."

Patton sipped his coffee. "I'd surely like a part in that."

"Bored with my company, Lieutenant?"

"No, sir. It's just that fighting men are meant to fight, not sit on their ass."

"Get to my rank and it seems like that's all they let you do."

"With all due respect, sir, I'll never get there if I keep sitting on my ass."

"Hmm, true enough. I can't promise you action, but at least I can get you into the field. Foulois tells me that between crash damage and mechanical failures, his squadron is officially grounded. We have to rely on couriers to fill the gaps in telephone and telegraph communication. I can attach you to Tompkins temporarily if you like."

"You may recall, sir, the Major and I have a bit of history."

He bit off a smirk. "Oh, that's right, Major Tompkins has a problem taking orders from a Lieutenant."

"I simply made your intentions clear, sir."

"And you were right, as usual. I suspect he still didn't like it. Well, George, you have a choice. Do you want to get off your ass or steer clear of Tompkins?"

"Get off my ass, sir."

Buoyed by the prospect of getting into the field, Patton resolved to make good on a promise he made to himself in Sierra Blanca.

Sierra Blanca seemed a long time ago, yet the lessons imprinted on his memory there remained with him. He found Henry Vaughn at the corrals shortly before lunch.

"Mr. Vaughn, I wonder if I might impose on you for a favor."

Vaughn paused, currying the sturdy chestnut he favored when given the opportunity to ride. "Sure thing, Lieutenant. Please, though, Henry will do."

"Very well then, Henry, I was wondering if you would accompany me into town. I'll buy lunch and you can help me with a little shopping errand I'm planning."

Vaughn shrugged. "Best offer I had all day, though, I'm sure I don't know what sort of shopping you think I might help. I don't know much about them frilly women's things, 'cept for maybe appreciatin' what's in 'em."

Patton chuckled. "No, not that. I'm looking for a revolver."

He tilted his chin. "Yup, I know somethin' about them all right. But what'd ya want with one of these for?" He spun the Colt out of his holster. "You got one of them pretty new automatics."

"It's a long story, Henry. I'll tell you over lunch."

The bespectacled scarecrow of a shopkeeper bent over the glass case and removed the pistol. He wiped it on his apron and handed it to Patton. "Finest piece I got in the store. Model 1873 Colt, it's got genuine carved ivory grips, hand-etched nickel plate. The man puts that piece on his hip says somethin' about style."

Patton passed the pistol to Vaughn. He checked the cylinder, worked the action and sighted it. He gave it a spin, testing the balance. He handed it back to Patton. "It's a little stiff for my taste, but it's new. Kind of fancy for a man like me, but if you was fixin' to wear it on parade, Lieutenant, it'd look right smart."

He smiled. "Yes, I expect it would. Nothing wrong with that, hell, Custer had that buckskin jacket."

"Well, I cain't say I recommend followin' his footsteps."

Patton caught Vaughn with a twinkle in his eye. "Not likely, Henry. I listen to my scouts."

Vaughn laughed. "Well, hell, Lieutenant, then buy yourself that gun. Just remember to holster it the way Dave Allison told you."

"Hammer on an empty chamber." He turned to the shop-keeper. "I'll take it."

2100 Hours

Dearest Beat,

Separation without worthy purpose grows increasingly difficult. Opportunities to distinguish one's self for advancement abound here though thus far, they remain beyond my reach. Two days ago a more junior officer than I engaged one of Villa's generals in an ambush and killed him. Surely the man set himself up for promotion and did so without the benefit of academy training. As I contemplate the frustrations here and your encouragement to a civilian life, I compose my thoughts in these verses.

> *Oh Beatrice, sweet Beatrice*
> *Inspire my heart to love*
> *Oh Beatrice, sweet Beatrice*
> *My wreath of triumph for your head*
> *What moment waits, uncertain fate*
> *A tale to be yet told*
> *Were I to fail approval*
> *Your love would be enough*
> *Should I attain to glory*
> *My portion you shall share*

> *But should it pass without you*
> *Life trumpets hollow brass*

I remain hopelessly divided by love and ambition. Love for you. Love for little Bea. Yet I am beset by dedication to the military and ambition to greatness. Time and opportunity slip away. Why can I not face it? Why can I not be other than who I am?

The general has given me an opportunity for temporary assignment to field duty. Perhaps it will afford the antidote to exorcise these demons. Your love and patience sustain me.

Love,
George

Juárez
Customs House
April 30

The sleek black open-top touring car rolled across the International Bridge, gleaming in reflected sunlight. The driver coasted to a stop in front of the Mexican Customs House. The honor guard lining the walkway snapped to attention. A ceremonial band struck up an unfamiliar martial tune.

An orderly jumped out of the front passenger seat and opened the rear door. General Scott unfolded his bear-like frame and straightened to his full height. General Funston followed, his bandy rooster stature dwarfed by Scott. The two started up the walkway. They were greeted by the imposing figure of General Alvaro Obregon. Obregon retained his presence despite the loss of his right arm. He extended his left hand in welcome.

"General Scott, General Funston, good of you to come."

"General Obregon, thank you for hosting our meeting."

"The pleasure is mine. Please, come in." He led them down a dimly lit, polished corridor that smelled of fresh floor wax. The hallway opened to a large sunny room. A long table of rich polished wood dominated the spare furnishings. The Mexican flag stood in a standard beside a freshly hung portrait of President Carranza.

Obregon took his seat at the head of the table. Scott led Funston around to the far side of the table, putting the sunlit windows at his back where he could read Obregon while the Mexican squinted. The Americans took their seats. Scott opened the meeting.

"We should have had this meeting before we began the current operation. It is fine for the politicians to agree on broad diplomatic outlines, but it is perhaps more important for the military to agree on specific rules to govern operations. Had we done so, I'm quite sure we could have avoided that regrettable incident in Parral."

Obregon nodded indulgently. "I should hope so, though the meeting seems somewhat unnecessary by now."

"I believe there are things we might yet agree on. The first, with your permission, is a rather urgent need to use your railroads to supply our troops."

Obregon knit his brow, his mustache drooping around a frown. "Supply operation? I see no need. Our government has requested that your forces leave Mexico immediately."

Funston straightened in his chair. Scott raised a cautionary hand. "Our forces are here by mutual agreement, General. Our mission is the removal of a threat common to the security of both our nations."

"That may have been so at one time, but Villa is either dead or rendered no further danger. That purpose has been accomplished. Now it is time for your troops to leave Mexico."

"I'm afraid that is a diplomatic matter, General. It is not something I am authorized to discuss."

"Pity. I am."

"Our job is to agree on terms for continuing the search cooperatively."

"That may be your job, General. My job, to use your term, is to obtain the immediate withdrawal of your troops."

"President Wilson and President Carranza agreed to cooperate in the effort to track down Villa and bring him to justice. He is known to be in Mexico. Our troops are here in accord with that agreement and that mission."

"That agreement was then. This is now. Villa is dead or of no further concern. The need for cooperation is past."

Funston's neck pulsed, red above his collar. "Is that why your men fired on my men at Parral?"

Obregon glared at Funston's show of pique. "Your men entered Parral illegally."

"They entered Parral under an agreement of cooperation and were fired on for it!"

"That will be all, Frederick." Scott silenced the outburst. "Please excuse my colleague, General. He is rightfully sensitive where the safety of his men is concerned. I'm sure you understand."

"Of course. I'm sure if we agree on a speedy timetable for your troop withdrawal, we shall have no further incidents of misunderstanding."

Scott shook his head. "As I said, General, withdrawal is a diplomatic matter and not something I am authorized to discuss."

"Then I suggest you consult with your diplomats, General. I see little more we may accomplish here today."

Scott clenched his jaw. He rose, towering over the seated Obregon. "No need to get up, General. We can find our way out."

CHAPTER THIRTY-SIX

Rancho Rodriguez
May 10

Late morning sun baked the Plaza beyond the shaded veranda. A gentle breeze rendered the shade preferable to the stuffy confines of the hacienda. Villa sat in the shade, his injured leg propped on a cushioned stool. The sweet smell of bougainvillea wafted on the breeze. He drummed his fingers on the table beside the dregs of a near empty milk glass. The confines of recovery fretted his temper. The wound improved, though he still could not walk without the aid of a crutch. The doctor doubted he would regain full use of it.

The days dragged long with nothing to amuse him other than the German woman's visits. She'd come several times. He might not be the full measure of himself, but she proved more than willing to release his frustrations. This time she came to stay for a few days. Her superiors must be getting anxious. They were sure the Parral fight would provoke war. Now they faced the fact it did not. He could have told them that. Carranza was too piddling a coward to go to war with the Yanquis. Pancho Villa could make war, if only he could get off his ass.

"Francisco."

Her voice sounded of butter and honey wrapped in a warm tortilla. He cocked his head with a playful twinkle in his eye. She wore a silken white robe, clinging to curves plainly naked beneath. Her corn silk hair, still tossed from the bedclothes, rustled in the breeze.

"Buenos tardes, Señorita. Did you plan to sleep the day away?"

She padded across the veranda, her bare feet silent on the terracotta tiles. She rested her bottom on the edge of the table beside him, her eyes liquid. The robe parted ever so slightly above a golden tanned knee. Fingers delicate yet strong caressed her silver cigarette case. She placed a cigarette between full lips and lit it with the snap of a pearl lighter. Silk-covered breast swelled, releasing a mask of blue smoke to the breeze.

"I missed you this morning."

"Morning passed hours ago."

She pouted. "At least you haven't forgotten me." Half smiling, her eyes wandered shamelessly to the effect she had on him.

Boots clipped the tiles, rowels ringing to staccato percussion.

"Jefe, forgive me."

"What is it, Nico?" His eyes never left her hardened nipples.

Elsa tugged the robe, covering herself with her arms as she smoked.

"I have bad news."

"What now?"

"Candelario is dead. The Yanquis killed him near Namiquipa."

Villa slammed his fist in his palm. "Candelario was a loyal compadre and a tiger in battle. I thought he and his men were safely in hiding."

"The Yanquis found them in Tomochic. They escaped. Candelario sent his men home. He was on his way to Namiquipa when a Yanqui patrol caught him."

"Yanqui patrol?"

"Sí, Jefe. The Yanquis have pulled back. They now have camps in San Geronimo, Namiquipa, El Valle and Colonia Dublán."

"Pulled back, this is good, Nico. I want you to go to Durango. Begin gathering the men. Send word to the men in Sonora." He lifted his leg. "This thing should be healed enough for me to return to the field in a month. If the Yanquis have withdrawn, it is time to give them a kick in the pants. Candelario would expect no less of us."

"Sí, Jefe." Fernandez turned on his heel. The melody of boot falls followed him across the veranda.

Elsa stubbed out her cigarette. "Back to the field, Francisco, I find that very exciting." She lowered a curtain of lash, the tip of her tongue moistened her lip between even white teeth. She slipped off the table, carelessly the robe fell open.

Gaul

Bone snapped like the crack of a whip. The stallion's head dropped with an anguished bellow. His withers crumpled left over the ruined foreleg, pitching the Centurion forward. Instinctively he rolled, taking the force of the fall with his shoulder lest he break his neck. Still he struck his helm on a stone, stunning him senseless.

The ground shook to the thundering hooves of a thousand shaggy mountain ponies. The Hun, he shook his head, willing away the darkened red haze. He struggled to his knees and returned his helm to its rightful position. His sword hilt swam before his eyes. He grasped it, a fighting chance. It felt wrong, too light. He raised the blade, broken by the fall. He lifted his eyes to the hairy horde pounding down on him. He dropped the useless blade, prepared to meet his ancestors.

He woke drenched in sweat. The heat in the dark confines of the tent was stifling. A dream, he sighed. The fallen horse, the broken blade, it all seemed so real. He sat on the edge of his cot and wiped sweat from his face. A faint shaft of starlight sliced through the tent flap, illuminating the ghostly white grip and silvered plating of his pistol where it hung in its holster on the back of a camp chair.

He considered the weapon. Beside the broken blade and fallen horse, it seemed a concession to the contemporary. A concession yes, but one made with reservation, something old with which to face the new. A timeless weapon in the hand of a timeless warrior, he'd take it for a fighting chance.

Colonia Dublán
May 14

Patton stepped out of his tent. Three touring cars waited, their engines idling just beyond the headquarters quadrangle that billeted Pershing, the expedition headquarters and his staff. Henry Vaughn waited at the running board of the lead car. Sergeants Thomas and Baker sat in the passenger seats of the other two with their drivers. Three riflemen were mounted in the rear seat of each vehicle. Patton set off to take his place at the head of the column.

Pershing looked up from his morning coffee. "Where are you off to, Lieutenant?"

"We're going down to Rubio, sir. We think we've found a grain supplier."

"That almost looks like a full-scale patrol."

"I always have my eyes open, sir. You never know what you might run into in these parts."

"Is that regulation?" He gestured to Patton's side arm with a half smile.

He flushed slightly. "Not exactly, sir. I prefer the, ah, reliability."

Pershing stood. "I see. May I?" He held out his hand.

Patton drew the Colt, flipped it around butt first and handed it over.

Pershing hefted the weapon. "Very impressive, it'd be the envy of Wyatt Earp himself." He handed the pistol back. "I don't expect the grain supplier will haggle over the price much. Good hunting, Lieutenant."

"Thank you, sir."

Rubio

The convoy rolled into Rubio at midmorning trailing the ever present dust cloud. The driver braked to a slow roll through town, scattering chickens and stray dogs. Here and there dirty children stopped their play to gawk at the unfamiliar vehicles.

"Well, look at that." Vaughn pointed his rough-shaven chin at a dozen horses tethered outside a local cantina. A knot of tough-looking men lounged near the door eyeing the Yanqui soldiers. "Them's some bad hombres."

"Villistas?"

"Most of 'em now and again."

The General was right. The grain seller didn't haggle over the price much beyond who picked it up and delivered it. Patton decided to send his own trucks. They could divide the shipment for delivery to each of the four base camps. As they remounted the cars for the ride back to base, Patton paused.

"That ranch is nearby, isn't it, Henry?"

"San Miguelito? Sure is."

"What say we pay 'em a call?"

"With so many of his friends in town, it sure couldn't hurt."

San Miguelito rested on a broad plateau northeast of Rubio. Patton halted the patrol a mile below the ranch. He assembled the two sergeants and Vaughn. Vaughn sketched a crude map in the roadside sand.

"The road comes in to the main entrance here." He drew a line to the northwest corner of a large rectangle with a smaller rectangle inside. He drew *X*s at the southeast and southwest corners of the large rectangle. "The walls are gated here and here."

Patton scratched his chin. "Sergeant Thomas, Sergeant Baker, I want those south gates covered. Mr. Vaughn and I will take the main gate. We'll move in and search the premises. This ranch is known to have harbored Villistas in the past. Expect hostile action from anyone you encounter. Is that clear?" Both men nodded.

"Mount your vehicles." *Mount,* the irony appealed to the erstwhile poet cavalry officer.

CHAPTER THIRTY-SEVEN

San Miguelito

Patton's car took the point rolling up the road at the head of the convoy. A quarter mile from the ranch he gave a hand signal, sending the Thomas and Baker cars overland to positions at the south gates. He signaled the driver to slow, approaching the main gate. They stopped twenty yards short of the arched entrance to the walled yard.

He stepped out of the car. Vaughn followed. Crouching low, he ran forward to the low wall running along the north perimeter of the ranch yard. He paused beside the gate. His eyes swept the quiet yard. Three horsemen burst from behind the hacienda, galloping toward the main gate. Confronted by Patton and Vaughn they pulled their horses to a sliding stop.

"Halt!"

The horsemen ignored the order. They wheeled away, spurring their horses toward the south gates. Thomas's riflemen greeted them at the southeast gate. The leader spurred west and drew rein again at the sight of Baker's men. He spun his horse and raced back across the yard to the north gate followed by the other two. He leveled his pistol and fired.

Bullets bit the adobe wall, showering Patton in chips and dust. He drew his Colt. He sighted the pistol and fired. Powder smoke bloomed, the charge recoiled. The action slowed. He stood his ground and fired again. A surge of exhilaration coursed through his veins, filling the void where fear might have taken root.

Riflemen cut loose at his back, the volley knocking one of the riders off his horse. The body bounced, skidded to a stop on the hard baked dirt yard and lay still. Effectively trapped in a box, the leader and the other rider slid to a stop, spun their horses and broke back to the hacienda. Thomas's troops opened fire, killing the second rider. The leader disappeared behind the hacienda.

Patton ducked behind the gate. He flattened his back to the pillar, supporting the entry arch. He released a breath he hadn't realized he held. He took another and let it out slowly, calming the excitement. He opened the cylinder gate and ejected a spent cartridge. He slipped three bullets from the loops in his cartridge belt and fitted the first in the empty chamber. He repeated the mechanical motions, steadying his breathing as he reloaded the gun, all six chambers this time.

He snapped the cylinder closed and listened, nothing stirred beyond the gate. He glanced around the post. The yard stood deserted. Neither fallen Villista moved. He caught Vaughn's eye across the open gate. The scout shrugged. Patton stepped into the yard. He moved cautiously along the wall, approaching the hacienda. A shaded portico ran along the north wall. He slipped into the shadow, measuring his steps to the courtyard at the back of the house. A rider bolted into view.

"Halt!" Patton leveled his pistol. Dave Allison called the shot. The muzzle exploded. Powder charge blossomed over the target. The bullet struck the horse in the hip. The animal squealed, twisted violently and fell, taking the rider down and pinning his leg. Desperate, the rider struggled to free his leg of the thrashing animal. The horse attempted to rise. The man wrenched his leg free and struggled to his feet. Patton held his pistol steady. "Stay where you are."

The man turned, his face contorted in frustration and rage. He reached for his gun. Patton fired. The man's eyes froze in disbelief. Dark red stain splashed across his breast. The Colt roared again. The Villista staggered, dropped his gun, sagged to his knees and pitched forward unseeing into the sand beside the thrashing horse. The acrid scent of powder smoke drifted off on a soft breeze. The scene turned eerily quiet despite the horse's struggles. The Centurion stood alone, bloodied in battle once more.

He finished the last steps to the mouth of the portico. He glanced around the corner of the hacienda. Nothing moved in the yard. He stepped out of the shadows, cautiously approaching the fallen Villista. The wild-eyed horse flailed its forelegs in a futile attempt to stand. The sound of running boots came from the ranch yard behind him. He spun in a crouch, pistol ready. Vaughn's lanky frame flashed in the sunlight beyond the portico followed by his riflemen, their Springfields at port arms. He stood, turned back to the horse. He pressed the Colt to the animal's temple and fired. The flash suppressed, the horse jerked convulsively and fell still.

Troopers fanned out around the hacienda and yard, alert to the presence of additional Villistas. Vaughn stopped beside Patton. He pushed his hat back off his forehead and looked from the front yard to the back.

"Hell of a shootout, Lieutenant. Wyatt Earp could'a used you at the OK Corral."

Patton took the comment in stride. He ejected a spent cartridge from the Colt and reloaded the chamber. Dave Allison would have approved. He noticed the saddle first. Fine-quality polished leather studded in intricate silver work with a broad bone pommel in the Mexican style. The dead Villista wore an officer's saber.

Vaughn examined the sombrero, lost in the fall from his

horse, a silver Dorado emblem affixed in the center below the crown. He recognized the body. He pointed the stubble beard on his chin at the fallen Villista.

"Julio Cardenas, Dorado commander, carried the rank of General. You got yourself a big one there, Lieutenant."

Boots sounded on the walkway under the portico.

"Yard's clear," Sergeant Baker reported.

Patton glanced up at the flat hacienda roof. Tactically that's where he'd go in the same situation. "We need to secure the roof."

Vaughn jerked his head toward the north wall. "That log over yonder looks like it's fit to climb."

"Sergeant, get it up against the wall."

Baker's men carried the log to the hacienda and propped it against the north wall. Patton climbed to the roof.

"Clear." He stepped onto the adobe-covered timbers, moving cautiously across the roof. The adobe gave way with a brittle crack. He had no chance to step back before he found himself wedged through a hole in the roof up to his armpits. His lower body dangled from the ceiling of an unknown room below. He realized he made a defenseless sitting duck completely compromised by his circumstance.

"Damn it! Get me out of here!" He heard men climb the log behind him. "Hurry!"

Vaughn reached the top of the log and broke into laughter.

"Shut up, Henry. Get me the hell out of here."

He scrambled onto the roof followed by Baker. Both men suppressed laughter as they hauled their commander out of the hole in the roof.

"Damn lucky one of them hombres didn't take a machete and use your privates for a piñata, Lieutenant."

"I'm well aware of the possibilities, Henry. Sergeant, search the house!"

A room by room search found no Villistas. They did find Cardenas' wife, daughter and mother hiding in a root cellar below the kitchen.

"Sergeant Thomas, we will take the bodies back to base. Tie them on the fenders of the cars. We don't want to ride with them, and it will send a message to Villa's sympathizers. Oh, and Sergeant, get that silver saddle off the general's horse and put it in the back of my car along with his saber."

Thirty minutes later as they prepared to depart, Vaughn pointed southwest toward Rubio. A dozen or so horsemen boiled out of the hills, bearing down on the ranch. "Might be best if we get the hell out of here, Lieutenant."

"Might indeed. Mount up! Driver, let's go."

The convoy accelerated out of the ranch yard in a shower of dust and stone. The three cars raced down the drive to the main road. The horsemen cut across the plain behind them, giving chase. They fired pistols at a distance too far for effect on horseback. Thomas's men in the last car returned fire, downing one horse head over first, scattering the riders behind it. The Villistas gave up the chase by the time the convoy turned north on the road to Colonia Dublán.

The convoy rolled into base camp under late afternoon sun slanting over the western peaks. Flushed with the excitement of his first combat, Patton ordered his driver to proceed directly to Pershing's command quad. He had the car door open before the vehicle came to a complete stop.

"You'd best come see this, sir." Lieutenant Collins summoned Pershing from his command tent. The General stepped out. A beaming Patton stood beside the body lashed to the fender of his lead car. Other bodies were similarly tied to fenders of the other two cars. Pershing smiled to himself and walked down to the road to have a look.

"Well, Lieutenant, what have we here? Doesn't look much like horse fodder."

Patton saluted. "The fodder will be along soon enough, sir. This gentleman is, or was, General Julio Cardinas, chief of Villa's Dorado guard." He nodded to the cars behind him. "The other two were friends of his."

"Well done, Lieutenant. I'm surprised you found him selling horse feed."

He permitted himself a smile. "He wasn't, sir. We noticed some suspicious men in Rubio and since we were in the neighborhood we decided to pay a call at San Miguelito. The general, it seems, took offense when we interrupted his siesta."

"Siesta, how inconsiderate of you, George."

"You know I can be a pain in the ass, sir."

"I know. Not this time, though. Hell of a fine piece of work. I'll expect a full report. With a man this close to Villa's inner circle in the area, maybe we're closer to him than we think."

"I hope so, sir."

The saddle in the back of the car caught Pershing's eye. "What's this?"

"The general's saddle and saber, sir."

"Saber, he actually carried a saber?"

"Yes, sir."

"Too bad you didn't have yours. You might have had a first-class duel."

"I'm afraid I had to shoot him first, sir."

"So those bothersome modern armaments have their place after all."

"Not entirely, sir." He patted the ivory handle in his holster. "I took him with my six-shooter."

Pershing laughed. "Touché, Lieutenant. A shootout with a well-mounted adversary. Well, keep the saddle and the saber.

They'll make fine mementos of our first mechanized cavalry operation."

CHAPTER THIRTY-EIGHT

Villa General Slain in Columbus Reprisal

On May 14, American expeditionary forces struck a blow in response to Pancho Villa's March 7 raid on Columbus, New Mexico. Elements of the Thirteenth cavalry under the command of Lt. Geo. S. Patton encountered members of Villa's elite Dorado guard while on a routine supply mission near the town of Rubio in northern Mexico.

Entering the town Lt. Patton and his men noted suspected members of Villa's insurgent band known as Division del Norte. Lt. Patton determined to search a ranch in the area known to harbor insurgent forces. He led eleven men accompanied by a civilian scout in a motorized convoy of three open touring cars.

Upon approaching the ranch, Lt. Patton deployed his vehicles to cut off escape routes from the ranch. The action, believed to be the first mechanized assault by United States Cavalry, trapped members of Villa's elite guard inside the ranch compound. The Villa men attempted to escape on horseback. A gunfight ensued in which three of them were killed. The dead included a man identified as General Julio Cardinas, Chief of the Dorado guard. Lt. Patton is personally credited with killing Cardinas. A thorough search of the ranch failed to locate any others responsible for the Columbus raid.

279

2200 Hours

Dearest Beat,

I hope this finds you well. By now I expect you've read the newspaper accounts. I've seen one or two, but I am told the story made the rounds of most of the major dailies. The general calls me "Bandit Killer" and accuses me of basking in celebrity. That seems a bit exaggerated, though I admit I do enjoy the notoriety.

I finally feel as though I have a military accomplishment to distinguish my career. It may have been little more than a skirmish, but I faced enemy fire and did so without hesitation. I know you may have concern for the danger, but I assure you I felt none. Should that surprise you, know that it also surprised me. Instead, I found the experience thoroughly exhilarating. I also face the realization I killed a man and contributed to the shooting of another. While I understand the inherent evil in unjustified killing, killing the enemy in battle for a righteous cause gives me no discomfort of conscience. It tells me in some way, I am suited to the life of a soldier. If only I were better prepared for the future.

The newspapers speak of San Miguelito as the first mechanized assault by United States Cavalry. My first combat engagement and I did not ride a horse. I shot a man who did. The man carried a saber. The Saber Master did not. On leaving the ranch, we were pursued by mounted cavalry. We escaped by car. Had we been mounted, fresh horses would have easily overtaken us and perhaps given a rather different ending to the story. I am continually confronted by change and confounded to find my place in it.

Love,
George

War Department
May 23

"Welcome back, General." Tasker Bliss rose from his desk to greet Scott. "How was General Obregon's humor this time?" Scott folded himself into a leather upholstered side chair and stretched his legs. Bliss resumed his seat.

"Well, we managed to reach an agreement of sorts, though in the end, it may have been a concession to exhaustion. In broad terms the agreement allows Pershing to carry on with his regional deployment strategy. He'll have to play nice with the local garrison commanders which he won't like, but he can still take the field when he has reason to do so. Obregon doesn't like the agreement, but he couldn't argue the point about Villa being neutralized after the Cervantes incident."

"Will Carranza approve the agreement?"

Scott shrugged. "Your guess is as good as mine. I doubt he'll get much encouragement from Obregon. I think the old bear went away feeling he'd given more than he got."

"Place your bets on machismo."

"Likely so."

"So the cotillion continues until we get lucky and get Villa or we run out of the need for a show."

"That's about the size of it."

Colonia Dublán

Patton trudged down the dusty camp street amid the burgeoning construction of temporary facilities. He found Pershing in the command quad seated at a camp desk in the shade of a tent canvas.

Patton saluted. "You sent for me, sir?"

Pershing smiled, returning the salute. "I did, George. At ease." He picked up a brown envelope from the stack of paper on his desk and held it out. Congratulations, First Lieutenant. It's been a long time coming and long overdue."

Patton took the envelope, pleasantly surprised and bittersweet with the realization "Long overdue" may indeed mean too late. "Thank you, sir. I'm sure you played a part in this. I appreciate it."

"You're a soldier, George, a damn good soldier. This Army needs men like you, now more than ever."

"It's kind of you to say so, sir."

"Nonsense, it's the truth. Have a seat."

He drew a camp chair up beside the table.

"Look, George, I know something about ambition. We all come out of the academy full of it. A peacetime army doesn't generate near enough opportunity to go around."

"I understand that, sir. Still, I look back at officers whose careers I admired as a cadet and wonder what's to become of me. Jeb Stuart and Custer made brigadier before they turned thirty."

"Those were wartime promotions, George. You prove my point."

"Please don't think me ungrateful for this, General." He held up the envelope. "At this rate, I may not see colonel by retirement. It's not the career I bargained for."

"Be patient, your time will come."

"Time will come to do what? That's the other question. Have you ever wondered if this might be the last United States Cavalry campaign?"

Pershing considered the question. "I can't say I've framed it with quite that finality, but I do see your point."

"The signs are all around us. If that is indeed the case, I'm left to wonder where that leaves me."

"Give it time, George. Your call will come. It may not be Boots and Saddles this time, but your call will come."

"I hope you're right, General." He rose. "Thank you, again."
He turned to the command tent opening.

Quo vadis?

Chapter Thirty-Nine

Handmade Italian shoe heels clipped the polished tile as he crossed the office to the massive ornate desk. Venustiano Carranza sat at a desk, arraigned more like a king on a throne than el Presidente of a republic. Sun slanted through floor-to-ceiling windows, rendering Carranza's bespectacled eyes patches of golden light. He sat beneath his own portrait flanked by a Mexican flag. Von Kreusen felt the intended diminishing effect of the setting. The Indio irked his aristocratic sensibilities. Carranza needed props to assert strength. Von Kreusen thought it the surest sign of weakness.

"Herr Presidente, thank you for agreeing to see me."

Carranza inclined his head. "Señor von Kreusen, you are always most welcome. Please be seated."

Von Kreusen took one of the side chairs arranged in front of the desk. He noted the desk sat on a low platform, forcing visitors to look up to Carranza.

"Now, Señor Ambassador, what is on your mind today?"

He polished his monocle in the folds of a kerchief, choosing his words carefully. He fitted the piece in his eye and fixed it on the panes, shielding Carranza from his gaze as though he could indeed penetrate the facade. "My government wishes to understand your intentions concerning the American occupation of Mexico."

Carranza braced ever so slightly at the suggestion his government permitted the American occupation of his country. The proximity of the accusation to the truth pained him as intended.

"The Americans are here by mutual agreement, though I admit they may be overstaying the purpose of that agreement. How is that of interest to your government?"

"Let us be candid, Herr Presidente. The world is drawn up in alliances. The Americans profess neutrality to the conflicts in Europe, but their sympathies are well known. Germany would be pleased to welcome Mexico into the circle of our friendship if your intentions toward the Americans were clear. Should Mexico engage them at home it is unlikely they will join the British and French against us in Europe. You can count on our support if you act. The question is, have you the will to do it?"

Carranza braced again. Von Kreusen had prepared his message carefully. Carranza's government is weak. He knows it, but he does not appreciate having his nose rubbed in it.

"The matter of American troops on Mexican soil is a matter between the United States and Mexico. German interests have no standing in the matter."

"That may be so, Herr Presidente, but if the Americans mount a full-scale invasion, where will you turn for aid?"

"The Americans have no such intention toward Mexico."

"You say so now, but what happens if the matter is taken out of your hands?"

"You talk in riddles. What do you mean?"

Von Kreusen sat back, a faint smile tucked under his goatee. "Pancho Villa."

Carranza dismissed the suggestion with the wave of a hand. "Pancho Villa is either dead or wounded and in hiding. His military force is destroyed. His revolution has been defeated."

"Not so, Herr Presidente. Villa has declared the Americans his enemy. As we speak he reorganizes División del Norte. If he strikes the Americans, they will use it as a reason to invade your country in force. They will occupy your northern states on the pretense of securing their borders."

"Presidente Wilson has no stomach for such an action."

"Our sources monitor the Americans closely. This plan has already been advanced by members of their general staff, including General Pershing who commands the forces already in Mexico. So, as I see it, Herr Presidente, you have a choice." He leveled his monocle for emphasis. "You can show the people who is in charge and throw the Americans out with Germany's support, or you can face the Americans and the Villistas alone."

Carranza felt boxed. He had no appetite for all-out war with the United States. He could take his chances on controlling Villa, though part of neutralizing him as a revolutionary force would require showing the people strength. He could save face at the Americans' expense. Perhaps enough to garner German support, which would surely transfer to Villa should he refuse to act. Diplomacy and drama, one could seldom tell the difference.

"What form of aid might we expect?"

The German smiled. "That is what I admire about you, Herr Presidente. You are a realist."

Colonia Dublán
June 16
The sleek tan touring car trailed a dust cloud through town to the American base camp. It rolled to a stop at Pershing's command quad. An aide seated in the forward passenger seat stepped out of the car and opened the door to the rear passenger seats. Obregon unfolded his bulk and helped himself out of the car with his good hand.

Pershing stood in the shade of a canvas canopy waiting for the Mexican general. Obregon requested the meeting. He saw little harm in granting the request though he knew from Funston's account of his meeting with the man, Obregon had little use for the American presence in Mexico. He'd reluctantly agreed to their continued presence in a subsequent meeting with Scott. He'd already gotten that message, so he had to wonder what Carranza's man had on his mind. He caught Patton's eye across the quad and waved him over. He came at a jog.

"Sir?"

"Stick around, George, I may need a witness."

"Yes, sir."

Obregon's polished brown riding boots crunched up the quad from the road. The sun beat hot, casting the long shadow of an imposing figure. He wore a neatly pressed uniform with polished brass. Battle ribbons decorated his left breast. The pinned-up right sleeve of his tunic flapped in the breeze. His cap insignia bore the Mexican golden eagle over a polished brown leather visor. A broad red, green and white striped sash draped from his right epaulette to his left hip. Pershing smiled to himself. Whatever the old peacock had on his mind, he'd given it all the military ceremony he could muster.

"General Obregon, welcome." He extended his hand.

Obregon took it in his left. "General Pershing, I am pleased to make your acquaintance."

"This is my aide, Lieutenant Patton."

Obregon nodded. "Patton, Patton, you are the one who shot Cardenas, are you not?"

"Yes, sir."

"You are to be congratulated, Lieutenant. One does not come that close to Villa's inner circle every day."

"Thank you, sir."

"Right this way, General." Pershing led the way into the dimly lit command tent. "Please, have a seat." He gestured to a camp chair, scarcely large enough to accommodate Obregon's bulk. "You must forgive our somewhat humble circumstances here, General."

"I have spent my career in the field, General, I understand the necessities."

Pershing took his seat at his desk. "Now, what can I do for you?"

"As you know, your presence in Mexico is by the mutual agreement of our governments to cooperate in the pursuit of the bandit known as Pancho Villa."

He nodded.

"Thanks to the work of your men and mine, Villa's forces have been disbursed or destroyed. Villa himself is in hiding. The Mexican government believes the threat he once posed has been eliminated. Your presence here is no longer required."

"That is a political matter. I believe you've discussed it with General Scott."

Obregon pursed his lips. "Yes, well, I've been instructed to make certain your position here is quite clear."

"I have my orders from General Scott."

"I am sure. My superiors want to be sure the men in the field understand our little agreement as we do. We would not wish to have a repeat of that regrettable incident at Parral."

"Of course not."

"Good, then we understand one another. We expect you to hold your current positions and take no action in the field without the consent of the local Federal authorities."

"Even if they are protecting Villa or elements of his command?"

"I don't know what you are talking about."

"I'm talking about Parral, General. The 'incident' as you refer to it occurred because your garrison commander refused my men when they asked to search an area where Villa was reported hiding."

"Your men entered Parral illegally and precipitated a riot."

"My men were pursued and fired on by your regulars as they withdrew in compliance with your garrison commander's request. Had our forces cooperated in a proper search, we may very well have captured or killed the bandit. If that were the case, we would have accomplished our purpose in entering Mexico. Once that is done, we will be more than happy to leave Mexico to the Mexican people."

"Your purpose here is finished. Villa is no longer a threat to either country."

Pershing shook his head. "You don't seriously believe that, do you, General? We have information that even now Villa is reorganizing División del Norte. Surely your intelligence must be better than ours. He's not finished. My orders are clear."

Obregon set his jaw. "My orders are also clear. You are to hold your present positions. Any further incursion into Mexico will be regarded as hostile action. I am instructed to use all means at my disposal to resist such action on your part."

The sweltering heat in the tent cooled noticeably. Pershing locked Obregon's black eyes in icy steel. "General, I am in Mexico on a mission. I will prosecute that mission as I see fit until such time as I am relieved or ordered to stand down. If you or any of your troops use force to interfere with my men in carrying out our mission, I can assure you your action will be met with every measure available to me. Do we understand one another?"

"Do not act irresponsibly, General. I assure you the gravest of consequences are at stake."

"I suggest you review your instructions with your superiors. It would be unfortunate if some rash action foolishly precipitated armed conflict between our two countries."

"I suggest you also review your orders with your superiors."

"I have."

Obregon rose, turned on his heel and left. Silence followed in his wake. Moments later his car started, engaged its gears and roared out of the camp in a cloud of dust.

"Do they mean it, General, or is he bluffing?"

"I'm not sure he knows. Carranza could answer that question. Unfortunately, he won't be commanding the troops in the field and that's what makes the situation dangerous."

CHAPTER FORTY

White House

June 18

Wilson hated these meetings. National defense, it seemed, forever intruded on his domestic agenda. Besides the distraction, he never felt comfortable with military matters. The general staff made such cut-and-dried assessments. They gave little or no consideration to the political nuances. Some criticized his choice of Newton Baker for Secretary of War. Admittedly, Baker had no military experience. Those who criticized the choice had no appreciation for the fact he needed a like-minded voice of reason in his dealings with the War Department.

He glanced around the table as he entered the room. Scott and Bliss sat on one side of the table, Baker and Lansing on the other. Typical, adversarial alignment, he resigned himself to his role as mediator.

"Gentlemen, thank you for coming." He took his seat at the head of the table and turned to Lansing. "Robert, I understand we've had another disappointing contact with the Carranza government."

Lansing nodded. "I received another protest late yesterday. It seems General Pershing made some rather inflammatory and threatening comments in a meeting with General Obregon."

Scott shifted in his chair. "I've looked into that personally, Mr. President. I got General Pershing's report from General

291

Funston. I called General Pershing this morning to get his account of the meeting. General Obregon advised General Pershing that in the opinion of the Mexican Government, the threat posed by Pancho Villa is over and that our presence in Mexico is no longer required. General Pershing pointed out the fact that such determination is a diplomatic matter. General Obregon then ordered him to hold his present positions until the matter could be satisfactorily resolved. General Obregon stated that Mexico would regard any further incursion into its territory as a hostile act. General Obregon advised General Pershing that his instructions were to resist further incursion by force. General Pershing responded that he had a job to do and that if Mexican Federal forces attacked his men in the performance of their duties, his men would defend themselves vigorously."

Lansing glanced at the President. "General Scott, General Pershing had it right when he said our presence is a diplomatic matter. He should have left it there. The last thing we need is an aggressive rooster strutting around another man's barnyard threatening his chickens."

"I'm sorry, Mr. Secretary, General Pershing's response was reasonable under the circumstances. We can't allow our men in the field to be bullied out of political convenience. Carranza agreed to this arrangement. He can't unilaterally change his mind and start shooting at our people. Now if the President decides to withdraw our troops, that is a different matter."

"And that is precisely what we should do, Mr. President." Lansing said. "President Carranza may be diplomatically clumsy, but he's right about the fact that Villa's forces are disbursed and no longer a threat. We have no further need of troops in Mexico."

"Secretary Baker, do you agree with Secretary Lansing?"

"The Secretary makes a strong argument. On the other hand, we have reports that Villa may be attempting to reorganize his forces. Is that correct, General Scott?"

"We do have reports to that effect, Mr. Secretary. General Pershing believes the situation in Mexico remains unstable. The Carranza government is weak. If Villa raises a new army, Carranza will be powerless to control him."

Wilson removed his spectacles and rubbed the bridge of his nose. "Didn't Mexican Federal forces inflict two rather sound defeats on Villa this spring?"

"Only because Villa made two rather ill-advised attacks on heavily fortified positions. He blames us for the defeat at Agua Prieta. He's sworn vengeance on American interests. If he raises a new army, I believe he will leave Carranza alone. We will be the target."

Wilson rubbed his chin. *Five months to the election, we can't have that.*

Lansing shook his head. "That's pure conjecture, General."

"Call it conjecture if you like, Mr. Secretary, but it is based on information that comes from sources on the ground in Mexico." He turned to Wilson. "Would you like to know what your commander in the field really thinks, Mr. President? General Pershing recommends we send a second expeditionary force south from El Paso to seize Juárez, the railroads and Chihuahua. Pershing will send elements of his command west to Sonora. The only way to secure our border is to occupy the whole of northern Mexico until the country stabilizes politically. The Carranza government is incapable of controlling Villa."

Wilson pressed his lips to a distasteful frown. "Why, that constitutes a full-scale invasion and occupation of a sovereign neighbor. He can't be serious."

"He's dead serious if you want to secure the border."

"Yes, well, we may be able to accomplish something short of that. Secretary Baker, I believe a naval presence off the coasts of Mexico would send a signal to the Carranza government that we mean business. Perhaps you could arrange appropriate demonstration maneuvers?" Baker nodded. "General Scott, instruct General Pershing to remain in Mexico, using every effort to avoid confrontation with Mexican federal forces. Secretary Lansing, you may advise President Carranza that we find General Obregon's bellicose language offensive. That will be all, gentlemen."

Wilson stood, ending the meeting. As the President left the room Secretary Lansing jumped to his feet. "Mr. President." He scurried out of the room after him.

Bliss hadn't said a word through the entire meeting. Alone in the car with Scott on the way back to the War Department, he finally spoke up. "Pershing's right, you know."

Scott stared out the window as the car cleared the White House grounds. A few large raindrops splashed the wind screen ahead of black clouds gathering over the Potomac. He smoothed his moustache and nodded. "We should respect the opinion of our men on the ground. 'A naval presence,' 'Offensive language,' 'Avoid confrontation,' it's all political bullshit. Five months to the damn election is what that was all about. Well Tasker, we're going to draw up Pershing's plan, because before this is over we may yet find ourselves at war with Mexico."

Colonia Dublán
June, 19
Pershing replaced the telephone receiver. "Son-of-a-bitch! 'Avoid confrontation.' What the hell is that supposed to mean?"

Patton looked up from a supply manifest. He could almost guess what that was about. "Sir?"

Pershing got up from the camp desk, clasped his hands behind his back and paced the spacious command tent. "That was Funston. Scott met with the President yesterday. Our orders remain unchanged, though we are reminded to 'Avoid confrontation' with Mexican federal forces. The Mexicans threaten to fire on us and we're told to put our hands in our pockets."

Hoof beats announced the arrival of a rider. Patton looked toward the sun glare beyond the double tent flap. Henry Vaughn stepped down and ground-tied his horse. He appeared silhouetted in the entry. "Beggin' your pardon, sir."

Pershing motioned. "Come in, Mr. Vaughn. What have you got?"

"I'm not sure, General. Maybe nothin', then again maybe somethin'."

"You're talking in circles, man. Spit it out."

"I was in town at the market. Took a look at some nice melons and overheard these two peons talkin' kinda quiet in the next stall. The one says a little bird told him to get over to Carrizal before the ice cream melts."

"That doesn't make any sense."

"I know. That's what made me think it might be some kind of code."

"Code for what?"

"Well, sir, ice cream ain't real plentiful in these parts."

"Neither are talking birds. What's your point?"

"It minded me of a man with a powerful weakness when it comes to ice cream."

Pershing snapped alert, *Villa.* "Where is Carrizal?"

Patton set down the manifest. "Seventy miles northeast."

"Lieutenant, find Captain Boyd on the double."

CHAPTER FORTY-ONE

Carrizal
June 21

Captain William Boyd led a detachment of the Tenth Cavalry out of Colonia Dublán on the seventy-five-mile trek to Carrizal. He had C Troop under Lieutenant Henry Adair and K Troop under Captain Lewis Morey. Bill Bell scouted for the column.

They cut Boyd out of the same pugnacious bolt of cloth as Frank Tompkins. He'd seen enough of this Punitive Expedition to know that most of the punishment being handed out was heaped on the backs of the American forces. The Carrancistas were obstructionist at best and outright sympathetic to the bandits at worst. He hadn't had a decent fight in three miserable months in Mexico.

Two days out, Carrizal came into view the morning of the twenty-first. It sat on a low rise surrounded by broad fields scored by irrigation ditches. Scrub brush and cottonwood trees lined the banks of the ditches. Boyd drew a halt to water the horses at an irrigation ditch southwest of town.

"You figure we should request permission to enter the town, Captain?" Lieutenant Adair had heard the Parral stories.

"It might be good form. Not that it matters much."

"Might not be needful, Captain." Bell stuck his chin up the slope toward the adobe walls and low roofs of the town. A hand-

ful of uniformed horsemen jogged down the hill and drew to a
halt waiting to meet them.

"Captain Morey, position K Troop on my right. Lieutenant,
take C Troop on the left. Let's move out."

The column splashed across the ditch and spread out,
advancing up the rise toward town and a second irrigation ditch.
Boyd signaled a halt a quarter mile west of the irrigation ditch.

"Captain, Lieutenant, hold your positions here. Mr. Bell, let's
see what the Federales have on their mind." He spurred forward
followed by the scout.

The Federale Commandante sat ramrod straight astride a
flashy palomino flanked by a squad of a half dozen troopers.
Boyd jogged up to him and drew rein. He touched his hat brim
with something between a salute and a tip and smiled. "Captain
William Boyd, Tenth Cavalry."

The Federale nodded. "General Felix Gomez. State your
business."

Bell translated.

"We have information that Pancho Villa may be hiding in
Carrizal. I intend to search the town."

"I must ask you to halt your advance and return to your
base."

"I am under orders to search the town."

"General Obregon has informed your General Pershing he is
not to advance any further into Mexico. Your presence here
constitutes such an advance. If you do not heed my order to
return to your base, I will use force to stop any further attempt
to advance."

"I have my orders. I will search Carrizal."

"Then the responsibility for what happens here is yours." He
wheeled his horse and led his detail back up the hill into town.

Boyd scratched his chin. "I think he means it."

" 'Pears so."

Boyd followed Bell's gaze to the cottonwoods along the irrigation ditch north and south of town. Troops spilled out of town taking positions along the banks in the trees.

"What d'ya figure to do, Captain?"

Boyd cocked an eye at the scout and shrugged. "Search the town." He wheeled southwest and squeezed up a lope to Captain Morey's position.

"Captain, we advance on my command. I expect we will be fired upon. Have your men ready their weapons."

"Are we starting a war, Bill?"

"We're not, Lew. They are." Boyd loped across the field to Adair's position.

"Ready weapons, Lieutenant. We advance on my command."

"You expect trouble, sir?"

"I'm sure of it."

"Ready arms!" The sounds of slapping stocks and bolts slamming cartridges into chambers rippled through the ranks.

Boyd waited for the sound to fade away, signaling arms ready. "Forward, ho!"

He led C and K Troops forward at a walk.

Wind ruffled Elsa's hair. Her pulse quickened with excitement. He stood beside her, sloped shoulders hunched against the tile-capped top of a low adobe wall at the roof's edge, his dark silhouette lost in a sea of flat roofs. His eyes crinkled at the corners, intent on the scene unfolding below.

The Americans rode forward. She glanced to the north. She could see the Federale Commandante in the cottonwoods on the east bank of the irrigation ditch. He watched the Americans through field glasses. The advance drew them into crossing fire lanes formed by the sloping curve of the irrigation ditch and the troops positioned behind it.

"*Fuego!*" The command echoed faintly.

The banks of the ditch exploded in machine gun and small-arms fire quarter-flanking both Troops. The initial volley lashed the column, cutting down horses and riders.

"Fire at will!" Adair and Morey relayed Boyd's command to their troops. The Springfields responded with deadly accuracy. The machine gun on the north flank went silent. Boyd rallied C Troop to charge the Federale position anchored by that gun. A new gunner scrambled into position and lay down a curtain of death, blunting Boyd's vanguard with dead horses. The charge broke under sweeping sheets of machine-gun fire.

A heavy-caliber machine gun bullet struck Boyd. He pitched from his horse, hitting the ground hard and knocking the breath out of him. He fought to recover his breathing, only to discover searing pain in his right shoulder. Blood stain spread down the sleeve of his useless right arm. He turned to Morey's troop, frantically looking for an opportunity to flank the Mexicans and roll up their positions.

Powder smoke spread like a fog up the south bank of the irrigation ditch. Morey's men shrank under a withering fire storm. Boyd's shout penetrated rifle and machine-gun reports.

"K Troop, cross that ditch!"

Morey turned to Boyd, bewildered by the order. Boyd's eyes went wide in that instant. His right temple shattered in a vaporous red exit wound.

Adair rushed the north end of the ditch with a handful of men. They made it across under heavy fire, giving as good as they got. Adair clamored up the east bank of the ditch only to catch a bullet in the chest. The impact threw him back into the men, following behind. The attempted assault melted in retreat.

Morey fought to hold his position pinned down in the crossfire. Mexican troops advanced across the irrigation ditch under the cover of trees and scrub along the bank. One of his sharpshooters found a shadowy figure among them watching the action through field glasses. Recognizing the man for an officer, he took careful aim and squeezed. The man crumpled like a string-cut marionette. Morey rallied his men to counter attack when a bullet caught him in the shoulder. He staggered and fell. With Boyd dead, command fell to him. He rose to his knees. The sight of Mexican cavalry taking the field sealed his decision.

"Retreat!"

The withdrawal began in good order until the Federale cavalry stormed out of the trees in pursuit. What remained of Boyd's command broke and ran, scattering across the fields and roads to the north and west. The Federales soon lost interest in pursuit, preferring instead to loot the bodies of the fallen and round up the easily overtaken as prisoners.

He pushed away from the wall and stood, clasping his hands behind his back. He cocked an eye at her with a satisfied smile. "You see, my sweet, it is as I told you. It takes no more than a little bird."

She smiled. "Francisco, you are such a devil."

CHAPTER FORTY-TWO

Fort Sam Houston
June 22

The annoying bell jangled.

"Funston."

"Scott here. How the hell did this happen again?"

Funston moved the receiver away from his ear. "How the hell did what happen?"

"Pershing had another firefight with Mexican federal forces."

"He what?"

"You heard me."

"I'm as surprised as you are, General."

"Not half as surprised as the President. He read it in the damn newspaper. I spoke with General Pershing this morning. He mentioned they had a lead on Villa, but nothing about a firefight. If he knew about it he certainly would have said something. Where the hell is Carrizal and what was Pershing doing there?"

Funston turned to the theater map on his office wall. Thankfully the name came to his glance. "All I can tell you is that Carrizal is seventy-five miles from Colonia Dublán."

"Well, it might as well be next door to Washington."

"I spoke to General Pershing this morning. He had no information. He didn't even know it happened."

"So the only thing we've got is what we read in the newspapers, is that it?"

"I'm afraid so."

"We get our asses whipped by a bunch of Mexicans, the President reads about it in the papers and the chain of command doesn't know shit. We look like idiots! We don't have casualties, MIAs, prisoners, anything."

"No, sir."

"Son-of-a-bitch. I want information as soon as Pershing can get it even if he has to round up the stragglers personally."

"Yes, sir."

"Put your command on alert, Frederick. General Bliss and I have a plan for the occupation of northern Mexico. It looks like the President is prepared to ask Congress for the authority to implement it. You could be days away from an order to invade Mexico."

Presidential Palace
Mexico City

"Congratulations, Herr Presidente. You have struck a blow for Mexican independence." Von Kreusen beamed, floating across the polished tile floor.

"Mexico is independent, Señor Ambassador."

"Yes, of course. I came as quickly as I could after checking with my superiors. I have information that may interest you. As you know already, my government monitors conditions in the United States somewhat closely. We have learned that the naval presence off your coast is but the overture to a much broader plan. President Wilson is prepared to ask Congress for the authority to invade Mexico. They plan to occupy the states along your northern border until such time as a stable government can be established in Mexico. Stable I think is a euphemism for a government acceptable to the United States. We thought you should know."

Carranza gazed out the window. He knew this could happen. Realistically he didn't have the forces to resist an invasion in force across the breadth of the northern border. If he tried, Villa would rise up against him, virtually unopposed. Simply put, he could not afford to invite invasion by the Americanos. They could occupy his country and in doing so demonstrate that his government was powerless to do anything about it. The German waded into his thoughts.

"Of course, you should expect our support with whatever materiel we have in our power to supply."

"Of course. I don't imagine that includes a half million men under arms."

The diplomat shrugged with an exaggerated pout. "You must realize, Herr Presidente, our military forces are somewhat occupied at the moment by the conflict in Europe."

"Hmm, then I suppose that leaves us to our own devices, doesn't it?"

The German took his turn at silence.

"Very well then, Señor Ambassador, I will let you know should we need anything *within your power to provide.*"

Carranza had no fight in him. Von Kreusen could feel it.

White House
June 24

"Mr. President, Secretary Lansing to see you."

Wilson set aside the draft of his speech to Congress and motioned for his administrative aide to send the Secretary in. He planned to stop short of a formal declaration of war. He'd toyed with calling the action a Security Intervention, though he puzzled over how that might play in the press. Lansing broke his train of thought as he approached his desk.

"What is it, Robert?"

"Carranza blinked."

"Blinked?" He folded his hands over the speech. "Have a seat."

"The Mexican Ambassador just delivered an offer to return our prisoners as a gesture of good faith, if we agree to discuss terms for limiting further incursion into Mexico."

Wilson smiled. "His hold on the country truly is fragile, isn't it?"

"It would appear so. We now have some options. We can continue with the planned invasion knowing he can't possibly mount a serious resistance, or we can negotiate a favorable continuation of the current operation. We could even agree to withdraw."

"No. No withdrawal, not yet. Columbus is still a tender nerve along the border. I'll not let it appear as though we backed down over the Carrizal defeat."

"Then, do we refuse and proceed with our invasion plan?"

The President drummed the desk with his fingers. He shook his head. "I was prepared to accept that option as an alternative to declaring war, but I'm not comfortable with it. I'm running a campaign based on keeping us out of war. Occupying the lawless border region of a neighbor nation is a poor compromise to keeping us out of war. No, we'll negotiate new terms, allowing the Punitive Expedition to stay. As long as we can keep our forces between Villa and the border we shall have done enough."

"I can hear the howls over at the War Department from here."

"Yes, well, the generals can scream all they want. That is Baker's problem. You get me an agreement that keeps us out of war and gives me political cover along the border. That's your job."

"Yes, Mr. President."

Colonia Dublán

"Put on the whole armor of God, that ye may be able to stand against the wiles of the devil. For we wrestle not against flesh

and blood, but against principalities, against powers, against the rulers of the darkness of this world, against spiritual wickedness in high places." (Eph. 6:11–12)

Pershing tossed the thick sheaf of papers onto the desk. "Well, George, it looks like our mission here is firmly in the hands of the politicians and the diplomats."

"How's that, sir?"

"New orders. We are to withdraw to base camps in Colonia Dublán and El Valle and stand down. We are not to pursue Villa unless we have reason to believe he is moving toward the border. If we have information to that effect we are to share it with our Mexican counterparts. If Carranza's man agrees, then and only then may we pursue the son-of-a-bitch."

"They might as well bring us home."

"No, no, we couldn't have that. Why that might give the appearance we had one skirmish with the Mexicans, turned tail and ran. No, we'll bake our asses here the rest of the summer. They'll call us home, oh, say, the day after the election."

"That's bullshit, sir, if you don't mind my saying so. Military operations run on clearly defined objectives. Politics run on the line of least resistance. You can't run an army that way."

"That doesn't mean the politicians won't try if you let them. There's more. General Scott was kind enough to alert me to the fact the President is about to issue a statement that may have implications on our situation down here. He plans to call for an end to the Mexican revolution. He'll call on the Mexican people to unite behind Carranza as the country's legitimate government."

"That'll piss Villa off."

"Yes, well, General Scott thought it might irritate certain elements down here."

"Irritate certain elements, may I speak freely, sir?"

"When has ceremony ever stopped you before, George?"

"Wilson is a spineless idiot. His socially progressive idealism renders him incapable of carrying out the responsibilities of commander-in-chief."

"I'm inclined to agree, though men in uniform are best advised to keep their own counsel on such matters."

Presidential Palace
Mexico City

Wilson pide que la Unidad de Mexico

Carranza reread the morning headline and tossed the paper into the island of light on his desk. "The arrogance, the audacity, who does he think he is? He presumes to dictate to the people of a sovereign nation."

The cleaning lady hurried to empty the wastebasket and disappear into the shadows, clearly uncomfortable in the presence of el Presidente's anger.

He messaged the dull onset of a headache. Does he think this benefits my government? The Mexican people could give pig feces for his imperial opinion. He gives credence to Villa's claim we are nothing but a Yanqui puppet. The Americano professor sees none of this. He hears only the rattle of his own empty words.

Frustration fed the ache in his head. What could he do? Once again demand the Yanquis leave Mexico? They would remain unmoved until the Professor had his re-election. Confront their forces? This only risked a war he could neither afford nor win. German promises of aid rang as hollow as the prattle of the Yanqui Presidente. Crush Villa? This he might do, but even this carried risk. His actions might be seen as doing the Yanqui's bidding just as Villa claimed. Worse, it might rally the people's sympathy to the bandit's rebellion. Everywhere he turned obstacles beset him. He saw no way out of the dilemma until after the Americano election. Damn the accursed bandit!

Rancho Rodriguez

Villa wiped tears from his eyes. He burst into another peal of laughter. "I tell you, Nico, I have not had such good humor since Guerrero. The Yanquis retreat into hiding, giving their lap dog the appearance of victory, only to have their foolish Presidente cover him in pig shit! If Carranza didn't look so good covered in shit, he would almost be worthy of pity."

Fernandez smiled at the indignity of el Presidente's predicament. "Sí, Jefe. You could not have done as well as this by your own hand."

"Now we shall see whose ice cream melts, eh? It is time to call the men from Durango. We will show the people who stands for Mexico and who squats a fool for the Americanos."

Fernandez shifted uncomfortably, gazing at the toes of his boots.

"What is it, Nico? Is something the matter?"

"It is the recruiting, Jefe."

Villa sensed trouble. His eye flashed a warning light. "What is it? What is wrong with the recruiting? We have German guns. We have German pesos. We have the justice of our cause. What could possibly be wrong with recruiting?"

He bit his tongue.

"Out with it, Nico. The truth, tell it now."

He shrugged. "It is only that some men no longer wish to serve."

"They deny the cause of revolution? Impossible! It must be something else." He read more to tell in Fernandez. "You will tell me now, Nico."

He took a breath. "It is the losses, Jefe. So many have died, the men are afraid."

Villa nodded. He wagged a finger. "The men are afraid to fight. Nico, Nico, Nico, truly this is not a problem. They only need to fear refusing to fight more than they fear fighting. Go back to the towns and villages. Offer the men the opportunity to join our glorious revolution. Shoot the first man to refuse. Shoot the next one who refuses. Soon after, we shall have our army."

CHAPTER FORTY-THREE

Columbus

August 1916

The black touring car rolled up Deming Road past Camp Furlong. Notoriety had turned Columbus into a boomtown. Cars, trucks, horse-drawn wagons and pedestrians clogged dusty streets soaked in blazing summer sun. Everywhere the sights and sounds of rebuilding assaulted the senses. Hammers rang a staccato beat to the hum of saws. Raw lumber and paint scented the breeze. A new frame skeleton rose from the ashes of the Commercial Hotel.

The car rolled through town past burnt battle scars awaiting their turn at the building boom. Heads turned to the low-slung black car with the blue pennant and its single gold star affixed to the right front fender. Word spread. Pershing is back.

The car turned east on Broadway, threading its way through town to the Hoover Hotel where it braked to a halt. Patton leaped out of the car and held the passenger door as Pershing climbed out. Beat stepped onto the hotel porch flanked by Nita. Pershing smiled. He clapped George on the shoulder with relaxed familiarity and led the way up the steps. George took his leave to kiss Beat. Pershing took Nita's hand in his and held her eyes. Her cheeks colored.

A bellman fetched the suitcases out of the car's package boot. Beat took control. "Come along, George. Let's get your things settled in our room."

"Shall we meet for cocktails at seven?" Pershing's eyes never left Nita's.

"That would be very nice, sir."

"Please, George, John will do. We're on leave."

Beat led the way up the stairs to their room.

Pershing found Nita's eyes. "Would you care to take a walk before we meet George and Beatrice?"

"That would be lovely."

"Give me a couple of minutes to get my bag settled and I'll be right down."

She nodded. Five minutes later he returned. She took his arm and followed him out to the hotel veranda. They took a leisurely stroll up the boardwalk to the corner and turned west on Broadway.

"Columbus is rather more rustic than Washington," Pershing said.

Nita squeezed his arm affectionately. "Washington was lovely. I'm sure Columbus will be every bit as enjoyable, considering the company."

Evidence of the raid could be seen everywhere. "It must have been horrible that night," she said.

"Villa and his men understand violence."

"Will you capture him?"

He furrowed his brow, considering the question. "I don't think Pancho Villa will threaten our border again."

"Good."

They paused at a corner for a truck loaded with lumber to make its turn, belching clouds of inky black exhaust. Nita put a hand to her nose to stifle the smell. They stepped off the boardwalk and crossed the street.

"If you don't mind my asking, how is Beatrice holding up at Fort Bliss?"

Nita gave him a sidelong glance, considering what to say. "Tolerably well, I expect. West Texas is primitive by her standards. Separations are never easy, but women who marry military men know that when they enlist."

He chuckled. "They do enlist after a fashion, don't they?"

"Why do you ask?"

"I'm concerned about George."

"George? Why ever for? No one is better able to take care of himself than George. Some might say he's too able."

"He's a good soldier, a fine officer. The army needs men like your brother. I'm afraid he is having second thoughts about his career choice."

"The only career George has ever dreamed of is becoming a cavalry officer."

"Yes, I know, and therein lies part of the problem."

"I don't understand."

"The day of the horse soldier is coming to an end, Anne. Neither one of us has been on a horse since we first entered Mexico. Modern ballistics, aviation, motorized vehicles all conspire to assign the cavalry service to the pages of history. It's progress of course, but it also means change. The light is going out on George's old dream. He needs to find a new one."

"I see, though I'm quite sure I do not understand all the reasons."

"There's more to it. I'm sure he's disappointed in his rate of advancement."

"He's only recently been promoted."

He nodded. "Recognition that was long overdue. I'm sure by his age he expected to be captain or even major."

"He's never been short on ambition. Why do you think he has not achieved more?"

"It's not for lack of ability. It's just hard to advance in an army at peace. I'm afraid the day is coming when the army will need men like George. I only hope he does not become discouraged and resign his commission."

"Do you really think he might?"

He shook his head. "I don't know. That's why I asked about Beatrice. She and the little one will surely weigh on his thinking."

"Can't you help him appreciate his possibilities? I know he thinks the world of you and with good reason I might add."

The dimple showed in his smile. "I can try. Friendship aside, I am his commanding officer. I musn't try to do more than I'm asked. You know your brother better than I. He wouldn't accept favor."

The bellman set the suitcase inside, accepted his tip and departed. George took Beat in his arms. "Now let's have a proper kiss for a man who's been away these long months." She settled against him, her lips soft and sweet and welcoming. At length she breathed.

"Ah, that's better. It's been ever so long, Georgie." She rested her head on his chest. "How much longer must we endure this?"

He could take that question at face value or choose the deeper one that lay behind it. For the moment he preferred the simple answer. "Not much longer. Our new orders have stripped the mission of its original purpose. Our presence in Mexico is now symbolic. The General believes we will be recalled as soon as the election is over."

"That will be nice." She too could let it rest for the moment. "Come have a seat."

The room was small though comfortably furnished with a bed, dresser, nightstand and two stuffed chairs separated by a side table. Beat took one of the chairs.

"The general seems quite pleased to see Nita."

"Yes, he does. I think we should get used to having him

around. You know she met him in Washington the last time he returned for a briefing."

"She did mention that. I think the feelings between them are quite mutual."

"He's a bit older, but Nita is a big girl and he is a fine man."

"It can't hurt your career either I suppose."

A jaw muscle tightened. "That's not how I mean to advance my career, Beat. I am learning a great deal from him. I suspect he had a hand in this." He fingered the new gold bar on his collar. "Perhaps if I had come into his command earlier in my career it might have made a difference. It's late for me now, Beat, probably too late."

"Well, you did have your brush with fame over that business with Cardenas. The papers were full of your exploits. It made me ever so proud of you."

"Proof I have the mettle, but mettle for what? The days of cavalry glory are past. I could dismiss Villa's defeats as the undisciplined performance of untrained irregulars. How do I explain the defeat of some of our best at Carrizal? I am as obsolete as my beloved saber. The army moves slowly. Nothing will happen overnight, but the way of the future is clear." He sighed and smiled. "Let's not speak of such things now. How is little Bea?"

The dining room shimmered with a glow different somehow as he remembered it from the night of the officers' dinner. He suspected the presence of women softened it, allowing touches of elegance to shine through. The tables were laid in starched dark green linen. Bone white china trimmed in gold ordered each place setting, flanked by polished silver. Flickers of candlelight reflected in crystal goblets and wine glasses. The Hoover dining room created an island of style and grace removed from the dust and heat of recent weeks.

Nita looked radiant in a sunny, light summer frock. A splash of color touched her cheeks and lips, accenting a flawless alabaster complexion. The general seemed totally captivated. Beat wore an understated gray gown, a blank canvas made for a quiet portrait of her beauty. She spread relaxed comfort to those around her, glossing over Patton's tendency to discomfort in such situations. With Beat at his side, no one noticed an overserious demeanor that masked his awkward feelings of shyness. In truth he felt more at home in the heat of the San Miguelito shootout than he did sipping sherry from cut crystal. Fortunately casual conversation came easily to women. He heard the admiration Nita felt for the general in her voice.

"John took me for a walk this afternoon. It must have been terrible that night, the night of the raid, I mean. They are rebuilding and repairing everywhere you look. It's one thing to read about it in the newspaper and quite another to see the devastation firsthand. You read of people being shot down in the streets, but words on paper render the news quite abstract. Then you see bullet holes in the buildings, in this building mind you, and you better understand the horror those poor people must have suffered. It makes one appreciate what you men are doing down here."

Pretty and thoughtful, he liked that. "Unfortunately, I doubt we will actually get the man responsible."

"Why not?"

"Washington seems satisfied we've done enough."

"I don't understand."

"Our presence in Mexico is embarrassing to the Carranza government. It makes them appear weak. President Carranza would like us to withdraw. He's ordered his troops to resist our advances. We've had two skirmishes with Federal forces, the last one nearly led to war."

"Oh, my. Well, if we are satisfied that we have done enough

314

and the Mexicans want us to leave, why doesn't President Wilson bring you home?"

Patton glanced at his sister. "Politics."

"George." Beat cautioned.

"It's all right, Beatrice. George and I discuss such matters, though at times I share your concern for his, shall we say, candor. The border states expect the President to protect them. That is why he sent us here and that is why we will stay until after the election."

"Somehow that doesn't seem right."

Pershing smiled. "Politics are a fact of life where the military is concerned. Social order often depends on the judicious use of force. Politics thrives on deciding what terms like 'judicious' mean. Villa did an evil deed here. He's suffered for it. Has he suffered enough? It depends on who you ask. If you ask President Wilson, he'd say yes. If you ask the people rebuilding Columbus, you might get a different answer."

Nita nodded. "I see."

"I don't." Patton shifted uncomfortably in the straight-backed chair. "It's damned awkward policy for dealing with a border bandit like Villa. I shudder to think what it might mean should we face a determined national threat from, say, German aggression. You can't fight threats like that for show. You must thoroughly defeat an enemy like that."

"You're right, George. Pray God we are given that order should time and circumstance draw us into the European conflict."

Beat looked from the general to George. For all the faults and failings of human endeavor, she saw devotion to duty between them. Could such character be satisfied by the pastoral pursuits of raising horses? she wondered.

"George, I believe we've bored these two lovely ladies too long with such serious matters. The concierge tells me they have an orchestra playing at the Moose Lodge tonight. I think a little dancing might be a far more pleasant way to spend our evening. Don't you agree?"

Beat caught Nita's eye for a chorus. "We do."

He lay awake, staring into the darkness. He felt Beat beside him, soft and warm, her steady breathing the echo of their love-making. Leave had come to an end too soon. Tomorrow they would part again. He smelled tent canvas and felt the lonely discomfort of a cramped camp cot. God, he missed her already. He denied himself these comforts. His ambition denied them both the happiness they shared, and for what? What lay beyond this futile campaign? The President would win his re-election and with it four more years of pacifist isolation. In four years, he'd be thirty-six and likely as not, a First Lieutenant still. The general said his call would come, but when? What if this was it? What would happen when the last of the Army's mules were turned out to pasture? His dream, his career would be turned out with them. Beat had the right of it. It was time to grow up. The time had come to face the facts. The dream was at an end.

He had the metal, to be sure. He'd proven that to himself. He'd faced Cardenas and his men gun in hand and given good account of himself. He had the metal. He could lead. The general saw it. Glory followed from preparation meeting opportunity. Time had passed his preparation by. Destiny it seemed would accord him no opportunity. He had his duty. This last campaign, he'd see it to the finish and face his future then.

The car rumbled south on the return to Colonia Dublán. Wind streaming through the open top softened the worst of the day's heat. Pershing lounged in the rear seat, thoroughly rested and relaxed after his week with "Miss Anne." Patton too had enjoyed his time with Beat, though the burden of separation hung over them. The pain of yet another leave-taking came laced in the question of his future.

"She's quite the woman, your sister, George."

He smiled. "We had our sibling moments as children, but she's grown up much to my liking."

"I should think so. I find her quite fascinating. I hope you don't mind."

"Not in the least. She quite enjoys your company too, I've observed."

"I hope so. I should like to see more of her. I enjoyed getting to know Beatrice better too. She is a lovely girl. You're fortunate. A good Army wife is an asset."

He looked at the passing desert. It simply wasn't fair to ask that of her. He doubted he should ask it of himself.

"Look, George, it's none of my business, but I know you are having second thoughts about your career."

He turned back to the general.

"It's natural enough. We all come out of the Academy with expectations. We're trained for war. In times of peace, we wait. You're a good soldier, George. You've the makings of a fine field commander. We live in uncertain times. Your time will come."

"You've said as much before, sir, and I appreciate it, but time is passing. Time is passing me and my family. I'm not a young man anymore. Beat knows it. I know it. My pride refuses to accept the truth of it."

"Don't make too much of the moment. The time is coming when the Army will need officers like you."

"A horse soldier and Saber Master? That strikes me as unlikely."

"The days of the cavalry may be numbered, but they are not over. The army doesn't move that quickly. I've just been asked to write an article on cavalry training. You can help me with that while we let time and training deal with the shape of the future. Be patient, George. You'll find your rightful place. Men of ability always do."

"I'll consider it, sir. Thank you."

CHAPTER FORTY-FOUR

South of Parral

September 9

Villa called a halt. He bridled at the confinement of riding in a carriage. It struck him as unmanly. His men expected more. He should be at the forefront, leading the charge. His leg would not yet permit it. And so he was left in the care of fifty Dorado, an invalid carried in comfort. He still had the mind and heart of the Jaguar. He only needed the legs of another.

"Nico!"

Fernandez peeled away from the head of the column and galloped to the side of the coach. "Sí, Jefe. Parral lies just ahead."

Villa chuckled. "Nico, I thought you knew me better by now."

Fernandez knit his brow and leaned forward in the saddle. "The sun makes me stupid?"

Villa laughed again. "Not the sun, the little bird."

"What bird?" Jefe's riddles could be maddening.

"The bird sings Parral. He has the Carrancistas bunkered in behind their machine guns and trenches. We are not going to spill our blood on that trap. Lead us east swiftly, Nico. Jimenez is fat with Carrancista arms and supplies. There are no machine guns and trenches there because of the little bird."

Fernandez sat back in his saddle and smiled. He wagged a finger. "There is a reason we follow a fox, Jefe."

"Sí, Nico." He smiled. "Now swiftly."

Jimenez
September 11

Villa wiped tears from his eyes. He burst into another peal of
Division del Norte swept out of the predawn gray. They overran
the small town and the federal arms depot. Carrancista guards
stationed at the depot offered no resistance. They ran from their
posts at the first sound of the charge. Villa's men captured German arms and ammunition including machine guns and light
artillery. The Germans played both sides to no one's surprise.
They gathered the food stores they needed and distributed
surplus to the poor. A grateful people spread the word: "Pancho
Villa has returned."

Presidential Palace
Mexico City
September 12

Villa wiped tears from his eyes. He burst into another peal of
Obregon's polished boots clipped the black and white tiles as he
crossed the spacious office to Carranza's desk.

"You sent for me, Presidente?"

"Sit."

The general's eyes darkened behind a composed mask. He
did not appreciate being ordered about like a schoolboy by a
pompous politico.

"Explain for me how Villa was able to plunder federal stores
at Jimenez without the slightest opposition?"

"We had information that he would strike Parral. We
reinforced the garrison there to provide him a proper reception."

"Clearly your information was wrong. He got no reception.
You served up a fat prize for him instead. Arms, ammunition,
machine guns, even cannon. He has an army again! We look
helpless and foolish!"

Obregon fumed to himself. *Looks may be deceiving, in this case perhaps not.*

"Do I have to take the leash off the Americanos to bring this cur to heel?"

"That would be most unwise." He paused. "Excellency."

"Don't patronize me, General. I made you when I allowed you to take this city. Perhaps I should have left it to Villa. He may be a brigand, but he is a reliable brigand. Now, thanks to you, he has a well-armed revolutionary army. The question is what is to be done about it?"

This popinjay made me? He sat on his ass while fighting men won his revolution for him. He is weak. He knows it. I know it. Villa knows it. The Yanquis know it. He has no choice.

"El Presidente, you have a choice. You may leave Villa to me or give your problem to the Americanos. You and I both know what that would mean. The people would flock to the one true revolutionary. Men and arms would rally to the cause of preserving Mexico for the Mexican people. No amount of German promises will save your government from that. Now, I suggest you leave Villa to me, before the situation gets out of control." He stood, turned on his heel and strode out of the office, leaving Carranza staring after him open-mouthed.

Ciudad Chihuahua
September 16

The carriage clattered across the plaza to the gates of the Governor's mansion. Distant rifle and pistol fire was all that remained of the Carrancista security force's waning resistance. Dust and powder smoke drifted over the tiled roofs of the city. Villa's Dorado guards rode through the gates and dismounted. They rushed inside to search the mansion.

Villa rose from the carriage seat, braced himself on the door frame and stepped down, favoring his stiff leg. He limped into the shade of a pillared portico, covering the massive double-door entryway. He paused at the sound of a galloping horse. Fernandez wheeled through the gate, circled the courtyard fountain, drew rein and swung down.

"The Carrancistas have been driven out of the city, Jefe."

"They will come back with a much larger force, but for now we may enjoy the comforts of victory."

"My men have opened the jail. We found two hundred willing recruits."

"Excellent, Nico, assemble them in the Plaza. I will address the people today."

"Should I prepare my men to defend the city, Jefe?"

He pursed his lips in a disparaging scowl and shook his head. "I have no intention to hold it. Let the men rest and enjoy the spoils. We will be gone before the Carrancistas return."

A crowd packed the sun-soaked plaza. Villa rode out to address them, standing in his carriage where they might see him.

"Amigos!" He paused, waiting for quiet.

"Amigos."

"Amigos, once more I, Pancho Villa, am your humble servant." He bowed.

"Viva Villa! Viva Mexico!" The roar of the crowd was deafening

"Together we have fought tyranny and oppression these many years. We fought for land reform. We fought for your rights. We defeated the tyrant Diaz under the leadership of the great Francisco Madero."

The crowd cheered wildly. He paused, measuring the effect of his words.

"Francisco Madero was the people's hero. For this they killed him."

The throng roared disapproval.

"We had no time to mourn this injustice. The usurper Huerta showed himself no better than Diaz. He ground his boot on the neck of the people. Again we rallied together in the cause of revolution. We trusted Carranza. Venustiano Carranza is no Madero."

They cried out with condemnation of Carranza. He had them eating out of his hand.

"He makes no land reform. He enriches himself by the sweat of your labor. Worse, he has sold you out to the Americanos. At this very moment, Yanqui soldiers occupy El Valle and Colonia Dublán. Yanqui war ships sit off the coast of Vera Cruz."

"Muerta Americanos! La muerta de Carranza!"

"No, no, amigos." He wagged his finger at the crowd in mock admonition. "You must not say such things. The Yanqui Presidente says the Mexican people must put down your revolution. You must unite behind Carranza. He is the Yanqui choice to be your Presidente."

"Muerta Yanqui Presidente! La muerta de Carranza!"

"It will be as you say. I your humble servant say death to the Yanquis. Death to their lap dog Carranza! Once again, I, Pancho Villa, have answered your call."

"Viva Villa! Viva Mexico!"

"División del Norte once again takes up the cause of revolution. This time the people shall have justice. This time the people shall have true reform. We shall never again entrust these things to faithless imposters. This time we shall have true revolution. This time we shall throw off the yoke of Yanqui oppression. This time we shall defeat the tyrant and his lap dog." He spread his arms, embracing the sky. "This time the people shall have Pancho Villa!"

"Viva Villa!"

"Viva Villa!"

"Viva Villa!"

Colonia Dublán
September 18

Patton folded the newspaper, tossed it on his desk and bunched his fists. He looked across the headquarters tent at Pershing.

"So, who the hell is winning here? Carranza? Villa is on the march again. He took Chihuahua City a couple of days ago and Wilson's choice for President couldn't do a damn thing about it. Worse still, now we know where the son-of-a-bitch is and we can't so much as send out a patrol. Bad as he is, Villa's the one we should have backed. He's the French Revolution gone wrong, but who knows, with a little help we might have steered him right."

"Right, wrong, it doesn't matter. There's not a damn thing we can do about it."

"Hell of a way to run an army in the field. Wilson has no stomach for the hard work before us. He'll have us sit in this godforsaken, snake-infested hell hole until he's got political cover to tuck our tail between his legs and drag our sorry asses home."

"I understand your frustration, George, but be careful. Politics and a military career don't mix. I've got some of my own concerns, but there's a time and a place and a way to express them without getting your tunic buttons handed to you."

"What do you mean, sir?"

"Well for starters I don't know how much longer we can maintain a position of neutrality on the war in Europe. Sooner or later we will be drawn into it. Our experience down here demonstrates how ill prepared we are to take on a major military conflict. We lack men, material and weapons. We grounded our air service down here in little more than a month. We lag far behind the Germans, French and British. We have given no thought to the realities of modern warfare and the need for modern weapons. The officer cadre is woefully depleted. We've got too many experienced men at the end of their careers. If we are drawn into a wider conflict, a massive effort will be needed to effectively arm the nation."

"That's a pretty grim assessment, sir, though I agree with you. So what do you do with that?"

"It's the sort of conversation I have behind closed doors with General Scott. It's the kind of conversation he has behind closed doors with Secretary Baker and the President."

"I was with you right up to the last. Political neglect is how we accumulated all the problems you just cited."

"That may be so, but we live under a constitution. As soldiers we operate within a chain of command. The principles may be imperfect, but they've kept things in order for a hundred and forty years now. I expect they'll serve in the current circumstances."

Patton drew his pipe from his pocket. "Fortunately, I have no political aspirations. I'd never be any good at the subtleties. I'm too plain-spoken."

Pershing chuckled. "Plain-spoken, is it? You are that, George. Political aspirations or no, a soldier needs to manage his opinions for his own good. You'd do well to remember that."

CHAPTER FORTY-FIVE

Colonia Dublán
September 25
1700 Hours

The supply convoy rolled into camp on the return trip from El
Valle as late afternoon sunturned the southwestern peaks orange
gold. The lead truck braked to a stop opposite the command
quadrangle. The passenger door swung open. Patton dismounted.

"Carry on, Sergeant." He slammed the door. The truck
ground into gear and drove off to the motor pool. Patton
trudged up the stone path to the command tent. He stepped
inside, allowing his eyes to adjust to the low light. Pershing sat
at his desk, too absorbed to notice his presence. He crossed the
dirt floor to the desk and saluted.

"If I may offer my congratulations, sir?"

Pershing looked up and smiled. A second star twinkled on his
collar. "Indeed, thank you, George."

"Well deserved, sir."

"It's kind of you to say so. I suspect the War Department
wants to make it clear that our limited success down here isn't
wholly our fault."

"Nonsense, sir, it's well-deserved recognition." He glanced at
his watch. "I know it's early by your standards, but it is a civil

quitting hour by most. I'd be pleased to buy you a drink to celebrate."

Pershing looked at the stack in his in-box. "I guess this will still be here in the morning. A drink does sound good."

They crossed the dusty quad to the company street and made their way north to a large tent that served as the Officer's Club. Inside a crowd was beginning to gather. Pershing led the way to a back corner table. A waiter in a white starched jacket met them at the table.

"What may I get for you, sir?"

"Scotch whiskey."

Patton nodded to the waiter. "I'll have the same."

The waiter returned by the time they'd settled in their seats.

"Service is pretty good when you drink with a Major General." Patton's eye twinkled. He lifted his glass. "Again, congratulations, sir. Best wishes for continued success."

Pershing lifted his glass. "Thank you." He savored a swallow. "That's pretty good. My compliments to whoever runs our supply operations."

Patton smiled. "It's all about choosing the right supplier, sir."

"I'm sure it is, George. Nonetheless, well done."

"Your promotion couldn't have come at a better time. It puts you in line for a major command should we enter the war in Europe."

"Hmm, the President's protests aside, I do think it is a possibility."

"I can't imagine we'll stay out much longer. We're far too closely allied with the British and French. Even Wilson can't deny German submarine provocations. We know they've meddled against us here in Mexico. My gut says Carranza has played us both to his advantage."

Pershing swirled the whiskey in his glass. "It wouldn't surprise me if they had a hand in Villa rearming División del Norte."

"He did manage that rather quickly, didn't he?"

"He did. Now he's a thorn in Carranza's side again. It appears Villa's learned his lesson. He's picking his targets with a bit more care, attacking Carranza's weaknesses and avoiding his strongholds. Taking the governor's mansion in Chihuahua had to be embarrassing for El Presidente."

Patton patted his pockets, producing his pipe and tobacco pouch. "Embarrassing, hell, newspaper accounts of the speech he made from the governor's mansion had to be salt in an open wound. Well, Villa's Carranza's problem now. This one is over for us. I expect you'll be on your way to France before long." He filled his pipe. He scratched a match and puffed a fragrant cloud.

"I studied the terrain while attending the cavalry school at Saumur. It presented some interesting tactical challenges and that was before the Hun dug in defensive positions."

The waiter arrived with a tray carrying two fresh drinks. "Colonel Slocum sends his congratulations, sir."

Pershing glanced across the room. Slocum raised his glass. He accepted the drink and returned the toast. "If I stay here very long, Lieutenant, they'll have to carry the two of us out of here."

He shifted the pipe stem to the side of his jaw. "We'll not let that happen, sir."

"I don't know much about France. If you are right about our entering the war, your knowledge of the country will be useful."

"It would be an honor to serve with you, sir."

"So you've gotten over your misgivings about your career prospects?"

"No, I can't say that I have, but I haven't brought myself to resignation yet, either. I have a duty to finish this assignment. At my age, I can't invest four more years in a peacetime army career. If we do enter the war, perhaps my call will come. I know you shall have a prominent command."

"Let's don't get ahead of ourselves, George. We haven't entered the war yet and we both know the President has little appetite for the sort of work we do. Still, if you're right, and I happen to think you could be, I'll find a job for you in whatever part I'm given to play."

"Thank you, sir." *Make it a line command. I've had enough logistics.*

They knocked back their drinks.

Colonia Dublán
October

Filling a kerosene lamp in the dark with cold hands made for sloppy work without wind whipping the stream of black fuel, spilling into the lamp well. It was either that, or have no light to read his Bible. These days the Bible and Beat's letters were all that broke the monotony of sand, dust and insects, unless of course the damn wind blew. The election loomed in the coming month. He could only hope they'd be headed home in time for Christmas.

Shit! The overflow served notice, the lamp was full. He capped the fill hole and trudged back to the quad, his shoulders hunched against wind gusts and stinging sand.

He pulled the tent flap back and fumbled in the dark for the crate that served as a bedside table. He set the lamp on the crate and sat on the cot. The smell of kerosene filled the small tent space. He fumbled in his blouse pocket for a match, lifted the chimney to expose the wick and struck the match.

The flash exploded in his face, blinding him in bright hot light. Fire spread across the crate and leaped to the blanket. Light blindness cleared. His hands were on fire. He lunged for the tent flap, diving into the sand outside. He planted his face and hands and rolled, fighting the spread of flames. Somewhere in the back of his throat he must have screamed.

He lay still, feeling for the effects of flame on his body. Nothing. Shock. The burning tent crackled behind him. The oily smell of kerosene hung in the air. Somewhere in the darkness he heard people running.

"Holy shit, sir! Are you all right?"

He lifted his face out of the sand. "I'm burned." Darkness dropped like a curtain.

Light again. Harsh light overhead behind a shadowy figure blinded him. Light blinded him, not darkness. He could see. *Thank God.* His hands and face burned like fury. He remembered the flash, the smell of kerosene and burning hair. Or was it flesh?

"He's coming around."

A needle stabbed his arm. The light went out.

Morning light chased shadows into the dimly lit canvas corners of the field hospital. He held up a bandaged hand. He could feel more of them wrapping his face, *mummified.* No, burned.

"Are you having any pain, Lieutenant?"

Her voice sounded soft, concerned.

"Some."

"Would you like something for it?"

"How long have I been out?"

"Since they brought you in last night."

"How bad is it?"

"I'll let the doctor give you his opinion, but there is good news. Your senses don't appear to have been damaged. We won't know how serious the burns are for a few days, but you put yourself out quickly and that limited the damage. Do you want something for the pain?"

"No. Thank you. When will the doctor be around?"

"He's here now." The voice sounded behind the nurse. She stepped away from the bed. A man with a Medical Corps insignia on his collar appeared. Pershing stood beside him.

"You gave us a bit of a scare, George."

"I'm sorry, sir. The lamp exploded, I think."

"The Lieutenant is a very lucky man, General. His eyes could easily have been damaged." He held up a finger and moved it from side to side. "Can you follow my finger, Lieutenant?"

He did.

"Good. A few days' rest and we'll be able to assess the tissue damage. Right now I'm guessing it should heal satisfactorily. Then I'd say you're in for some medical leave.

Lake Vineyard
Los Angeles, California
November

The trail climbed gently along a coastal ridgeline. Far below, dark gray-green surf splashed sunlit white foam against rocks and sand. To the east, the ridge line fell away to a lush grassy valley turned golden brown in late autumn. A sun-silvered clear creek meandered out of the northeast to the southwest, searching some secret fall to the seashore below. Pine thickets dotted the meadow along the creek banks and hillsides.

The horses climbed easily to the crest where Beat drew a halt. She shook her hair to the sun and sea breeze, taking in the beauty around her, her eyes merry with contentment. She made a picture he could carry in his heart.

"Look at it, Georgie." She swept her arm across the valley below. "Can't you just see a herd of fine horses down there? We could build a lovely house where the creek bends around that pine grove. I wager you'd find trout in that stream."

"It is lovely, Beat, a horseman's dream."

She stepped down, ground-tied the little roan mare she was

riding. She climbed out on a rock outcropping and sat on a large, flat stone, dangling her legs over the side. George followed and took a seat beside her. Light bandages still covered his cheeks and the backs of his hands where new pink skin pushed back the ravages of his burns. White puff ball clouds rolled east on the breeze, painting the valley floor in a kaleidoscope of light and shadow.

"Can't you just picture it? It could be ours, you know."

"Is that your dream, Beat?"

She caught his profile in the arch of her brow. "Is it yours, Georgie?"

He knit his brow. "I don't know. Sometimes I think it is. Those times I think I'm most rational. But then something happens to encourage my current path, the Cardenas affair, the promotion, the General's promotion. If we enter the war in Europe, he will have an assignment in the upper echelons of command. He's promised to take me with him."

Beat's eyes narrowed. The smile lines tugging at the corners of her mouth sagged ever so slightly. "Do you think that is likely now that the President has won his re-election? He seems more committed than ever to maintain our neutrality."

He shook his head. "I don't know. It is one of the facts that vex me. If we don't enter the war, in four years I will be a thirty-six-year-old junior officer. Whatever career prospects I might have had will be over by then. If we do enter the war, I see no place in modern warfare for the horse soldier or the saber. The general says the army doesn't move that fast. He's right, I suppose. A peacetime army doesn't move fast. A wartime army becomes another matter. Where is there a place for a horse soldier and Saber Master in that? I just don't know."

"There is a place for a horseman down there." The jut of her chin took in the whole of the valley.

"Perhaps, Beat. I can't yet say. The general says time and

invention have a way of correcting shortcomings in modernizing the army. He says time and experience will lead me to new opportunity. Perhaps he is right. Then again perhaps too much time has already passed. It may be too late.

"I do know this Punitive Expedition marks the end of an era. The end of the era I'm best prepared to serve. What can I learn in the middle of a lackluster career that may yet reverse the fortunes of my future? I wish I knew. I do know this, I'm grateful you showed me this place. I can see a future down there. Soon I shall have to choose."

She rested her head on his shoulder. He wrapped an arm around her. She lifted her lips to his. "Whatever you think best, Georgie."

CHAPTER FORTY-SIX

Columbus

November 14

"Next stop, Columbus." The blue-coated conductor passed up the aisle. "Columbus is next in fifteen minutes." The soulful hoot of the whistle punctuated the announcement.

Patton watched the high desert roll by the Pacific and Southern coach window. Here it began. Here soon it would end. With the election over, he expected Wilson would yield to Carranza's whining and withdraw the Punitive Expedition. They'd handed out some punishment. He'd had a hand in it and took some satisfaction from that. Still they'd fallen short of accomplishing their purpose, something the United States military wasn't known for. He'd asked to return to duty even though his recovery might have allowed him to skip the final act in this play. He felt the need to be here. History would be recorded here among the sand and scorpions and snakes. None would mark it the finest hour of the storied American horse soldier. Nonetheless, the story of the United States Cavalry made her final hour historic.

Somewhere up ahead brakes squealed. The train slowed. He wondered if this historic hour might indeed be the end of the line. He remembered the brash optimism of his last days at the Point. He'd been prepared to join the tradition. He expected to embrace it and in turn be embraced by it. He remembered his tactics course, the dashing account of J. E. B. Stuart, victorious at Brandy Station in the greatest cavalry battle ever fought on American soil. Young Stuart, Brigadier General at twenty-eight, Cadet Adjutant, George Smith Patton had foreseen such a future for himself. He would never have accepted the expectation of a First Lieutenant's bar at thirty-two. A sun-drenched seaside valley with a lovely home on the bend of a creek called out to him. There were fish in the creek. He knew it. But first, he had one job left to finish, one last page of this history yet to be written.

Camp Furlong appeared in the window south of the tracks. He'd find a convoy there bound for Colonia Dublán. The train lurched to a halt. He stood and pulled his valise down from the rack. He squared his shoulders and started up the aisle, First Lieutenant, George Patton, reporting for duty.

Colonia Dublán

The driver braked to a stop north of the quadrangle.

"Welcome back, Lieutenant."

"Thanks for the lift, Corporal." He jumped down from the cab and slammed the door. He presented himself at the command tent.

"Lieutenant Patton reporting for duty, sir." He snapped off his salute.

Pershing stood. "George, welcome back. How are you feeling?"

"Fine, sir. It still itches some but Beat says I'm pretty well healed, so I guess that's that."

"Sound medical opinion to me. You ready to get back to work?"

"I am, sir."

"Good, because I could use some help."

"Tell me what you need."

"You remember that article I agreed to do on cavalry training?"

He wrinkled his brow. "I seem to recall something about that."

"Well, it's coming due and I must confess I'm nowhere near as far along as I need to be. Would you take a crack at finishing it up?"

"Me, sir? I don't think lieutenants draw the same water as major generals when it comes to training."

Pershing chuckled. "Nonsense, George. You're a first-rate cavalry officer. You'll write a fine article. I'll help you with the editing and take half the credit for your work."

"Sounds like a hell of a deal."

"Splendid! I knew you'd appreciate opportunity when you saw it." He handed over a thin folder. "Here are my notes."

"When is it due?"

He glanced at the calendar on the desk. "Ah, week after next, I think. Yes, that's it, end of the month. Of course, I'll need a couple of days to review your draft."

"Looks like I'm behind schedule already. I best get my ass in gear."

"Capital assessment, Lieutenant!"

Patton hefted the thin folder and started for his desk.

"Oh, George, one more thing."

"Sir?"

Pershing's eye twinkled. "Do be careful if you decide to burn any midnight oil."

"Thank you, sir."

November 23
1900 Hours

"Not bad, George, not bad at all. Actually, it's quite good considering you've had little more than a week to finish it. Sit down, sit down."

Patton took a seat across the camp table that served as the general's desk. "Thank you, sir."

The general sat in a pool of lamplight, a draft of the article fanned in one hand. "Your recommendations on marksmanship training are perceptive and innovative. Where did you come up with the idea of simulating combat situations on the range? It's far more engaging than simple target practice."

"Thank you, sir. In thinking about the shootout at San Miguelito I realized the best shot I may have made was shooting the horse. Dave Allison taught me to do that. I'd never have learned that on a target range."

"Dave Allison?"

"He's Sheriff in Sierra Blanca."

"Oh yes, the father of your Wyatt Earp revolver, isn't he?"

Patton ignored the jibe. "It's a practical example of tactical shooting. We don't teach that sort of thing with tightly scored bull's eyes."

"I see the point, excellent. Let's see." He thumbed through pages scribbled with marginal notes. "Most of these comments are semantic suggestions. Ah yes, page five, the section on tactics. You devote a good deal of attention to the charge. Again I like the idea of getting the training off the parade ground and into simulated combat situations. That said, I think you've given the charge too much emphasis. Thanks to our friend Villa, we've seen what happens to the cavalry charge against modern firepower. In my mind the advisability of the charge is severely diminished in modern cavalry tactics. You've even included exercises in the saber charge. I know your affection for the saber, George, but really a saber charge against machine-gun emplacements? Mass suicide comes to mind."

"Sir, not every enemy position will be protected by machine guns."

"It's only a matter of time before they are. Our regiments carried machine guns in offensive operations and may I remind you, we didn't carry sabers."

"But sir, the saber charge is the signature of the cavalry."

"The nineteenth-century cavalry, George, this is the twentieth century. No, the article needs to stress a reduced reliance on the charge and a similar de-emphasis of the saber on pages nine and ten. You can accomplish that by taking out the saber charge and reducing saber training to ceremonial drill."

"Sir—" He cut off his own objection. There seemed little point. The general clearly had his mind made up. He took it for another of those cold splashes of reality. "I'll make the changes, sir." He gathered his papers and turned to go.

Pershing grasped the moment. An army facing world conflict as ill prepared as this one could not afford to lose a warrior of young Patton's stripe. "George!" He stopped at the tent flap. "Leave the saber in."

He smiled. "Thank you, sir." The tent flap closed behind him. Cool night air mindful of a cold splash slapped him. The general conceded his point, against the weight of his own argument. The feeling of vindication notwithstanding, he realized the General was right. The cavalry as he'd known it had come to an end. There could only be one reason the general conceded the saber point. *The General saw a future for him.*

Colonia Dublán
December

> *Dearest Beat,*
>
> *In my mind's eye I take my reflections on the future to the top of that ridge where I sit by your side. If I was sure that my present circumstance saw no chance of improvement, I would see a future in that lovely valley, for these long days of separation are painful and filled with tedium punctuated only by the chance*

of action as a means to glory. If I knew that would elude me, I should happily settle down to more pastoral pursuits and yet I cannot tear myself away from the gleam on the prize. Life is a risk. It seems I take it for both of us. Be patient with me. The moment I see I cannot achieve the greatness I aspire to I shall give up this quest and come home to you. They say ambition may be blind. The goal may also be illusion. If it be no more than a dream, for better or worse, it is mine.

Love,
George

Columbus
January 19, 1917

The mobile command rolled up Palomas Road in a cloud of dust south of Camp Furlong. A sharp wind accompanied a gray flannel cloud deck running out of the northwest. Patton's lead car pulled off the west side of the road, made a wide circular turn and braked to a stop facing the road. Pershing's command car followed, pulling up beside Patton. Collins pulled in alongside Pershing. Pershing stood in his open-top car and picked up his salute joined by his officer staff. The general recognized this unceremonious parade for a historic moment. Patton felt it too, perhaps with an even deeper sense of loss.

Worn and weary troops and horses seemed to sense the moment too. Riders straightened in their saddles. Horses picked up their step, a mottled column of black and bay, chestnut and roan tossed their heads with a prideful spirit. The gentle jangle of tack served for the lack of a regimental band. Column formations drew tight and sharp as the United States Cavalry passed in review.

The Seventh led the way as it should. The familiar bars of Gary Owen, the Seventh's traditional regimental song, played in Patton's mind. The cavalry's most celebrated unit, famously

339

distinguished by the exploits of its flamboyant former commander, Lieutenant Colonel George Armstrong Custer. Custer proudly led his beloved Seventh through the plains' Indian wars. Courageous to the point of foolhardy he led them to the gravest defeat ever inflicted on the American horse soldier. Still he led them to glory ever to be remembered.

The Tenth followed. The rugged all-black unit known as buffalo soldiers. They served on the plains and in Cuba. Pershing himself led them to the nickname "Black Jack." He snapped a salute full of respect. He knew Roosevelt's legendary Rough Riders might never have taken San Juan Hill were it not for the courage and tenacity of the Tenth, holding his flank.

The Black Horse Eleventh served with distinction in the Philippines and here again in Mexico. Slocum's Thirteenth traced its roots to the war of succession. The Thirteenth bore the brunt of the Columbus raid. But for the defense they mounted, the raid might have taken a far greater toll in lives lost and property destroyed.

And so they passed. George Smith Patton saluted them with a heavy heart. The cavalry traced its roots to ancient times when man first found his seat on a horse. He'd ridden the horse to battle in ages past. He'd met the enemy with a bright blade and swept the field to glory. Glory drove him. Glory all but eluded him. He'd ridden into Mexico that spring, a horse soldier, the fulfillment of lifelong aspiration. He returned to an uncertain future, mounted on a open top touring car, witness to the end of an era. The United States Cavalry passed in review that day, and into the annals of history.

Afterword

Pancho Villa negotiated an agreement of amnesty with the Mexican government, following the assassination of Venustiano Carranza. Under terms of the agreement, he retired to Canutillo, a 163,000-acre estate in Durango. He turned the estate into a fortress for his personal protection. He maintained a personal security force of fifty Dorado guards and surrounded himself with a small, intensely loyal staff. Other members of División del Norte and their families settled adjoining estates, further solidifying Villa's protective perimeter. He lived quietly for two years, actively cultivating cordial relations with the government and his old adversary Alvero Obregon.

Obregon turned power broker, maintaining close ties between the military and the political power of the presidency. In time, Villa's mystique drew his name back into political discourse. Villa allowed his opinion to be courted at a time and in a fashion that made him appear a threat to Obregon's handpicked successor to the presidency. Obregon had had enough of the old bandit. He determined it was not possible to penetrate Villa's security at Canutillo. He sent a team of assassins to nearby Parral to wait for an opportunity. Opportunity presented itself when Villa agreed to serve as godfather at a christening in the village of Rio Florido.

Returning from the christening, Villa stopped in Parral to visit one of his mistresses. His spies in Parral gave him an all clear for the visit. Following the visit, he took the wheel of his

Dodge touring car for the drive back to Canutillo. He was accompanied by his chauffer, secretary, an assistant and two bodyguards. As they approached an intersection to the only road out of town leading to his estate, an old man selling candy at a roadside stand sang out, "Viva Villa!"

Villa flashed a broad grin and waved as he turned the corner. The assassins fired from the windows of a house beside the road. The volley struck Villa in a hail of bullets, killing him instantly.

War Department
Washington, D.C.
May 1917

Secretary of War Newton Diehl Baker gazed out his office window. The gardens below spread a carpet of delicate spring blossoms against a blanket of thunderheads, darkening the horizon across the Potomac. The President despised war as much as he. Still Wilson petitioned the Congress and Congress had enacted a Declaration of War. The United States would enter the war in Europe. Why? Because public opinion demanded it after British intelligence reports revealed German intentions in Mexico? Was it because German submarine atrocities continued to target our shipping? Or was it because the President saw no other way to gain a seat at the table for the treaty-making that would create a new world order after the war? Who could say? Baker could only speculate. A soft knock at the door called him back from his reflections.

"General Pershing is here, sir."

And so it begins. Baker felt the weight of a responsibility he never sought. A responsibility he thought himself unqualified to assume. A responsibility thrust on him by times and circumstances beyond his control. As such, responsibilities were demanded of men down through the ages. "Send him in."

The General's presence crackled with confidence. He strode across the room, crisp as the creases in his uniform. He stopped before Baker's desk, his cap tucked under his arm, clear-eyed, ramrod straight.

"You sent for me, Mr. Secretary."

Baker nodded imperceptibly to himself. "So I did, General. So I did. Please have a seat." He waited for Pershing to settle himself. "Let's get right to the point. The President has named you Commander of American Expeditionary Forces in Europe." He paused, allowing the import of the assignment to deliver its own message.

"I'm honored, sir. A little surprised, but honored."

"Don't be. You are without question the most qualified general officer we have for this command."

"It's just there are others more senior."

Baker cut him off with a wave of his hand. "You are the most qualified man for an assignment of historic importance and, I might add, significant difficulty. I am here to see to it you get what you need."

Pershing fixed him with an ice-blue gaze. "Then, sir, we share this assignment. In some ways your share may prove the more difficult."

Baker's puzzlement spoke without words.

"Declaring war is one thing, Mr. Secretary. Going to war to win is another. Going to war requires men, materiel and national will. The President has asked me to take responsibility for the boots on the ground in theater. Providing those men and supplying them will determine the prospect for victory. The Punitive Expedition, whatever its merits, exposed the fact we are woefully unprepared to undertake war on a global scale. We have an army of barely one hundred thousand men. Winning this war will require a force ten times that number. The entire air service consists of fifty-five obsolete aircraft. This war will require five thousand or more. I doubt we have sufficient artillery munitions to sustain a full day's bombardment on the scale required by the European conflict. Other modern weapons from small arms to machine guns and vehicles including armored vehicles are in short supply or nonexistent."

Baker rubbed the bridge of his nose between a thumb and forefinger. He nodded to himself and met Pershing's level gaze. "You've given me my assignment, General. I accept. For you, I have only two orders. I have given you the first."

"And the second?"

"Come home."

Chamlieu, France
November 1917

Patton stood in the shadowed entry to the massive mechanics barn. *Barn.* The air chilled his cheek; it smelled of gasoline and grease. The warmth of animals and the sweet smell of hay had no place here. The steel monster he'd bet his newly minted Captain's bars on towered in a flood of ceiling light. It looked every inch a war machine, though of some otherworldly time and place. They called it the Renault FT-17 light tank, light at 7.2 tons being relative to the heavier British Big Willies. The FT-17 discredited the notion of armored artillery he remembered discussing that long-ago night in Mexico. The body supported a top-mounted rotating gun turret. The armament consisted of a 37 mm gun flanked by dual 7.62 mm machine guns. Yet the formidable firepower seemed dwarfed by the oversized propulsion system.

He stepped out of the shadows. His boots echoed hollow on the concrete floor of the cavernous maintenance shed. He stepped into the spotlight next to the front fender. The tank propelled itself on wide steel tracks driven by parallel rows of wheels arranged by size from the largest at the front of the vehicle to the smaller at the rear. The configuration gave the FT-17 the appearance of perpetually going uphill. According to the performance manuals, this enabled the tank to maneuver over rough terrain, climbing over obstacles in its path or out of depressions such as trenches.

He walked slowly around the vehicle, running a hand along the fender as he might have familiarized himself with a newly drawn mount. Just over sixteen feet long, he rounded the rear skirt, not quite five feet wide. He found a step at the back that allowed the two-man crew to mount the vehicle. He stepped up and walked along the deck to the turret hatch. The height, the mass, the steel, the weapons, the vehicle exuded a feeling of mythical power.

He pulled the crew hatch open. The metal hinges groaned. He made a mental note. They needed oil. Light from the powerful overhead lamp spilled into the cockpit, dimly lighting the gun controls and the second seat. He climbed inside to the gunner's seat. The driver's seat and controls were barely visible forward and below. He sat back, closed his eyes and tried to imagine what an enemy might see in this fighting machine.

No, not a single vehicle integrated with infantry the way the Brits used them. No, concentrate force. The tank must be the point of attack, the tip of a new, more powerful spear. They must be massed in squadrons, platoons, companies, battalions. Speed and concentration of force, these decisive strategic principles of the ages suited the tank. He remembered another manual entry, *top speed 4.35 miles per hour, range 40 miles*. Little more than a day's ride, he shook his head. Not fast enough. He smiled. *"Time and invention,"* the general said.

He climbed out of the gunnery seat up through the hatch and sat on the turret. *Magnificent,* a weapon this powerful deserves a name. He smiled again at another memory. He'd call his *Buster.* Somewhat melancholy, he admitted, the saber would be useless as a matchstick against such a weapon. He dismissed the disappointment in favor of a new realization. This is the future, his future. It hadn't eluded him. It had merely changed. He'd found the future of the cavalry, the armored cavalry.

Gaul
Early morning fog concealed his ranks from the Hun across the plain. The Centurion strained in vain to penetrate the folds of a moist gray curtain. Those he could not see could not see him. Caesar spoke from the mist. Audaces fortuna iuvat.

Meuse-Argonne
France
September 26, 1918
Guns thundered in the distance. Bombardment recalled him to the present. He checked his watch. Zero hour, exactly as Pershing had ordered. *Forward!* The command echoed down through the ages. Engines rumbled, spouting gouts of black exhaust. Treads clanked. The Centurion's tanks rolled forward, their line stretched across the plain.

LAST WORD

The last United States Cavalry campaign may not be remembered as the storied American horse soldier's finest hour. It should be remembered for the imprint it left on American military leadership in the two great wars that followed.

AUTHOR'S NOTE

Most of the characters and events recounted here are based in historical fact. The author has taken creative license in characterizing individuals and describing events to suit the story. While German agents were active in Mexico during the Punitive Expedition, von Kreusen and Elsa Lieben are fictional characters. The roles of General Obregon, Lem Spillsbury, Henry Vaughn, and one or two others have been expanded to limit the number of characters presented to the reader. Researching historical events invariably uncovers inconsistencies that contribute to creative interpretation. Where there is any conflict between historical fact and the author's portrayal, it is the author's intent to present a fictional account for the enjoyment of the reader.

SELECTED SOURCES

Axelrod, Alan. *Patton* (New York: Palgrave Macmillan, 2006).

D'Este, Carlo. *Patton: A Genius for War* (New York: HarperCollins, 1995).

Lacey, Jim. *Pershing* (New York: Palgrave Macmillan, 2008).

McLynn, Frank. *Villa and Zapata: A History of the Mexican Revolution* (New York: Carroll & Graff, 2001).

Pratt, Fletcher. *Civil War: Ordeal by Fire: A Short History* (Mineola, NY: Dover, 1948).

Welsome, Eileen. *The General and the Jaguar: Pershing's Hunt for Pancho Villa: A True Story of Revolution and Revenge* (New York: Little, Brown, 2006).

ABOUT THE AUTHOR

Paul Colt creates historical fiction that crackles with authenticity. His analytical insight, investigative research and genuine horse sense bring history to life. His characters walk off the pages of history into the reader's imagination in a style that blends Jeff Shaara's historical dramatizations with Robert B. Parker's gritty dialog.

Paul's first book, *Grasshoppers in Summer,* received finalist recognition in the Western Writers of America 2009 Spur Awards. *Boots and Saddles: A Call to Glory* received the Marilyn Brown Novel Award, presented by Utah Valley University for excellence in unpublished work. To learn more, visit *www.paul colt.com.*